The
Daring Heart

The Highland Heather and Hearts Scottish Romance Series, Book Three

by
Carmen Caine

This book is dedicated to my family

… for being so patient with me.
I love all of you.

Author's Note to the Reader

Though Julian and Liselle never existed, the true story of Thomas (Robert) Cochrane, King James III of Scotland, and his brothers, continues where "The Bedeviled Heart" left off. And while Dolfino Dolfin did exist and sold trade secrets that played a hand in starting the Venetian Salt Wars, the Vindactim never existed.

And while my goal is to weave history throughout these stories in an effort to make them all the more entertaining, they will always be romances first and historical second, my focus being on the human relationships between the characters.

"The Kindling Heart" begins the story with Bree and Ruan in the Isle of Skye.

"The Bedeviled Heart" covers Cameron and Kate's dramatic romance against the backdrop of court intrigue and witchcraft.

"The Daring Heart" brings the adventure of Lord Julian Gray as he meets his match in the Venetian assassin, Liselle.

"The Bold Heart" (formerly known as "The Loyal Heart") weaves the spell of fated love with Merry rescuing Ewan in the events leading up to the Battle of Sauchieburn and completes the circle of how it all began.

1

A WICKED MINX

Sarlat, France
May, 1482

Lord Julian Gray's dark lashes flew open.

He became aware of the sharp blade pressed against his ribs the exact moment the door to his bedchamber crashed open.

'Twas not the way he preferred to awake from a deep sleep.

The Venetian assassin he had been trailing the past week stood framed in the door, observing him with the deadliest of expressions. He was a lean, dark-haired man possessing an air of refinement. His nose was long and thin, and he peered across the chamber at Julian with one hand holding a torch aloft and the other firmly clasped upon the hilt of his sword.

The bed jiggled a little as the blade in Julian's ribs dug a little deeper into his flesh, and then a woman's husky voice whispered softly in his ear, "Play nice, if you wish to live."

"Explain yourself, knave!" the assassin at the door roared at the same moment.

Julian's gray eyes narrowed.

Under the covers, the blade slid along his chest and he caught his breath.

Ach, but he could recognize his own blade anywhere.

The canny vixen had stolen his own dagger from under his pillow!

Startled, he cast a quick sidelong glance at his bedmate assailant, and his lips parted in surprise.

Even in the flickering torchlight, he could see the lass was a feast for the senses! Honey-colored tresses cascaded over a creamy, naked shoulder. Her lips were wide and full, her nose pointed at the tip, and her lashes fluttered over stunning hazel eyes.

She nudged the dagger again, dangerously close to piercing his flesh.

There was a rasp of steel as the assassin crossed the chamber and pulled out his sword, cursing, "I'll have your head, knave!"

"It's too late, Orazio!" The hazel-eyed lass threw herself over Julian's bare chest. "We are wed, and the marriage has already been consummated!"

Julian choked.

His reward was a twist of the blade. This time, he was *certain* it had drawn blood.

Orazio drew a sharp breath. "Liselle! What have you *done*?"

"I'm a grown woman, Orazio!" she replied. "I've reached my twentieth year and can do what I please!"

"Did you find her?" a hauntingly familiar voice asked from the passageway outside.

Julian blinked in astonishment as the dark-haired, sultry-eyed Lady Nicoletta, lady-in-waiting to Princess Anabella of Scotland, appeared in the doorway swathed in a velvet mantle, her full lips drawn in a tight, worried expression.

They stared at each other in shock.

"Lord Julian Gray!" Nicoletta was the first to regain control.

Julian licked his dry lips. "Nicoletta? What are ye doing in France?"

But Nicoletta was not listening to him. Running to the side of the bed, she placed her hands firmly upon her hips and glared at the lass still draped over Julian.

"Liselle, get out of that bed at once! Lord Gray is a man of the most disreputable ilk. You'll have naught to do with him!"

Julian began to snort in wicked amusement, but after one look at Orazio, quickly changed it into a cough. Adopting an insulted manner, he began to protest. "Ach, 'tis not true, Nicoletta! Ye've always misunderstood me!"

Orazio's dark brow swept up in astonishment. "Do you know this man, Nicoletta?"

"Does it matter?" the lass at Julian's side asked pointedly. "He is my husband. The deed is done!"

Nicoletta gasped, clutching her heart. "Husband?"

Julian opened his mouth to object but shut it quickly when the tip of the dagger poked him again.

"Lord Gray, did you truly wed our sister?" Nicoletta asked in a strangled voice.

Julian caught his breath. Was the wee, malevolent beastie spilling his blood drop-by-drop, the sister of the deadliest and most-famed Venetian assassin? As was Lady Nicoletta?

He really had no choice but to go along with the vixen's farce.

The man glowering above him, weapon drawn, was intent only upon securing his sister's honor. He could read it in the assassin's eyes.

"Aye!" Julian growled with a flash of annoyance.

The blade beneath the covers bit him deeper.

He clenched his jaw.

Ach, but he was going to discipline this wee terror the moment they were alone. Clearing his throat, he confirmed in a strong tone, "Aye, I wed ... Lady Liselle ... last night."

But Orazio's eyes had narrowed suspiciously. "I would see both of your hands first, Liselle—and *then* hear the man speak."

With a smirk, Liselle arched her back and slowly lifted her hands out from under the covers. Dropping one hand to thread her fingers through Julian's fair hair, she lightly skimmed the palm of the other over his naked chest. "We've been properly wed, haven't we now?" she asked Julian in a low, provocative voice.

Beneath the covers, a new blade needled his flesh.

Had the lass found his dirk as well? And was she using her knees?

By the Virgin, but her skills were impressive!

At that, Julian paused, and for the first time in his life, experienced a ripple of genuine interest. He subjected the mischievous lass to a second, deeper look. She had the most unusual eyes he had ever seen; they were green, flecked, and ringed with gold.

And the expression in them was charmingly malicious.

He stared at her in wonder.

How had she slipped into his tightly locked chamber, avoiding the snares he had set just the night before at each door and window? And how had she slid into his bed and used his own dagger against him?

But most importantly, in just what exactly had the wicked sprite embroiled him?

"Then it appears I must welcome you into our family, Lord Julian Gray." Orazio laughed, but there was little humor in his tone and no sign of mirth in his eyes.

"This simply cannot be!" Lady Nicoletta wailed.

And then suddenly Orazio escorted Nicoletta out of the chamber, and closing the door, left Julian alone with Liselle.

The latch had scarcely fallen into place before Liselle sprang from the bed, sweeping up her gown from the nearby chest to shrug into its soft, vibrant green velvet. As the material fell in loose folds over her shoulders, she began to laugh.

It was a husky, throaty sound, one that Julian found strangely appealing.

"There's no need to hurry, lass. I wouldna mind if ye tarried a wee spell," he invited with a cheeky grin, patting the bed.

"Orazio will have your blood when he learns we've not been truly wed," she said sweetly, quickly capturing her shimmering waterfall of hair with a jeweled net. "You had best leave Sarlat, and right quickly!"

He knew that was sound advice. Orazio was a dangerous man, but at the moment, Julian found himself immensely distracted by the wee lass smiling down at him, her hazel eyes hinting of dangerous pleasures.

"Then let's not tell the man we're not, aye?" he suggested, eyeing her curves appreciatively.

Liselle leaned down to walk her fingers up his arm. "Alas, but I've no further use for you, Lord Gray." She shared the same pouting lips and sultry smile as her sister, the Lady Nicoletta, but she was clearly younger and certainly more mischievous. And then she added in a whisper, "You are far too aged for me."

Recalling she had just claimed to be twenty, Julian laughed. He was only a decade older. "Ach, just take a wee look at me, lass! I'm as brawny and virile as any man! Mayhap even more!"

She did take a look. A long, slow one, and then her lip crooked and a devious expression crossed her face. "Would you rather hear that you are simply not man enough to interest me, Lord Gray?"

Julian raised both brows. "No lass has ever said so of me afore!" He laughed outright, his curiosity growing even deeper in the trickster fluttering her lashes at him. Folding his arms behind his head, he settled back and asked, "Would ye care to enlighten me as to why ye've made your brother my enemy, then?"

"I haven't the time," she said, shrugging nonchalantly as she fastened the laces of her dress and stepped into a pair of finely embroidered slippers. Pointing a delicate toe at a coil of rope on the floor, she raised an eyebrow up at Julian.

He distinctly remembered tying the very same rope into a snare around the window the night before, in order to catch unwary intruders.

She had evidently read the confusion in his expression. With a smug but irresistible smile, she said, "You should really protect yourself better, Lord Gray. The incensed husbands and brothers of France are not as … *gòfi* as the Scottish! Ah, how shall I say it so you may understand?" She paused and tapped her lip, and then her eyes lit with a devilish glint. "Ah, you are like a lumbering ox … a bumbling jester, as well as a scandalous fool."

Julian's lips parted in surprise. While he readily embraced scandal— nay, he relished scandal—he was anything but a lumbering ox!

In reality, he was *Le Marin,* arguably the most famous and daring spy in Scotland, England, *and* France. And no one, not even his closest friend, Cameron Stewart, Earl of Lennox, knew that Lord Julian Gray and *Le Marin* were one and the same. Cameron thought Julian was an exceptional spy, but he little knew just *how* exceptional. The feats of *Le Marin* were legendary, and numerous were the theories of just whom *Le Marin* might truly be, theories that Julian found terribly amusing, especially in how far they fell from the truth.

Amusing … until now.

But there was little he could do about the matter. No, it was better the lass continued to think of him simply as the scandalous Lord Gray, the shockingly disgraceful young Scottish lord intent on gambling away his family fortune and bedding every maiden he encountered.

Brushing his momentary touchiness aside, he rose from the bed and peered down at her with an easy grin. Clad in his close-fitting breeches, his chest was bare, exposing hard muscles that never failed to elicit sighs of admiration from any lass that beheld them.

"Tarry a wee spell, my lady," he murmured in a suggestive tone. "And ye'll soon see how mistaken ye are."

But the wicked beastie was clearly unaffected by his physical prowess. Lifting a mocking brow, she scooped up his white shirt from the foot of the bed and tossed it over his broad expanse of naked chest.

"Impressive, mayhap, for a Scotsman. *Bondagnénte smoroxéto,*" she replied with a coy smile. "But in my land, men like you are of the most common kind!"

Common kind? He highly doubted that. Would an ordinary man know that she'd just called him a *good-for-nothing* gallant in Venetian? Aye, but how could she know he'd been mentored by a Venetian master spy and was fluent in their language. His grin broadened as his interest ignited even more.

"I must be gone, Lord Gray." Liselle gave a laugh as a wicked smile curved her full lips. "This has been a pleasant diversion, but the sun is rising."

Blowing him a kiss, she turned lightly on her heel and headed for the door.

He watched her go with a twinge of disappointment and a full measure of admiration. But, as the door closed behind her, he quickly donned his shirt and collected his weapons, shaking his head all the while.

Now there was a lass worth kissing. And the fact that such an act might be rewarded with a knife in his gut made him all the more interested in attempting the deed. What a delightful challenge she would be!

But alas, he had not the time for such pleasantries. He was on a mission. Alexander Stewart, Duke of Albany, and the last surviving brother of King James III of Scotland, appeared to have embarked, yet again, on another foolish attempt to wrest the throne from his brother.

Just a few years prior, the king's lowborn favorite and latest lover, Thomas Cochrane, had accused Scotland's youngest prince, John Stewart, the Earl of Mar, of witchcraft, and had murdered and buried him. Albany, afraid for his own life, had then fled to France with Julian's help.

Julian sighed, pushing back his shoulder-length blond hair and pulling on his black leather boots. He despised Albany. He'd only aided the man as a favor to his friend, Cameron.

The instant Albany had set foot in the French court of King Louis XI he had embroiled himself in one treacherous plot after another.

Aye, the prince was angry over Mar's unjust death; it was an anger that most in Scotland shared. But Albany was no better than James; the king was a fool, but Albany was unscrupulous.

In the bid to gain the French king's favor and support, Albany had unceremoniously dissolved his marriage to Lady Katherine—disinheriting his three grown sons and daughter in the process—and had then married Anne de la Tour. After which, he redoubled his pestering of Louis to put him on the Scottish throne.

But the French king would have none of it.

Now banned from court, Albany was skulking in Sarlat, a town nestled in a hollow between the hills and the Dordogne River in Aquitaine, in southwestern France.

Julian had been almost relieved last week to discover a man shadowing Albany, a man who proved to be the Venetian assassin, Orazio di Franco.

But as Albany continued to walk in the light of day, Julian had become intrigued, knowing that if Orazio had truly wanted the treacherous prince dead, he would be. And then Julian would even now be standing on Scottish soil with Albany buried six feet beneath him.

No, Orazio clearly had other designs in pursuing Albany. And those designs were fair interesting to Julian as *Le Marin*. And mayhap this Liselle was even part of that plan, a thought Julian found even more enthralling.

Aye, something was brewing, and he more than ached for a game of wits with worthy opponents.

He knew little of his sister, but from what he knew of Orazio, the man would be the worthiest of opponents.

Crossing the chamber, Julian cracked a shutter open.

His room was on the top floor of the inn, affording him a stunning view of the sun which was now rising on the sleepy town of Sarlat and bathing its shale roof tiles in a warm red glow.

Voices drifted up from the cobblestoned street below, and he glanced down to see Orazio standing almost directly beneath him.

The man was pacing, appearing genuinely agitated as he waved his hands at Lady Nicoletta who was standing nearby.

Liselle was nowhere to be seen.

With his eyes trained on the pair below, Julian strained forward to catch his words.

"... and we must not fail!" Orazio made a harsh chopping gesture with his palm. "Not again!"

"She is no longer a child, Orazio." Lady Nicoletta heaved a great sigh, laying her hand on her brother's arm. "We have held her back long enough."

"And you know *exactly* why that's so! She's too passionate. She leaps and then looks to see where she's falling!" Orazio growled. "And now she's playing some ill-thought-out game with that fool!"

Julian grinned, and tilting his head to one side, took a cloth from his pocket and absently began to polish one of his blades.

"Indeed, I agree, of all men, why that one?" Lady Nicoletta waved a disgusted hand in Julian's direction. *"Macarón!"* She began to pound her chest with her palm.

Julian's grin widened. He and Lady Nicoletta had never seen eye-to-eye. She'd called him the demeaning term at every opportunity.

Lady Nicoletta's wailing stopped abruptly as a man stepped out from the shadows to murmur something into Orazio's ear.

The effect was immediate. "Then, to the market square with haste!" Orazio ordered, and all three whirled upon their heels, their cloaks billowing out behind them as they disappeared into a nearby alleyway.

Julian's eyes lit with exhilaration. Finally, the game was afoot! Quickly, he inserted a blade into each boot and concealed a third within his sleeve. Grabbing his cloak, he slipped out of his chamber and went down the narrow, dark stairs of the French inn, *Les Trois Couronnes.*

At the bottom of the stairs he spied the flat-faced innkeeper huffing about the common room, poking several snoring men with the handle of a broom.

Julian chuckled under his breath. He'd never met a more righteous innkeeper; the man should have been a priest. Taking a deep breath, he stepped into the room, lurching sideways in feigned drunkenness. After all, he had a reputation to uphold as the irresponsible, reckless Lord Gray.

"Did ye see a lass run through here a wee bit ago?" he asked the innkeeper, slurring his speech and bracing himself unsteadily against the doorpost. "A green gown, I think she wore!"

The innkeeper brushed back his gray hair which hung in straggly, limp strings, and his long face lengthened even more as he eyed Julian with rank disapproval. "No, my lord."

"Well then!" Julian blinked as if in surprise and stepped back, weaving a little before adding with a grin, "I'll take any lass then ... or two. Can ye send a few to my chamber and more of that fine Frankish wine of yours, aye?"

The frown on the man's face deepened. "I run a respectable inn, my lord. I do not employ *demoiselles* of the kind you seek."

Julian gave a loud groan, but judging he was on the verge of losing Orazio's trail, he heaved a disappointed sigh and stumbled towards the front door. He paused on the threshold a moment and grinned at the innkeeper who huffed in disgust, and then Julian stepped out into the cobblestoned street.

Once out of the innkeeper's sight, Julian dropped the act and set off in hot pursuit of Orazio and his companions.

Shafts of morning sunlight fell in crisscross patterns through the narrow, crooked lanes as he hurried to the market square in the center of the town. It was still early, and most of the stalls were closed, but for a thick-lipped man with a bulging belly arranging baskets of mushrooms, and a lad with a face more fit for a lass, driving a flock of geese into a pen.

At the edge of the market square, he caught sight of Orazio and the others striding determinedly towards a stone cottage with a walled courtyard and red-shuttered windows. Herbs grew in pots on the sills, and ivy covered the courtyard walls and half of the brown slate roof as well.

Pausing before the cottage's gate, Orazio peered over his shoulders in both directions.

Quickly, Julian ducked into a nearby alleyway, inadvertently startling a flock of pigeons. He frowned as the birds fluttered to rest on the rooftop ridges of the narrow buildings flanking him. No doubt, Orazio would see and know he was being followed.

Cursing under his breath, Julian waited longer than he liked before peering cautiously around the corner, just in time to see Orazio disappear behind the gate.

Apparently, the man hadn't suspected he'd been followed.

Julian expelled a breath of relief, stretched, and glanced around.

Already, there were more people on the street, and they were growing more numerous by the moment. As a cart rumbled by, Julian stepped out of the alleyway to casually weave through the square, approaching the stone cottage from the back. It was easy enough to scale the courtyard wall and peer inside the enclosure.

There was a garden, and it was small, barely room enough for its single raised herb bed and several large clay pots. A tree grew near the smoke-stained sandstone wall of what appeared to be the cottage's kitchen. Swinging his legs over the wall, he dropped lightly on his feet and swiftly darted to the nearest window.

The soft murmur of voices met his ear, but he couldn't make out any words. He was ready to move on when a loud laugh caught him by surprise.

He would recognize that laugh anywhere.

It was Albany.

"… and I've been assured that ye are the finest spy in Christendom," the Scottish prince was saying gruffly.

Julian rolled his eyes in scorn. The fool had been misled. Orazio was an assassin, not a spy. And even if he were a spy, he was nothing *akin* to *Le Marin*.

"Aye, the reason I've need for your particular kind of service is that I'm on my way to England and will need my own man to watch my back and to uncover what those treacherous English rats will undoubtedly try to hide from me!" Albany continued, clearing his throat. "I'll expect ye to journey with me the whole way to Fotheringhay, where 'tas been arranged I should be a fortnight hence."

Sweet Mary! Julian's gray eyes widened. Fotheringhay? England? If Albany were to gain the support of Edward, King of England, then

Scotland was in serious danger.

"I will send a man of mine to accompany you—" Orazio's unmistakable tones began.

"Nay, not so!" Albany interrupted angrily. "'Twas *ye* I was told to hire, not another!"

"My man will suffice! As I have said, my lord, you will be pleased with my services—services, may I remind you, that you've yet to pay for." Orazio's voice hardened.

Julian frowned. Orazio was not a gatherer of information; the man was an assassin. There could only be one reason for the deception. His true target must be a man of Albany's acquaintance.

"Aye, aye," Albany mumbled. There was the sound of a wooden chair scraping against a stone floor, and then the prince's voice floated through the window from different angles as he began to pace. "Then, I've nae choice but to trust ye. Ach, 'tis a princely sum that ye've asked of me! I dinna have such a sum of gold at hand! I can only pay ye half now."

At that, Julian raised a brow in admiration. Aye, Orazio was a wily one to collect the prince's gold while at the same time using him as a tool to gain access to his true target! 'Twas no wonder the man was infamous. Such deviousness could only be admired.

"I see," Orazio replied. His tone was cool. "Then perhaps our services are not really what you need."

"Nay!" Albany quickly inserted. "I'll see ye paid the rest soon, I swear it! But give me time!"

"No, my lord," came Orazio's reply. "I require the entire sum first, as I have said. When you have it, send word and—"

"God's Wounds!" Albany swore loudly and there was a crash, as if he'd kicked over a chair. "Surely, the word of the future King of Scotland means something to ye?"

There was a long pause.

And then Orazio's deep voice dropped. "Mayhap ... mayhap there *is* a way, my lord."

"A way?" Albany seized the words eagerly.

"Mayhap..." Orazio murmured. There was a drumming sound, as if he were drumming his fingers thoughtfully upon a table. "On this one occasion, my lord, I could wait on the full payment in return for a favor."

Albany's voice turned suspicious at once. "A favor? What favor is this?"

"A simple request. 'Tis my sister, the Lady Nicoletta. I must see her returned to the Scottish court to the care of Princess Anabella, and I cannot accompany her myself," the man answered calmly.

Julian raised a brow, wondering what kind of threat Orazio might pose to the Scottish court if he were using his relationship to Nicoletta as part of his scheme. It was something that he should delve into, and forthwith.

"Nicoletta?" Albany cleared his throat and paused a moment. "Is the lass a spy as well?"

Orazio laughed, and Julian found himself laughing silently along with him.

The concept was ludicrous. Nicoletta was anything but a spy. She was a mere lady-in-waiting. Aye, every time he'd ever been in her presence, she'd spoken only of court etiquette, and specifically his own great lack in observing it. Rumors and intrigue didn't appear to interest her in the slightest.

"My sister Nicoletta is naught but a *trusted* companion to the princess, my lord," Orazio replied in a derisive tone. "And you would do well to remember that our mother is the Lady Catelin le Brun, a long-time favorite in the French court and a personal friend to Princess Anabella of

Scotland. My sister knows nothing of my more *adventurous* activities."

Albany cleared his throat. "Aye, now, I meant nothing by it. Indeed 'tis a fair barter. I'll see to her safe passage for ye," he said, sounding distinctly embarrassed.

Suddenly, the clap of a closing door startled Julian.

Someone was approaching.

With nowhere to hide, he had no choice but to abandon his eavesdropping. Leaping lightly onto the top of the wall, he dangled one leg over the side and hesitated just long enough to catch a glimpse of a vibrant green gown before jumping to the other side.

Was it Liselle?

He was half-tempted to leap back over and see. But the news that Albany was traveling to Fotheringhay in England was beyond alarming. If he were to gain the support of the English in his quest for the throne, Scotland would be doomed. Cameron had to know. Scotland had to prepare. They could very well be headed for the war that they'd been working for years to prevent.

For a moment, he pondered what Orazio's scheme might be and if the man he was sending with Albany was also an assassin. But even if he were, it appeared they were traveling to Fotheringhay and that meant his intended victim would most likely be English. Julian smiled to himself a little. One less Englishman conspiring to wage war against Scotland wasn't particularly troubling news.

Striding through the marketplace, Julian headed back down the walled streets of Sarlat. He chuckled once or twice at the mere thought of Nicoletta being a spy, but Albany's treachery was enough to turn any man's mood ultimately somber.

He had to leave for Scotland at once, but not before he left a parting message for the treacherous Scottish prince. Aye, the man was a cur. And he should remain in France, where deception was the way of life. That a Scottish prince would scheme with the English was beyond repulsive.

Julian blew a breath in disgust.

Heading for the inn where he knew Albany to be staying, he fished a length of fine silver cord from his pocket.

God's Wounds! He'd leave the man a message—a message that would strike fear in his very soul.

Anger boiled in Julian as his nimble fingers began to weave a Turk's head knot, the well-known trademark of *Le Marin*. Years ago, he'd taken to leaving the knot behind whenever he wanted to alarm his adversaries. He'd leave it as a warning but also as a brazen clue to his actual identity. His family had been in the shipping trade for centuries, and the ornate silken knot was an outright declaration of his seafaring heritage. But no one had yet pieced together the clues. They had simply taken to calling him *Le Marin,* assuming that only a sailor-turned-dangerous-spy would leave a Turk's head knot behind as a token.

Finishing the knot with a flourish, Julian slipped it into his pocket. Aye, he'd leave his token on Albany's pillow, knowing the man would quail in his boots upon seeing it.

Turning up a narrow street, he arrived at Albany's inn. And with a confident step, Julian strode through the kitchens, past a man with a face that reminded him of a rat, and up the creaky stairs leading to the Scottish prince's rooms.

He nodded at every gent and winked at every lass he met along the busy passageway, grinning as the maidens blushed and giggled. One bright-eyed girl caught his attention in particular. Aye, she might have proved worthy of a diversion if he wasn't in such a hurry.

Soon enough, Julian spied the entrance to the prince's rooms, seemingly left unguarded. He made short work of picking a few locks and was soon placing the Turk's head knot on Albany's silken pillow. His deed accomplished, Julian swiftly left the chamber and made his way back to the kitchens, snagging a carrot from the bowl of an unwary cook. Stepping out into Sarlat's narrow cobbled streets, Julian took in his surroundings. A short distance away, a group of traveling jongleurs were performing in front of a church. They balanced wooden staves upon their heads as a thin and wiry young man held out his cap to collect coins from the clapping bystanders.

Julian paused to watch them for a moment, leaning against a rough sandstone wall.

"You mend right swiftly, my Lord Gray," Liselle's alto tones whispered by his side. "When you left your inn not long ago, I was concerned for you. You could scarcely stand."

Deep lines of laughter creased his cheeks. So the wee imp had been watching him? Turning, he leaned down, and brushing the top of her ear with his lips, he whispered in reply, "French wine is water to a Scotsman, lass."

Her hazel eyes flashed with amusement, and gathering her green gown, she moved as if to step past him, but he caught her about the waist and pulled her back, effectively caging her against the rough stone wall.

"There's no need to leave, lass," he said with a chuckle. "We are wed, are we not?"

Smiling demurely, she reached up and let her finger trail down his cheek in a manner he found most seductive. "You really should be leaving Sarlat while you still yet live, my lord."

He would have thought of a witty reply had not a particularly captivating and voluptuous brunette chosen that particular moment to pass by. And then Liselle's slender fingers slid up the side of his neck to catch his chin, drawing it back towards her.

Dragging his gaze away from the brunette, he peered down into a pair of dangerous green eyes flecked with amber.

With a smile, Liselle pulled his head down with an unusually strong grip. "No man looks at another woman whilst in my company, Lord Gray," she warned, breathing softly into his ear before nipping it with her teeth.

His pulse quickened, and his lips slowly stretched into a predatory smile. Aye, the wicked lass had his full attention now. Scotland could wait a wee bit. After all, Albany's riding skills were nothing compared to his own. His hot breath brushed her cheek as he lowered his lips to hers, but at the last moment, she twisted away, easily slipping out of his arms.

"I'm afraid we shall not meet again, my lord." Her eyes sparkled with amusement. "And for your safety, I certainly hope not."

Julian's eyes slid over her appreciatively as she pivoted on her heel, and without a backward glance, the lass strode down a cobblestoned lane bordered with fruit trees.

He frowned.

Alas, but he had not the time to pursue her further. 'Twas time to ride to the coast as fast as a horse could carry him.

Aye, but 'twould do him good to ride.

With a pronounced sigh of regret, he straightened his shirt and headed for *Les Trois Couronnes* for his horse.

2

LOVE IS AN ILLNESS

The sun was high over Sarlat's rooftops before Julian finally galloped across the bridge over the Dordogne River and onto a steep road leading up the nearby hill.

With his thoughts now firmly on Scotland's safety, he urged his horse through narrow valleys, over hills covered with numerous flocks, and under the wind-rustling leaves of chestnut trees. The roads were difficult, and by the time he finally stopped to tend to his horse and a tankard of ale, he was fair exhausted.

The village was a small one, boasting only a single inn with two rooms, and the best his coin could buy was the least crowded bed. But he was tired enough to sleep through the snores of his bedmate, a stolid-looking man with wide cheekbones and a broad nose.

Morning saw him refreshed, and after giving the bosomy serving lass a healthy pinch, he was madly galloping once again.

Images of Liselle strayed across his mind the next few days, but when he finally reached the port of Bordeaux, she had faded into a distant, amusing memory.

Pausing in the shadow of Langoiran Castle perched on the hills overlooking the Garonne River, he eyed the banners hanging from the tower windows with a rueful grin.

In three days' time, the scandalous Lord Gray was expected to appear there for a week of hunting, feasting, and wagering. Alas, but he would not be arriving as anticipated. And while he longed for a goblet in his hand and a lass on his knee, he had to reach Scotland, and right quickly.

A short time later, he was dismounting at the docks with a gleam in his eye upon catching sight of *The Yellow Carvel* moored in the harbor. Fortune was favoring him to find the Scottish king's own ship at a French port.

He had to listen only a moment to identify which tavern along the docks housed the Scottish ship's captain and his crew; it was the only one filled with Gaelic drinking songs, Gaelic curses, and the sound of men actively brawling.

The sand was gray and springy beneath his feet as he made his way to the rickety structure, and a woman with a wrinkled face and sagging skin met him at the door. In response to his query, she waved him to the back to where the Scottish captain sat drinking with his men.

"Lord Gray!" the captain recognized him instantly.

With an easy grin, Julian bought the man another tankard, and in moments had secured his passage to Edinburgh.

"But I've nae mind for the king's black money, lad," the captain insisted gruffly, spitting a little as he talked. He was a middle-aged portly man with a stubborn air but a sincere face. "Ye must pay in good honest silver. I'll nae accept the Cochrane Plack, no matter how many laws the king passes!"

"Aye," Julian agreed without hesitation, pressing a silver coin into the man's palm.

The captain eyed the coin and then punched Julian on the shoulder, a smile hiding in his unruly beard. "Then dinna be late, lad. We sail with the dawn!"

Julian smiled, downing a tankard himself as he listened to the men complain about Thomas Cochrane's latest scheme to debase the king's coin by mixing good silver with copper. "Black Money", most called it, and some called it "Cochrane Plack". And few, if any, would accept the coinage in payment for goods, in spite of the numerous laws the king had issued to make them do so.

Growing weary of hearing Cochrane's name, Julian left to sell his horse, and then wandered aimlessly along the docks for a time, watching the bank of clouds roll in with the tide.

The night passed quickly, and soon enough he was leaning against the deck railing of *The Yellow Carvel* watching France dwindle into the distance. Next to him stood a somber woman holding a bairn whose wee face contorted into tears the moment Julian looked at him.

Quickly, Julian moved away.

Ach, he would never understand bairns nor why anyone would want one of the complicated little beasties.

As the ship plowed through the sea, wave by wave, he let his mind wander over Albany's latest treachery and the very real threat of war. And by the time the afternoon sun finally pierced the pearly haze that shrouded the sea, his head was aching. Aye, he hadn't thought it possible, but he now detested Albany even more.

Days passed, and at last they were sailing up Scotland's black, jagged coast.

Opening his arms wide, Julian breathed deeply of the fresh chill air, eyeing the sea cliffs sprinkled with tufts of grass. Standing on the deck with a cool breeze at his back and the sun warm on his face, he questioned, as he had upon occasion, if he were finally growing tired of *Le Marin's* escapades. There were times he wondered if he should abide by his mother's advice to stay in Scotland and preside over Castle Huntly.

Fortunately, the feeling never lasted very long.

Soon, *The Yellow Carvel* made its way up the Forth, lined with thatched cottages on either side, and finally to the docks. Once disembarked, Julian lost no time in securing a horse, and then proceeded to gallop madly to Edinburgh.

Before him, the dark and mighty Edinburgh Castle grew steadily closer, rising high upon the rocky cliffs surrounding the town and the Forth Valley. And soon enough he had entered the city gates, guiding his horse up the cobblestoned streets leading straight to the castle's main entrance.

The guardsmen let him in at once, and taking the steps two at a time, he arrived at Cameron's private apartments quite out of breath.

Pounding on the door, he rested his head momentarily against his arm.

He was unprepared for the door to be yanked open immediately, and that by Cameron Stewart, the Earl of Lennox himself.

"Come in, lad! They told me ye'd arrived with haste!" Cameron pulled him inside at once. "Ach, ye look haggard, Julian!"

The Earl of Lennox was a tall man, dark haired, broad-shouldered and imposing, but the smile in his penetrating eyes was mirrored upon his chiseled lips. "'Tis good to see ye again!"

"Aye," Julian agreed in a heavy tone.

Cameron's eyes darkened and his lips thinned. "It canna be good tidings, then."

Julian grimaced in answer.

The earl expelled a breath. "Then let it wait a moment. Drink first."

Wearily, Julian followed him across the chamber to a small table laden with goblets and a platter of sweetmeats.

"Take a seat, lad," Cameron ordered, pushing him towards the nearest cushioned chair. "It's been too long since I've seen ye. What has it been? A year almost?"

"Aye," Julian grinned tiredly, accepting the proffered goblet and draining it in a single draught. He had last seen Cameron upon the birth of his second daughter. Sizing the earl up and down, he added, "Matrimony and fatherhood becomes ye, lad, though ye'd best be wary of going as soft as a monk."

Nothing could have been further from the truth. The earl was as fit as he'd ever been.

"'Tis time ye found a lass yourself, Julian." Cameron's lip crooked upwards in his version of a laugh.

"Love is an illness, a wretched disease!" Julian tossed his head back with a wide disparaging grin. "Love is a malady *I'll* never suffer from."

There was a scuffling at the door as the latch lifted, and a group of little girls poured into the room to descend upon Cameron. As they began to squeal, Julian flinched.

"Julian! 'Tis been far too long!"

Rising to his feet, Julian turned to see Cameron's wife, Kate, the Countess of Lennox entering the chamber, balancing a plump babe on her hip. The diminutive countess glowed. Her cheeks were rosy and her brown eyes sparkled with laughter.

As she drew closer, Julian could see the smooth curve of motherhood announcing she was expecting her third child. Bending low over her hand, he said with a humorous glint in his gray eyes, "My most beloved Countess of Lennox, 'tis your favorite onion-eyed varlet come to greet ye!"

"Will ye never forget my foolish words, my lord?" Kate laughed, her nose wrinkling in delight. "Ye know well that I thought ye a thief when I called ye that, nigh on three years ago!"

Pressing her hand dramatically against his heart, Julian grinned. "I shall never forget, my lady. I half fell in love with ye myself that night."

"Ye've yet to know what love truly is, ye foolish lad!" Kate laughed again, peering up at her husband with a sly twinkle in her eyes. "But, well do I remember that night."

As Cameron sent his wife a smoldering look, Julian glanced away.

In some ways, he couldn't understand Cameron anymore. And as the little lassies ran about in circles, shouting with excitement, Julian winced outright.

Ach, he didn't have anything directly against bairns, but he did privately view them as a wee bit of a nuisance. Cameron had shared that opinion in the past, but it was quite obvious the man had gone a bit daft since meeting Kate. By all appearances, he not only didn't seem to mind the lassies hanging off his arms, he actually looked as if he enjoyed it.

Moving to tower over his wife, Cameron captured her hand in his long fingers and gave it a soft kiss. "I'll join ye soon, my sweeting."

"Then I'll see that your chamber is readied, Julian," Kate said, and ordering the chattering children to her side, bustled them out the door.

Once they had gone, Julian shook his head with a droll laugh. "Ach, Cameron, 'tis no wonder affairs of state have deteriorated of late," he observed wryly. "Another bairn? 'Tis three in as many years as ye've been wed! If ye spent half as much time in court as ye do with your wee wife in bed, James would be sitting on the throne of not only Scotland but of England and France by now."

Cameron tapped his fingers on the table, a touch amused. And then his face grew serious.

"Aye." Julian sighed, reading his expression. "But ye won't like what I've come to say."

And he didn't.

It didn't take long for Julian to relate Albany's latest treachery.

"Then England prepares for war and so must we," Cameron said softly when Julian had finished. "I'll send word to the clans to gather their men."

"And I shall ride to Fotheringhay with the dawn," Julian offered.

"We must discover who is supporting his cause."

"Aye." Cameron nodded grimly.

A silence fell for a time, a silence Julian finally broke. "And how is the king? Is Thomas Cochrane still the cat who manipulates the royal mouse? Or does James caress Hommil the Tailor and Torfifan the Fencing-Master once again?" Both lowborn men had been royal favorites in the past, before Thomas Cochrane had arrived.

Cameron shot Julian a dark glance.

Thomas Cochrane was a sore subject with the earl; he had nearly lost Kate over the man's schemes, which had seen the king's loyal brother, Mar, accused of witchcraft and then murdered.

"Aye, 'tis still Thomas alone who receives the fond kisses and favors of the king, and he is well-guarded," Cameron finally answered with a sardonic twist of his lip. "My time for vengeance hasna yet come, Julian. I must wait still."

"Mayhap not long," Julian said with a yawn. Rising to his feet, he stretched before adding, "He's a rash, overbold fellow. He might well have made a fatal error with this unsavory black money plot."

"Aye, the anger amongst the people has grown uncommonly strong, but dinna underestimate him," Cameron warned softly. "Though I dare say justice will prevail in the end, Julian."

"Aye, but it oft needs a helping hand," he replied with a hollow laugh. "Very well then, I'll be off to England with the sun."

"Have a care, lad," Cameron cautioned, escorting him to the door. "These are dangerous times. Have a care."

3

THE HAND OF FATE

Liselle leaned out of the second-story cottage window, soaking in the warmth of the sun as the soft summer winds caressed her face.

There was more to the handsome young Lord Julian Gray than met the eye.

Of that, she was certain.

His charm, combined with an air of mystique and a smile of pure decadence, made him fascinatingly irresistible. And his shrewd, gray eyes reminded her of a hawk in search of prey—far from the drunken fool that Nicoletta claimed him to be. Her sister had sworn to her that he was a simpleton and a scandalous lord, intent only on securing his own pleasure.

Liselle smiled a secret smile. She might have agreed with Nicoletta if she hadn't accidentally stumbled upon him one evening perched on the rooftop above the Scottish prince's window. He crouched there, listening to the man's pompous ranting for a time, before dropping lightly to the ground and disappearing into the darkness.

Intrigued, Liselle had begun to follow Julian, much to Nicoletta's annoyance and Orazio's concern.

Santo Ciélo! Liselle rolled her eyes. They trusted her so little!

Their response to her initiative had been to accuse her of *falling in love* and so they'd promptly assigned her cousin, Pascal, to watch and dictate her every move since.

Liselle had retaliated by evading her vigilant cousin, and it hadn't been easy. Once free, she had slipped into Julian's chamber at the inn, her goal being to find proof that the man was more than Nicoletta claimed.

Indeed! He could well be a potential adversary and mayhap someone to watch closely in Scotland!

Pure instinct and training had helped her to narrowly avoid the snare set by his window. Thus forewarned, she had tiptoed through his chamber with extreme caution.

And then she had seen him sleeping in his bed.

Her heart had pulsed in excitement as she'd crept closer to stare down at him in admiration. And she'd stared for far longer than was prudent, but only because his chest had been bare, exposing firm muscles in such a way that left her deliciously breathless. But then she had spied a bundle of parchment resting upon his saddlebag nearby. Reminded of her purpose, she'd just taken a step towards it when Nicoletta's wail had drifted up from below.

Dedia! Her sister could be overbearing at times! And *for* sure, it must have been that fool, that *bábio* Pascal, who'd betrayed her whereabouts.

As Nicoletta's shrieking grew closer, accompanied by the pounding of feet up the stairs, Liselle had succumbed to the temptation of annoying her sister just a tiny bit more. In one fluid movement, she had slipped out of her gown and into the bed of the sleeping Lord Julian Gray.

But she hadn't expected Orazio to be the one to burst through the door.

Nor had she expected Julian to be so warm, and even more handsome up close.

She smiled, reliving again the moment he'd discovered her next to him.

"Liselle!"

Liselle jumped, startled out of her pleasant memory.

Nicoletta's voice was far too close. It was too late to escape. Turning, she spied her older sister charging up the steps, her red-velvet skirts firmly clutched in both hands.

"Do not even *think* of running from me!" Nicoletta warned, punctuating each word with an angry huff. "Lord Gray? Why Lord Gray? And just *what* have you done with him?"

"*Òsti,*" Liselle scowled, tossing her hands up in the air. "I am not a child, Nicoletta!"

Nicoletta arrived out of breath, but still managed a snort of disgust. "*Ah sì,* and toying with a shameful buffoon proves that?"

Liselle lifted her chin, letting her hazel eyes flash, but remained silent. Crossing Nicoletta was always a dangerous proposition.

"Lord Gray is of the most scandalous ilk, Liselle!" Nicoletta continued passionately, wiping her brow and fanning her cheeks. "And you know my plans for him! He is the perfect dupe, and if the need were to arise, I could lay the blame of any action I must take at his feet! I just pray your foolish prank hasn't ruined my designs, and that you haven't ruined yourself as well!"

Liselle's scowl faded slightly. Her sister's complexion was sallow and her forehead beaded with sweat. "You look unwell, Nicoletta," she observed with concern. "What ails you?"

"*Àu!* Do not think to distract me!" Nicoletta replied sharply and then repeated for emphasis, "*Lord Gray is of the most scandalous ilk!* He is naught but a gambling drunkard—*un farabùto!*"

But Liselle was not so sure. Recalling the wide variety of snares and weapons the man had hidden in his chamber and bed, she knew there was more to him than just wagering, wine, and women.

She hesitated, smoothing invisible wrinkles in her skirts as she weighed the choices before her.

Nicoletta was clearly feeling indisposed. And Liselle knew right well that her older sister sought only to protect her. The bond of sisterly love was fiercely strong between them. It would be kinder to apologize, make peace, and let her rest rather than engage in a conversation that would likely end with Orazio negotiating yet another truce between them.

"Your hot-blooded nature will be your downfall!" Nicoletta was still speaking in furiously short, clipped tones. "And your lack of judgment is astounding! You are behaving quite rashly, and I'm having Orazio send you *straight* home!"

The single word of *home* wrested the choice of restraint from Liselle's hands. All at once her anger ignited. *Home?* How dare they even *consider* sending her home! She was more than ready to practice the family craft. In fact, she was long past due for her first real assignment.

"*You* are the rash one, Nicoletta!" The words burst vehemently forth from Liselle's lips. "And your plan is flawed if you seek to use Lord Gray as any sort of dupe! He is *not* what you think. He would not stand by to take the blame for your—"

"*Esumimi! God help me!*" Nicoletta's beautiful eyes blazed as she lifted an imploring hand to the heavens. "How could you fall for him so swiftly? You are blinded by foolish fancy! I had thought you wiser than this! Did all of those years of learning teach you *nothing*—"

"*You* are the blind one!" Liselle interrupted heatedly. "Your distaste colors your reasoning! You see only the man he wishes you to see!"

"Can you even *hear* yourself speak?!" Nicoletta bristled in response. "Can you see what harm you have done? He was *perfèto! Perfèto*, I tell you! No one at court doubts his flawed, impetuous nature. It would have been easy to implicate him for anything I had to do."

Liselle threw her hands up in exasperation once again and retorted, "Not so! He would have found a way to turn the blame back on to you, and you would have paid the heavy price. That is why I sought to discover his secret! I've been watching him—"

Placing both hands on her hips, Nicoletta cut her short with a snort of disdain and pinned her with a withering glance. "At least in that you speak the truth! Now that I think on it, you have done little more than watch him on every occasion. And his *secret* is nothing more than constant practice, Liselle, practice at bedding every maid he sees!"

"Then, is this jealousy?" Liselle's eyes narrowed speculatively. "You seem to know so much about his character! Are you a jilted lover or—"

Nicoletta rewarded her with a sharp slap across the face. "That you would say that proves you are not thinking—"

"*Basta!* Enough, Nicoletta!" Orazio's deep baritone startled them both.

Liselle stepped back, cupping her palm over her stinging cheek, and then both sisters turned on him at once.

"She lacks prudence, Orazio! And—" Nicoletta began.

"And *she* lacks skill!" Liselle inserted quickly. "My talents overshadow hers by far! You know this to be true!"

"And you *both* lack discretion! I could hear you from the streets!" Orazio laughed, stepping in between them and shaking his head as he peered down at his sisters in amusement. But then observing Nicoletta, his astute brown eyes grew serious all at once. "You look ill, Nicoletta. What is it?"

"*Santa pazienza!*" Nicoletta tiredly waved her hand at her younger sister. "This one will soon send me to my grave."

Liselle rolled her eyes at the all too familiar words. "You are not *mama*, Nicoletta."

"But now I understand her so well," Nicoletta sighed heavily. "I see why she says that of you so often." And then her knees suddenly buckled, and she would have fallen had not Orazio caught her by the shoulders.

"Rest," he ordered, his distinguished features suffused with concern. "I will … handle Liselle."

Liselle tensed. It never ended well for her whenever they decided she needed to be *handled*.

"Yes. I could rest," Nicoletta whispered, closing her eyes for several long moments before lifting her dark lashes to glower at Orazio. "You will keep your word?"

At Orazio's barely imperceptible nod of reply, Liselle's heart sank further. It was true. They were sending her back to Venice.

"Very well then," her older sister heaved a deep sigh. And then without another word or a backward glance, she left the room.

Liselle waited until Nicoletta was out of earshot before turning to Orazio and demanding in outright alarm, "What ails her? Is she ill?"

Nothing—even the threat of being sent home—was more important than her sister's health and well-being.

Her brother arched a dark brow. "Have you ever known anything to daunt her, *sorèla cara*?"

His response was comforting. As maddeningly overbearing as Nicoletta was, life would be torture without her. But all warm, sisterly thoughts evaporated instantly upon hearing Orazio's next words.

"Pascal will escort you home on the morrow, Liselle."

"No!" Her anger returned full force. "I refuse! My abilities are far superior to Nicoletta's, Orazio! You know this!"

He tilted his head, looking down at her from the lengths of his long, angular nose before observing coolly, "Mayhap your skills are, but your judgment certainly is not."

"Simply because of Lord Gray?" Liselle exploded, her hazel eyes flashing with fire. "He did not touch me, Orazio! I swear it! Nor did he see my viper mark! He only discovered I was there the moment you burst in. *Cà de dìa*, Nicoletta was making such a racket! I heard her coming up the stairs and slid into his bed simply to aggravate her!"

"Indeed, that is my point, *cara*," Orazio replied softly, but his dark eyes held a glint of humor. And then the humor faded to an almost paternal kindness. "She speaks the truth, Liselle. Your passionate nature blinds you. You are too impulsive and impatient. You are not yet ready."

Struggling to control her temper, Liselle almost choked on her own words. "*Ridicolóxo!* Are you both truly that blind? The man is not what he seems! For Nicoletta's own safety, I went to his chamber to see what he's hiding!"

Leaning down, Orazio placed a heavy hand on her shoulder. "Liselle, Lord Julian Gray is Nicoletta's concern, not yours. You were to find Dolfino Dolfin, not to spy on a foolish Scottish lord."

She wanted to scream out of pure frustration. She had told them repeatedly that the old salt spy, Dolfin, had fled to England after his audience with Albany. And she knew very well that Orazio secretly believed her. Why else would they be in Sarlat, courting Albany's favor in order to find out where in England the old man had gone?

"Who is truly concerned with the fate of Dolfin any longer?" Liselle muttered rebelliously. "He is ancient in years and will soon be dead. And even if he were young, he is now exiled. He can no longer return to *La Serenìsima* to cause harm."

"He betrayed his own country," Orazio indulged her with the reply. "You know well that he sold secrets of the salt trade."

"Salt!" Liselle rolled her eyes in contempt. "No man ever died by his hand. It is over salt, Orazio! Salt!"

"Men will die soon because of it, *cara*," her brother patiently explained. "Already, we have received the Pope's blessing to take arms against Ferrara. Men *will* die to protect our salt trade."

"But—" she began.

Orazio's expression hardened. "*Basta*, I will speak of this with you no more. You were to find the man, not question the reason. You were to find him before he left France, and you failed," he pointed out mercilessly. "The man's trail clearly led to Albany, and you lost it."

Chastened, she sealed her lips. His words were true enough. She had lost interest in finding Dolfin the day Lord Julian Gray arrived in Sarlat. The Scottish noble had been a much more fascinating concern.

Still, ferreting out information was a child's task, and a note of irritation crept into her voice as she asked, "Why do you only give me useless tasks? I grow weary of decorating the arms of men and dining on partridges and sweetmeats simply to learn where an old man might be hiding."

"And if you had found him, Liselle, can you surmise the next task I would have assigned you?" Orazio's dark eyes gleamed with challenge. "Dolfin may be old, but his folly of selling our homeland's trade secrets to our enemy of Ferrara has plunged us into war. There is vengeance to be had, dear sister. The man must pay for his foul deed!"

A sudden chill hung on the edge of his words.

Liselle blinked, taken aback.

"See, *cara*." Orazio sighed, patting her sympathetically on the shoulder. "I gave you an important task. I merely asked you to find him first. Your next step would have been ... different."

Liselle blanched. The thought of assassinating an old man was abhorrent, especially over salt, but she quickly buried the thought. She had been trained from an early age on the many ways to make a man die, but she had yet to actually *use* her schooling. Most likely, it would be easier to do when the time came.

Glancing up, she caught her brother closely watching her face. Though she knew herself to be exceptionally skilled, she also knew he wasn't so confident in that.

"Go home and wait a bit, Liselle," he said with a compassionate smile. "Your time will come."

"When I am old and gray!" she countered, but without venom. The heat of her anger had inexplicably dissipated. There was an expression in his eyes that bothered her, something left unsaid, and she suddenly wanted the truth. "I left childhood several years ago, Orazio. And Nicoletta was younger than I am now when you sent her to the Scottish courts. Why do you hold me back?"

He heard the sincerity in her voice, and his answer was long in coming. Finally, he replied, "You have the skills, Liselle, *mi digo!* You are even extraordinarily talented, but you haven't the heart to truly be one of the Vindictam."

She recoiled in alarm. "What do you mean, Orazio!"

"Be at peace, Liselle," he said, reaching over to place a comforting hand upon her shoulder. "As the Magno Duce I have the authority to withhold you from missions until you are truly ready." Nodding at her ankle, he added, "And you have yet to receive the final marking. There is still time for you to withdraw and take on a different role for the Vindictam. You are a dreamer, and … I believe you were made for … something else."

"Something else?" Liselle repeated, disheartened. "Pray, what do you mean?" How could she be made for *something else* when she'd spent her entire life learning the ways of an assassin?

He took so long to reply that she thought he wasn't going to answer, but then he murmured, "This past fortnight, I have seen the manner in which you have watched Lord Gray, and I would hazard to guess you are already in love with the man. You were meant to love, Liselle, not … destroy."

Liselle's mouth gaped open. How could he misunderstand her so completely? "Absurd! He is nothing to me!" came the fervent denial, and never more genuinely felt.

It was clear that he didn't believe her. He just stood there, and then his eyes darkened with the soft inquiry, "Could you assassinate him then? To protect us all, could you take his life?"

"Yes!" she swore without hesitation. How could her brother doubt her loyalty? Her voice caught a little as she added, "I am a di Franco first and foremost, Orazio! Nothing comes between blood bonds! *Nothing!*"

Orazio watched her for a time, his shrewd eyes boring through hers, and then he simply said, "Then prove your loyalty and go home."

There was nothing she could say to that. Her shoulders sagged. Her dreams had just come to an abrupt end. Bowing her head, she turned on her heel and made her way down the stairs, caught between anger and sadness.

How could Orazio doubt her loyalty?

It did not take long to pack her belongings. And as the tantalizing whiff of rosemary and roasted meat filled the air, Liselle made up her mind. Joining the others for the evening meal would be preferable to spending the night alone with bitter thoughts, even if it meant risking another clash with Nicoletta.

But the dining chamber was empty save for her cousin, Pascal, a tall, lanky youth with angelic looks and long, dark hair.

He glanced up as she came in, and a scathing smile formed on his lips. "*Bábia!* As I predicted, the moment you thought yourself free you foolishly jumped into the flames."

Refusing to take his bait, Liselle sat down and helped herself to the rosemary suckling pig and red partridge before asking, "Where is Orazio? And Nicoletta?"

If he was disappointed by her response, he didn't show it. "Not here."

He shrugged, downing his goblet of wine.

Liselle sent him a dark look. Of all her cousins, she cared for Pascal the least. And she knew the feeling was mutual.

Absentmindedly, she ran her finger along the lip of her goblet.

Soon she would be home again, aimlessly wandering in the Piazza San Marco, wearing the finest of gowns and a fortune in jewelry about her neck. Her days would be spent chatting with the merchants at the Rialto Bridge, smelling spices, inspecting silk, and bargaining with the jewelers selling pearls and precious stones.

She expelled a heavy breath; it was not the life she wished for.

No, she longed to escape the confines of her prestigious family. She wanted freedom. She wanted to experience the world. She wanted to engage in a game of wits, to use the skills she had honed her entire life.

"Pah! The best French wine is worse than the dregs of the vilest vats in Greece!" Pascal complained, draining yet another goblet.

Liselle eyed him sourly. "Then why drink so much of it?" she muttered.

Pascal's carved lip lifted in a slight sneer. "*Ciò*, and what else am I to do? I'm to be sent home—yet again—because of you! It seems I am nothing but your donkey!"

Slamming her goblet down, Liselle rose to her feet. "I've no reason to stay here and listen to your yapping." Indeed, she would hear nothing but a litany of complaints all the way back to Venice. There was no point in subjecting herself to it more than necessary.

Taking a baguette with her, she retired once again to her chamber.

The amber glow of the candles was soothing, and after a time, she prepared for bed.

Slipping out of her green gown, her eyes fell on the small coiled viper tattooed on her left ankle. She heaved a long sigh and knelt in the candlelight, slowly rubbing a finger over the small tattoo she had been given at birth.

The viper. The assassin's sign of the Vindictam.

Her tattoo *still* lacked the tongue.

"I'm hexed!" she wailed in a whisper and softly tapped her chest. "*Sò falimènta, a failure!*"

She could only receive that final mark upon accepting her first mission. The mark of authority. The mark of no return. Once her viper had its tongue, she could only leave the Vindictam through death. But, she didn't find that particularly troublesome. She had dreamt of receiving the full mark her entire life. There was no higher honor.

She was a di Franco! The di Francos of Venice were wealthy and respectable salt merchants, powerful leaders in the European salt trade. But few knew the name they called themselves ... or what they truly were.

The shadow of her family stretched far over the lands. They were a part of the Vindictam, a group of elite assassins.

But the secrets did not stop there.

Only the women in the Vindictam were given the assassin's mark, the viper tattoo. And only the women were trained from birth in the many ways to kill a man, from poisons to strangulation, to the most effective use of the infamous, needle-pointed stiletto, their dagger of choice. Liselle even knew how to drown a man with mere drops of water.

The men of Vindictam were the decoys, spies, and protectors. They dealt with those seeking the family's services, issued the orders, and acted as escorts for the women as they went about their darker deeds.

Liselle frowned at her viper tattoo. Never had an assassin taken so long to receive her final marking. Already, she had failed. All of her older sisters and cousins had been sent to royal courts throughout Europe in preparation for the day when their services might be required. But whenever she had asked for which country she was bound, the only reply had been to *wait*.

Well, she would have to *wait* even longer now.

With a resigned scowl, she rose to her feet, and quenching the candle, plunged the chamber into darkness. The stars were bright, and a chill wind blew through the open window as she struggled to latch the shutters closed.

She would miss the town of Sarlat, and she would miss trailing Lord Gray. But there was nothing she could do now, save devoutly pray he truly was the fool Nicoletta thought him to be. It would be the only way her sister would be safe to use him as a dupe.

With a heavy heart, she stumbled to her bed.

* * *

Liselle woke to the sound of rain pattering against the shutters mingled with Pascal's curses outside her chamber door.

With a surge of annoyance, she yanked the door open, preparing to scold her cousin, but one look at his face caused her stomach to lurch in alarm. "What is it, Pascal? What has happened?"

"Nicoletta—"

At the sound of her sister's name, Liselle shoved him aside and flew down the passage towards Nicoletta's chamber, colliding with Orazio halfway.

"Nicoletta?" Liselle gasped, shaking his arm. "What has happened?"

He held a finger to his lips and replied softly, "She's ill, *sorèla mia*, but she will live. Do not fear."

Relief flooded through her at once.

"She's been struck with the ague," Orazio explained, sliding his arm about her shoulders as he guided her towards their sister's chamber. "But she has asked to see you ... before you leave. She is weak, so speak quickly." He paused, and then warned with a wry expression, "And control your temper, Liselle. She needs to rest as much as you need to leave."

Liselle scowled, and shrugging away from her brother's embrace, placed her hands on her hips to confront him. "How can you ask me to go home when she is ill? I will stay—"

Orazio silenced her with a look and then asked, "Will you ever listen, Liselle?"

She would have protested further had not they already arrived at Nicoletta's door. And then she was stepping into her sister's room filled with the heavy fragrance of lavender to ward off the bad air.

Approaching the bed, Liselle saw her sister huddled beneath the coverlet, shaking with chills, puffy-eyed, white-lipped, and with dark circles under her eyes.

"You are strong, Nicoletta," Liselle said, her voice catching a little as she knelt at her sister's side.

"I'm sorry, *sorèlina cara*," Nicoletta apologized with a feeble smile. Wisps of damp hair framed her face, and her eyes were bright with fever.

"No. *I* am sorry," Liselle replied quickly. "I beg forgiveness for my rude words yesterday—"

Nicoletta gave a weak humph and rolled her eyes. "I'm not speaking of that! I speak of Albany and Scotland. And for what you must do now in my place." The expression on her face was one of genuine regret.

Liselle caught her breath. Could it be? Had they changed their minds? A ripple of excitement washed through her, even as she worried for the health of her sister. Choosing her words carefully, she managed to answer in an even tone, "I would do anything for you, Nicoletta. You have only to name it."

"You must be cautious," Nicoletta replied, managing to look stern even as she shook with fever. "And you must be wary."

"Always, Nicoletta," Liselle replied, torn between exhilaration and worry.

Her sister grabbed her arm. Her grip was surprisingly strong. "And you must guard your heart. If you see Lord Gray, do not even speak with him! Do you understand? Not one word!"

Liselle's eyes widened. Were they truly sending her in Nicoletta's place?

"Orazio, *fradèl mio*." Nicoletta lifted a frail hand. "I fear for her so!"

Crossing the room, Orazio leaned down to cover her hand with both of his. "She is strong, Nicoletta."

"*Che scalògna!* Why has ill-fortune touched me?" Nicoletta wailed, turning once again to Liselle. "Remember, *cara*, beauty can be the deadliest weapon when used well."

"But beauty fades," Orazio inserted skillfully, glancing over to meet Liselle's eyes. "Live by your wits. And remember, you have passed every test of stealth and cunning, but you still fail in patience."

Liselle held still, too stunned to respond. There was no doubt now. They were sending her out.

Dimly, she heard Nicoletta continue to fret. "But she is too young!"

Her brother responded in consoling tones, but Liselle did not hear his words.

And then Nicoletta's fingers dug into her arm once more. "I have something for you, Liselle. A gift." She lifted a fragile hand to pat Liselle fondly on the cheek.

"A gift?" Liselle repeated numbly, still in shock.

"Give them to her, Orazio!" Nicoletta whispered, shaking with chills.

"I will," he promised, gently squeezing her shoulder. "But now you must rest. Say your farewells as Liselle must leave straightway."

Liselle scarcely heard Nicoletta's words of advice as she bade her farewell. She only saw her sister's resigned face as she fell back tiredly into the pillows. Nicoletta had clearly accepted her fate, and for some reason, Liselle found that sobering.

And then Orazio drew her from the room and guided her to another.

"Will she live, Orazio?" Liselle asked, consumed with worry. "Oh, Orazio! She cannot die!" Sudden tears filled her eyes.

"Hush, *mia cara*, she will not die. She is strong," Orazio assured, pointing to a carved rosewood box on the surface of a small table. "'Tis Nicoletta's gift. You must take her place until she is well. And you must leave at once."

It was difficult to concentrate on his words at first, but gradually excitement won over the anxiety of Nicoletta's illness. After all, as Orazio had said, Nicoletta was strong.

"Then, I'm truly not returning home?" Liselle asked suddenly.

Orazio laughed a little and reached over to tousle her head as if she were still a child. "You are going to England with Albany," he repeated in amused tones. "You will accompany Albany until he delivers you to the Scottish court. So you will have much time to perhaps learn from him just where in England Dolfino Dolfin is lurking."

"Then you *do* believe me that he has gone to England!" Liselle's lips parted in surprise.

"I've always thought your instincts were exceptional," Orazio replied, drawing his fine, aristocratic lips into a thin line. "It is your heart I fear for, little one. Do you remember the tale of Pippa?"

Liselle heaved an internal sigh. Her family took every opportunity to remind her of the ill-fated Pippa, the beautiful Venetian assassin who had betrayed her own land for the love of a Scottish highland lord—and how she had lost her life for it. Frowning, she reminded him tartly, "I've already told you I care not for Lord Gray."

"It is your nature that concerns us, Liselle. You are a dreamer," he said softly. And then he pushed the carved rosewood box towards her. "Nicoletta wishes you to have these. Keep them well."

Holding her breath, she unclasped the lid to reveal a pair of finely made stilettos with bone handles wrapped with leather cording. She ran a light finger over the cool steel of the sharp blades. Her hands were trembling, but whether from apprehension or excitement, she could not tell. She had spent her entire life waiting and countless hours of studying and training, all for this moment, to be sent out on her first serious assignment.

"I will keep them well, Orazio," Liselle whispered the vow. "And I will make you proud."

Orazio was silent a moment and then asked, "Then are you ready for your viper's tongue, *cara*?"

Her heart leapt. "My viper mark? Will you finish it now?" she asked breathlessly.

Crossing his arms, Orazio peered down at her from the lengths of his long nose. "You are merely to find Dolfin and not yet to dispatch him."

She dropped her eyes to hide her disappointment.

"Stay with Albany, Liselle," her brother continued. "And when you find Dolfin, send for me. I have words that must be said to the man ere he dies."

Liselle nodded and glanced up as Pascal arrived to slouch in the doorway.

And then Orazio took out a needle and a small pot of ink from a leather pouch about his waist. "But I shall not send you forth without authority, *cara*," he said with a half-smile.

Liselle caught her breath in excitement.

"*Diàmbarne!* That is a dreadful mistake!" Pascal objected with a curse. Holding up a hand to forestall Orazio from cutting him off, he continued, "Do not give her the tongue! You know that she does not have the heart to become one of us!"

Orazio raised a surprised brow at the youth. And then reaching over, he caught Liselle's wrist. His dark eyes searched her face. "Are you truly ready for this, *cara sorèla*? If not, I can find another to replace you. Are you certain you wish for the pigeons and the viper tongue this day?"

Liselle's eyes lit. Finally, she was being given what she had spent her life waiting for—the tongue to announce her position in the Vindictam, one of respect and authority. And the pigeons would be given to her at her destination, pigeons that she would use to immediately inform the Vindictam of her success.

She glanced down at her ankle, hidden by her skirts. Once he added the tongue to her viper tattoo, there was no return. She would have to succeed or lose her life trying.

Resolutely, she lifted her chin and assured, "I am ready!"

Orazio was watching her closely. "Then heed my words well. When your path is unsure, *cara,* focus only on the next step before you and nothing else!"

She nodded firmly.

"And always be suspicious of those you trust first—the ones closest to you," he warned, his fingers still gripping her wrist hard.

"Then, that would be you, Orazio." Liselle smiled sweetly in reply. She knew he was worried, but she was too thrilled to share his concern. "Do not fret, Orazio *caro*. I will be like *Le Marin*! I will always be successful and never be caught!"

He grimaced at that. *Le Marin* was a sore subject with Orazio. Three times the French spy had bested him in the past few years.

And then she had to ask, "But if I should fail?"

Orazio hesitated and then replied, "Even I could not save you."

She blinked in surprise.

Pascal expelled a breath and rolled his eyes. "She is not ready, Orazio!"

"Those who carry the viper's tongue cannot walk the earth if they've failed, *cara sorèlina*," Orazio said, ignoring Pascal huffing by the doorway. "As Magno Duce, I would be called to slay you myself should you fail. And if I did not, then any member of the Vindictam to travel with us, such as Pascal, would be required to slay us both. And should he fail, the Quattuor Gladiis of our family would hunt us down to slay us all."

A shiver of trepidation ran down Liselle's spine, but she quickly brushed it away. There was no possibility that she would fail.

"I am ready," she said, lifting her chin in determination.

"*Ah sì*? Then one day, no doubt, I shall be called upon to slay you," Pascal muttered from the door with a dark look.

Orazio sent him a glance of mild reproach and then dipped the needle into the inkpot.

Liselle didn't even feel the needle drawing through her flesh. She could only stare in fascination at the tongue forming upon her tattoo.

"It is done," Orazio said at last, giving her tattoo a gentle pat.

Liselle didn't respond. She couldn't remove her eyes from her ankle.

"That mark alone will give you authority wherever you may travel," he said, wiping the ink from his fingers. "I will join you when I may."

"Then I'm going alone?" Liselle gasped, surprise overcoming her distraction. "You are not coming with me?" Heavens, surely they weren't sending Pascal with her in his stead!

"Pascal will travel with you as your decoy and protector," Orazio said, peering down at her with a slight air of apology.

Liselle scowled. "But you should be going with me!"

Orazio hesitated, and then leaning close, confessed in a soft tone, "I have a most pressing concern. There are rumors that … *Le Marin* is here in Sarlat."

In spite of her annoyance, Liselle's hazel eyes took on a sparkle of humor. "Ah! I see! What is it now, Orazio? Is it three times that *Le Marin* has outwitted you?"

"He's a dangerous man, Liselle, and not one to be taken lightly!" He sent her a disapproving frown. "And the fact that he has rescued Dolfin from my clutches more than once can only mean he is of the Saluzzo family, working for Ferrara. We must do whatever it takes to protect our homeland!"

She smiled. She was so different from her brother. He preferred to stay close to Venice, to protect it and its precious domination of the salt trade. He thrived on subverting enemy spies and delighted especially in sabotaging the schemes of the enemy city-state of Ferrara.

Not her. She wanted nothing more than to leave Venice once and for all, and to explore far-off lands. "Then I wish you fortune in finding the man," she said.

At that, Orazio snorted, and then he ordered Pascal to make ready to join Albany's party and to leave for England at once.

Slipping past her arrogant cousin, Liselle skipped to her chamber as her spirits took wing.

At last, she had her tongue. She was truly an assassin, and she was truly on her way to her first mission. She could only hug herself in anticipation.

Taking a deep breath, she warned herself aloud, "Patience, Liselle. You must stay focused on your task."

Her foolish fascination with Lord Gray had nearly sent her back to

Venice. She would never make that blunder again. Yes, the man was striking, with a rugged jaw, lean hips, and strong, muscular legs. And yes, the soft, rolling vowels of his Scottish burr sent chills down her spine. There was no doubt that Lord Julian Gray had been fascinating.

But then, so were many other men.

He certainly wasn't worth the risk of being sent back home.

Shrugging all thoughts of him aside, she quickly changed into a golden gown adorned with velvet and silk ribbons and slipped the stilettos into the hidden pockets sewn in the sleeves just for them. And then throwing her green, fur-lined mantle about her shoulders, she ran down to join Orazio at the garden gate, shaking raindrops off the leaves of the shrubbery as she passed.

He said nothing as they set off through the rain pelting the cobblestoned streets. And in a matter of minutes, they had entered the inn housing Albany and were immediately escorted to where the prince was already waiting.

Nobly attired in crimson velvet, Alexander Stewart, the Duke of Albany, was tall in stature, broad-faced, red-nosed, and large-eared. His hair was also red, but the brows over his brilliant green eyes were dark, almost black.

He stood before the fire crackling on the hearth, clutching something in his hand and demanding that Orazio take care of the matter at once.

As her brother joined him at the fireplace, Liselle moved to the window, shaking the rain from her mantle.

"What does it mean?" Albany was asking Orazio, his face darkened in worry.

At Orazio's sharp intake of breath, Liselle's interest was piqued. Leaving the window, she crossed the room to stand at her brother's side.

"The Turk's head knot," Orazio murmured softly, gingerly taking the fine gray corded knot from Albany's outstretched hand.

"Is it *Le Marin?*" Albany cleared his throat nervously. "But what has *Le Marin* to do with me?"

Orazio was silent for a time, inspecting the knot closely before finally admitting, "It appears genuine."

As Albany began to curse, Liselle reached over him to pluck the knot from Orazio's grasp. Curiously, she turned it over in her palm. The fine gray cord appeared vaguely familiar, but she couldn't recall where she'd seen it before. And as Albany and Orazio's conversation turned into a heated debate over *Le Marin's* possible concerns in Albany's doings, she lost interest entirely. After placing the knot on a nearby table, she returned to the window.

Le Marin was Orazio's business. Not hers.

4

THE QUATTUOR GLADIIS

Sometime later, after Albany's fear of *Le Marin* was appeased, Pascal arrived and Orazio introduced him as a master spy to satisfy Albany's every whim. Pascal was tall and thin, and with his arrogant air, dark cloak, and black doublet, he certainly looked the part.

Albany was pleased immediately.

And when Orazio explained that Liselle would be traveling in Nicoletta's stead, Albany's pleasure increased. Apparently, the man detested Nicoletta as much as she did him.

As the conversation waned and they made ready to depart, Liselle caught Albany's lecherous gaze upon her more than once. But it wasn't particularly troubling. She knew many ways of handling such men, with methods ranging from cold words to sharp stilettos.

A short time later and with rising excitement, Liselle found herself mounting a black mare and waving her farewells. And then, carefully fanning her green mantle out across the horse's flanks, she turned her mare's head and joined Albany's party, bound for Bordeaux and thence to England.

It was still raining as they set off, but as the day wore on, the clouds drifted away. They stopped for only brief periods of rest, pressing on until finally the last rays of the sun swiftly faded into darkness. And the moon was high in the sky when they finally arrived at a small inn to take rest.

Liselle retired at once to her small, assigned chamber, but she was too excited to sleep. She stayed awake until the first signs of dawn, staring out of her window and listening to the crickets and frogs singing in a nearby pond.

The morning found Albany in a particularly lusty frame of mind, and Liselle wasn't surprised when the red-haired Scottish prince caught her about the waist and pulled her down to his knee.

"Give us a wee kiss now, lass." He laughed suggestively. "A kiss for luck!"

From the corner of her eye, Liselle spied Pascal gracefully slouching against the wall with a smile of perverse amusement playing across his handsome face. It was clear that he had no intention of rescuing her. Not that she needed him to. But she found his attitude and lack of action annoying all the same.

As Albany's hand inched towards her breast, Liselle refocused her attention upon the man. And sliding a stiletto from her sleeve, she whispered into his ear, "I pray you, my lord, please remove your hands."

"And why would I do that?" Albany chuckled in delight. "My hands are quite pleased to remain where they are!"

Liselle lowered her lashes with a lazy smile. "But I would fain see you keep them, my lord," she breathed softly as her blade lightly pierced the flesh beneath his ribs.

Albany jerked and removed his hands at once, but the interest in his eyes only deepened.

Rising swiftly to her feet, Liselle stepped away, relieved that the prince was not one to force his interests. Returning her blade to its hiding place, she paused to send Pascal a disapproving look.

He responded with an exaggerated yawn that plainly signaled boredom.

And then Albany swept his arms in a grand gesture and announced he was ready to leave at once.

The rain returned, and the going was slow. But finally, after several days of squelching through the mud, they arrived at Bordeaux where the burly Scottish captain, James Douglas, awaited them on his ship *The Michael.*

Once settled in her small cabin, Liselle gratefully peeled off her wet clothing, and after slipping into a dry gown, wandered curiously around the deck for a time. But, as the looming dark clouds overhead threatened even more rain, she returned to her cabin and spent the evening listening with unease to the waves slapping the ship's side.

In spite of having been born in Venice on the edge of the sea, she had never cared for sailing.

She could only pray the journey to England was a smooth one.

But, alas, her prayers went unanswered.

They set sail with the dawn, and shortly afterward the gusty winds ratcheted to a near gale force, tossing the ship about in the waves like a toy.

At the captain's insistence, Liselle remained below deck, huddled in her cabin as the ship heaved and rolled.

Day upon miserable day passed as the incessant winds mercilessly pounded *The Michael,* each day an eternity in which she could do nothing more than groan as her stomach lurched and churned with the ship. And each night the snapping of the sails and creaking of the ship's timbers made sleep impossible.

Several times each day, Pascal poked his head through her door to mercilessly tease her about her green complexion. And on each occasion, she found his smug grin even more aggravating than before.

The storm finally stopped, and she fell into the first deep sleep she had known since the voyage began. And when she woke once again, it was to find her cousin's smirking face planted mere inches from hers.

"You'll never find Dolfin skulking below decks like this," he observed with a careless shrug. "And I'm not finding him for you."

Straightening, he adjusted the red-velvet sleeve of his doublet and meticulously brushed imaginary lint from his gold-colored hose.

Scowling, Liselle swung her feet over the edge of the bunk. "When have you ever done anything that wasn't in your own best interests, Pascal?" she asked in a scathing tone.

"Does anyone?" he queried philosophically, tossing his long, dark hair over his shoulder.

She eyed him from head to toe and didn't bother to reply.

"Albany's quite fascinated with you," he drawled, raising a brow. "You should use that to your advantage."

Liselle snorted. "Why? I've already learnt all that I can from the man. He's no longer useful to me. He scarcely knows Dolfin." Picking up her mantle, she threw it about her shoulders and added, "Dolfin was looking for someone—someone he was certain would appear wherever Albany tarries. I believe we will find the old man in Fotheringhay."

"So you say." Pascal yawned as if he found conversation with her tedious. "And I still doubt your reasoning."

"I care little what you think, dear cousin," Liselle replied sweetly as she shoved him away from the door.

Brushing past him, she strode down the narrow passage and up to the ship's deck.

The retreating storm hung low on the horizon, and the gulls rode the winds high above her head as she emerged from below, wincing in the bright light.

As a sudden gust of cold, bitter wind tore through her garments, she scowled, "Will this journey ever end?"

"Look there, *bábia*," Pascal's lip curled into a superior smirk as he pointed behind her.

Scowling at being called a fool, she turned to see a long dark ribbon of land painting the horizon.

"*Inghilterra. England,*" Pascal murmured in her ear. "We've arrived."

They watched in silence as the land rose to fill the skyline. And soon they were sailing past the dramatic white cliffs of the Isle of Wight and heading inland up the river, past the reedy salt marshes to the sheltered port of Southampton.

Eager to get off the boat and to leave the tempestuous winds and stormy waters behind her, Liselle followed Albany down the rough-hewn gangplank at the earliest possible moment after the ship dropped anchor.

They were met by a red-haired, square-jawed man with a bushy beard and a small scar under his left eye. Grinning widely, he strode forward to soundly slap Albany's back in greeting.

"That is Archibald Douglas, the Fifth Earl of Angus," Pascal softly informed Liselle. "A Red Douglas."

"Because of his hair?" Liselle whispered, her mouth twisting in wry humor.

Pascal sent her a dark look. "Heed my words well, *bábia!* You must learn these clans if you wish to succeed!" He waited until she erased the smile upon her face before continuing. "The Clan Douglas is a great clan holding vast lands. The Black Douglases were named so for their dark deeds, and nigh on thirty years ago sided with the Yorkist kings of England against the Scottish crown. The Stewart king only survived with the help of the Red Douglases of Angus. Yon earl's father fought with the Stewarts and drove their own kin, the old Black Douglas and his men into exile in England, where they've lived ever since."

Liselle lifted a brow at the red-haired earl still speaking with Albany. "Then is it not strange that this Red Douglas also now betrays the Scottish crown and a Stewart king by seeking Yorkist aid?"

Pascal's dark eyes glinted dangerously. "Men betray much for power," he said softly and in an almost jaded tone. "Even their brothers."

Liselle shot him a puzzled look.

"Be careful, *bábia*," he warned, not bothering to explain himself. "Archibald Douglas may appear humble and pleasant, but do not underestimate him. He's one of the craftiest noblemen of Scotland."

Liselle watched him a moment, wondering what secrets he harbored. "And how do you know of these Scottish clans?" she asked softly.

He didn't seem bothered by the question in the slightest. Leaning close, he retorted, "Unlike you, *bábia*, I seek knowledge. You would be wise to do the same."

And then with a blasé shrug of the shoulders, he moved off to join Albany and Douglas and proceeded to murmur something that was met by hearty bursts of laughter.

As they suddenly turned to her as one, Liselle sent her cousin a disapproving look. He'd clearly made a jest at her expense. But she joined them all the same.

"The Lady Liselle," Albany introduced her to the red-haired earl. "Nicoletta has fallen ill with the ague. Liselle will be taking her place as a lady-in-waiting to the princess."

The Earl of Angus' beard widened into a smile as he bowed and said politely enough, "'Twill be a pleasure to have ye in Edinburgh, Lady Liselle."

But she had scarcely curtsied in reply before he was waving them all to a group of horses waiting nearby.

"We'll stay for a wee night's rest with the monks at Netley Abbey," Douglas explained, catching his horse's head and giving the great beast a fond pat. "But we'll leave at dawn and ride hard for Fotheringhay. King Edward's own brother, the Duke of Gloucester is waiting ye there,

Albany, and his tidings will please ye greatly."

"The only tidings to please me would be those of an army," Albany retorted, mounting his horse. "An army that will make me King of Scotland."

"Then be pleased." Douglas laughed, urging his horse forward.

As their conversation continued along the same lines, Liselle fell to the back of the party. There was nothing to be learned from them now; they were too busy congratulating each other on having won a war yet to be fought.

They took a woodland path running along the river through clumps of birches and spreading ancient oaks. And the slight chill in the air made her shiver despite the sun filtering through the canopy of leaves overhead.

Soon enough, she saw Netley Abbey with its tall tower and painted glass windows perched on a gentle slope rising from the banks of the Southampton waters. There were several buildings south of the abbey's church, half obscured by ivy and surrounded by green trees and traces of a moat.

They had scarcely dismounted before an austere, blunt-faced monk came out to greet them at the main gate. Once they were inside the courtyard, he motioned a fellow brother to escort the men to one side of the abbey, as he escorted Liselle to a small one-room guesthouse on the other. And after promising her sustenance, he shut the door and left her alone.

Taking a deep breath, Liselle stretched and glanced around, grateful for the feel of solid earth beneath her feet. The room was a simple one, comprised only of a bed and a small wooden table with a single candlestick.

Moving to the window, she let her thoughts wander until a knock on the door revealed another monk bearing a simple meal of mutton stew and brown bread. After placing the meal upon the table and lighting the candle from his own lamp, he nodded kindly and then exited the chamber, never having said a word.

Liselle ate peacefully, lost in thought, listening to the cry of the gulls outside her small window for a time. She was relieved that she was no longer on a rolling ship or wasting away from boredom in Venice.

Finally, exhaustion overcame her. And as the sun set, she crawled beneath her woolen cover and fell asleep in moments.

The storms that had plagued their journey returned in the middle of the night, waking her on several occasions. But when she rose at dawn, the heavy drumming of the rain had subsided to gentle showers.

In a short time, she was dressed and ready to leave, and it was only a little time later that another soft knock on her door heralded the return of the kindly nodding monk, and with him, a breakfast of bread, fish, and a few honey-spiced almonds.

She ate quickly in silence, and then wrapping herself in a soft, hooded cloak and lacing up her sturdy boots, she slipped outside in search of the others.

She had almost reached the abbey's main gate when Albany's laughter sounded from inside a nearby building. Peering through an open door, she caught sight of the prince and Douglas still at table, slapping one another on the back. She rolled her eyes contemptuously. Apparently, the prospect of starting a war was an occasion to be overjoyed. Finding no sight of Pascal, she resumed circling the abbey grounds.

Stepping out from behind a long, low building near the stables, a flash of black caught the corner of her eye. Instinctively, she ducked back, and crouching low, leaned forward for a better look.

A short distance away, Pascal stood with his head bowed, murmuring to a man clad from head to toe in black.

Liselle frowned, watching as the two clasped forearms and pressed their cheeks in farewell. The gesture seemed strangely familiar, but she hadn't recalled seeing the man before. Most likely, it was a new messenger. Curious, she rose to her feet, preparing to join them.

But then a shrill whistle pierced the air, and as Pascal whirled with his stiletto appearing in his hand, she instinctively darted back.

Pascal was behaving unusually. But then, she'd never bothered to observe her cousin much before. Perhaps he always acted in this manner.

The whistle shrieked again, and the sound of Douglas' booming voice quickly followed it.

Reluctantly, Liselle gathered her skirts and withdrew. It was time to leave. She'd have to pry into her cousin's affairs later.

Picking her way a short distance through the wet grass, she arrived at the main gate just as Pascal stepped around the opposite side of the building. And as he caught the reins of her gray mare and moved to assist her to mount, she saw an unusually dark expression written upon his handsome face.

"What is it?" she whispered curiously in his ear. "Have you received new orders?"

He raised a scathing brow, but his voice was soft. "Orders? What madness is this, *bábia*? It's time for you to wake from your dreams now!" He snapped his fingers in front of her face.

Liselle scowled but nodded her chin towards where she'd just seen him. "Did you not receive tidings, behind yonder building?"

His dark eyes flickered, and she could tell that he knew what she meant, but he denied it anyway. "I know not of what you speak!" he said in a belittling tone. "You would do well to remember that my business is no concern of yours. I am not yours to command."

"You're lying," she accused, irritated.

But he was clearly done speaking of the matter. Stepping away, he complained loudly, "England is a miserable place." He held out his hand and eyed the raindrops falling into his outstretched palm with disgust. "Do they ever see the sun in this accursed land?"

"'Tis better than Venice," she retorted in annoyance and snatched the reins from his hands.

"I think not!" he grumbled and then abruptly walked away.

She watched him go with a scowl. Why was he lying to her?

And then as he leapt gracefully into his saddle and smoothed his black cloak, she suddenly recalled where she'd seen the farewell gesture before.

Several times, as a young girl, she had spied upon Orazio meeting secretly with the member of the Quattuor Gladiis that presided over their family. Just the title *Quattuor Gladiis*—the four swords—inspired fear. They were the four men who controlled the destiny of the Vindictam, and only they were allowed to know and speak with the Dominus Granditer, the Grand Master of them all—the one man who held the fate of everyone in the palm of his hand.

Her frown deepened.

Perhaps she was mistaken; it made little sense that Pascal should speak with one of the Quattuor Gladiis. Only the captains, the Magno Duce, such as Orazio, had that right. And although Pascal was a member of the powerful da Vilardino family, he was still her cousin. She would know if he were a Magno Duce.

She shook her head, perplexed, and then decided she must have misunderstood.

Pascal was far too young and arrogant for a member of the Quattuor Gladiis to speak with him and show him such respect as the gesture implied.

Deciding to brush the matter aside, she urged her horse forward, and then Archibald Douglas sounded his hunting horn and they left the abbey behind them.

For a time, they galloped along the river path, and then took a northerly road out of Southampton.

Albany and Douglas were both battle-hardened men with a purpose. Their pace was brisk, but Liselle found the ride exhilarating. And they rode hard each day, rarely stopping and speaking little as they headed north towards Fotheringhay as fast as their horses could carry them.

Far sooner than she'd expected, Liselle spied the high, thick walls and lofty towers of the formidable Fotheringhay Castle in the distance. And shortly after, they were clattering over the bridge spanning the River Nene and under the ancient stone gate to be met by a party of English nobles and a gray-haired grizzled man in a plaid that Liselle could only assume was the Black Douglas.

Maneuvering his gray gelding to her side, Pascal pointed with his chin. "The small one is the Duke of Gloucester," he muttered disgustedly under his breath.

"And is that the Black Douglas?" she whispered the question.

"Then you *do* listen upon occasion, *bábia*," he observed with a smirk.

Liselle scowled at him, but then strangely, the fleeting image of him greeting the mysterious black-cloaked figure at the abbey crossed her mind.

"Ah, but I spoke too soon!" Pascal's grating tones interrupted her thoughts. His fine nostrils flared. "Pay heed to my words! Must I ever remind you of your duties? Look to the English king's brother, the fool giving Albany an army!"

Gritting her teeth at him, Liselle turned her gaze to Gloucester.

The expression on the man's face was proud and fierce, resembling anything but a fool. He was a delicate man with almost feminine features, long dark hair, an arched nose, and thin lips. He stood hunched to one side, and it took her a moment to see that his spine was dramatically curved, lifting one shoulder noticeably higher than the other.

He must have sensed her eyes upon him, for he looked her way, and for a brief moment, their eyes met.

The man's expression soured at once.

A little surprised by his response, Liselle bowed her head, but when she glanced up again, Gloucester had disappeared into the castle along with Albany and both Douglases, the Red and the Black.

"Strange," Pascal commented in a snide tone. "Gloucester seems impervious to your charms. How amusing." He began to chuckle softly under his breath.

Scowling, she dismounted, and leaving Pascal to his own designs, followed a chubby, rosy-cheeked maid to a small chamber in the northwest tower.

"There's no lady present, my lady," the maid informed her, bobbing up and down. "This is a place of war."

Liselle smiled. With no lady present, she wasn't expected to waste time engaging in idle gossip. "Then I'll have my cousin escort me to the feast," she said, thinking aloud. "There's no need to trouble you further."

The rosy-cheeked maid seemed all too pleased at that and left quickly before Liselle could change her mind.

"I am *fortunà*," she murmured to herself as she selected a green embroidered gown with a pearl-lined collar and a matching set of earrings to wear. Changing her hose, she paused a moment to stare at the viper upon her ankle.

She had a mission. She had to find Dolfin. Quickly donning her new hose, she changed her shoes and took a deep breath.

There were many nobles in the castle. Perhaps one of them had news of an elderly Venetian.

Cautiously, she slipped out of her chamber and down the tower steps to the great hall.

The great hall was a massive room with arched windows lining the western wall above a magnificent fireplace. The air was murky and filled with the smoke and scent of roasted meat as servants scurried about with platters for the evening meal. Men discussing battle plans sat around tables—or on top of them. And as the wine flowed freely, Liselle knew their tongues would quickly loosen.

Keeping to the shadows, she slowly circled the room, searching for a talkative man to suit her purposes and listening to scattered fragments of conversation. She was surprised to see a number of Scottish men in plaids mingling with the English, but she could only assume they had been exiled with the old Black Douglas from years before.

And then she heard a loud, overbearing laugh and moved closer.

"The men are mustering at Alnwick," a particularly pompous young English knight was saying. Draining his goblet, the lanky youth wagged his head and continued self-importantly, "Albany is a fool, I say! If I'd a moment alone with the man, I could persuade him merely with the promise of two warhorses to grant me twenty Scottish castles! But of course, before I'd accept them, the smell of rotting peat would have to be purged from them first!"

"But he's already promised Edward half of Scotland, Baldric!" one of his companions observed.

"Then why not the rest of it?" the portentous Baldric asked.

The men around him laughed.

Liselle paused. This Baldric was perfect for her purposes. Such men loved to talk; in fact, it was difficult to get them to stop.

Making her mind up all at once, she stepped forward and, lowering her lashes, pretended to stumble, nearly landing straight into his lengthy arms.

"My lady!" Baldric dropped his goblet in his haste to catch her. "Are you well?"

As his strong hand lifted her up, she hid a pleased smile. She had netted her prey.

"*Gramersè*, many thanks, my lord!" she gasped in an exaggerated Venetian accent. Clutching his arm tightly, she gave a helpless shrug and pretended to search for words. "My lord ... your *bravàso*, your strong... strong arm has saved me from a ... an injury most *grève*!" She gave her best, simpering smile.

"'Tis my pleasure, my lady!" Baldric beamed. Patting her hand, he focused his entire attention upon her, already forgetting his companions.

In minutes, he was telling her the history of his family name and all about his *vast* estate in the south. And after allowing him to guide her to a private table, she sat by his side and permitted him to pick the choicest morsels for her to eat as the evening progressed.

As expected, he never stopped talking. He kept speaking even as the announcements were made, giving his opinion on a notice of a public execution and then on a fellow knight's betrothal. He even rendered his judgment upon a minstrel, just awarded a fine woolen cape for having composed a wondrous new song; it had seemed a mediocre piece of the most common kind to Baldric.

As time passed, it became increasingly difficult to tolerate his company. Her head began to pound from his endless spouting. She was almost ready to leave when his conversation took an abrupt and interesting turn.

"And your native tongue, your accent, my lady, 'tis so lovely. It sounds the same as the merchant who arrived here a fortnight ago. Now, whence did he come? Venice! Ah yes, Venice, the city of Saint Mark, it was!"

"*Mercànte?*" she asked in her huskiest voice, taking care not to appear too interested. "*Venècia* is famous for its traveling merchants."

"But clearly, even more so for its beauteous ladies!" Baldric smiled widely, unaware of the piece of chicken stuck betwixt his teeth.

He leaned close. Too close.

Wanting nothing more than to slap him across the face, she forced her lashes to lower and her lips to smile. "You flatter me, *bòn cavalièr*! But mayhap your merchant has news from my homeland. Is he still here, so I may ask?"

But Baldric was clearly more interested in the possibilities of a kiss than any more speaking. His lips wiggled mere inches away from her own.

All of a sudden, a booted foot planted itself on the bench between them.

And then Liselle heard a rich, deep voice with a familiar smooth Scottish burr interrupt. "My bonny wee wife, 'tis a wondrous miracle to find ye here."

Liselle's heart lurched, and her eyes widened in genuine surprise. She would recognize his voice anywhere.

Turning, she glanced up directly into the searching gray eyes of Lord Julian Gray.

Clad in a crisp white shirt and a dark green plaid, he merely stood there, looking down at her with his broad shoulders shaking in silent laughter.

"Lord Gray!" Liselle quickly composed herself to dip her head in greeting. "I am pleased to see you this fine evening."

Slanting forward to rest his arm upon his knee, Julian's hot gaze licked her from head to toe. "As I recall, Lady Gray, when we last parted ways, ye warned me that no man looks at another lass whilst in your presence, aye?"

Liselle smiled a superior, secretive smile. So, the man remembered that, did he?

And then he added with a challenging gleam in his eye, "So what is your husband to say about ye kissing another man whilst in his company, then?"

At that, Baldric jumped to his feet, upending his wine goblet. And with a hastily mumbled apology, he fled from the table before either of them could scarcely utter a word.

Julian laughed. It was a pleasant, deep sound. And with his cheek creasing in humor, he helped himself to the seat vacated by the English knight.

"I fear I frightened your lover away, Lady Gray," he said without an ounce of remorse in his tone.

Liselle let her eyes twinkle. "And I thank you for saving me the effort of frightening him away myself, Lord Gray."

"Aye, I imagine ye could frighten a man right well," he replied with an appreciative wink.

The man's self-assurance and easy confidence were captivating, and the way the muscles on his arms strained against his shirt caused her heart to quicken.

For the very first time, Liselle wondered if Nicoletta had been right. Had she let herself become dangerously infatuated with the man? Was that even possible after such a few brief encounters?

Concerned, she rose to her feet and dipped a curtsey. "I thank you for your services, but I shall retire now, Lord Gray."

As expected, he didn't follow her, but she felt his piercing gaze track her across the hall until she dodged behind a screened alcove. And then, mounting the stone steps worn smooth by countless feet before her, she quickly returned to her chamber to collect her wits.

It was unsettling to find Lord Gray in Fotheringhay. What was he doing there? Fotheringhay was not the place to indulge in wine, women, and wagering; it was a place now of war and strategy.

And his arrival had been most ill-timed.

She'd been on the verge of discovering vital information concerning Dolfino Dolfin's whereabouts.

Feeling unusually hot, she threw her shutters open wide and stared into the night sky, her thoughts consumed with the possible reasons for Julian's presence. It took some time, but gradually her mind calmed, and finally she was able to put all thoughts of him aside and return to her original purpose of finding Dolfin.

If Dolfin had travelled through Fotheringhay disguised as an ordinary Venetian merchant, the servants were more likely to know more about his current whereabouts than the English knights. Her best course of action would be to listen to the maids' gossip about where to buy fine trinkets— trinkets needed to aid them in their quest to catch a knight's eye.

But already the hour was growing late. She would have to hurry.

Her hand was on the latch before she paused. With a castle filled with men and very few women, it would be wise to take additional precautions. Searching through her belongings, she found a small velvet pouch and opened the drawstrings to shake out a small glass vial.

Indormia, a secret of the Vindictam. Something that Pippa, the mistress of poison, had devised before her ill-fated destiny led her to an untimely death. A few drops from the vial would cause even the strongest man to fall into a deep sleep. And a few more drops would cause him to never wake again.

Smiling in satisfaction, she tucked it into her sleeve next to her stilettos, and feeling confident of her success, once again slipped into the dark maze of passages outside her chamber door.

The feasting in the hall had ended, and the knights and their men were settling down for a night's sleep. Skirting the hall, she headed for the kitchens, descending down the narrow steps winding into the darkness below.

But to her disappointment, the kitchens were already deserted, save for the pot-boy snoozing next to the banked fire. She stood for a moment, wondering where the maids might gather to gossip, when once again, a silken voice whispered into her ear.

"And why is a swan-necked beauty such as ye wandering in the castle kitchens at this late hour?"

Liselle froze.

For the second time that night, Lord Julian Gray had surprised her.

5

A WEE NIP OF WINE

Amused, Julian leaned against the kitchen wall and observed Liselle from under half-closed lids.

"I could ask the same of you, my lord!" Liselle's throaty voice held a note of humor as she slowly turned to face him. "What business does a Scottish nobleman have in an Englishman's castle?"

Julian stirred, whistling under his breath as his eyes traveled slowly from the river of her dark, honeyed tresses, over the sinfully decadent pout of her lips, and down to the curves that promised heaven. She was a torture of the most delicious kind.

"Ach, family ties know no borders, Lady Gray," he lied with a shrug as his eyes continued to ravish her. He had no family here, but the truth mattered little. He knew right well that he was eyeing her far too long, but the wee lass didn't seem to mind. In fact, she was practically purring, and her eyes held a wicked glint in them.

And then she said, "You are overly bold, Lord Gray."

A smile creased Julian's cheek even as he knew her presence in Fotheringhay signaled that Orazio was undoubtedly close by. Ach, the man apparently used Liselle as a lackey of some sort. But the covert air of deceit swirling around her intrigued him. And in spite of knowing that any reason she had to be there wouldn't be a good one, or perhaps because of it, he caught her wrists and pulled her to his chest.

"Bold?" he repeated with a suggestive lift of his brow. "Ye dinna know what bold is, lass. Mayhap I should show ye." He lowered his voice into an intimate rumble that never failed to affect any woman.

Except this one, he amended dryly as she deftly maneuvered out of his grasp.

"'Tis strangely hot," she whispered, trailing her fingers evocatively down her throat and over the bodice of her emerald gown. "Perhaps wine would be in order, my lord. Would you care to drink with me?"

Julian's eyes lit even as his suspicions kindled. The wee vixen was obviously toying with him. That only meant she had something to hide. Could she be a danger in her own right? The thought heightened his interest.

"Where is the harm in a wee nip of wine?" he asked, crossing his arms to lean against the wall again. Aye, he'd play the wee devil's game. Perhaps he'd loosen her lips along the way as well. "But I expect ye to join me, lass," he added.

Moving to a shelf littered with half-empty bottles, Liselle selected one, and finding a goblet, filled it to the brim with a deep burgundy wine. With her eyes locked on his, she slowly returned, swaying her hips as she walked. And then offering the goblet to him with both hands, she murmured, "Have a drink, my lord."

Clearly, she was plotting something; her movements were too refined and her tone too seductive. Aye, she had been well-trained. Giving no sign of his inward thoughts, he quirked his lip in a half-smile and rumbled, "And who could tell such a siren no?"

Her lashes fluttered as he took the cup. He glanced down, wondering if it had been poisoned. He swirled it several times, and lifting it to his nose, inhaled the aroma as if in enjoyment. He could smell nothing suspicious.

With his eyes riveted upon hers, he ran his tongue along the goblet edge and took a small sip as if to savor the sweet taste. Aye, he couldn't taste any poison, either. And he had tasted many over the years.

And then he saw that her eyes had gone wide and her breath had quickened. He hid a smile, noting her reaction. So the lass was smitten with him, after all.

Suddenly, he found her game even more interesting.

"Do you not care for the wine, my lord?" she asked, knitting her eyebrows into a frown.

He didn't answer as she tore a piece of bread from a loaf resting on a nearby table. Moving so close that he could feel the heat of her skin, she dipped the bread into the wine and trailed it over his lips before popping it into his mouth.

And then placing her lips on the edge of the cup, she whispered, "May I taste, my lord?"

He raised a brow. Tilting the cup forward, he watched her drink deeply and then lick her pouting lips.

The gesture was his undoing.

He drained the goblet in a single draught. And tossing it over his shoulder, he caught her hand fervently into his own. And bringing it to his lips, kissed each tapered finger slowly to at last suck her fingertip as he stared into her fiery eyes.

A flicker of delighted surprise suffused her features. And then her luscious lashes dropped again.

"You are arrogant and overconfident, my lord," she said, removing her hand.

He laughed. "Am I, Lady Gray?"

But even as he laughed, a strange relaxation mixed with a vague sense of unease descended upon him.

Liselle was pressing closer. Her lips were almost upon his, and as he watched, they parted slightly to blow a seductive breath in his face.

With a groan, he caught her to his chest, and giving way to desire, he pressed his lips against the sweet, soft expanse of her long, slender neck.

And as her hands slid up his chest to lock behind his head, he nuzzled her ear and nibbled one of her pearl earrings, removing it quickly with his teeth.

"Lord Gray!" she protested in mock outrage.

But her voice echoed eerily in his head.

In outright alarm, he reached behind his neck to pry her fingers away, but the effort cost him his balance. And as he lurched unexpectedly to one side, the answer raced through his mind.

The wicked minx *had* poisoned him!

"Sleep well, my lord," she whispered into his ear.

She said something else, but he couldn't understand her words. And suddenly, it was too difficult to speak or even think.

And then he was falling, and his world went black.

* * *

Lord Julian Gray became aware of the voices first and then the cramp in his leg.

With a groan, he lifted leaden eyelids to find himself surrounded by a bevy of tittering maids.

"My lord!" A pleasingly plump red-haired lass snorted with a giggle. "Would you care for your shirt now, my lord ... or would you rather wait a while?" She snorted and giggled again.

Julian frowned and then glanced down. Both brows rose in startled surprise.

He was lying on the floor, stark naked, his shirt and plaid neatly folded on top of a nearby wooden barrel. Glancing around, he spied the sun streaming through a tiny window.

Sweet Mary, but his head ached!

He frowned, puzzled. And then with a rush, the events of the evening before returned to him.

The wicked minx *had* drugged him! Why would she do such a thing? What had she been looking for in the kitchens? A quick inspection of his flesh assured him that she hadn't harmed him—beyond giving him a slight headache, he amended with a wince. It made little sense. What had been her purpose?

It had been quite some time since he'd fallen victim to such a ploy. And then strangely, his annoyance turned into admiration. Chuckling under his breath, he rose to his feet, muttering, "The wee canny vixen! What a lass!"

It was then that he realized he was still surrounded by giggling, ogling maids.

With a wink, he pointed to his shirt and plaid. "Aye, I'll need my clothing, lassies," he replied, wiggling a brow, and then with a devilishly charming smile, added, "And were it not for a most pressing matter, I'd not ask for them mayhap the entire day."

The result was a chorus of giggles and snorts from the entire lot.

Amused, Julian fetched his shirt and plaid himself. But, as he dressed, his thoughts were fully occupied with Liselle.

The wee beastie surely had a wicked sense of humor. He'd do well to discover her purpose and just how she figured in Orazio's schemes. 'Twould be done easily enough; he planned to stay on at Fotheringhay at least a day, mayhap two, in order to learn more of Gloucester's army whilst mingling among the Black Douglas' men. Taking a deep, invigorating breath, he smiled to himself. Aye, spying on Liselle would be a pleasure.

"Well met at last, *caro vecio*!" A familiar, crusty voice shattered his thoughts. "When I heard Albany was headed here, I knew I would find you not too far away!"

Buttoning his shirt, Julian cocked an eyebrow in the direction of the door, and then a wide grin spread upon his face.

Dolfino Dolfin stood at the scullery entrance, shooing the maids away by shaking his rich velvet mantle in much the same way one teased a Spanish bull. He was a spare, elderly man with white hair, slightly bulging eyes, and a friendly ever-present smile.

Taking in Julian's state of undress, he shook his head in amusement and said, "Finish dressing yourself, *caro*. I see you have fallen prey to a woman once again."

"Ach, but what a woman!" Julian chuckled. Diving into his shirt, he tossed his plaid over his shoulder and turned to face the man.

Dolfino Dolfin had been a master spy in his prime. Their paths had crossed in Italy, many years before, and the man had become Julian's instructor, his *Istruttore,* helping to shape him into the man that was now *Le Marin.* And as the years had passed, he'd become a second father to him.

Stepping forward, Julian swallowed the old man in a warm hug. And then throwing an arm around the Venetian's stooped shoulders, guided him out of the scullery, through the kitchens, and into the gardens outside.

"'Tis well to see ye once again, *Istruttore!*" Julian exclaimed, once he was certain they were alone. "'Twas fair troubling to hear tidings of your trial in Venice. I should have ignored ye and ferreted ye out of there!"

Dolfin heaved a weary sigh. "I had hoped it wouldn't end in my exile," the old man admitted in soft regret. "I prayed they would remember my life of service on their behalf, especially my work ensuring the blessed Pope himself would continue to support Venice in the salt trade. But in the end, they were afraid. The Doge himself was convinced that I had … I had…truly betrayed secrets to Ferrara for …"

A shadow touched his face as his voice trailed into silence, and he looked away with a pained expression.

Julian waited for him to continue, but as time passed, he gently probed, "What happened, then?"

Dolfin jerked a little, as if in surprise. "Happened? With what?"

"Your trial?" Julian pressed, frowning a little. "Ye said they thought ye had sold secrets."

"Ah, yes!" Dolfin closed his eyes for a moment, and his mouth twisted down. "Gold! They refused to see the lie. They … believed that I … I … would betray *La Serenìsima* for *gold*!" He sniffed in disgust at the word and repeated it several times.

Julian eyed his mentor curiously. Dolfin was an elegant man of courtly articulation. His halting speech was a bit unusual, but then perhaps it was to be expected. The man was aged and had suffered greatly of late.

"Gold!" Dolfin whispered once again, his eyes taking a far-off look.

"By the Virgin! How could they think ye'd betray Venice … ever?" Julian mused. Such a man would never betray his land for anything.

Dolfin's shoulders sagged, and the eyes that met Julian's were sharp and shrewd.

"The truth is … I know too much, *caro vecio*," he said. "But they could not reach me in *La Serenìsima*. They had to flush me out."

Julian speculatively tilted his head to one side. Perhaps Orazio *was* after the old man.

"Then 'tis best ye leave at once, methinks," he muttered as if to himself before clasping his mentor firmly by the shoulder. "Hie ye off to Scotland, *Istruttore*. There is more than one Venetian hereabouts. But, ere ye go, tell me, have ye had dealings with one Orazio di Franco?"

Dolfin paled, and stepping out of Julian's grasp, quickly drew his hood and covered his face.

Julian couldn't help but notice the old man's trembling hands. "What is it?" he asked grimly. "What are ye not telling me?"

"It is nothing," Dolfin replied, but his voice had become guarded all at once, and his tone signaled that no other information would be forthcoming.

"Are ye sure 'tis better left unsaid?" Julian pressed anyway.

"I am simply a weary old man," his *Istruttore* answered, drawing deeper into his hood. "I should not have come here."

"Nonsense!" Julian protested and gave him a hearty clap on the shoulder. "Many a time I've dragged myself bleeding to your door, do ye not recall?"

Dolfin didn't reply, but his eyes twinkled in response.

With a nod of satisfaction, Julian continued, "Then hie ye off to Channelkirk forthwith and wait for me at the inn there. I'll see ye sent where no others can find ye, I swear it!"

The aged man hesitated a moment, but then gripping Julian's forearm in agreement, he spun on his heel and disappeared into the kitchens.

Julian watched him go.

Dolfin was in danger, that much was certain. But was Orazio plotting to see the old man who'd been so faithful to Venice for so long, killed—over a few secrets of the salt trade? And what did Liselle know of it? The whole matter was odd, but most importantly a distraction from his most pressing concern—that of Albany and the fate of Scotland.

As a rare clap of thunder resounded across the sky, Julian grimaced at the dark clouds rolling in from the north; they heralded nothing but more rain. Already, the river was breaching its banks. He didn't relish the thought of riding back to Scotland in the mud.

Adjusting his plaid, he ducked under the low door leading back to the castle's kitchens; it was the shortest way back to his chamber. Spying a bowl of fruit on a nearby table, he deftly snagged a strawberry and popped it into his mouth.

The cooks were suitably shocked.

"'Tis dangerous to eat that raw, my lord," one of the men warned as he left.

Julian grinned, certain he was far more likely to die by a sword than a strawberry.

He'd scarcely stepped into the hall when a sudden fanfare of trumpets sounded from the castle courtyard. And as the barking of a dozen scent hounds joined the fray, Julian curiously pushed his way through a group of jugglers and sprinted up a nearby stairwell to peer through a narrow window slit.

The Yorkist King Edward IV of England had arrived.

Julian frowned.

Edward's presence meant that Albany's army had likely already mustered, and that meant that matters had taken a perilous turn for Scotland.

Dressed in a dark crimson mantle and with a great sword belted about his waist, the war-weathered king sat astride a white charger. Raising his hand, he signaled the large retinue of royal attendants following him to halt, as his brother, the Duke of Gloucester, came forward to greet him.

"Your Sovereign King hails you!" Edward's powerful voice carried up to the window.

The duke's reply was lost as the hounds began to bark once again.

Julian raised a thoughtful brow as he watched the English king dismount and then hurry inside the castle just as the rain began to fall in earnest.

Rumors had run rife around the hall the evening before—rumors that Albany had promised half of Scotland's land to Edward. In exchange, the monarch would lend an army to place the prince upon the Scottish throne. Apparently, Albany was more than ready to shed the blood of his own kinsman just for a crown.

Grimly, Julian folded his arms.

Cameron would need to know just how big an army Scotland faced in order to band the clans together, along with proof of Albany's betrayal.

A sudden gust of cold air blasted through the window, and Julian grimly stepped back.

'Twas time to spy upon Edward.

As he turned, a flash of green skirt from a nearby intersecting passage caught his eye.

Instinctively, he crouched and flattened against the wall, and drawing his dirk, extended the blade at an angle to catch the passageway's reflection on its well-polished surface.

He couldn't see any green.

He waited patiently for some time, but when nothing moved, he sheathed his dirk.

The moment he'd done so, he heard the soft click of a latch.

Peering cautiously around the corner, he saw a woman scurrying away from him. Aye, he'd recognize that green-velvet gown and cascade of honey-colored tresses anywhere.

It was Liselle.

He eyed her retreating form with interest. Had she been spying on him? And if so, was it at her brother's behest or out of her own curiosity?

Rising to his feet, he stalked her through Fotheringhay's twisting passages until she stopped before a heavy oak door guarded by two burly men. Bowing her head, she exchanged a few words with them, and after a moment, they moved aside and allowed her to pass.

As the door shut behind her, Julian tilted his head thoughtfully to one side. The two sentinels by the door wore the garb of the king's bodyguard. For certain that meant Edward was nearby.

But Liselle's presence was a curiosity. What had she to do with the king?

He cast a sharp eye at his surroundings. He was quite familiar with Fotheringhay Castle, and he knew there was a chamber directly above the one Liselle had just entered. 'Twould be a simple enough task to leap from that chamber's balcony to the one below; aye, and most likely, that point of entry would be unguarded.

Dashing up the nearest stair, he slid into the chamber he sought and found it to be empty. Thanking his luck, he threw the shutters wide open only to wince sourly at the driving rain that stung his face in greeting. He'd be swimming his way back to Scotland if it kept pouring with such fervor.

As expected, the balcony below was unguarded. Apparently, they thought only a fool would try to jump from above.

Ach, but they had not reckoned on *Le Marin*.

As *Le Marin*, he'd scaled and jumped from many a castle wall in pursuit of elusive answers. He'd also done so many a time as Lord Julian Gray, but in pursuit of willing maidens.

Balancing on the window ledge, he gauged the distance and angle, and then easily leapt to land lightly on the stone railing. Dropping onto the balcony floor, he listened at the window for a moment but could hear nothing. And then taking advantage of the wind rattling the shutters, he used it to mask the noise of his dagger lifting the latch.

As the shutters cracked open, he cautiously peered inside.

The room was dark, gloomy, and bare of furnishings. But to the right, a beam of light fell through a partially opened door, and in the shadows nearby, hovered Liselle.

Julian's eyes lit with interest.

Plainly, the lass had no legitimate cause to be there lurking in the shadows. With a catlike grace, he slipped into the room.

He was behind her in an instant, and before she could utter a word he had clamped one strong hand over her mouth and had slid the other about her waist.

Liselle went rigid.

"I must beg your forgiveness, Lady Gray. I've no excuse for falling asleep so unforgivably early last night," he rumbled in a soft, low whisper.

She relaxed at the sound of his voice, and he felt her lips curl into a smile beneath his palm. And then the scent of her hair filled his nostrils and his pulse quickened.

"Wed Cecily?" Albany's angry voice rang from the adjoining chamber. "How can I?"

Upon hearing the man's voice, Julian's expression hardened.

Tightening his grip on Liselle, he leaned forward to see Albany pacing in agitation, running his hands nervously through his red hair.

A fire crackled on the far wall, and seated on a polished ornate oak chair was King Edward. A small writing table had been placed at his side, and he drummed his fingers on its shiny surface as his sharp blue eyes pierced the Scottish prince before him.

"And has your heart grown feeble already?" the English king asked in a tone riddled with disdain. "Do you reject in taking our daughter to wife as your queen?"

Albany drew up short. He swallowed several times, and then protested weakly, "But I've only just wed Anne! And Cecily has been betrothed to James' son for nigh on several years!"

Julian rolled his eyes at the man's diplomatic clumsiness. Any refusal to divorce Anne de La Tour to wed Edward's daughter, Cecily, meant that the Scottish prince still hoped to retain ties with France. How could such a man beg for England's army?

Insulted, the king flared his nostrils as his strong voice pressed, "You still wish to curry favor with Louis, but has he lent a hand to your cause? Did we not agree that you would renounce your alliance with the French?"

Albany mumbled something incoherent.

"Answer us!" King Edward demanded.

"I'll sign your treaty, Edward," the Scottish prince growled in frustration. "Aye, I'll sign both agreements!"

With a calculating but vastly pleased smile, Edward waved his hand.

And then another man bearing a carved wooden coffer stepped into view, and Julian caught his breath, scarcely able to believe his eyes.

It was Archibald Douglas, the Earl of Angus, a man whose loyalty to Scotland no one doubted. Ach, the man was a Red Douglas, a staunch supporter of the Scottish Crown! If the powerful earl had betrayed Scotland, it could be a fatal blow.

"God's Wounds!" Julian whispered under his breath.

Archibald Douglas placed the wooden box on the table and traced a stubby finger along the fine filigree lid several times before finally lifting it to remove several sheets of parchment.

"Aye, I'll sign!" Albany snorted nervously, snatching the pages from Douglas' hand. Grabbing a quill, he pressed it so hard against the paper that the nub broke, and he required several attempts before both agreements were finally signed.

And then Gloucester appeared and Edward's demeanor turned even colder. With a flick of a finger, he ordered his brother to take the documents from Albany.

No one spoke as the duke seized the papers from Albany's rigid fingers. Placing them on the table, he proceeded to drip red wax upon them and affix Edward's royal seal.

"Now, tell me of my army!" Albany demanded, pounding on the table even as his eyes fixed with horror on the red wax seals, as if he couldn't believe what he had just done.

"Gloucester's army," Edward corrected frostily. "But you may ride with him to the mustering place."

At that Albany lost his temper and began to shout. "Then I'll see him leave at dawn! I"ll nae wait a moment longer for my crown!"

"You will leave when Gloucester chooses," Edward retorted in disgust.

As the monarch rose to his feet, Julian drew back at once, pulling Liselle with him.

It was time to leave.

Twisting free, Liselle caught Julian's sleeve and tugged him across the chamber towards a brightly painted door.

She paused to twist a key into the lock, and they stepped through, discovering yet another door opening to the outside passage.

"Not yet, ye wee devil," Julian growled, blocking her escape with his arm.

She glanced up in surprise.

Bracing his palms on either side of her shoulders, he caged her against the wall. And with a devilish grin, he asked, "What cause have ye to lurk in the shadows listening to the private words of a king?"

"And what cause have you, Lord Gray?" she asked in turn, her voice adopting a subtle purr.

"I was merely chasing ye, lass," he lied easily enough. "I thought to find myself in your chamber."

Uncertainty entered her eyes as she searched his face, and then her lips parted to reply, "And I came when Albany summoned, my lord. I had no knowledge of his visitors."

"Albany?" Julian cocked a brow. A twinge of jealousy flared to life. "Have a care with the man, lass—" he began.

"*Basta!*" she interrupted. Recoiling at the implication, she pinched her nose in disgust. "Have a care where your thoughts lead you, my lord! Albany has promised my brother that he would safely escort me to the Scottish court. That is all!"

"Scottish court?" Julian repeated with narrowed eyes. So, Orazio wasn't in Fotheringhay? That could be good news for Dolfin. "What business have ye in Scotland?"

"And I will answer, though you have no right to pry into my concerns," Liselle replied, her voice adopting a low, melodic pitch. "I journey to Edinburgh in my sister's stead, Lord Gray. Nicoletta was struck with the ague."

"Then I wish Nicoletta well," Julian replied courteously even as he eyed Liselle from head to toe. His distrust of her was growing by the moment, but the thought of seeing her often in the Scottish court was an exhilarating one.

"But do not allow me to delay you, my lord," the lass was saying. "Should you not be in the hall, drinking wine and trading kisses with any maiden that catches your eye?"

Refocusing his attention upon her, Julian chuckled. "Is that an invitation, Lady Gray?" he asked in a suggestive tone.

She lowered her eyes demurely, but he knew it was an act. Aye, but the wee beastie was wickedly enthralling. Sliding an arm about her waist, he pulled her close, locking her in a possessive grip.

"I'll nae be sharing wine with ye again, ye shameless lass. But I'm still right willing to taste your lips," he said, his voice hard and low. Aye, he'd play upon her interest in him and find out why she had drugged him.

Liselle shook her head. *"Che bixùco pitóxo"* she whispered, sliding her hands to rest on his chest.

Shivering at her touch, he was careful to hide the fact that he knew quite well she'd just called him a *piteous fool*. Faking ignorance, he whispered, "Ye speak in such seductive words, lass. I'll take ye up on the invitation!"

He lowered his head.

With a coy smile, she tapped him lightly on the nose with one finger and said firmly, "My kisses must be earned, Lord Gray."

Suppressing a grin, he pretended to be affronted. "Ach, ye'll beg for my kisses soon enough, Lady Gray," he murmured, running his thumb lightly over her bottom lip.

She froze under his touch, but then clearing her throat, managed a small laugh. "Will I?"

A strange mix of suspicion and desire flooded through him as he looked deeply into her hazel eyes and asked, "Aye then, mayhap ye'll confess why ye poisoned the wine and left me naked?"

Something he couldn't interpret flashed across her face, but she masked it well, and scarce a moment later her eyes twinkled up at him mischievously. "Wine, my lord? *Cà de dìa!*" She rolled her eyes a little before explaining with a distinct note of humor, "It was the bread, my lord."

His lip lifted in mild surprise. Aye, the lass was a cunningly clever one. Leaning closer, he lowered his voice even more as he whispered into her hair, "And did ye find what ye were seeking, lass?"

"Yes, my lord," her voice hitched a little. "Your safety was all I sought."

Safety? He frowned at the unexpected answer. He stayed where he was a moment, inhaling the fragrance of her hair. He could hear her soft, rapid breathing, and his pulse quickened in response. Ach, that would never do. He couldn't develop a real attraction to the lass; he only meant to find answers.

Taking a deep breath, he stepped back and repeated, "Safety? Safety from whom?"

But she pushed him away. Placing her hand upon the door latch, she countered coolly, "And what of you, Lord Gray? What is the *real* reason you are here at Fotheringhay? I'm told you travel the lands indulging your whims, but from what I can see, your actions are more befitting of *Le Marin* than a scandalous drunkard."

He drew a sharp breath in astonishment as his gray eyes swept over her face.

Le Marin. Most likely, she'd only referenced *Le Marin* coincidently, but she was the first to come so close to the truth. Even by accident.

Mayhap the less seen of this particular wee devil, the better.

Tossing his blond head back, he forced himself to roar with laughter. "And if I were to claim that I was *Le Marin*, lass, surely that would deem me worthy of a kiss now, aye?"

She stared at him then, and his pulse leapt once again as he suddenly found himself drowning in her hazel eyes. The wee lass was complex and most likely dangerous. Why did he find that alluring?

And then she pulled the door open. Pausing on the threshold, she said, "We must leave separately, Lord Gray. It would not do to let Pascal find us together. He is not as … understanding as Orazio."

"Pascal?" Julian inquired, careful to sound only mildly curious. Pascal. Yet another Venetian he must investigate.

"My cousin," she explained, dipping a curtsey. And then a gleam of wicked amusement entered her eye. Pointing to the shuttered window, she added, "Perhaps you should leave the way you arrived. It might be safer."

Julian chuckled. "Mayhap 'twould be, if your kinfolk are prowling about, ye wee beastie. But I've no mind to risk a broken limb. Ye can avail yourself of the window if ye desire. I'll be leaving through the door."

"Then remember that I warned you, *bixùco pitóxo mio*," she said, shaking her head in mock pity. "I wish you well."

"Until we meet again, Lady Gray," he replied, bowing with a flourish.

She did not reply, and then slipping through the door, she was gone.

He did not hesitate.

After all, he scarcely trusted the lass. She could very well be setting a trap.

Exiting the chamber, he boldly strode down the passageway and past the two royal bodyguards still standing by the door. Surprised to see him, they glanced at each other nervously as if trying to assemble the courage to accost him. But he was long gone before they'd succeeded.

He had much to do. Not only did he have to secure proof of Albany and the Red Douglas' betrayal, but he had to get a firm count of the soldiers under Gloucester's command.

Exiting the stairwell, he paused for a moment to peer through the narrow window slit. The rain had ceased; the clouds were breaking. Perhaps the sun would be shining soon.

With a deep yawn, he lifted his arms to stretch when he felt the cool steel of a blade suddenly pressed against his throat.

"Leave the Lady Liselle alone if you wish to live, Lord Gray," a grim voice warned.

6

THE MYSTERIOUS RING

It had to be Pascal.

Swatting the blade from his neck, Julian summoned a mask of arrogant astonishment and turned to face a slim, dark-haired aggressor. "And who dares to threaten Lord Julian Gray?" he demanded with the affected disdain of a slighted noble.

"A man who would defend his cousin's honor," Pascal replied in a deadly soft tone.

Affecting a clumsiness in keeping with his character, Julian fumbled with his dirk and waved it towards the youth.

Pascal sidestepped him with an easy grace. Any man could have, but it was the way in which the lad had done it that caught Julian's attention. He moved with the expertise of one highly trained.

There was more to the lad than met the eye.

"And who might ye be?" Julian asked, surveying him as if bewildered.

Twirling his own blade, Pascal sheathed it in a single fluid motion. His gaze was shrewd, his handling of the dagger sure, and he stood with the poised stance of an accomplished swordsman.

Ach, were all of Liselle's kin assassins?

Pascal's eyes glittered dangerously through his dark lashes. "As we should never meet again, Lord Gray, you need not know my name," he replied with a contemptuous tilt of his chin.

There was a moment of strained silence, and then brushing imaginary lint from the sleeve of his black-velvet doublet, Pascal spun on his heel and set off down the passageway without a backwards glance.

The corner of Julian's lip lifted in a knowing smile. Such youthful conceit was prone to beget mistakes.

He waited until Pascal had entered the stairwell before following.

"Aye, 'tis time to unearth secrets," he muttered under his breath. The task of procuring Albany's proof was better left to the darkness of night, anyway.

Fotheringhay bustled with activity, and it was easy enough to lurk in the great hall unnoticed, keep an eye on Pascal whilst listening to the words of pompous English knights for secrets that might be used to Scotland's benefit.

Liselle's cousin strolled aimlessly about for a time. Periodically, the young man would pause to squint through the narrow window slits at the foul weather outside and tap his fingers nervously on the stones.

Finally, the rain stopped. And as a ray of sun broke through the dark clouds, the slim youth threw a cloak around his shoulders and slipped out of the hall.

Julian was only a few steps behind, shadowing him out of the castle and into the village below. Once or twice along the way, Pascal had glanced back over his shoulder, but Julian kept a safe distance and remained undetected.

The village of Fotheringhay was a bustling one in spite of the wet weather. Men and women slogged through the muddy streets, dogs barked, wet-feathered chickens scrabbled in the muck, and the occasional cart rolled through the mire headed to or from the castle.

Bowing his head, Pascal strode with a purpose towards the towering Church of St. Mary and All Saints when a short man with thick stubby eyebrows fell into place behind him. But the stranger had taken no more than three paces before the slim dark-haired youth whirled and lunged for him.

The scuffle was short-lived, but it was long enough to let Julian close the distance between them and find cover behind a stack of oaken barrels nearby.

"*Diàmbarne!*" Pascal spat a series of vehement curses. Gripping the short man by the throat, he hissed, "*Ale!* Get you gone, Saluzzo!"

With an adept maneuver, the man twisted and broke free. "You have no power over me, you fool!" He stayed his ground, sizing Pascal up and down before continuing with a sneer, "I would know why Pascal da Vilardino walks so far from *La Serenìsima!*"

Julian raised a curious brow; but then, from the corner of his eye, he spied a brilliant flash of green scuttle across the castle drawbridge.

It was Liselle.

The lass certainly had a knack for interrupting him. And judging by the speed of her gait, he had less than a minute before she'd see him crouched behind the barrels, eavesdropping on her cousin.

A quick search of potential escape routes settled upon the rotund jolly-eyed friar headed his way, driving an ancient cart pulled by an even older donkey. It would be easy enough to take advantage of its cover to switch hiding places.

Casting a gauging eye at Liselle, he still had seconds to spare. She couldn't see him yet. Leaning forward, he turned his attention once more upon Pascal.

"I owe you no explanation, Saluzzo," the youth was saying in an arrogant tone. Impaling the thick-browed man with a chilling gaze, he continued, "Get you gone from my sight! I care not for this mistake of a truce between our families, and I will not vouch for your safety should you tarry a moment longer in my company!"

The man sniffed in disgust. "You are but a pup still suckling milk! I will see that Orazio hears of your words."

"I do not fear *Orazio*," Pascal replied with a careless laugh and a proud toss of his head. "Be gone! For I swear if my eyes fall upon you once more, I will right gladly send you back to Ferrara colder than stone!"

The Saluzzo faltered back a step, clearly shocked. And then his voice dropped in warning, "The Saluzzi will not be the first to shed blood. But if blood is spilled, I will devote my life to see that not a single trace of the Vindictam is left!" His eyes lit eagerly at the very thought. And then he spat in the mud at Pascal's feet.

A blade suddenly appeared in Pascal's hand.

And it was at that moment that the friar's cart rolled between them, blocking Julian's view.

"Ach, what timing!" Julian swore under his breath. Rising to his feet, he sauntered alongside the rickety contraption, ducking down a little just as Liselle passed on the other side.

She didn't see him, her hazel eyes were focused straight ahead.

And then for one gloriously suspended moment, he saw nothing but her flawless skin, her impossibly long dark lashes, the soft curve of her neck, and her pouting lips clamped tightly shut with determination.

And then she was gone, and he shook his head as if to wake from a dream.

Straightening a little, he maintained his pace with the cart.

What ailed his reasoning? He knew better than to allow himself to become enamored with such a devious lass. Aye, he was fair worn. 'Twas time to return to Scotland, deliver the news to Cameron and then rest a wee spell and spend his days with a lass on his knee and drowning his thoughts in wine as befitted the scandalous Lord Gray.

Shaking his head to clear it, he leaned over the cart's edge to inspect its cargo with a keen eye. It was filled with a variety of items, from wine caskets to crates of vegetables, but a monk's robe thrown over a bundle of hemp gave him a sudden idea.

Sprinting forward, he caught the donkey's head and pulled the cart to a halt.

"Good day, my son." The jolly-eyed friar dipped his double chin in greeting.

"And a good day to ye, father," Julian replied with a grin. Fishing a silver coin from his sporran, he tossed it onto the wooden seat next to the man. "Stay and take refreshment ere ye swim home."

"Bless you, my child," the friar replied with a hearty laugh as he pocketed the coin. "'Tis more than enough to buy a keg!" And then with an encouraging cluck, he urged his donkey forward.

Nodding a farewell, Julian waited until the cart had almost passed him by before reaching in to pluck the robe free. It only took a moment to slip it on and draw the cowled hood low over his face.

Cautiously, making his way back to the stack of barrels, he saw no sign of the Saluzzo or of Liselle, but Pascal was crossing the market square and had nearly reached the threshold of the churchyard.

Adopting a stooped shuffle, Julian kept his eye trained on the youth from under his monk's hood as he threaded his way through the crowd. Villagers lugging mud-spattered baskets of fish and vegetables dipped their heads in respect, and he faithfully responded to each one with a benediction and the sign of the cross.

Pascal stopped in front of the church's massive doors a moment and then swiveled on his heel to cross the street and lean against the stone wall of a simple thatch-roofed cottage. Folding his arms, he immediately began to tap his fingers in impatience.

Shifting his course, Julian ambled towards the church's entrance, picking his way through the mud.

Several times he felt Pascal's eyes upon him. But the dark-haired youth lost interest the moment Julian placed his hand on the latch of the church's heavy oak door.

Entering, he dipped his finger in the basin of holy water before him and made the sign of the cross. The church was quite empty save for several craftsmen busily at work on a pulpit which had newly been gifted by King Edward. So focused on carving and painting the hexagonal structure, the men never even lifted their heads to acknowledge Julian as he made his way down the wide nave and towards the western aisle of church. He slipped behind a tall screen and exited the church through a small doorway that was meant only for clerks.

Crossing to the nearby cloister, he heaved himself up onto its lower roof, and racing over the sloping tiles, crouched down near the ridgepole to peer down at the street below.

Pascal was still slumped against the cottage wall, idly inspecting his hands.

Expelling a long breath, Julian settled back on the lead tiles to wait for Pascal's next move. His rooftop perch afforded him a good view of the bustling marketplace. And as time passed, he found himself searching time and time again for any sign of Liselle amongst the ever-changing crowd, but he never saw her.

Pascal fidgeted continually, at times tapping his foot, pacing up and down before the cottage wall, or stretching and yawning out of pure boredom.

And then the church bells began to ring, and Julian winced, covering his ears.

But, as the last strains died away, two lean, black-cloaked men approached the thatched-roofed cottage. Upon catching sight of Pascal, they threw back their hoods to reveal dark angular features and grim faces.

Pascal straightened at once and stepped out into the street to greet them by clasping his forearms with theirs and kissing them upon the cheek.

But then, to Julian's surprise, Liselle's cousin extended his hand and both men sank immediately to their knees.

First one man, and then the other, seized Pascal's hand to reverently kiss a golden ring upon his finger.

And then Pascal murmured something, motioning for them to rise. Huddling close, the three men bowed their heads to speak in low whispers.

Julian grimaced.

He'd never hear what they were saying from his current position on the roof. He needed to get closer, and judging by the attention lavished upon the ring, it would be useful to get a better glimpse of that as well.

But first, he had to create a diversion.

An inspection of his surroundings afforded only one viable option. Swine. Fat sows with multitudes of piglets squealed and rooted in their market pen scarce ten feet away from Pascal and his whispering companions.

Crossing back over the roof, Julian dropped to land softly on the stones. Quickly, he drew the cowl over his face once more, and catching the ear of the nearest ragamuffin, he whispered his request.

Upon seeing the coin, the lad's mouth spread into a wide toothy grin, and the bargain was promptly sealed with a handshake.

In less than a minute's time, the swine were free and mayhem ensued.

Piglets scattered in all directions. And to Julian's delight, a particularly large sow charged the two men, effectively driving a wedge between them and Liselle's cousin.

Pleased, Julian tossed the ragamuffin his earned coin and swiftly stepped into the street. Piglets wove around his feet as he advanced on

Pascal, and it was with some small measure of amusement that he collided directly into him to send him sprawling into the mud.

Alarmed, Pascal's two companions surged forward as Julian watched, etching their faces into his memory. They were distinctive enough, boney and sharp-featured, with eyes like hawks.

But before they could navigate through the squealing piglets to reach him, Julian had grasped Pascal's hand. With a gruff-voiced "Forgive me, my child", he hefted the slim youth to his feet, taking the opportunity to study the signet ring from beneath his cowl.

The ring was unusual. The symbol carved on its gold surface was one he wouldn't forget easily, a bold 'V' entwined with a crown and a sword.

And then Pascal was snatching his hand free, but his tone was respectful enough as he replied, "'Tis no fault of yours, father."

"Bless you, my son," Julian grunted, and with a hobbling step, headed back to the market square, keenly aware of Pascal's riveting gaze observing his every move.

Aye, the lad was suspicious of him. Likely, he'd send one of his men to investigate.

Quickening his step, Julian ducked into the back of a weaver's shop. Discarding the monk's robe, he straightened his plaid and strolled through the place, past the startled weaver measuring ells of cloth, and out the front door. He then casually leaned against the sun-warmed wall next to a basket of wooden spindles and unspun wool, looking to all the world as if he'd been standing there for hours.

Casting a quick glance around, he spied Pascal standing alone in front of the churchyard; his men were nowhere to be seen.

Julian grinned.

No doubt, they were looking for the clumsy priest. And almost as if on cue, one of Pascal's men burst through the door beside him.

"What's the hurry, aye?" Julian asked him in amusement.

The man eyed him suspiciously.

With a careless shrug, Julian turned away to survey the women in the market crowd. And spying a particularly comely lass nearby, he gave a piercing whistle and raised his hand to hail her, "Come hither for a wee kiss, ye bonny blue-eyed maid!"

The maiden glanced his way and smiled.

The suspicion on the face of Pascal's grim-faced companion disappeared. Assuming an arrogant stance, he asked Julian instead, "Have you seen a priest pass through here?"

Julian hid a smile. "Aye," he replied in a distracted tone, waving his hand in the opposite direction. "A cowled priest just entered yonder inn, methinks."

The man bolted towards the place scarcely before the words had left his mouth. Julian shook his head with a wicked smile. It was unlikely the fool would find a priest at the inn, but perhaps he'd find a wild goose being served for supper.

Stretching and taking a deep breath, Julian decided it was time he'd returned to the castle. He'd learned enough of Pascal's doings for now. Aye, the lad was an enigma, as was his bonny cousin, Liselle, but he wasn't yet certain if the Saluzzi and the Vindictam, along with Pascal's distinctive ring, truly had anything to do with him or Scotland's affairs.

Of more pressing concern was the army headed north, its exact size, and procuring documented proof of Albany's betrayal.

Heading back to the castle, he had just neared the gate when he heard Liselle's distinct throaty voice.

"But it's not worth buying, even for the cutting of bread, good sir!" she said in a slightly outraged tone.

Julian paused.

Liselle stood before a craggy-faced man in front of a blacksmith's forge, squinting at a dagger driven deep into the wooden lid of a rain barrel. A thick strand of her hair had escaped her jeweled hairnet to fall forward and frame her face with a spiraling curl.

"You haggle worse than a fishwife, my lady." The blacksmith gave a rough laugh. "A finer blade you'll not see in Fotheringhay! I stake my life on it!"

"Then you will not live to see the sun set," Liselle responded with amusement. "I would see your finer wares."

Julian raised a curious brow. The lass and her kin only grew more interesting by the moment. Most likely, she knew of Pascal's doings. And since she was standing only a few feet from him, mayhap it would be worth a few minutes to dally with her a wee bit and charm answers from her pouting lips.

Brandishing his smile like a weapon, he stepped forward. "May I be of assistance, fair maid?"

Liselle glanced up in surprise. And the responding delight in her hazel eyes was unmistakable. "Well met, Lord Gray!" she greeted him warmly.

Julian's pulse leapt a little. But he grimaced the moment he became aware of it. He'd do well to remind himself that the lass was a source of information and naught else.

Joining her side, he grasped the dagger and yanked it free to heft it in his hand. Although it was polished brightly with a sharp edge and solid leather-corded hilt, it was clearly of inferior quality and would not endure much use. Recalling the skillful way she'd maneuvered his own knives against him, it should not have been surprising that the lass could tell a good dagger from a bad one, but still he couldn't help but glance at her in bewildered admiration.

And then turning to address the craggy-faced blacksmith, he tossed the weapon to him, "The lady is right. 'Tis a trinket, not a real dagger. And though I dinna know what cause she has to arm herself, surely, ye have finer wares to show?"

"Well then," the man grunted in mild irritation. "Give me a moment. I might have another." Grumbling, he disappeared into the shop.

Julian's cheek creased into a grin as he glanced down at Liselle.

"I thank you for your assistance, Lord Gray," she purred sweetly, yet there was a decidedly wicked glint in her eyes. But then, casting a quick glance over her shoulder, she suddenly swore, "*Orponón!*"

Following her gaze, Julian caught only a brief glimpse of Pascal striding their way before Liselle caught his wrist, and pulling him into the blacksmith's shop, shoved him out of view.

"And who—" he began, but she silenced him with a swift jab in the ribs and then clamped her hand firmly over his mouth.

"Not a sound!" she whispered, holding a warning finger up to her lips.

So the wee lass sought to hide him from her cousin, did she? But even as he wondered why, her presence invaded his thoughts and he became aware of just how close she was pressed against him. He felt the beating of her heart against his chest. And as the light perfume of her hair teased his nostrils, all other thoughts fled, save the temptation of burying his face in the wealth of her honey-colored tresses.

Slowly, he lifted his hand and twisted the escaped curl around his finger.

Liselle froze.

A genuine spark of desire rippled through him, and as he looked deeply into her amber-colored eyes, he was certain he saw in them an answering flicker.

He didn't know how long he stood there, pressed close with his fingers entwined in her hair, but suddenly his reason returned, and he let his hand drop.

Aye, how could he forget, even for a moment, that the lass was of the most devious kind? He sought information from her, nothing more. And while he'd never encountered a lass more bewitching he knew it was never more important to remind himself—repeatedly—that she was treacherous.

Swallowing hard, he pulled himself away and broke the spell.

It was not a moment too soon.

He had been dangerously close to kissing her.

Taking a deep breath, he recovered enough to grin down at her with a roguish lift of his brow. "Evading your cousin, are ye?"

"Cousin?" she repeated, glancing sideways at him in surprise. "How did you know that man was Pascal?"

"The lad introduced himself," he explained with a chuckle. "He seems an interesting fellow. Reminds me of the sort who can make a man disappear or find one who doesna want to be found." He studied her face for any sign of a reaction.

Liselle's brows tangled into a frown, and her voice took on a somber cast as she replied, "'Tis true, my lord, that is why for your sake, I pray you're a man of many skills. My cousin will not take it kindly when he finds you've been following me."

Julian tilted his head to the side. He hadn't expected such a gloomy response. And before he knew it, he was once again standing close, cupping her cheek with his hand and wondering what he could do to wipe the sorrow from her brow.

Ach, he scowled at himself.

Did he have no willpower at all?

Clenching his jaw, he backed away once again, and excusing himself with a bow, quit the place as fast as he could.

* * *

Liselle watched Julian stride away in the direction of the castle. The man became more of a distraction every time they met. How could any woman resist his charm?

She stared after him for a moment, biting her lip.

And then she rolled her eyes at herself. She was no swooning maid! No, she was an assassin, or would soon be one!

She had mysteries to unravel, and the strange doings of her contemptuous cousin to decipher.

There was no time in her life for one Lord Julian Gray.

Gathering her skirts, she set off towards the castle, picking her way through the mire as raindrops once again rippled the puddles. Cold mud oozed into her shoe and she grimaced. Venice was never so cold and miserable!

A strong wave of homesickness rose to overwhelm her. It was amusing, in a strange way. She'd spent her entire life attempting to escape *La Serenisima*. And now that she had, in less than a month, she found herself pining for the canals, piazzas, and masquerades.

Snorting at herself in derision, she squared her shoulders, marched across the drawbridge, and into the castle.

Once in her chamber, she kicked off her muddied shoes and lit the tapers. And then with a slow, almost ritualistic precision, she laid out her collection of knives upon the table.

Blades were her specialty. She was talented, and her aim was extraordinary. For her, there was nothing more exhilarating than to hit a target dead on. And she found throwing knives relaxing; it offered her clarity of mind.

With a smile, she held one of the bone-handled stilettos up to the candlelight in admiration. The blade was sharp and the balance keen.

And then with a quick flick of her wrist, she sent the slim weapon flying through the air.

It made a satisfying thud as it struck the center of the door.

Nodding in approval, she picked up the next blade and raised her hand when a sharp series of raps sounded on the other side of the door.

Liselle gritted her teeth. Only Pascal knocked in that manner.

"*Òsti,* I've naught to say, Pascal," she said pointedly, taking aim once again.

"But I have enough words for us both, *bábia!*" came his muffled, sarcastic response.

Liselle hesitated, but she knew that if she didn't let him in, he'd most likely spend the rest of the night causing a commotion outside her chamber. With a growl of exasperation, she stalked to the door and slammed the latch back.

Her tall cousin slouched against the wall with folded arms. "Your games with Lord Gray end this day," he stated with a dark look.

The mere mention of Julian's name elicited a wealth of conflicting emotions, and the memory of his muscular chest made Liselle's lips curve in a delightfully wicked smile. The smile hastily disappeared under Pascal's disapproving glare.

Entering the chamber, he kicked the door shut behind him.

"Why, whatever do you mean, *cuxìn caro?*" Liselle asked sweetly, assuming an innocent expression.

Shoving her aside, he strode to the table and ran a finger over her collection of knives.

"There's not a tongue in this castle that isn't wagging over your doings with the man in the kitchens last night," he said, picking up a large blade and twirling it through his fingers. "Did you really think I'd not discover that you drugged him? Is he such a danger to your heart that you seek to hide and protect him from me? I am not blind, *bábia!*"

Liselle drew back in surprise. Her cousin was proving to be anything *but* blind! What could she possibly say? She *had* sought to hide Julian from Pascal to keep him safe! And maybe even protect her heart in doing so.

"Mayhap I should eliminate him after all," her cousin drawled, "Mayhap then you could focus on your task of finding Dolfin and free me from this mockery of a country." He waved his hand in an all-encompassing gesture and heaved a great sigh. "And to think I found the French wine lacking! I am convinced that the English merely bottle their pig swill and are too dense to know better!"

Liselle tossed her head. She'd dealt with Pascal her entire life. She did not fear him.

Especially when she knew of his secret doings.

"If you suffer so, *cuxìn caro,* I'm sure you can find your way home," she said with a false smile.

"One would think I could, *bábia,*" he agreed easily enough before adding in a biting tone, "I have escorted you home in disgrace oft enough, have I not?"

And then locking his dark eyes on hers, he sent the large blade flying across the room to embed itself next to her stiletto with a loud thwack.

With an even sweeter smile than before, she continued in a voice that dripped honey, "And who are you to demand anything? You, who have dealings with the Saluzzi and other members of the Vindictam in the shadows, behind Orazio's back."

She could tell by the way he stood there, silent and still, that she had stumbled upon a secret he *had* wished to keep. How fortunate she had followed him!

Moving to the door, she yanked the knives out and returned to the table, her face still brandishing a smile.

"How observant of you," Pascal murmured with a strange gleam in his dark eyes. "I would that you knew so much of Dolfin."

Liselle scowled, and raising her wrist, took aim.

And then Pascal's lip curled into a smirk. "Focus on your task, *bábia*! Cease following me and cease your games of seduction with Lord Gray, or Orazio will be sure to send you back home on the first ship he can find! And by yourself! I'll not be your donkey again!"

But at the mention of her brother's name, Liselle tensed, and the stiletto flew wild to bounce off the stones next to the door. "Orazio?" she asked, "Is he here? Have you had word? Were those men messengers—"

Pascal's response was immediate. "Forget you ever saw them, *bábia*," he ordered in a tone of authority that she had never heard before. But then he shrugged and pretended to brush a speck of dust off his sleeve as he added nonchalantly, "And if you do not, I shall relish the opportunity to inform your brother that you prefer to spend your evenings disrobing Lord Julian Gray rather than to follow orders."

Liselle rolled her eyes, but she was quick to respond with a threat of her own. "Do not even think of it, *bábio*. If such words were to fall from your lips, Orazio just might hear of your harsh words to the Saluzzo in the marketplace."

They stood there, glaring at one another, and then Pascal threw his head back in a scornful laugh. "Fine then, dally with him as you may, Liselle. A drunken fool is a fitting match for you, I must admit."

"*Basta!* Enough of this dithering!" Liselle snapped. Returning to the door, she wrenched it open and ordered, "You may leave now! Go! *Marcìa via!* Put wings upon your feet!"

To her surprise, he stalked past her straightway, but on reaching the threshold, he paused to peer down at her and say with a disdainful twist of his lip, "If you thought of Dolfin even half as much as you do of Lord Julian Gray, you would have found the old man by now!"

"Did you say Lord Gray?" Liselle gasped, drawing her hands to her mouth as if shocked. And then she reminded him harshly, "I forbid his name to cross your lips! Remember well, or else I might find myself inadvertently speaking of your visitors, fair cousin!" With a scowl, she jiggled the door handle.

Pascal's fine nostrils flared. "Then seal *your* lips, *bábia*. You've been naught but a thorn in my side from the start!"

Liselle gritted her teeth in a fake smile, a smile he matched with one even more false.

And then Pascal turned to leave, but he had taken only a step before he paused and asked as an afterthought, "In your prowling about the village, did you see a cowled monk?"

"Many!" she retorted. "Which one?"

He hesitated and then cursing under his breath, strode away.

With a burst of temper, Liselle kicked the door shut and leaned against it. *Santo Ciélo,* but Pascal was difficult to deal with!

After a time, her temper cooled to be replaced by a perplexed feeling of unease.

She never would have imagined Pascal could be so easily blackmailed. It was disturbing. What could possibly be the secret he protected so dearly? She had not known the two men that had met him, but for certain she'd recognized the distinctive greeting. But why had they kissed *Pascal's* hand? No one had ever kissed Orazio's hand.

Clearly, Pascal had a mission that neither she nor Orazio knew anything about.

But who had given it to him and what was it? Orazio was his Magno Duce. And if Orazio had no knowledge of it, then only the Quattuor Gladiis could have given Pascal such a charter. But why would someone so powerful in the Vindictam stoop to deal directly with her arrogant cousin?

Diàmbarne! But it was enough to make her head split.

Annoyed to be thinking so much of her cousin, Liselle tucked the bone-handled stilettos back safely into her sleeves. And then freeing her hair from her net, she picked up a fine silver-handled comb and ran its teeth through her tresses, directing her thoughts once more to a far more pleasant subject.

Lord Gray.

The man certainly had a mysterious habit of showing up everywhere of late. A fact she found quite delightful. Absently combing her hair, she recalled his muscular, hard body and his piercing gray eyes.

For one brief, glorious moment at the blacksmith's, she thought she'd seen in those eyes a look of real hunger, hunger for *her*. She shivered, reliving the moment, and then her lashes flew open in outright alarm.

Santo Ciélo, but Pascal was right! She spent far too much time thinking of the seductive Scot. And in all likelihood, Nicoletta was right as well. The man probably was a rogue and thought of nothing other than satisfying his own needs.

Expelling a breath, Liselle leaned her head against the window and looked out. Dusk had fallen. The dark clouds rolling in from the north hid any sign of a sunset.

The dogs were barking in the courtyard once again, and she saw that some new knight had just arrived riding a black charger as a score of soaked and muddied soldiers stumbled behind him on foot.

"Fools," Liselle whispered. It made little sense for them to die for the pompous Albany's meaningless crown.

It was then that she noticed a solitary man standing near the stables observing the new arrivals with interest.

Her heart flopped.

Even from this distance, she knew it was Julian.

Biting her lip, she peered down at him for a time, wondering what he sought and, despite herself, admiring his sharply defined muscles and shoulder-length blond hair.

It seemed he would stand there all night, a prospect she quite looked forward to, until she noticed a man swathed in a black cloak observing him from the battlements above.

Her eyes widened in alarm.

Was it Pascal? Had he broken his word?

Without hesitation, she made for her chamber door.

Her cousin's nature had always been scheming and deceitful, but she had never known him to so deliberately cross her. Flying down the stairwell, she ordered her beating heart to slow, but it did not obey.

Bursting out into the courtyard, she pushed her way through the men thronging about in the rain. Ignoring their calls for her attention, she finally broke free of the crowd just to see Julian stride into the stables.

There was no sign of the dark figure on the battlements. Wiping the rain from her face, Liselle searched the surrounding area.

Almost immediately, the dark shadowy form appeared behind the stables, and she caught her breath in a mixture of relief and concern. The man was much too short to be Pascal.

But then, who could it be?

One of his mysterious companions? Or, *cà de dìa,* a Saluzzo?

As she watched, the figure darted into the stables through the back entrance.

She was behind him in a flash.

Instinctively unsheathing a stiletto, she stepped inside the building. The stench of foul straw met her nostrils. The interior was so dark she couldn't see, but then at the far end, Julian's blond hair gleamed in the sudden flash of a torch flaring to life.

Squinting, Liselle saw only piles of straw, saddles, and ropes.

There was no sign of the furtive stranger.

Ahead, Julian dropped the torch into an iron sconce and entered one of the stalls.

A horse whickered loudly in greeting.

"Aye, 'tis time to be leaving soon, lad," Julian chuckled fondly in response.

Cautiously, Liselle crept closer and dropped to a crouch, leaning forward for a better view. The stones dug roughly into her knees.

"Easy, lad," Julian was crooning as he led the beast out of the stall. "There's a lad now."

And it was then that Liselle saw a glint of metal from above.

It *was* the Saluzzo from the market pace. Immediately, she recognized the wiry man with dark stubby brows crouched in the rafters, a sharp blade glittering betwixt his teeth and a heavy coil of rope in his hands.

And then he lunged forward to spring down upon Julian from above.

7

THE PROTECTION OF THE VINDICTAM

Liselle didn't hesitate. She let her stiletto loose. It wouldn't be a serious strike, but it would be enough to prevent the man from harming Julian.

The Saluzzo made a shocked, gargling sound as her blade struck home. Landing off balance, he dropped the rope and stumbled forward with the bone-handled stiletto protruding from his shoulder.

Startled, Julian stepped back, unsheathing his dirk in a single movement.

And then the Saluzzo straightened, and his blade appeared in his hand as he crouched as if ready to strike Julian.

"Who are ye?" Julian thundered as he lunged forward.

With a curse, the Saluzzo began to retreat.

"Have a care, Lord Gray!" the man rasped in warning. "Your friends in the Vindictam will not protect you for long! We will find you!" For one brief moment, he glared into the darkness in Liselle's direction, and then turning on his heel, fled the stables.

Liselle closed her eyes and swallowed.

What had she done?

She felt ill.

But not because she had just attacked a Saluzzo from Ferrara, an action that, should they hear of it, would surely shatter the fragile truce between the Vindictam and the Saluzzi family.

No, it was the sight of blood that had made her nauseated, the first drops she had ever spilled.

What kind of assassin *was* she?

And then Julian's Scottish burr commanded, "Reveal yourself!"

* * *

Silence was Julian's only answer.

He'd recognized his assailant as the Saluzzo in the marketplace. But what cause had the man to attack *him*? He prodded the coil of rope with his boot. Or had the man been trying to abduct him? For what reason?

And who had averted the attack and perhaps just saved his life?

God's Wounds! He hadn't the time for this mystery! He still had to procure proof of Albany's betrayal. Chasing would-be abductors and assassins would be a distraction.

When nothing moved, he sheathed his dirk, aggravated at the delay in his plans. And slapping his horse on the rump, he guided the beast back into the stall.

"I'll be back soon, lad," he promised.

Aye, he'd throttle some answers from the Saluzzo, and right quickly!

Quenching the torch, Julian headed outside the stables to search for the man. It wasn't hard to pick up his trail. Immediately, he found traces of blood, and judging by the size of the drops, the man's wound wasn't as trivial as it had first seemed.

He hadn't tracked the man far before screams resonated from the kitchens.

His quarry had been discovered.

Sprinting towards the commotion, he arrived to see a maid waving her hands frantically at the scullery door.

"Lord Gray!" She seized his arm. "Signor Balbus has been sorely injured! Oh, please help him straightway!"

Julian strode into the scullery and peered down at the unconscious man at his feet. Prodding him with a booted toe, he glanced up at the maid and asked, "And how do ye know this man's name?"

"Oh, he's a rich merchant, my lord!" She gasped, and then stepping closer, she lowered her voice and hissed conspiratorially, "But he's really an Italian prince in disguise! He made me swear to tell no one!"

Julian suppressed a snort.

And then the place filled with more maids pleading, "Please help him, my lord!" and "Send for the herb-wife at once!"

Julian stifled a growl of frustration. He'd never be able to wring answers from the man under such circumstances, even if he *were* to regain consciousness.

As if on cue, the Saluzzo moaned.

Kneeling by his side, Julian heaved the assassin onto his back, and under the guise of staunching the blood, swiftly searched the man.

There was little on him, save for a small velvet pouch attached to a leather belt. But, it was an unusual belt. Upon closer inspection, Julian saw that it was quite intricate, a parchment-thin strip of leather wound loosely on top of a more serviceable belt of thick hide.

Ordering a maid to press down on the stab wound in his stead, Julian swiftly unbuckled the looser belt and slid it and the pouch under his knee. As he did so, a bloodied bone-handled stiletto fell to the stone floor.

He recognized it at once; the small knife had subverted the attack. Wondering at the identity of his savior, he wiped the blood off the blade and slipped it into his boot.

And then the herb-wife arrived to issue orders, and Julian seized the opportunity to pick up the pouch and belt and then to slip away.

Threading his way through the maze of castle passages, he swiped a torch, and returning to his chamber, began his inspection.

Fishing the stiletto out of his boot, he eyed it curiously. It was well made, aye, exquisitely made, even. Small, deadly, and bearing no identifying mark.

The Saluzzo's velvet pouch held nothing but coins and what looked like a small bottle of ink. Julian frowned, a little puzzled, before tucking it away into his sporran. Why would the man carry ink?

And then he turned his gaze upon the belt.

The top strip was of stretched leather, resembling parchment more than anything else. It had been folded lengthwise into thirds and unwrapping it revealed a series of dark letters written at different angles and of varying widths apart.

Julian's eyes lit.

A message!

He scanned the groups of letters with interest, recognizing only fragments of what appeared to be Latin. Peering closely at the slanted characters, he looped the leather around his hand, wondering if the matching angles would form full words.

His first few attempts produced nothing.

But then his eyes widened in surprise as two words formed: *Giuliano Gray.*

Glancing about the chamber, he searched for something long and thin to loop the leather around. The only thing remotely suitable was the iron candelabra with its narrow tapers.

It took several attempts at wrapping the belt in different patterns around bars and tapers of varying widths before he finally saw a coherent series of Latin words form.

"Dolfin veniet si Dominus Giuliano Gray timetur.
Electus eis invenire et occidere."

Julian caught his breath in alarm, whispering the words aloud, "Dolfin will come if Lord Julian Gray is in peril. Find the Electus and slay them all."

Aye, even unconscious, the Saluzzo had given him the answer to why he'd been attacked. They sought to use him as a hostage to flush Dolfin out of his hiding place. But who was the Electus? And had they discovered that he was *Le Marin*?

Closing his eyes, he tapped his fist lightly against his forehead.

Matters had taken a dangerous twist. He couldn't afford to ignore these strange doings any more.

Nor could he delay much longer in gathering the information that Cameron would so desperately need!

It was a long, aggravating night. Julian found no new answers, nor was he successful in finding the treaties signed by Albany's hand.

And when the sun finally rose, it found him sitting in the great hall, exhausted and ill-tempered.

The day only worsened when Gloucester arrived, issuing orders to ride.

Wincing at his overly loud voice, Julian watched the men leap from their seats around him and scurry out of the hall to saddle the horses and make ready to depart.

Weary of the hall, Julian made his way to the courtyard and cast a critical eye at the gray and drizzly sky. He didn't relish trailing after Gloucester in such miserable weather, but it had to be done. Leaning back, he stretched his arms with a loud yawn when his eye caught Albany's red head bobbing across the ancient drawbridge spanning the roaring waters of the River Nene.

Julian's jaw clenched, and filled with a mixture of curiosity and anger, he slipped outside the castle walls in hot pursuit.

The rainstorms of the night had caused the river to flood its banks, eradicating any sign of its usual graceful curves and forming lakes in the nearby fields. Those lakes had swallowed stands of birch and weeping willows, making for an eerie countryside.

Albany was already out of sight, but he'd left a trail of fresh footprints already half-filled with water, and those led over the boggy ground to a nearby spreading oak.

And it was there that Julian found the prince huddled in the company of a flock of rain-sodden sheep.

Albany stood silent, on the edge of a muddy hillock overlooking the turbulent waters. His head was bowed and shoulders hunched in a manner most forlorn.

Aye, the man had cause for a guilty conscience!

"'Tis odd to find ye here in England," Julian said by way of greeting. The sarcasm was rife in his tone.

Albany jerked in surprise. "Aye, Julian. 'Tis strange to see ye here in Fotheringhay."

"Strange?" Julian repeated, adopting a belligerent tone. "I but visit kinfolk. I come here oft enough, but I've never seen ye here afore."

Albany glanced away, and then replied, "Aren't ye as angry as I? Do ye nae wish for vengeance on Mar's behalf? 'Tis not right that cur, Cochrane, succeeded his earldom!"

Julian raised a brow, surprised Albany would be thinking of his murdered younger brother. "Aye," he agreed truthfully. "I'm angry for Mar."

But Albany wasn't listening. "I loved my brother," the Scottish prince admitted gruffly. "He was always seeing naught but good. He was a dreamer, that lad."

"Aye, he was a dreamer," Julian agreed as his gray eyes narrowed. "And he'd not want to be the martyr who ignited treason—caused brother to fight against brother, aye?"

Albany went pale, and his hand began to shake. And then he whirled on Julian and shouted, "And what would ye know of it? I'll see justice done, Lord Gray! I'll see myself King of Scotland even if I have to use a Yorkist bastard to get me there!"

A curse left Julian's lips. "God's Wounds, but ye've gone daft, Albany! Don't ye see you're giving the King of England our land for naught but an empty title? There's no justice for Mar in that. Ye've only drafted a surrender of Scotland!"

"Spare me your lofty speech, Julian! Why would *ye* care which king sits on the throne? The wine will flow for ye just the same!" Albany's nostrils flared, and he gave an irksome bray of a laugh.

Wiping his hand over his brow, he stumbled back a little.

And then suddenly he was sliding down the riverbank and tumbling backward into the slow-moving current.

He began to thrash then, flailing in the muddy river water and struggling for breath, and it took Julian a moment to recognize the wild desperation in the man's eyes to be genuine panic.

The fool couldn't swim.

It was tempting to leave him there and let fate take its course. And he almost walked away.

Almost.

But then Albany gave a gargled sort of scream. And as he was swept downriver a bit, Julian grudgingly searched for something with which to fish him out.

A short distance ahead he spied a coil of rope tied to a tree, the kind used to guide boats to the other side of the shore. 'Twas cumbersome, but it would have to do.

Sprinting past the flailing prince, he heaved the coil up and tossed it in an arc. Miraculously, Albany managed to catch hold.

Julian eyed him a moment and then lounged against the tree to watch. Aye, he'd not be reeling the shameful prince in like a fish. The fool deserved to thrash about and fight for his life. After all, he was preparing to wage war on his own kinfolk.

It took some time, but Albany finally struggled ashore, his lips trembling as he shivered uncontrollably.

"I'll be your king soon, Julian!" The man seethed through chattering teeth. "Have a care!"

"Then it behooves me to see that ye never be king." Julian growled. The words were like a gauntlet, flung down at the prince's feet.

Albany's mouth dropped open.

But Julian didn't give him a chance to respond. "Stop this madness, Albany! Dinna doom Scotland to servitude and dinna spill the blood of your own kinfolk!"

Albany's mouth snapped shut, and his shoulders sagged once more. And then, without a word, he pivoted on his heel and headed back to Fotheringhay.

Julian watched him go, shaking his head in disbelief as the sudden raucous calling of crows caught his attention. And as they flapped off squawking in alarm, the rain suddenly began to fall in driving sheets.

Squaring his shoulders, he set off after the prince.

'Twas time to leave.

* * *

"Liselle! Do you know what you have done?"

Liselle whirled to look straight into Pascal's accusing, dark eyes.

Glaring at him, she put her hand to her heart. "Are you trying to frighten me?" She gasped. She hadn't heard him sneak into her chamber. *Santo Ciélo*, he was as silent as a cat!

She sent him a scathing look.

He matched it.

"Show me your stilettos!" he ordered forcefully, "Both of them! *Ale!*"

Liselle tensed.

He didn't miss it.

In a flash, Pascal twisted her arms behind her back and snatched the stiletto from the hidden sheath within her sleeve.

He was so astonishingly quick that she had no time to react. *Òsti!* Her cousin grew more surprising by the day! Where had he learned such speed?

"Where is the other one?" he asked as he tossed the bone-handled stiletto onto the table.

Wrenching herself free, Liselle faced him, haughty and proud.

"Yes!" she confessed boldly, raising a clenched fist. "Yes, I attacked the Saluzzo last night. But I did not kill him!" She'd been ill enough at injuring him. She couldn't imagine what it would have felt like to have taken his life.

Pascal loomed over her, his handsome face rife with disapproval. And then to her utter astonishment, he shrugged and observed softly, "'Tis a pity that you did not kill him, *bábia!* Ridding the world of a Saluzzo would have atoned for the entirety of your follies. And, I feel compelled to remind you, your follies have been *numerous!*"

Picking the stiletto up, he held it aloft a moment. And then, taking up her hand and spreading her clenched fingers apart, he placed the hilt of the slim weapon into her palm and closed her fingers around it.

"Tell no one of what occurred last night," he commanded with his arrogant eyes boring into hers. "No one! Not even Orazio!"

Liselle was shocked. "How can I not tell my Magno Duce?"

"He needn't know," Pascal answered with a superior smile.

"You have gone mad, Pascal!" Liselle accused. Bowing her head, she whispered the words that had kept her up all night. "They will find out. The Saluzzo survived. He will tell them, and they will know the treaty has been broken. I have rekindled the war betwixt our families! They will demand retribution! And—"

"I grow weary of quarreling with you!" Pascal interrupted sharply before adopting his trademark smirk. "The Saluzzi are nothing. I do not fear them. The Vindictam should not live in the shadow of fear, *bábia, and especially* if that shadow belongs to a Saluzzo!"

Liselle tilted her head suspiciously. "What game are you playing? Have you no loyalty to the Vindictam—to our families?" she asked, feeling more than a little trepidation.

Pascal sent her a black look. "*Game*? Perhaps I only seek to protect you! Why would you accuse me of playing a game?" But he couldn't refrain from sarcasm for long. Shaking his head, he clucked, *"Ah sì,* what is 'blood loyalty' anyway, when the recipient of that loyalty isn't—how shall we say it—*loyal?"*

She didn't answer. She merely narrowed her eyes.

"Well then!" Pascal gave a graceful shrug. "We have an understanding. If you speak of this to anyone I shall send for Orazio and inform him that merely to save Lord Gray's life, you became the first member of the Vindictam to spill Saluzzi blood since the treaty was forged. Won't he be pleased that his own *sorèlina cara* was the one to start the war!"

Liselle swallowed. "Unthinkable!" she whispered. It was *unthinkable* precisely for the fact that it was horrid to think it was exactly what she'd done!

"Or," Pascal continued with a black look and a gleam in his eyes. "Or remain silent and perhaps this Saluzzi fool will be *permanently* silenced as well."

She could only stare at him, wondering how much she really knew her cousin, after all. Was he offering to protect her? Was he even *capable* of that? Or, as was more likely, was he using this incident as an excuse to rid the earth of the Saluzzi that he so desperately hated?

Suddenly weary, she sank against the table.

And then Pascal said in a soft voice, "Pack your things, *bábia*. We leave straightway for Alnwick."

And without a backward glance, he quit the room.

Subdued, Liselle quickly packed her belongings, and a short time later, clad in a French riding gown and a tightly woven russet cloak, she picked her way across Fotheringhay's courtyard.

Horses stamped and metal swords clanked. Men cursed as the rain poured upon them.

She glanced up at the dark sky. The storm showed no signs of retreating. It would be a miserable ride.

But, it matched her mood.

Spying Albany and Pascal astride their horses near the castle gate, Liselle drew her hood low over her face and hurried to join them.

Dressed in royal plaids and a dark green mantle, Albany waved a hand as she approached. "We'll have ye cozy in Scotland soon enough, lass!" he promised, wiggling his brows.

A sudden clatter of hooves behind her made her glance back to see the fierce Duke of Gloucester bearing down upon her.

"Get you gone, woman!" he ordered brusquely. Sitting in the saddle, his curved spine was not as pronounced.

Liselle blinked, unprepared for the vehemence in his voice. "My lord, I am to be escorted to Edinburgh—" she began, dipping a quick curtsey.

"But we ride to war, woman!" The duke peered down the length of his long nose at her disdainfully. "This company is no place for you."

"My lord—" she began.

"Silence!" he cut in curtly and lifted his hand.

Liselle snapped her mouth shut and turned to Albany.

For a moment, she feared the Scottish prince would agree with the duke, but then Pascal chose that moment to urge his mount forward and to casually rest his hand upon the hilt of his sword.

Albany didn't miss the gesture. Clearing his throat, he addressed the duke gruffly, "I'm sworn to deliver the Lady Liselle to the Princess Anabella in Edinburgh, Gloucester. When we reach the borderlands, I'll send her on her way with a few of my men."

Gloucester's forehead creased with displeasure, but then with a grunt, he spurred his horse and was gone.

Sending him a dark look, Liselle mounted her gray mare. She'd scarcely done so before the horns sounded and the company of horsemen under Gloucester's command unfurled his royal banner emblazoned with a white boar, and began to march out of Fotheringhay Castle with the duke and Albany at the head.

Sitting on her mare, Liselle watched the men file before her.

She'd spent the night fretting over Lord Julian Gray. Where was the man? She knew the Saluzzo lay ill under the care of the herb-wife, but could there be others? Had Julian escaped harm throughout the night?

She waited until the last possible moment, desperately seeking any sign of him before reluctantly nudging her mare to follow the other horses plodding over the drawbridge and through the village.

They had just reached the far side of the marketplace when she saw Julian near the churchyard astride a red roan.

She caught her breath in relief.

He wore no cloak, only his dark plaid and a white shirt, plastered to his muscular body by the rain. He'd unfastened the top button of his shirt, and as they passed by him, she couldn't prevent her gaze from dropping to catch a glimpse of his bare chest.

She bit her tongue. Hard. And then she lifted her lashes and their eyes locked.

But her horse chose that moment to sidestep into another, and when she'd regained control of the animal, she looked back at the church.

But he was no longer there.

She didn't see him again in the days that followed.

Gloucester's party had headed north through rolling hills, fragrant meadows, and vales clothed with ancient forests. Pascal had informed her that their destination was Alnwick, but the name meant little to her beyond the fact that it was a castle close to the Scottish border.

She lost track of the days.

And then finally one afternoon, they left a forest and rounded a bend in the road to arrive at the mighty Alnwick Castle sprawled over the hill guarding the northern borderlands.

It was a magnificent place, one that inspired awe.

As their horses clattered over the drawbridge straddling the River Aln and a deep ravine, Liselle could only stare in awe at the fortress rising before her, its battlements adorned with the figures of stone warriors. She passed through three sets of gates before finally reaching the center of the great citadel.

Men dressed for battle were everywhere, and the smell of horses filled the air. There was an army here. And a large one.

She turned a questioning gaze to Pascal riding beside her.

"Thousands," he answered softly, reading her unspoken question. "There are thousands of men here. It does not bode well for Scotland."

Liselle followed in silence.

122

A short time later, she curtsied before the elderly lady of the castle, and begging weariness from the journey, retired at once to her assigned chamber.

Dusk was approaching. With so many men in such a place, Alnwick Castle was a treasure trove of information. And once darkness fell, she could slip unseen through the passages and learn much—perhaps even a secret or two to serve her well in the future.

Plaiting her hair to the side, she rummaged through her clothing and selected a simple dark gown and soft leather shoes, shoes the Vindictam fashioned for silence.

A servant appeared with a meal of roasted fowl, bread, and nuts. And after eating, Liselle sprawled comfortably in the window seat, waiting for the sun to set and allowing her thoughts to rove where they would.

As night approached, campfires dotted the hillside, accompanied by the sound of stamping horses and the low, gruff voices of men.

And then finally, it was dark enough.

With a beating heart, Liselle slipped silently from her room. She stood still, staring wide-eyed into the inky darkness, waiting for her eyes to adjust. And then with a wary step, she crept down the passageway to the grand staircase expanding below her like a fan.

The main hall of Alnwick Castle was still a hive of activity. Tables ran down the center of the room, loomed above by braided-iron chandeliers. Tall windows in arched alcoves lined one wall and a massive fireplace graced the opposite. It was framed on either side by richly woven tapestries, and before them stood ancient suits of armor on display. Men clustered in groups, their heads bowed together as they used various table items to model battle strategies. Women bustled about, filling cups of ale and bringing out great baskets of bread and cheese, while scullery maids hurried about gathering wooden trenchers and abandoned cutlery.

At the head table, Gloucester sat alone, hunched in his chair and drinking what looked like whiskey from a large glass bottle.

Liselle snorted.

She found it nigh impossible the man could ever imbibe enough spirits to render him in a more agreeable mood. Never had she met so cantankerous a man!

Slowly, she crept down the stairs, staying in the shadows when shouts sounded abruptly from behind her.

"*Le Marin!* My lord, *Le Marin!*" a man cried, flying past her down the stairs.

Gloucester leapt to his feet, nearly knocking the whiskey over as the new arrival thrust a gray Turk's head knot into his hands.

"He seized the contract, my lord!" The man gasped, trying to catch his breath.

"Contract?" Gloucester repeated, still stunned.

"Albany's betrothal contract!" The man gulped. "I could not stop him!"

Gloucester stared at him a moment, and then roared.

Men scrambled up from the tables, drawing their swords. And as a dozen bolted past her, Liselle saw a tall man—masked from head to toe in dark clothing—calmly enter the hall from the opposite side.

Excitement thrilled through her, though she did not know quite why.

Perhaps it was the sheer bravado of the man.

As she watched, the masked man leapt onto Gloucester's table, and then calmly proceeded to walk down the length of it, as if he were strolling down a road. Once he had reached Gloucester's place at the head, he paused as every eye in the room riveted upon him.

Reaching into his dark mantle, he withdrew a parchment bearing a red-wax seal. And then, dangling it in front of Gloucester's astonished face, he hailed him in a heavy French accent, "Your undertaking is doomed to fail, Gloucester!"

The vein on Gloucester's forehead bulged. Lunging for him, he cried, *"Le Marin!"*

But *Le Marin* sidestepped him easily enough.

Bending down, *Le Marin* swiped the bottle of whiskey and swiftly stopped it with a rag. And then catching hold of an iron chandelier, he swung over Gloucester's head, lighting the rag with a candle before letting go to land lightly on his feet in front of the window alcove.

No one spoke.

No one moved.

And then with a blow, *Le Marin* dashed the whiskey bottle to the stones.

A sheet of flames rose to engulf the window alcove.

Falling back before the intense heat, no one could pursue him or even see past the glow. And by the time they had doused the fire, the only trace of him was the open window in the arched alcove.

Liselle smiled in appreciation.

Le Marin was a man to be admired, and Orazio would be sore disappointed to discover that he'd missed a chance in snaring the man.

Taking a seat, Liselle watched with great interest as men rushed about the smoky interior of the hall, cursing and stomping their feet.

The entire place was in an uproar.

Gloucester's face was purple with fury as he screamed orders to his men. Albany and Douglas arrived, looking confused at first, and then even more angry than Gloucester upon discovering just exactly what *Le Marin* had taken.

And then amidst the chaos, Liselle heard a deep Scottish burr whisper in her ear, "How pleasant to see ye again, Lady Gray!"

Liselle jerked and half rose to her feet in astonishment. "Lord Gray! What brings you here?"

"I but journey home, Lady Gray." He laughed. And then catching her hand to press her palm against his chest, he added in a low rumble, "And if I may say it, ye seemed right pleased to see me!"

Liselle's heart lurched in response. He was a devastatingly handsome and charming man, and while she'd always thought there was a hint of something rough and wild about him, it was oddly more pronounced now.

He didn't appear to notice her distraction. Raising a curious brow, he eyed the commotion around them. "What has happened here?"

She didn't answer. He was still holding her hand, and her every sense tingled with excitement.

And then his searching gray eyes fell upon her once more as he repeated, "What has them vexed so?"

"*Le Marin!*" she answered a little breathlessly, but more because of his hard chest and beating heart beneath her fingertips than any doings of a French spy.

Julian gave her an amused wink. "And does the man affect ye so?"

"Affect me, my lord?" she asked in turn, studying him from under her lashes. The way his shirt strained across the well-defined muscles of his chest made her suddenly hot. *Santo Cielo,* but the man radiated a strength that she found irresistible.

Swallowing, she sucked her bottom lip between her teeth.

Instantly, a sudden hardness entered Julian's gaze and tension appeared in his jaw. But then it passed, and a wicked gleam of mirth entered his eyes. "If I recall, did ye not say ye'd right willingly kiss the man?"

Liselle frowned a moment before realizing he was still speaking of *Le Marin*. And then tossing her head, she gave a long, low laugh. "Even the mighty *Le Marin* must earn my kisses, my lord."

A deep dimple creased one cheek as he asked, "Truly? Tell me, lass, what must a man do to prove worthy of your lips?"

The question was a hard one. Any man she might wish to love must first be approved by the Vindictam, but she could hardly tell him that. "Why speak of such things?" she asked with a frown.

And then the expression in his eyes altered, sending her heart racing. And leaning close, so close that she could feel the heat of his skin, he whispered, "Few can resist the lure of such beauty, Lady Gray."

She had to clear her throat several times before she could reply, "And few can resist falling prey to sweet honeyed words, Lord Gray."

He had yet to let go of her hand. His touch was like fire, but his gaze was even hotter as his eyes dropped meaningfully to her lips.

Suddenly, she filled with fear. Fear that he really *might* kiss her.

As if in a dream, she forced the words from her throat to say, "I am, however, one who *can* resist, my lord." She *should* be one of them! She *had* to be!

"Are ye now?" He breathed a soft reply.

And then somehow, his lips were close, almost upon hers. She was mesmerized, unable to move.

"I admit, I'm intrigued," he murmured, slipping a strong hand around her waist. "I find ye fair—"

"Dare ye show your face here, Gray?" Albany's loud, questioning voice interrupted.

Liselle jerked back as Julian smoothly turned on his heel to face the Scottish prince.

Albany stood before them, his hands splayed upon his hips, and his dark brows drawn in an angry line.

Behind him, Archibald Douglas gaped as if in surprise to see Julian before he suddenly averted his eyes and took a quick step back.

"My lord!" Julian swept an elegant bow, and then leaning sideways, added deliberately, "And a good evening to ye, Douglas. What brings ye to Alnwick?"

"Aye, good evening, lad," Douglas grunted in reply, and then looking as if he'd much rather be anywhere else, fell victim to a fit of coughing.

Stepping close to the table, Albany pounded his fist upon its surface and raised his voice, "Dare ye show your face to me, Gray? After nearly drowning me in Fotheringhay?"

Julian blinked in surprise and repeated in shock, "Drowning, my lord? Surely ye are mistaken!" And then with a rueful grin, he added, "I admit, I was fair drunk there, my lord. If I caused ye—"

"What is this?" a new, commanding tone inserted itself into the conversation.

They all turned to find Gloucester standing behind them, eyeing Julian with rank suspicion.

"Who are you? What brings you here?" The duke shot the questions out in an irate, rough manner.

Julian appeared almost embarrassed. "'Tis only a small misfortune, my lord," he answered in a low tone and waved his fingers in a pleading motion.

"Misfortune?" Gloucester repeated tersely and with more than a little distrust in his voice.

"A lost wager," Julian answered with a slow, self-conscious grin. "And I heard Douglas was here. I came to borrow a wee bit of coin afore they find me and … well, there is a lady present." He nodded his chin at Liselle.

Liselle watched him in amazement. He was plainly playing Gloucester for a fool. Surely, the man could see it! Surely, Albany and

Douglas could as well!

But Douglas was groaning and rolling his eyes. "For the sake of St. Andrew, how much this time, Julian? Just know ye'll be paying me back anything I lend ye afore ye pay Cameron what ye owe him already! Do ye hear me, lad?"

"Aye, 'tis a mere hundred pounds." Julian's grin broadened.

Gloucester looked upon him, outraged. And then turning to Albany, he ordered through clenched jaws. "Remove this fool from my sight!" His temper was visibly boiling.

"My lord, the lad is a good friend of the Earl of Lennox—" Douglas began to protest weakly.

"Then the Earl of Lennox is a fool," Gloucester exploded. "He should choose his friends more wisely!"

As Albany and Douglas exchanged glances, Gloucester's mouth gaped, astonished at their visible reluctance.

"It will be no surprise when Scotland falls! The lot of you are fools!" he snapped viciously. "Is there not a man amongst you?"

And then his eyes fell upon Liselle.

Liselle froze, immediately regretting that she hadn't escaped whilst they had all been distracted. Well, she couldn't escape the man now!

With an outright snort of disdain, the duke hissed, "Get this woman out of my sight! Send them both away, and right quickly. Have the fool escort the lass to Edinburgh and have done!"

"Not wise, my lord," Douglas inserted quickly, his red face flooding in alarm. "I wouldna deliver any *lady* into Lord Gray's care."

"Aye, he'd bed the lass and then most likely leave her stranded," Albany growled, looping his thumbs through his belt. "I canna afford to anger her brother."

At that, Julian chuckled, and with a flippant shrug, said, "Then let it be as ye wish, my lord. Mayhap I should help ye search for *Le Marin* instead, aye?"

The vein on Gloucester's forehead nearly popped. "I've no time to bandy idle words with a pack of fools!" he said in a livid tone, and then shoving Albany aside, he strode away.

Refocusing his anger now onto Gloucester, Albany roared and followed the man, demanding an apology as Douglas muttered, "Julian, I'll find a way to pay your debt, for Cameron's sake."

And then he was gone.

Julian shook his head in disgust.

With a twinge of disappointment, Liselle watched him take a step as if to follow them, but then he suddenly turned and caught her wrist.

Startled, she looked up into his eyes and found them simmering with a sensual heat.

And then in one quick, fluid movement, he covered her lips in a scorching kiss.

8

"ACH, I SHOULDNA HAVE KISSED HER"

Capturing Liselle's bottom lip betwixt his teeth, Julian expertly deepened his kiss to interweave his tongue with hers.

Her response was immediate, filled with a fire and a wild abandon that made his blood boil as her tongue tangled deliciously with his. Slowly, she slid her palm over his chest, leaving in its wake a soft trail of burning sweetness that taunted him with the promise of more.

Lifting his hand, he cupped the delicate curve of her jaw as a groan of longing escaped his throat.

It was then that he knew he'd made a grave mistake. He should never have kissed her. She was treacherous, dangerous, and a relationship with her could not end well.

But it was already too late! A man could lose himself in her pouting lips.

How could he walk away now?

And then a new thought sprang to mind, a suspicion of a deeply buried fear. Was she a woman that he could *never* walk away from?

The thought was terrifying.

Abruptly, he tore his lips away. His chest was heaving and his breath ragged.

And then, hard fingers gripped his shoulders to sharply haul him back.

"God's Wounds, Julian!" Douglas swore in angered disgust. "Have ye gone daft? Ye canna toy with this *lady*! Even Cameron will have your head for it!"

And then Albany's rage-mottled face came into view. "Get ye gone,

Julian!" he roared. "Go afore ye bring the wrath of Gloucester down upon us all!"

Easily breaking free from Douglas' grip, Julian turned back to Liselle.

But she was already gone.

He stood there a moment, a little dazed, and then Douglas was pulling him out of Alnwick's chaotic hall.

"I'll see ye out the gates myself, Julian!" the Scottish earl barked, shouting orders to his men to ready horses at once.

It wasn't until Julian stepped out into the crisp evening air that his thoughts began to clear. Ach, where had his wits gone? He couldn't let a woman distract him from his true purpose!

Now it was time for *Le Marin* to escape.

Nothing else mattered, not even pouting lips and stunning hazel eyes.

As a stable lad came running with two saddled horses, Douglas turned on Julian and growled, "Make haste and get ye gone from here!" Withdrawing a small leather bag from his sporran, he tossed it Julian's way and added, "And take this as payment to your debts. But don't ye return for more. Gloucester didna take a liking to ye and will likely have your head!"

Julian caught the bag and grinned.

Acquiring the betrothal contract had been easy.

Escaping Gloucester's rage, jumping through the alcove window, and returning as the notorious Lord Julian Gray had been even easier.

But by far the easiest of all was leaving Castle Alnwick with none being the wiser.

His grin widened. *Le Marin* hadn't expected he would have a personal escort out of the castle, nor had he'd expected to be paid for his mission. Hefting the chinking bag of coins, he chuckled and tucked it under his shirt next to the evidence which would prove Albany a traitor—the betrothal contract.

With a deepening scowl, Douglas dug his heel into his horse's side and trotted through the gates at a fast clip, alongside Julian. They had scarcely exited the last one before he turned to Julian with his brows furrowed into a thick line of disapproval.

"'Tis only for Cameron's sake that I've given ye aid this night!" the earl spat. "I've nae the tolerance for your way of living!"

Julian suppressed a snort.

The man was absurd. How could he still claim Cameron's friendship whilst sitting on his horse with his plaids illuminated by the hundreds of campfires dotting the hillside behind him—campfires of an English army preparing to slaughter his own countrymen?

"Are ye out of your wits?" Douglas demanded impatiently.

"Aye," Julian muttered sarcastically. Aye, he was out of his wits for not throttling the man there and now as he deserved! There was much he wished to say, but alas could not.

Cursing under his breath, he gave Douglas a grim nod, and then wheeled his horse about. And as the clouds covered the face of the moon, he galloped away from Alnwick Castle.

Never had *Le Marin* escaped so easily. And never had he needed that ease more.

Just thinking of the numbers amassed at Alnwick Castle made his heart heavy. Gloucester had raised an army of over twenty thousand men with over two thousand sheaves of arrows and a hundred cart horses drawing siege weapons.

And all too soon they would march on Scotland.

Tiredly, Julian returned to the village inn where earlier he'd paid for a room to sleep the night. He'd rise with the dawn and hurry to Scotland to raise the alarm. There was naught he could do until the sun rose; the night was too dark to ride.

Collapsing onto a bed, he sought sleep, but it was long in coming. Scotland's woes preyed on his mind, joined at times by the uncertainties of Liselle.

"Ach," he muttered under his breath for the twentieth time. "I shouldna have kissed her."

Some small part of him had wanted to be disappointed, to find her kiss lacking. Aye, he'd become too enamored with her of late. 'Twas time to ignore the lass.

But the intoxication of her lips was far beyond anything he could have imagined. How could he shake his fascination with the lass now? Now, when there seemed little hope of quenching the desire raging in his blood?

Ach, had he known that her kiss would leave him so wanting, he never would have indulged his craving!

The hours of the night crept interminably on, and there was only the faintest glimmer of gray in the sky when at last he arose and set a furious pace north to Scotland, riding low on the neck of his horse.

Upon reaching the borderlands, he paused long enough at each village and hamlet along the way to raise the alarm that the English would soon be at their gates. No sooner had the words left his lips than he was off again.

Descending into the marshlands near the strong tower of Haggerston Castle, he guided his horse through the treacherous bogs to race along the rugged coastline, arriving at Berwick Castle just shy of noon. And after warning Lord Hailes of Gloucester's impending arrival, he traded horses and continued his journey up the coast to Dunbar.

Hawks and gulls soared over his head as the sun rose higher, and dark clouds gathered in the sky on the horizon. The air turned hot and muggy, and with nothing but miles of coastline to traverse, he allowed his thoughts to mull the mysteries surrounding him.

Who had thrown the bone-handled stiletto to aid him? The Saluzzo had named the Vindictam. And while Pascal clearly belonged to or knew of this mysterious Vindictam, the mere thought of the slim dark-haired youth assisting him—maybe even saving his life—made him laugh aloud.

No, 'twas most certainly not Pascal's doing.

But what of the hazel-eyed, honey-haired Liselle? She had already demonstrated an uncanny knowledge and skill where knives were concerned.

A shiver rippled down his spine at the thought. The more he learned of her, the more he found her bewitching.

Galloping up the coast, he spent more time thinking of her lips than he wanted to admit, but it made the time pass exceedingly fast.

Soon enough, he arrived at Dunbar with his horse all a-lather. The weather had turned foul, and dark clouds swept in from the sea to unleash waves of sheeting rain.

It was growing late and he had no choice but to stay. Repeating the warning of Gloucester's impending arrival to the castle caretaker there, he fell into an exhausted sleep.

The next morning found the rain gone, and the hot weather returned as he once again switched horses. Setting a heel to his new steed's side, he sprang away, eager to deliver his tidings to Cameron.

Galloping along the river, at last he saw the Forth stretched out before him and knew that his journey was almost at an end.

Ahead, the black, rocky crags of Edinburgh drew steadily closer until finally, he arrived. Drawing rein, he paused to wipe his brow under the shadow of the castle, high on the hill.

The past few weeks had been tiring ones.

But his task was almost over.

Urging his beleaguered horse up the Royal Mile, he wove his way through the crowds, threading past prancing horses and children chasing carts filled with produce for the next day's market. More than once, he narrowly sidestepped the contents of a chamber pot being tossed from above.

And then he was riding through the castle gates.

Sending word to Cameron, he retired quickly to his chamber to change his travel-stained clothing. He'd scarcely changed his shirt when he heard a knock on the door.

A young page bowed low in respect. "My lord, the Earl of Lennox, wishes ye to join him at once in the king's privy chamber, my lord," the lad's shrill voice piped ceremoniously.

With a crisp nod, Julian grabbed the betrothal contract from his belongings and sprinted down the steps towards the royal apartments.

He heard the outraged voices long before he entered the king's privy chamber.

And ducking his head through the doorway, he spied Thomas Cochrane posturing like a rooster before a dozen disgruntled nobles. The king's favorite was a brown-haired, young man with a sleek trimmed beard and a pale, sickly complexion. Dressed sumptuously in fine green velvets and wearing a thick gold chain about his neck, he stood before a splendidly framed portrait of none other than himself, hanging on the king's wall.

Rumors swirled around him, rumors that he was the king's lover. It was the only way his ascent from a low-born mason to the king's right-hand man made sense to the angry nobles gathered before him.

"The black money must be recalled!" one loud voice rose above the others. "Your Majesty, the people are suffering! They refuse to sell their goods for Cochrane's Plack!"

A short distance away, King James III sat in a carved chair, oblivious to the heated arguments surrounding him. The monarch was a prematurely aging man with a pallid face and heavy-lidded eyes. His pale red hair clung to his forehead in thin, wispy strings. And his thoughts were clearly elsewhere as he stared unseeing into the distance, toying absently with a gold-handled spoon. A platter of cured venison and sweetmeats on the table before him lay untouched.

Julian suppressed a snort.

Aye, the man would be the ruin of them all with his incessant pampering of favorites. Instead of governing his country, he spent the entirety of his time showering them with endless banquets and useless fripperies.

And then Thomas Cochrane stepped forward and raised his fist, rage staining his narrow cheeks as his nasal voice rose. "'Tis the law that they must accept my coin as they would any other!"

Voices burst out indignantly but then fell silent as Cameron pushed his way forward to tower over his cousin, the king.

The king swallowed visibly.

Cameron cut an imposing figure as he warned his cousin in a soft, chilling tone, "Your refusal to listen will prove dangerous to your grasp of power, James."

"And who are ye to utter such threats?" Thomas interrupted with a huff. Picking up his goblet, he stepped close to wag it in Cameron's face. "Dare ye address a king in such a manner?"

Cameron merely raised a cool brow, and the voice in which he replied was one of calm command. "Dinna interrupt me again, Thomas! Have a care. Your day of reckoning is near. Mar's title doesna befit the likes of ye. It will not wear for long."

Thomas started violently and licked his lips. "Are ye threatening me?" he mumbled in a choked voice. "I'll have ye banished from court!"

But Cameron had already turned away from him to clasp the king's shoulder, and he gave it a little shake. "James, 'tis time to wake from this madness! Listen to your people and ban the Cochrane Plack!"

The king turned his head to the side and drew his lips in an obstinate line as Thomas gasped in outrage.

"By the heavens above, 'tis only on the day I am hanged that the new coins shall be called in and not a day afore!" Thomas vowed, raising his fist once again.

The chamber erupted into angry shouts, and it was then that Cameron caught sight of Julian still standing in the doorway.

Waving his hand, Julian quit the place and stepped into the antechamber to wait.

It didn't take Cameron long to join him. Nor did it take long to give him the betrothal contract and to divulge the tidings that Albany was en route with Richard of Gloucester, leading an army into the heart of Scotland.

"Sweet Mary!" Cameron swore, his dark eyes smoldering. Beckoning to a nearby guard, he dipped his dark head and, in a lethally calm tone, issued a series of orders.

Julian nodded in satisfaction and gave a loud, long yawn, knowing that Cameron would see done what needed to be done.

"I've already warned the clans to ride at a moment's notice. We've heard rumors afore, but have not had the proof of Albany's betrayal nor an inkling of the numbers," Cameron said grimly and then weighed Julian with a measuring look. "Ye look fair dead on your feet, lad. Get ye off to rest. Ye'll be no good to me like this."

"I'm rested enough," Julian said with a tired grin, but then his mood darkened. "Aye, there's something else ye should know, Cameron." There was no good way to say it other than to say it quickly. "'Tis Archibald Douglas. He's joined Albany."

Cameron merely stared at him. Years of court intrigue had rendered him a master of masking emotions, and he betrayed no hint of surprise. "Are ye sure, lad?" he asked finally.

"Aye, as sure as I can be," Julian grunted in reply.

"I would speak with him first," Cameron murmured, and then laying his arm about Julian's shoulders, he guided him out of the room. "Let's see ye fed and rested. I'll be needing ye in a few days. I'll not see a drop of Scottish blood spilled over greed! We'll outwit Albany and avert this war."

"It shouldna be hard," Julian said with chuckle. "Albany could never outthink ye, Cameron, even when ye were lads."

"Albany, mayhap not," Cameron countered, "But the Duke of Gloucester is a highly able and ruthless man."

Entering Edinburgh's hall, Cameron chose the nearest table and waved for a serving maid as Julian sat down heavily and stretched out his long legs. Eyeing the various nobles conversing in the hall, he shook his head in silent disgust.

"And?" Cameron's dark eyes fell upon him, twinkling with amusement.

Julian nodded his chin at the men surrounding them. "'Tis right glad I am that I've no dealings with any in this nest of vipers," he said. "I'd wager over half are likely plotting this very moment to behead both James and Albany. Ach, and how many plots are directed against ye, do ye think?"

With a laugh, Cameron glanced around the hall before sitting on the edge of the table and resting an elegant boot on the wooden bench. "Come now, Julian," he said with a sardonic twist of his lip. "What would this place be without a good plot a-brewing? 'Twould be dull."

"Julian! Lord Julian Gray!" a feminine voice giggled from behind.

Raising a brow, Julian turned to see a fair-haired lass with milky white skin and bright green eyes smiling down at him. Aye, not long ago he'd played with the notion of courting her, at least for a few weeks. But looking at her now, he couldn't recall why he'd found her so interesting.

With a polite but plainly disinterested nod, he faced Cameron once more to prod, "And will the clans come to defend James, do ye think? Are there enough loyal to even raise a sufficient army?"

Cameron's dark eyes flicked to the lass in mild curiosity, but he replied to Julian's question easily enough. "No matter how angry they are with James, they're of no mind to let the King of England interfere. They'll come, lad. They'll come for the queen and the young prince, if naught else."

"My Lord Gray!" another woman's soft voice interrupted.

This time, it was a particularly comely serving maid setting down a platter of meat and a large mug of ale before him.

"Is there aught else I can do for ye?" she asked in a low voice, flipping a black braid over her shoulder and lowering exceptionally long lashes over a pair of stunning blue eyes. "I'd be more than pleased, my lord."

Julian's gray eyes swept her from head to toe. Aye, he knew quite well she sought an invitation to his bed, but oddly enough, he didn't find the prospect tempting.

"No, I thank ye, lass," he replied, and dismissing her with a nod the same as before, swiveled back to Cameron. "And when do ye think the clans will gather?"

Cameron folded his arms and tapped a long finger as his eyes narrowed in speculation. "Who is she, lad?" he asked, his voice rife with amusement.

Julian raised a puzzled brow. Glancing over his shoulder, he saw that the lass had already disappeared, but then Cameron's deep laugh rang through the hall, and Julian looked back at him in surprise.

"Not the serving lass, ye fool," Cameron explained with a chuckle. "I speak of the one who has captured your heart! Ye havena looked at a single lass since sitting, and ye've turned down two offers to warm your bed. 'Tis most unlike ye, lad!"

Julian opened his lips to protest, but the words stuck in his throat as he heard Liselle's sultry voice play through his mind. *No man looks at another woman whilst in my company, Lord Gray.*

"I must meet this astonishing woman!" Cameron was laughing outright as he slapped his knee with his palm.

Strangely bothered, Julian rose abruptly to his feet. "Ach, I dinna know what ye speak of! I'm overly tired, Cameron. That is all."

"Aye, then." Cameron graciously inclined his head, but it was obvious that he didn't believe a word of it. "Rest. Ye'll likely be riding in a few days. Sleep while ye may."

With a curt nod, Julian snagged the platter and escaped to his chamber, scowling as he walked and reassured himself that there wasn't a lass alive that could ensnare him!

He had been riding for weeks.

Cameron had merely mistook his exhaustion for something else.

Aye, he was just overly tired.

After devouring his meal and avoiding all thoughts of Liselle, he stretched out on his bed, one booted foot falling onto the floor. For a time, he absently flipped the bone-handled stiletto between his fingers, but

Cameron's words wouldn't leave his head.

Rising from the bed, he paced for a time.

He wasn't ensnared. He didn't love Liselle.

Aye, he found her fascinating, but what man wouldn't find such a bonny creature captivating? And what man wouldn't find her lips preferable to others? Clearly, there was no comparison.

'Twas quite unfair to the other lasses, but 'twas how it was.

And then, annoyed to find himself thinking of her yet again, he swore under his breath, and grabbing a bottle of wine and a length of gray cord, propped himself on the window ledge to weave a few Turk's head knots.

But he'd scarcely swallowed more than a few mouthfuls of wine before exhaustion overcame him. And tossing the knots to the side, he threw himself face down upon the bed and drifted off to sleep.

He'd slept through the remainder of the afternoon, night, and into the next morning before the plaintive wail of war-pipes roused him.

The clans were readying for battle.

Heaving himself from bed, he glanced out the window at the men moving about in the castle courtyard below. Aye, Cameron would be successful in outwitting Albany.

Julian stretched and gave a loud, long yawn.

Cameron didn't need him for a day or two, perhaps now was a good time to see Dolfin safe. The old man would have made it to Channelkirk by now.

Making up his mind, he dressed and began packing his belongings to ride yet again.

It was a good day for travel; there was not a single cloud in the sky. And even though the warmth of the morning sun promised an unusually hot day, he much preferred to ride in the heat than to swim through the rain.

Coiling the Saluzzo's leather belt, he placed it and the bone-handled stiletto into his sporran, and for a moment, stared down at his plaids.

Should he bring an extra plaid and cloak? Surely, the old man had assumed a disguise already? But 'twas strange that he hadn't in Fotheringhay, especially since he knew he was being followed. Such carelessness was quite unlike the old salt spy. Snagging the extra plaid and cloak as a precaution, Julian added his new collection of Turk's head knots to the bundle and left his chamber.

He found Cameron in the hall speaking with various chieftains, and after securing the earl's assurance that he could indeed be spared for day or two, Julian saddled his favorite gray mare and thundered down the Royal Mile.

He would reach Channelkirk by noon, escort the old man safely to Cambuskenneth Abbey, and mayhap along the way learn more about the Saluzzi and Vindictam.

Leaving Edinburgh behind him, Julian galloped down the King's Road, flying south over the heath towards the parish of Channelkirk. The day grew warmer with each passing hour as he flew across endless fields of bracken and fern, and seas of early-blooming purple heather and saffron-colored moor grasses. And by the time the Lammermuir Hills swelled on the horizon, both he and his mare were sweating.

Pausing to water his horse, Julian wiped the sweat from his brow and greeted a few carts as they creaked past him on the road. Mounting once again, he cantered down the King's Road at a brisk pace, but as he neared the old village of Channelkirk, the occasional cart had turned into a steady stream of wagons, all of them jolting towards the highlands.

Clearly, tidings of the English army's approach had spread quickly.

Trotting down the village's cobblestoned streets, Julian reined his horse before the only inn, *The Golden Cockerel*, a wattle-walled establishment with a mud-thatched roof and a stack of peat bricks by the door. And after seeing his mare watered once again, he tethered her to the post and ducked under the low doorway to acquire a refreshing drink for himself.

The common room was uncomfortably warm and heavy with the sweet smell of burning peat. An old woman with missing front teeth sat on a three-legged stool and was stirring the contents of an iron pot suspended over the fire. While, across the room at a small counter, a middle-aged balding innkeeper stood chatting with an elderly man who was quaffing a mug of ale.

There was no immediate sign of Dolfin.

"Aye, as if the king's black coins are nae enough sorrow to heap upon our heads!" The innkeeper clucked. "Now we have Albany bringing the English down upon us!"

"Aye," the elderly man grunted.

Stepping up to the counter, Julian tossed a coin and wordlessly pointed to a mug of ale.

"Aye, my lord, and what have *ye* heard of the English?" the innkeeper asked, sliding a full mug across to him.

"The English?" Julian repeated, taking his mug and moving to a nearby table to stretch out his long legs. He downed half his brew with a hearty swig and wiped his mouth before replying, "I've heard thousands are marching."

The innkeeper's eyes lit with a morbid thrill. "Vermin!" he said in a tone of vindication and snapped his fingers under the nose of the elderly man. "I told ye! They're coming just like rats!"

"Aye," the man grunted in response before downing some more ale.

Finding the scene strangely amusing, Julian suppressed a grin, but then turned his thoughts to the matter at hand.

Had Dolfin arrived yet? The man would usually leave Julian a sign.

Tapping his finger on the table, Julian cast a careful eye about the place. He didn't spot anything unusual until he spied a small bowl heaped with salt resting conspicuously on the windowsill. Raising a curious brow, he rose to inspect it.

"Ach, dinna touch it, lad!" the old woman near the fire suddenly spoke.

"And what is it for, my good woman?" Julian asked, nodding his chin at the small wooden bowl of salt.

"'Tis to ward off the nasty Spirit of the Hunchback, lad!" she replied with a huff as though astonished at his ignorance.

Julian grinned with relief. So, Dolfin *had* arrived. The bowl of salt was clearly a sign as well as a tale left by the old man. It was true of every Venetian he'd ever met that they were fair distrustful of hunchbacks.

The innkeeper rolled his eyes and sent Julian a rueful smile. "Ach, ye'll have to forgive my wee auld mother, lad. She listens to too many a traveler's tale!"

"He said 'twas not a tale!" the woman hissed at her son. "Not a tale! Not at all!"

The innkeeper shrugged and began to wipe the top of the counter with a rag.

"He?" Julian pressed softly.

"Ach, some auld merchant's been filling her head with wild fancies," the man explained, sending his mother an exasperated look.

She scowled at her son and made a whistling sound between her two missing teeth before she shook a trembling finger at Julian. "A wandering spirit is naught to make light of! Ye can ask him yourself, lad!"

"Aye, mayhap I will." Julian laughed lightly. "Do ye expect this tale-spinner to return soon?"

"He's looking after his horse in the stables, lad," the woman answered and turned back to her pot to taste a spoonful of stew. Smacking her lips, she added, "He'll be back soon enough!"

"Aye, then," Julian agreed with a thoughtful smile. It would be amusing to surprise Dolfin. His mentor had surprised *him* many a time over the years. "I shall see to my own horse as well."

Rising from the table, he finished off his ale and then ducked outside. Adjusting his eyes to the brightness of the sun, he took a step towards the post where he'd tethered his mare and promptly cursed under his breath.

The mare wasn't there. Someone had stolen his horse.

9

BLUE FINGERTIPS

Julian let loose a string of curses.

The gray mare was a favorite of his, and he'd spent hours training her to come whenever he would call. Still cursing under his breath at the inconvenience, he cupped his mouth and let out a loud, shrill whistle.

He waited.

There was nothing. Not even the faintest whicker in response.

"By the Virgin!" Julian swore louder just as the innkeeper joined him at the door.

Upon learning of the theft, the man shook his head gravely. "Ach, 'tis the times we live in! I'll round up my lads and we'll search the village at once!"

Julian cocked a brow at the line of carts disappearing towards the highlands. "Then have them be swift!" he said with a grim set of his jaw and nodded at the fleeing villagers. "That gray mare is special to me."

"We'll find your horse, my lord! And the thief as well!" the innkeeper promised before shouting over his shoulder and disappearing back into the inn.

Julian expelled a breath. He sprinted around the building to do a quick search himself, and whistled numerous times, but clearly his mare was gone.

With his brows knit into a scowl, he watched as the innkeeper and his sons spread out in different directions to begin their search of the village and figuring to use his time well, Julian headed for the inn's stables to find Dolfin.

The stables were housed in an ancient, half-crumbling building of moss-covered stones and a moldy, straw-thatched roof. The large doors were open, and stepping inside, Julian found the place stuffy and quite empty, save for an old donkey and a very familiar gray-haired man grooming a fine black gelding.

Julian grinned in relief.

It was Dolfin. The old salt spy was safe.

Moving closer, Julian opened his mouth to surprise his mentor when he noticed that the man's hands were shaking. Drawing his brows in consternation, Julian peered closer, detecting a frailness that he'd never discerned before.

He waited a few moments, and then changing his mind, announced his presence with a gentle clearing of his throat and a soft, "Well met, *Istruttore.*"

Dolfin jerked in surprise, but the eyes he turned upon Julian were smiling ones. "We meet again, *caro vecio.*"

Greeting him with the customary embrace, Julian's concern deepened. The old man looked ill. His face was haggard, his long sweeping cloak unusually soiled and mud-stained, and he stood slightly hunched to one side.

"There's no cause to fret over me." Dolfin's sharp eyes lit with amusement. "It is plain on your face that you think me an old dotard!"

"Not so!" Julian protested half-heartedly.

Dolfin slapped his horse upon the rump, and the animal flicked his ears immediately in response. "I was on my way to find you in Edinburgh," he said. "I've tarried here too long."

It was then that Julian saw the saddle and bags lying on the ground at his feet. He'd nearly missed him. "Then 'tis glad I found ye, *Istruttore!* Allow me to help ye!"

Ignoring the man's protests, Julian made short work of hefting the saddle onto the gelding and pulling the cinch tight. And as he buckled the saddlebags, he murmured, "I've a matter of mystery to discuss with ye ere ye leave this place."

Dolfin's expression brightened with interest, and seeing that his gelding was secure and busily feeding on a bit of hay, nodded towards the outside. Exiting the stuffy stables, the two men moved to a secluded stand of birch trees close by, a place somewhat cooler, and also one in which they would not be overheard.

"Ye've men on your trail," Julian murmured softly as he pulled the Saluzzi leather belt from his sporran and held it out for the spy to see.

Dolfin turned white and staggered back. He would have fallen had not Julian caught him with a steady arm.

"Ye recognize it? Tell me then, what does it mean?" Julian's brows rose, surprised at the strength of his mentor's reaction.

"You have figured out for yourself that it is a code, then. What are the words?" Dolfin whispered hoarsely.

Softly, Julian repeated the ominous Latin he had puzzled out before.

"Then even the Saluzzi know!" Dolfin swallowed, instinctively drawing his hood over his face. "And now they seek you as well." Raising imploring eyes to the heavens, he choked, "What have I done?" Grabbing the belt from Julian, he looped it around to read the words softly for himself, again and again.

His hands were shaking so strongly that Julian felt a ripple of unease. "Are ye ill, *Istruttore?*" he asked with a perplexed frown.

Dolfin straightened. And then in a sudden movement, he crushed the belt in his fingers and said in a horrorstricken tone, "I have brought death upon your head, Julian!"

Julian's first reaction was to smirk, but he managed to suppress it out of respect. Clearing his throat, he gently asked instead, "Then tell me why

I'm to die?"

But the old man didn't reply. Heaving a sigh, he braced himself against a slender birch and simply shook his head.

It was an obstinate gesture that Julian knew well. One that meant little information would be forthcoming. How could his mentor refuse to talk now? Pulling out the bone-handled stiletto from his belt, Julian offered it to Dolfin hilt first.

"Then mayhap ye'll speak of this instead?" he challenged with a half-grin.

Dolfin cast him a sideways glance and then his brows rose to his hairline. Snatching the stiletto, he gasped. "Where did you come by this? How? This blade couldn't have been seeking your blood! It would never have missed!"

"Aye, this blade prevented my abduction and mayhap saved my life in Fotheringhay," Julian answered with surprised curiosity. "It struck the Saluzzo who wore yon belt." He nodded at the stretched leather that Dolfin still clutched tightly in his hands.

The old salt spy stared at Julian as if he'd gone mad. "There is no doubt that they saved you! Had the Saluzzo taken you captive, you would not have lived long. But why? Why?" he repeated several times. "Why would they save you?"

"They?" Julian prodded when he fell silent once again. Ach, but the teasing of information out of the old man was proving to be an aggravating task!

And then, handing the blade and the belt back to Julian, Dolfin closed his eyes and murmured, "They must be at war again!"

And the man fell silent once more.

Growing impatient, Julian planted his feet wide apart and crossed his arms. And when Dolfin offered no further explanation, he peered down at his mentor from under his dark lashes and offered, "Then ye speak of the war between the Saluzzi and the Vindictam?"

Dolfin cast him a startled glance. "Already you know too much," he said in outright concern.

"Then tell me more!" Julian invited with a lopsided grin. "Ach, ye must! If 'tis already enough to kill me, then to have more can do me no harm, *Istruttore!*"

The old man bowed his head, and then his lips parted. "Know that the Saluzzi are to Ferrara what the Vindictam are to *La Serenìsima*. They are both families of powerful assassins, faithful to their city-states," he whispered. "Their names alone strike fear in the heart of any who hears them. For years, they were sworn enemies, that is, until recently. The families have forged an uneasy truce. But, if the Vindictam has spilled the blood of a Saluzzo, then the truce is broken."

Julian nodded slowly. He'd already surmised as much. "But tell me, why are the Saluzzi after ye now, *Istruttore*?"

Dolfin shuddered and then confessed in a voice so low that it could scarcely be heard, "I stumbled upon a secret, *caro vecio*, and for that, the Vindictam exiled me from my homeland. They sent me away from any who would protect me and even now seek my death to prevent this secret from being known."

"And?" Julian prodded when the silence became prolonged.

Dolfin's stooped shoulders sagged even more. "'Tis death to hear it Julian, but you have the right to know." He paused and swallowed several times. "The Dominus Granditer, the Grand Master of the Vindictam, is near death and has finally chosen his heir from amongst his sons. He has made his choice of who will rule one of the most powerful families of Europe. And he has chosen the youngest over the two elder sons, a choice that does not sit well with them, but it is the youngest who is the Electus."

"Electus," Julian repeated softly. It wasn't a question.

As he spoke, Dolfin picked up a stick and bent over to scratch the ground, murmuring, "I have seen his ring, his mark, the mark of the Electus. "

"Then the Vindictam seek to silence ye afore the Saluzzi can wrest his identity from your lips. And somehow, the Saluzzi have discovered our relationship and seek to use me as bait to loosen your tongue," Julian concluded. "Then they care nothing for their truce. The Saluzzi seek to slay the Electus."

"Perhaps," Dolfin said in a thoughtful tone as he continued to scratch in the ground. "There is unrest in the Saluzzi ranks. Perhaps not all would betray this treaty. This could be the work of few men, but even those few can ignite a bloody war. And if they succeed in slaying the Electus, the very ocean will turn red with blood."

And then dusting his hands, he rose shakily to his feet, and Julian glanced down at the symbol etched in the dirt.

His brows arched in shock.

He'd seen the mark before—a bold 'V' entwined with a crown and a sword. He could scarce believe it.

Liselle's cousin, *Pascal,* was the Electus? The arrogant, dark-haired youth who had threatened him in Fotheringhay.

"Soon, a new man will control the destiny of the Vindictam," Dolfin was saying. "And it is vital that his identity remains unknown in order to protect him. The Vindictam has many enemies. They will never stop searching for me, *caro vecio.* Both the Vindictam and the Saluzzi will see me dead." And then nodding at the belt, he added, "And mayhap you as well, though why the Vindictam would have saved you ... I cannot understand."

Julian made up his mind at once. Tugging a ring from his finger, he pressed it into Dolfin's hands. "Then I'll hinder your journey no longer. But do not tarry in Edinburgh. Get ye gone to Cambuskenneth Abbey straightway and find Father Ulric. Show him this and tell him that I request he provide safe passage for you to Dunvegan Castle in Skye, to a man I know there by the name of Ruan MacLeod. You will be safe there, at least, for a little while."

Dolfin took the ring, but his face suffused with concern. "But what of you, Julian?"

With a grin, Julian leaned forward and chuckled. "Your Vindictam and Saluzzi dinna know that I am *Le Marin, Istruttore*! Ye've taught me well. I'll not come to harm by them."

The old man winced a little, and his nod was an uncertain one. "But this is like nothing you have ever faced, *caro vecio*." He paused, and then added in a puzzled tone as if he had just thought of it, "Though why the Vindictam saved your life is a mystery. Something is amiss. Strangely amiss …" he repeated the words several times, still shaking his head.

Julian frowned. Aye, something indeed was amiss. Was the old man becoming forgetful? The sooner he had Dolfin safe in Skye, the better!

"Mayhap 'tis best that I travel with ye, at least as far as the abbey," he said, looping his arm around Dolfin's shoulders. "The lads should have found my horse by now. And if they havena, I'll get another—"

"Nay! I am not yet useless!" Dolfin interrupted, his eyes turning sharp once again. "Have I taught you nothing over the years?"

"Aye, but—" Julian protested.

"I will go my own way. It is safer for us both," his mentor insisted, and his voice suddenly sounded strong, more like his *Istruttore* of old.

Wincing, Julian nodded. "Aye then, go, though 'tis against my better judgment."

"Then allow me to say my farewells here." Dolfin smiled, clasping

Julian's shoulders in a warm embrace. "I will see you in Skye, have no doubt."

"Aye," Julian agreed. But he could not hide the uncertainty in his voice.

Dolfin gave a soft laugh. "Do not worry for me, *caro vecio*. It is you who walks the dangerous path. Be wary!"

They said little after that and returned to the stables. And leading the black gelding out of the stall, the old man mounted, and with a wave of his hand, trotted after a group of carts rolling down the King's Road towards the highlands

Following him a few paces down the path, Julian folded his arms and shook his head. Sweet Mary, but his mentor had grown frail! And his bouts of forgetfulness were disheartening. Dolfin had always been a man of sharp wit and keen eye.

Still shaking his head, Julian was of half a mind to buy the nearest nag and trot after him anyway, when he noticed the flutter of a black cloak near the edge of the inn.

Whirling, he caught a fleeting glimpse of a short dark form as it disappeared behind the building.

His eyes widened. There could be little doubt.

The Saluzzi had arrived in Channelkirk. Or mayhap it was the Vindictam.

Julian set off after him at once, but upon reaching the back of the inn, he saw no sign of the assassin.

"By the Virgin!" Julian swore under his breath.

Had the man simply vanished? Returning to peer down the King's Road, he took consolation in the fact that he could still see Dolfin in the distance, trailing after the carts headed for the hills. There were no signs of a dark figure racing madly after him.

Either the assassin was more interested in Julian, or he hadn't arrived in time to see the old man leave. In either case, Julian quickly decided that the best course of action would be to keep the murderer occupied whilst Dolfin made his escape.

"The lads are yet searching for yer horse, my lord!" the innkeeper greeted Julian as he stepped inside the common room. "They'll find her and the lout who dared take her, never fear!"

Julian grimaced. He wasn't so sure. If they hadn't found her by now, they likely never would. Still, the longer he kept the assassin in Channelkirk, the safer Dolfin would be. "Then I'll need a room this night, good man," he announced to the innkeeper and tossed a few coins onto the table.

Suddenly, the old woman sprang up from her stool with a spry eagerness that belied her age, and snagging his coins, bit them with her remaining teeth. Grinning, she tucked them away. "Aye, 'tis nae black money!"

The innkeeper clucked and sent his mother an exasperated scowl before nodding at Julian. "Pay my auld mother nae mind, my lord. Choose any room ye like, save the one in the attic. The foreign merchant paid good coin for a room of his own."

"Aye, then," Julian grunted in reply as a sudden draft of cool air filtered through the muggy, peat-scented room. He arched a brow. Had the assassin entered through the back door?

Heading up the creaking stairs, he peered down through the cracks in the steps and was rewarded with another brief glimpse of dark cloak.

Without a moment's hesitation, Julian dashed in hot pursuit of the assassin yet again. But once more, he could find no sign of the scoundrel.

Aye, 'twas aggravating; it was as if the man were a ghost.

Julian shook his head and with a quick step, made his way to

Dolfin's attic room.

The lodging was a simple one, consisting only of a bed, which nearly took up the entire room, and a single shuttered window that faced the cobblestoned road in front of the inn. Crossing the floor, he opened the window's shutters, but it provided little relief to the stifling air.

There was not much there that he could use to ensnare the stalker. Most of his belongings were presumably still in his saddlebags, which were most likely still on his horse. And that fine mare was probably trotting friskily towards the highlands at that very moment.

The heat was almost unbearable, and sweat beaded Julian's forehead.

Unfastening several buttons of his shirt, he fished about in his sporran until he found the small leather pouch he sought. Contained within it was a secret mixture of blue woad and other dyes that Dolfin had given to *Le Marin* as a gift several years before. By sprinkling the powder on the door latches and shutters, he could stain any unwary intruder's fingers blue long enough to aid in identifying the culprit later on, should he fail to trap them first.

It didn't take long, and surveying his handiwork with a grin, he tucked the pouch away.

Most likely, the assassin would wait for darkness before making his move. A bit of rope would prove useful to fashion a snare.

Not caring to turn his own fingers blue, Julian unlatched the door with the blade of his dirk and slipped down the stairs in search of rope.

He found it easily enough, a small coil resting on a wheelbarrow near the stables. And picking it up, he headed back to his room to fashion a snare.

Cautiously, he pushed open his door, but when the room proved empty, he quickly stepped inside. He'd just kicked the door shut when he heard the soft rasp of a blade leaving its sheath, and at almost the same moment, that blade was pressed against his throat.

He barely registered surprise before his knee was kicked sharply from behind, and as he half fell to the floor, a foot struck him on the side of the head, hard enough to knock him flat to the floor.

Cursing, Julian rolled sideways and leapt to his feet only to see the small, cloaked figure diving out of the window.

But by the time he reached it himself, he caught only a glimpse of the fluttering cloak as it disappeared over the edge of the thatched roof.

Julian didn't hesitate.

Squeezing through the window, he quickly slid down the thatching, and dropping to the cobblestoned street below, landed lightly on his feet.

But his assailant had already disappeared; nothing moved in the sweltering afternoon sun.

"Sweet Mary!" Julian swore. By the Saints, but the little man was quick on his feet!

And then a loud crack from behind shattered his thoughts.

He whirled to see a horse bursting from the inn's stables, bearing down upon him. And diving from its path, he rolled in the grass as it thundered past him with the slight, dark-cloaked form clinging tightly to its neck.

And then Julian let out a hearty laugh and leapt to his feet, recognizing his own favored gray mare in an instant.

Raising his fingers to his lips, he let out a shrill whistle.

The horse responded at once and nearly reared as she came to a halt. And then tossing her head, she swerved to gallop back to him.

The cloaked rider then pulled hard on the reins, and the mare's ears flattened in confusion.

Julian let loose another whistle.

This time, the rider vaulted out of the saddle and fled down the road towards a dense cluster of buildings.

Julian didn't hesitate to give chase, but he was surprised at the ease with which he closed the distance between himself and his quarry. For all of his quickness, the assassin was no match for Julian's speed.

Catching the man's shoulders from behind, Julian wrenched him back to fall hard upon him, pinning him to the ground.

And then Julian's mind went blank.

Dimly, he noted the narrow hips and the delicate waist. And the hands pushing back at him were elegant despite the slender fingertips stained blue. And were those *breasts* pressed against his chest?

Astonished, he pulled back and tore the dark cloak away from the assailant's face.

A river of honey-colored tresses fell from the hood, and Julian found himself staring into the depths of a familiar pair of stunning, hazel eyes.

"Liselle!" he gasped.

10

"DO YE HAVE SOME KIND OF SACK? I DINNA TRUST HER!"

Liselle hit the ground hard as Julian's unexpected weight knocked the air from her lungs, and it took several long moments before she succeeded in dragging a quavering breath.

He was stunned, his gray eyes wide with shock.

Neither moved.

And then his expression shifted, and all at once she was aware of the warmth of his skin, the hardness of his muscled chest, and the heat of his breath against the nape of her neck.

"Ach, but ye have a talent for mischief, Lady Gray!" he murmured.

She shivered at the sound of his smooth Scottish burr. Why did his voice affect her so?

He hadn't moved. He was still lying on top of her, every muscular inch of him. Strangely flustered, she dropped her eyes only to notice that his shirt was open, revealing a tantalizing glimpse of his bare chest.

Liselle bit her tongue. Hard. And suddenly, she was scarcely able to breathe again.

Santo Ciélo! The man was seduction itself!

Struggling to collect her wits, she turned her head away lest he somehow read her thoughts, but he caught her chin between his fingers and tilted her face back towards his.

"Just who are ye, ye wee devil?" he asked, shifting his weight to prop himself up on an elbow.

Her eyes flashed. *Cà de dìa,* but his new position was worse than the one before! Now she could feel his strong thighs pinning her down. How did he expect her to think when every sensual inch of him was pressed against her?

"Ach, and ye canna just be a simple lady of the court, can ye, ye wee devil?" he was asking with a wondrous shake of his handsome head.

And then Liselle found her voice at last. Placing her hands on his chest, she pushed him hard, and as he rolled away, she accused in turn, "And you are no mere drunken fool, Lord Gray!"

She managed to scramble to her knees before he grasped her wrist and pulled her down forcefully against him. Startled, she met his gaze and then caught her breath, unprepared for the smoldering heat in his expression.

And then all at once, she could only think of his devastating kiss, a kiss that had been impossible to forget. She had relived it again and again, more than she would admit. And now, pressed close against him, she wanted nothing more than to experience his lips again while running her fingers through his hair and over his sinewy chest.

Suddenly, a look of alarm crossed his face, and with a firm, yet gentle touch, he pushed her aside and rose to his feet with a fluid grace. His keen eyes inspected her from head to toe, missing nothing.

"And what manner of dress is this?" he asked, nodding at her dark tunic and leggings, clothes the Vindictam had fashioned for stealth.

Without waiting for an answer, he reached down and yanked her unceremoniously to her feet.

But he had misjudged his strength.

Unable to stop herself from propelling forward, she again collided against his chest. *Cà de dìa,* but his chest was captivating! Another button had become unfastened and she was suddenly filled with the temptation to rip the entire thing away.

But this thought was met by Nicoletta's disapproving face flitting across her mind.

Feeling all at once guilty, Liselle took a quick step back and masked her discomfort by wiping the dirt from the knees of her leggings.

Òsti, but her family would be disappointed in her! Nicoletta would be furious, but how could her sister truly expect her to resist him?

And Orazio! He would be shocked to discover that she had been caught. And by Lord Julian Gray, no less.

She didn't even want to think of Pascal's reaction.

"Sò falimènta!" she whispered under her breath. She *was* a failure of the highest order! And for all of her exceptional skills, she was proving to be a dreadful assassin.

She'd found Dolfin but had only followed the old man with the hope that he'd disappear again. Hopefully, for good this time, so she wouldn't have to kill him.

"And where have your thoughts flown?" Julian's voice pierced her mind.

Startled, Liselle glanced up at him. How had she become so distracted?

And how had she made such a mess of things?

Falling back on her training, she closed her eyes and took a deep breath as her brother's calming voice floated through her mind. *When your path is unsure, cara sorèlina, focus only on the next step before you and nothing else.*

Yes. She had only to think of the present.

Julian had asked her something. Searching her mind, she recalled his question and her lashes flew open. He had asked her what manner of dress she wore.

Summoning a sweet smile, she patted her leggings and slim tunic. "Venetian riding clothes, my lord," she answered, finally regaining control. "I wear the Venetian riding dress."

He lifted a suspicious brow at her delayed response, but murmured, "And 'tis deliciously revealing as well."

A thrill of delight leapt through her. "Delicious?" she repeated, pretending not to know the word.

But she didn't fool him. She could see it by the way his gaze dropped to linger on her curves. And then his eyes took on a challenging glint of humor.

"And what cause have ye to steal horses and leap from windows, Lady Gray?" he asked.

"Windows?" she replied, assuming a mask of mild surprise. "Surely, you're mistaken—"

Grabbing her wrist, he twisted her hand back to wag her fingers in front of her face.

"Blue," was all he said.

Liselle squinted at her blue-stained fingers and her eyes widened in alarm. "What is *this*? The plague? *Esumi*—"

"Nothing harmful, ye wee beastie!" he interrupted with a laugh but then grew serious all at once. "I know right well who ye are. Aye, and ye can deliver a message to your cousin, Pascal, that I desire to speak with him right quickly. Ye can tell him that the Vindictam will never find Dolfin."

Liselle gasped in shock. "How do you know of the Vindictam?"

The words shot from her lips. She couldn't have stopped them.

Julian's lips pressed into a tight line of disapproval. "And can ye be one of them? A lass?" His eyes raked her once again. "Are ye an assassin as well?"

Assassin.

He made the word sound so repulsive. How could he? It had been something she had spent her entire life to achieve!

All at once, she was angry. No, she was furious!

Tossing her head, she retorted, "You know so little, *bábio!*"

Anger reflected in his gray eyes as he snorted in response. "Do I? What cause could ye possibly have to harm an old man?" he challenged in a disparaging tone. "Have ye no heart?"

Of all things, how could he ask her that when she was already struggling with that thought herself?

Raising her chin in defiance, she retorted, "Some things cannot be questioned." And then bitter words followed, words she hadn't even realized she had been thinking. "Did I choose the family I was born to, Lord Gray? What choice do I have?"

Suddenly, he caught her arm, and pulling her close once again, dropped his head to whisper into her ear, "Nay, but ye have a choice now, Lady Gray. Let Dolfin go. Dinna aid Pascal in his unholy quest!"

In spite of her fury, her pulse leapt at his touch and his nearness. Once again, her gaze dropped to his collarbone and the skin of his exposed chest.

Òsti! But how could she feel anger and attraction all at once? Gritting her teeth, she reminded herself aloud in a choked voice, "There is no bond greater than blood loyalty!"

"Nay, 'tis not so!" Julian murmured, his lips lightly brushing her ear. "What of the bonds between a man and a woman?"

A shiver rippled down her spine at his words.

But then he abruptly stepped back. "Ach, I should send ye straight back to Venice myself, lass! Aye, that's what I'll do, and I'll do it right quickly!"

Without meeting her gaze, he brought his fingers to his lips and let out a piercing whistle.

A short distance away, the gray mare lifted her head to look back at him. Stems of grass protruded from her cheeks. And then flicking an ear, she cantered back to stop in front of Julian, stamping her foot in a soft whicker of greeting.

"Aye, ye wee lassie, 'tis right glad I am to see ye!" Julian murmured as he gave her withers a fond pat.

Liselle watched him numbly. How could she think of the bonds between a man and a woman? As a di Franco, an assassin of the Vindictam, she could not think of such things. It was a forbiddingly dangerous thing to do. Her loyalty was to the Magno Duce first.

No. She should focus on the matter at hand. And that matter was escape.

"And where is your horse?" Julian was asking, turning upon her.

Her lips were dry, but she managed to shrug and wave to where the carts had disappeared over the horizon. She'd only helped herself to his horse after someone had taken hers.

"Aye then," he grunted, patting his horse fondly on the withers.

Liselle eyed the gray mare sourly. Just like Julian, even his horse had secrets. Had she known the mare had been trained, she never would have taken her.

And she never would have been caught.

"Then ye'll be riding with me, lass," Julian said then. His voice was low.

Before she could even respond, he'd tossed her into the saddle and swung himself up behind to clinch a tight arm about her waist. And then digging his heel into the mare's side, he guided her out of the village of Channelkirk and headed north.

Neither spoke.

Liselle knew she should be thinking only of escape, but how could she? She could only hear Julian's voice continuously playing in her mind.

What of the bonds between a man and a woman?

What of them?

He had no such bond with her! *Cà de dìa!* It was foolish to dwell upon such words. A man such as he clearly meant nothing by them!

She knew she should escape. She had to return before Albany's men found her missing. *Santo Cielo!* But how could she evade the arm of steel banded around her waist, especially when she knew that she truly didn't want to escape at all!

Grimacing, she eyed the broad, sloping meadows and gentle hills with shallow burns winding their way through the heather. She was riding in the opposite direction of where she needed to go, and no doubt, Albany's men still thought her lying ill in her chamber at Thirlstane castle, a league from Channelkirk.

The day was waning, and her thoughts were still in a quandary when they crested the top of a hill, and Julian sharply pulled rein.

Following his gaze, Liselle spied a group of horsemen rapidly approaching from the west. But as a gust of wind unfurled a green and white banner emblazoned with a battle-axe, Julian laughed.

Urging his mare forward, he lifted his arm and let out a whoop of greeting. "A MacLean! A MacLean!"

The horsemen altered course at once, and shortly thereafter, they were surrounded by fierce highland warriors clad in full battle gear. The jingling of bits mixed with the chorus of their echoes of "A MacLean!"

"Well met, cousin!" the leader of the highlanders called, breaking away from the others to advance on a magnificent black charger. He was a young, lean man, broad-shouldered and with hair as fair as Julian's.

Julian met him halfway to clasp forearms in a fond greeting.

"It's been too long, Ewan MacLean!" Julian laughed as he held his young kinsman at arm's length and subjected him to a measuring look. "Ach, but ye've grown since I've seen ye last, lad!"

"Then 'tis been too long since we've met, cousin! I havena grown in a twelvemonth or more!" His cousin laughed with an easy grace of one accustomed to command. But even as his white teeth flashed in humor, one could see a distinct glimmer of some deeply buried pain in the depths of his blue eyes.

"What is it, Ewan?" Julian asked in sudden concern. "What of the earl and your mother?"

"There's naught to alarm ye, Julian. My parents are well," Ewan assured, glancing momentarily away before asking in turn, "And how fares my mother's sister?"

Julian hesitated a moment, clearly somewhat troubled, but he gave a snort of laughter all the same. "My mother is as she always is, sending weekly missives that demand my presence in Huntly to fulfill my duties as its lord."

"Aye and ye should," Ewan replied, clearly not finding the concept amusing. With a polite dip of his strong chin towards Liselle, he asked, "And is this your lady?"

Liselle felt Julian's chest heave behind her as her mouth opened in protest.

"Most certainly not!" she retorted.

"Sweet Mary, no!" he swore through clenched teeth at the same time.

Ewan raised a mild brow.

"'Tis too long a tale to speak of now," Julian replied tersely as his arm reflexively tightened about Liselle's waist. "But tell me, lad, what brings ye so far from Mull? Surely, Cameron's call-to-arms couldna have reached ye this swiftly!"

"Cameron's called at last, aye?" Ewan repeated, looking only faintly surprised.

With a grim set of his jaw, he raised an arm and ordered his men to make camp near a small copse of birches at the base of the hill. And as the men thundered away, he turned back to say, "We'll journey no farther this day. Join us. I would fain know more of what I ride into on the morrow. And 'twill soon be too dark a night and too treacherous a ride to tax a lady's strength, aye?"

"A lady, perhaps," Julian grunted in a perverse tone. "But ye know not of whom ye speak, lad."

Liselle turned enough to send him a scathing smile.

"Ach now, cousin!" Ewan chided mildly. For a moment, his sharp eyes swept curiously over Liselle's tunic and leggings. But he didn't mention them, and assuming a polite smile, he turned the head of his charger and cantered down the hill to his men.

"Ach, the lad's lost his sense of humor!" Julian clucked under his breath. "What ill has befallen him?" He remained where he was a moment, shaking his head and then followed.

Guiding the mare into the camp, Julian hailed a grizzled man with a jagged scar across his face and dismounted to exchange loud and exuberant greetings.

"And what ails Ewan?" Julian asked once their voices had settled.

"Ach, 'tis nae good, Julian!" The man turned his head and spat to the side. "The lad's nae been the same since the battle at Tobermory. We lost too many men to MacDonald's bastard, Aonghas! Aye, the lad saw too much, he did."

Julian frowned. "Ach, ye never mentioned it afore! Ye said only that he'd turned fearsome in battle—"

"Aye, and I've no doubt he'll soon become the most renowned warrior in all of Scotland," the man cut in, wiping the grime from his scarred face. "But at what cost, Julian? He's nae the same as he was. He had the heart of a poet, he did." Shaking his head, he moved away.

Julian stood there a moment and then reached up to pluck Liselle out of the saddle. Bending close, he placed his cheek directly against hers and warned in a whisper, "I'll have none of your tricks, lass. Dinna even think of escaping, aye?"

Liselle didn't answer. Instead, she fluttered her lashes and gave him a sickeningly sweet and devious smile.

Julian didn't miss the insincerity. "Sweet Mary!" he growled, "But ye'd best heed my words!"

And then dropping his hand to the small of her back, he pushed her toward Ewan kneeling before a pile of sticks and dry leaves. As they watched, he struck a flint and the fire caught and crackled into life, spitting sparks. And as several men set about fashioning a roasting spit, a few others began to pluck several large fowl they had apparently hunted earlier in the day.

"My lady." Ewan smiled at Liselle and indicated with a sweep of his hand a plaid spread upon the ground. "Pray, sit and rest."

Nodding her thanks, Liselle took the proffered seat and watched as Julian settled nearby to stretch out his long legs.

"So, what brings ye from Mull, lad?" he asked in a conversational tone.

Ewan grimaced. "Another battle brewing against the rebel MacDonalds," he answered shortly.

There was something in the way he said the name *MacDonald* that made the hair stand on the back of Liselle's neck.

Julian expelled a breath, and his eyes flashed briefly in sympathy. "Ach, Ewan. Not again. I'd hoped Ruan MacLeod had quelled those malcontents in the matter of his wee sister, Merry."

At that, Ewan's strong jaw clenched, and drawing his lips in a grim line, he vowed, "We'll see their wickedness purged, once and for all. Aye, the pain they afflicted on that wee innocent lassie still haunts me to this day, cousin." But then, he dipped his head ruefully to Liselle. "Forgive my dark words this night, my lady."

"There's naught to forgive, my lord," Liselle answered quietly.

They began to speak of other things, and as the savory smell of meat filled the air to mix with their soft Scottish burrs, Liselle was suddenly struck by the peace of the place.

The sun hung low in the sky to bathe the heather-covered hills and clumps of gorse in a warm red light. Already, the trees cast long shadows over the camp.

Soon, it would be dark.

She closed her eyes as a sudden cooling wind swirled the leaves above her head.

Men laughed as they dumped their saddles on the ground, resting their heads upon them as pillows and sharing spirits from small metal flasks. As several of them began to sing, she wondered what it would be like to live such a life.

Could she simply leave the Vindictam, the only life she had ever known?

Did she have a choice?

Caught in a strange fantasy, she stared into the flames, mesmerized by the burning embers, and let her thoughts wander a time before drawing back in disgust with herself.

Òsti! Pascal was right! She was a fool, a *bábia!* No one lived a life of calm evenings promising only stillness and rest! And she had no choice, no unbreakable bond with Julian.

She was an assassin for the Vindictam.

And it was long past the time for her to steal a horse and return to Thirlstane before her absence was discovered.

Julian had moved to have words with the scar-faced man on the other side of the fire. He wasn't even looking in her direction.

Liselle inched back.

He didn't react.

She waited several moments, studying his strong profile. *Santo Ciélo!* The man was enticing, but she could no longer afford such diversions.

It was time to leave.

The moon had just risen and the stars were bright, providing sufficient light for riding. If she hurried, she could be in Thirlstane within a few hours.

Assuming a bashful air precisely calculated to disarm the mountain of a man sitting next to her, she shyly murmured that she required a moment of privacy to tend to her lady-needs, and at his gallant bow, quickly stepped outside the circle of firelight.

She didn't waste a moment, knowing that Julian would not be fooled long.

Darting under the birch trees, she made her way to the grazing horses nearby.

With the highlanders using their saddles as pillows, she'd have to ride a horse bareback. It was not a particularly appealing prospect, but she was an excellent rider.

Grabbing the closest horse by its halter, she'd taken only a step when a heavy hand fell down hard upon her shoulder.

Instinct enabled her to lash out with a sharp kick, striking her assailant soundly upon the knee.

It was Julian.

"By the Virgin!" he swore, cursing at the impact. And then grabbing her about the waist, he tipped her over his shoulder to toss her upon her back.

She landed with a grunt in the bristly undergrowth.

He towered over her a moment before dropping to straddle her hips and grin. "Heaven have mercy, but it seems I've stumbled upon an imp from Hades!"

The touch of his thighs threatened to send a strong ripple of desire raging through her, but she could not let herself think such thoughts. *Diàmbarne!* She was an assassin of the Vindictam and she must escape!

He stayed there a moment, looming over her. The moonlight was bright enough to illuminate his stern brows, but his eyes were masked in shadows.

And then he rose to his feet, and she leapt to hers, striking out once more.

With lightning-quick reflexes, he caught her ankle in his strong hand and gave it a vicious twist.

Gasping, she fell back again into the heather and gorse, scratching the palms of her hands.

"Ruffian!" She scowled. For a drunk and scandalous lord, Julian Gray was exceptionally quick to react.

"By the Virgin, ye are a wicked wench!" Julian swore. "I'm of a mind to tie ye up and leave ye here!"

She grimaced. Her attempt to break herself free by brute force had failed miserably. Clearly, it was time to try another tactic.

"And you would abandon a woman?" she asked, adopting a low, pleading tone as she permitted her voice to waver, just a little.

She didn't fool him for a moment.

Julian snorted. "A woman? No. But a devil, yes," he exclaimed, yanking her to her feet and pinning her wrists roughly behind her back.

The movement had the effect of pushing her breasts tightly against his chest, and Liselle's breath hitched at the unexpectedly intimate contact. Suddenly, it was difficult to focus once again.

His face was easier to see now in the dim glow of the moon. His mouth was set in a grim line, but he didn't seem particularly angry. And then he abruptly lowered his face to hers.

Liselle could feel his hot breath upon her lips, and her every sense tingled. Would he kiss her again? She held her own breath expectantly.

And then Julian whispered, "Ach, I'll see ye off on the first ship I can find!"

Disappointment flooded through her. And even though she had heard those words so many times in her life, they never failed to anger her. "You have no power to send me anywhere!" she snapped, with a haughty lift of her chin.

"Oh?" he challenged, cocking a brow.

They stared at each other, breathing hard.

And then to her surprise, he looped his strong arm about her waist and heaved her over his shoulder like a sack of flour.

Striding boldly back to camp, his strong voice roared above the highlanders' raucous songs, "Do ye have some kind of sack, Ewan?"

Laughter met this query, along with a few comments.

"Aye, 'tis a wee abduction, then!"

"So 'tis love, aye, Julian lad?"

As Julian moved forward, Ewan blocked his way, his fair brows drawn together in alarm.

"Sack?" he repeated with a stern jaw.

"Aye! I'm putting her in it!" Julian bellowed in response and brushed him aside. "I dinna trust the lass!"

"Ach now, Julian!" Ewan protested, shocked. "'Tis no way to treat a lady!"

"Ye know not of whom ye speak!" Julian grated, tipping Liselle over his shoulder to plop her down in front of the fire. And placing his hand upon the top of her head in an aggravated gesture, he informed the highlanders, "This lass lives only to conspire and delve in continuous treachery! Dinna trust her!"

Liselle had only time to send him an injured look before he grabbed her wrist once again and pulled her to where he'd propped his saddle against the trunk of a slender birch.

"Aye, then. I'll tie ye like a beast!" he grumbled, drawing a length of gray cord from one of his saddle bags. "Sweet Mary, but ye must eat only mules! How else could ye be so stubborn?"

But she scarcely heard him.

She was staring at the gray cord as a sudden image leapt into her stunned mind. She'd seen that gray cord before. It was unique, fine of make, yet strong, and the most distinct shade of gray. There had been a great length of it in his chamber at Sarlat.

But more importantly, the picture in her mind was not of that. No, in her mind's eye, she saw a gray Turk's head knot resting in her brother's hand.

And then she knew.

Santo Ciélo! But it had been plain for all to see!

Catching her breath in awe, she looked up into Julian's eyes and accused in wonder, "You *are Le Marin!"*

11

THE LAUDER BRIDGE TRAP

Julian's eyes dropped to the gray cord in his hands and then back to Liselle in appreciation. There was little reason to deny it. He'd scarcely bothered to play a drunken and scandalous nobleman in her presence.

"Aye, but aren't ye a wee canny vixen!" he murmured softly.

Closing his hand over her mouth, he pulled her away from the highlanders' curious eyes, and once out of the firelight's glow, caught her by the waist again to pin her against a tree.

His intention was just to speak with her, but the moment he felt her soft curves and the thump of her heart beating against his chest, he wanted only to ravish her lips once more with his.

"We've a wee quandary now, lass," he all but growled.

Aye, and more than one.

He should be concentrating on matters concerning *Le Marin*, but her soft beckoning lips were far more fascinating. Aye, he'd been thinking of nothing else from the moment he'd placed her on his horse in Channelkirk.

"Let me go!" she demanded breathlessly. "You have no choice but to do as I say now! Else I will expose you!" She lifted her chin with an air of smug satisfaction.

"Aye, so ye think to spread tales of *Le Marin*?" He cocked an eyebrow, his attention momentarily diverted from her delicious curves. "Do ye trust the Scottish court will believe such wild tales of Lord Julian Gray, once they discover those tales come from the lips of a Vindictam assassin?"

She gave in at once. There was not even a moment's hesitation. "As you wish then, my lord. I will say nothing."

Intrigued by the speed of her concession, he leaned close and asked with a low, intimate chuckle, "Why do I feel that I've just made a pact with the devil?"

A hint of a laugh escaped her lips, and he could feel her breath upon his cheek as she replied, "*Il Diàvolo*, your devil, is more forgiving than the Vindictam, Lord Gray."

It was a warning.

So why was he smiling like a daft fool?

Her lips were perilously close, lips that could drive him to the brink of madness should he let them. And her eyes were like pools of liquid fire, filled with passion and with life. Eyes he could drown in.

"What should I do with ye, lass? I canna leave ye wandering about, can I?" he mused aloud. Aye, not when he wanted to bury his face in her hair and taste her pouting lips from dawn till dusk. Shaking his head to clear it, he forced himself to say, "I should send ye back to Venice forthwith! Aye, the only place for ye is far from here."

Or perhaps … she might remain under his protection.

The unbidden thought startled him, and he drew back sharply.

He was a hot-blooded and passionate man, accustomed to dabbling with his fancies and blithely moving on with only a prickle of conscience where women were concerned. 'Twas much simpler to leave afore either he or they grew too attached. But the mere thought of sending this one away already weighed too heavily upon his heart to ignore.

She wasn't easy to walk away from.

And that was dangerous, particularly with this lass—one with blood ties to the Vindictam. With such ties he shouldn't be walking, he should be running!

"You have no power to send me away," she was saying.

But he ignored her words. Lifting his hand, he gently traced her bottom lip with his thumb. "Aye, but ye must be a siren," he murmured, his heart beating an unsteady pulse.

And then his lips brushed hers in the merest whisper of a kiss, and as she arched her back into him, he was undone.

Hooking his hand behind her neck, he pulled her against him and sealed his mouth hungrily over hers, and as her lips opened to his in a tantalizing invitation, he caught his breath.

A hot current of desire surged through him. Never had a mere kiss inflamed him so.

And then her palms slid up his chest and he shivered. Mayhap the lass was the devil after all. Her touch held an unholy power.

Mesmerized, he stood there as she wrapped her arms around his neck and lightly nipped his bottom lip. And then succumbing to the pleasure lancing through him, he slid his hands down over her waist and hips, and groaned, devouring her lips in a ravenous and greedy claiming.

For several endless moments, they shared a mind-reeling passion, and then with a primal moan, he tore his mouth away and gasped, "No!"

She pulled back, breathing hard.

A shaft of moonlight fell upon them, illuminating her face and allowing him to see what he knew was mirrored upon his own.

Passion. Attraction. Desire.

And pure madness.

He had to send her back to Venice. "Nay, I *must* send ye back to Venice!" he swore, brushing his forearm over his face.

Grimly, he caught up the gray cord from where he'd dropped it, and quickly looped it around her wrists.

She didn't resist.

Staring at her kiss-swollen lips, he could scarcely recall how to tie any kind of knot. He could think of nothing more than the want to claim every inch of her as his own.

But finally, the deed was done, or so he hoped.

Patting the knot, he peered down at her and whispered, "What spell have ye cast over me?" He caught her chin in his hand and forced her eyes to meet his.

She didn't answer him. She seemed equally disturbed in her own right.

And then taking a deep breath, he turned away to collect his scattered thoughts.

He had no choice. He must send her away. He'd not even be able to focus should he let her stay. And he needed his every wit about him if he were to outfox Pascal and Orazio in order to protect Dolfin. Aye, he *had* to send the lass away. When she was near, he could think of little else than her maddening lips.

"Aye, I'll see ye gone from here," he said with a heavy heart. "I've no choice on the matter."

Silence met this statement.

Suddenly suspicious, he whirled to face her.

And then he swore.

She was gone. And in a neat little heap by the tree lay the cord that he'd used to bind her wrists, severed by a sharp blade.

"Liselle!" he roared even as he eyed the cord.

It was a razor-sharp cut.

Why hadn't he thought to search her for weapons? And why did he find that such a thrillingly seductive thought?

Dashing back into the circle of highlanders, he called her name again.

Taking one look at his face, the highlanders arose to the man.

"What is it?" their strong voices cried, accompanied by the rasping sound of steel as they drew their swords.

Julian grimaced. "The lass," he said. "She's gone."

Aye, mayhap the wee imp had been playing him all along, and he should count himself fortunate that he hadn't found her blade betwixt his ribs. But even as he thought it, he didn't believe it. Assassin or no, the passion on her face had been as real as his own.

"We'll search for the lady at once!" Ewan announced crisply, sheathing his blade.

Julian merely shook his head. "She's more akin to a viper than a lady. I'd say beware, and watch your horses—" he cut himself short as a new thought suddenly popped into his head.

Swearing profusely, he sprinted to where he'd tied his gray mare next to Ewan's black charger.

And then he swore even louder, uttering increasingly pointed epitaphs with each breath.

Once again, she'd stolen his gray mare. But this time, she was clearly prepared. Whistling produced nothing.

As the highlanders galloped in all directions, one of them brought Julian a saddled roan. He was at the point of telling the man there was little reason to pursue the minx. He only didn't because he wanted to ride, to escape the frustration mounting up within him.

Had she been toying with him all along? Surely, the passion in her kiss had been real?

The wind was picking up by the time he reached the crest of the hill. Pulling rein, he peered in all directions. The moon shone bright, casting an eerie glow over the heath and the rolling hills spread out before him.

Nothing moved. Liselle had disappeared like a wraith in the night.

Knowing it was futile, he cupped his mouth anyway and let out another whistle, but it was a half-hearted one.

Aye, Liselle was bold, brash, and meddlesome. But if she were riding across the heath in the darkness of the night, he'd want her on no other horse than his sure-footed gray mare.

"Sweet Mary!" he swore, striking the pommel of his saddle in aggravation. How could he still only want to protect her? Why was he worried only over her safety? Throwing his head back, he shouted, "Why? Why? Why?"

As his cries echoed through the night, hooves pounded from behind, and he turned to see Ewan easing his horse up to him.

"Don't come near me!" Julian thundered as his young kinsman drew near.

"Hold tight, cousin," Ewan greeted him in a mild tone, ignoring his demand. "We'll find her."

"Not if she doesna wish to be found," Julian replied grimly. He closed his eyes, but her fiery kiss and the passion in her eyes filled his mind. Ach, was there no escaping the lass?

"They say no herb can cure it, cousin," Ewan said in a quiet voice.

Julian gritted his teeth. He was hardly in the mood to chatter. Still, he cared for the brawny lad at his side, and so he forced his lips to reply, "Cure what, Ewan?"

"Love," Ewan said knowingly. "Ye love the lass, Julian."

Julian's eyes flew open. "Nay, this canna be love!" His voice came out raw and hoarse. "Nay! Never love. 'Tis more akin to hate or the result of some unholy spell! Ye dinna know the lass, Ewan!" Love? Pah! He was dedicated to the pursuit of women. He didn't stay long enough to love them.

"Aye, I'm told love is a cunning beastie," Ewan continued with a mischievous twist of his lip.

"I'll never be so daft as to fall in love, Ewan!" Julian objected strongly, but his objection rang false even to his own ears. "I'm not a man to be captivated by a single lass! I'll never make that foolish mistake!"

And then he clamped his mouth shut, knowing full well that the more he protested, the more he sounded like a drowning fool.

Ewan politely cleared his throat.

Clenching his jaw, Julian wheeled his horse around. "Aye, I've no concern for the lass. Call your men. We'll not find her, she's gone. 'Tis time to return to Edinburgh. Cameron needs us both."

And with a grim nod, he headed back to the camp.

Aye, his gray mare would see Liselle safe. He had faith in the animal. She'd never failed him. And Liselle, no doubt, had some skill of her own.

Aye, the lass would be safe.

Halfway down the hill, Ewan caught up with him to say, "Ye've changed, cousin!"

"Have I?" Julian replied. He'd always played the light-hearted fool in the lad's presence. Bitterly, he shook his head and muttered, "Mayhap 'tis time to reveal the many faces lurking behind the mask." He wasn't even sure to whom the words were addressed.

And then urging his roan to a fierce gallop, he thundered back towards the camp.

No one spoke as he settled in front of the fire and rolled into his plaid.

He'd find the lass. Or more likely, she'd appear in Edinburgh herself.

But he knew he'd see her again soon. *Le Marin* wasn't finished with her yet. *He* wasn't finished with her yet.

Sleep was long in coming.

* * *

Julian awoke to hear Cameron's deep voice calling his name as the bed curtains in his Edinburgh chamber were abruptly yanked aside.

"Up, lad!" Cameron smiled down at him. "'Tis time to ride."

Raising himself on his elbow, Julian glanced out the window to note the early morning sun. He'd arrived at Edinburgh with Ewan and his men just the day before, exhausted and worried about Liselle, though refusing to admit it to anyone, even to himself.

Ewan had dispatched several of his men to search for her, but it was too early yet to expect word.

"Julian?" Cameron's long fingers snapped in front of his face.

"Aye." Julian grunted, swiftly refocusing his thoughts. Cocking a brow at the rolled parchment in Cameron's hand, he asked, "And what's this?"

"The rotting stench of bribery and corruption." Cameron crooked a cunning smile as he tossed the scroll onto the bed. "'Tis a trap."

Julian swung his feet out of the bed and caught the plaid Cameron threw at him. "A trap?" he asked.

"'Tis written in my own hand, begging Albany to come to Edinburgh as our king," Cameron answered smoothly. "He will abandon all other plans once he reads it."

Julian paused. "Aye, he'll come at a run if he thinks that now even ye want him as king."

"Precisely," Cameron stated calmly. "I'll start with that as bait. I've only to bring Albany here and we've won. Gloucester doesna have siege weapons that can take Edinburgh."

"But Albany's anger will be unmatched when he discovers your treachery," Julian warned, sliding his feet into his boots.

Cameron didn't seem concerned. "The man loves Scotland and his brother more than even he knows himself, lad. I might yet talk sense into his thick skull," he replied with an elegant shrug. "And if I canna then I'll simply imprison him."

"Just imprison him *and* his brother and have done," Julian growled.

"Aye!" Cameron's eyes lit with laughter, and then he turned serious. "But if it comes to war, I'll have the clans support. Nigh on fifty thousand men have come to my call. Already, they are gathering at Burgh Muir."

Julian let out a long, low whistle of relief and chuckled aloud. "How could I have ever doubted ye, Cameron! Gloucester is doomed."

"We'll fight, if it comes to that," Cameron said, moving to peer out of the castle window. "But mayhap Douglas and Albany are men who can still be swayed. They hate the English more than most. Ach, they raided the borderlands for years! I dinna wish the blood of even one loyal Scot to be spilt over this, Julian. We've only to protect this land long enough for our young Prince James to become king, nothing more."

"Aye," Julian agreed. "Then I'll leave at once and see that Albany reads this on the morrow." He felt strangely restless. 'Twould do him good to be on the back of horse.

With Cameron's farewells ringing in his ears, he saddled Ewan's black charger—at his cousin's insistence—and galloped out of Edinburgh. And taking the same road that he'd taken just a few days before, he pounded across the blooming heather and rolling hills.

At Channelkirk, he paused at the inn, entering to the boisterous sounds of singing. Apparently, those who hadn't fled eagerly anticipated the impending battle with the English. The men were helpful, but none had seen any sign of Liselle or his mare.

Evidently, she hadn't returned to Channelkirk.

Resuming his journey, he continued south down the King's Road until the wide spreading oaks of the royal burgh of Lauder rose before him. And then turning his horse's head, he changed his course to the east.

As the sun rose in the sky, smoke began to drift toward him, casting a grim pall over the day, and as he crested a small rise, its pungent fumes assaulted his nostrils. Shading his eyes, he spied the distant flames and smoke of a burning village.

Cursing loudly, he reined the black charger in with a sharp jerk and pounded his fist on the pommel of the saddle.

He'd found Albany.

Was he even now watching the flames consume the thatched roofs and blacken the cottage stones of the homes of goodly Scottish folk? The very people he expected to cheer him as their new king?

Albany was even worse than his brother, James! Aye, the only Stewart worthy of the crown was Cameron, but he would never rise to take it.

Overhead, the sky threatened rain, but it would be too late to stop the burning. And by the time Julian rode through the thick black clouds of cloying smoke to arrive at the outskirts of the burning village, there were no folk left, English or otherwise.

The army's trail was easy enough to follow, but the going was rough.

Sometime later, Julian had just descended into marshlands when his horse began to favor a foot. Stopping at once, he grimly inspected the animal's hoof and dislodged a sharp stone. The fetlock was slightly swollen. Slapping at the cloud of midges surrounding him, he glanced up at the darkening sky. He'd have to find shelter and let the horse rest if he wished to make good time on the morrow.

Leaving the boggy ground behind him, he made camp at the edge of an ancient forest as a light drizzle began to fall. And using his saddle as a pillow, too weary and disheartened to think, he settled back to listen to the raindrops echoing like tiny drums on the thick canopy of leaves above his head.

The night passed quickly, and the dawn found the horse recovered. Still, it was early afternoon before he reached the border stronghold of

Edrington with its castle occupying the summit of the steep hill above Whiteadder Water.

Thick black smoke hung heavy in the air, and the mill and the village lay in ruin. Appalled, Julian skirted the destruction. Aye, by the time he finally did find Albany, he knew that he'd be sorely pressed not to strangle the man.

The bridge had been destroyed, and Julian was forced to ford the river. Clambering onto the far shore, he stood there a moment, surveying the damage before turning his horse's head east towards Castle Berwick. He then galloped along the banks of the deep churning river twisting its way through the valley.

Finally, he burst from the dense forest to see Castle Berwick rising against a sky streaked with black columns of smoke.

The siege of the castle had already begun.

Men on horses and on foot swarmed over the hillside like flies. Some were manning the siege weapons, while others burned outlying buildings.

A cluster of tents stood at the bottom of the hill with Gloucester's massive pavilion rising in the center, proudly flying a magnificent Yorkist banner. Albany's tent—half the size of the English duke's—was relegated to the outer edge.

Julian clenched his jaw.

The man was a disgrace to Clan Stewart!

Julian cocked a calculating brow at the sky. Already, the sun hung low over the trees. It would be easier to deliver the missive under the cover of darkness. Dismounting, he tied the black charger out to graze and settled back against a tree to wait.

Time passed with excruciating slowness.

It was fair difficult to simply lurk in the forest, listening to the angry sounds of war. And it seemed forever before the last bit of orange finally sank below the horizon to allow Julian to leave the cover of the woods.

Mingling with the English soldiers without rousing suspicion was easy enough. As *Le Marin*, he had learned long ago to act with confidence. Few ever possessed the courage to question him.

And gaining entry into Albany's tent was absurdly simple. The young lad posted as guard nearly tripped over his own feet in his haste to allow Julian to pass, pulling back the lamb's wool door-hanging.

"Aye, what is it?" Albany grunted, running his thick fingers through his red hair.

The treacherous prince sat alone behind a wide table graced with tallow candles that flickered fitfully in their silver candlesticks. The ground was covered with sheepskins and rugs, and nearby was a comfortable bed covered in fur.

As annoyed as he was, Julian quite enjoyed the look of abject astonishment on Albany's face.

"Julian!" The man cleared his throat in confusion. "What brings ye here?"

Throwing Cameron's parchment onto the table, Julian replied, "'Tis a missive from Cameron."

Albany stared at it a moment, rubbing his thumb and forefingers together in a nervous, circular motion.

"Well?" Julian prompted impatiently.

Taking a deep breath, Albany broke the wax seal and slowly began to read. But with each passing moment, a smug smile grew to spread across his face.

Inwardly, Julian heaved a breath of relief that Cameron's plan appeared to be working. With the smell of smoke and death in the air, heaven knew that they would need it to.

"Aye, 'tis as it should be!" Albany laughed outright in pleasure.

"Even Cameron himself wants me as king now, eh? Let's have wine to celebrate! Aye, and bring Douglas here at once!"

With a negligent wave of his hand, he pointed to the flask of wine and a goblet at the far end of the table.

Julian eyed the man in disgust.

The man had just burnt good Scottish villages. He'd not serve him a goblet of wine nor play his messenger lad. Aye, he had to get away, before he was tempted to tie the man up and deliver him to the newly-made homeless villagers for a bit of true Scottish justice.

Turning upon his heel, he strode through the tent door and quit the place.

* * *

Julian spent the remainder of the night lurking in the shadows and learning more than he wished to know of Gloucester's doings. And the following dawn saw him riding hard to Burg Muir, bearing the tidings that while half of the English army ravaged the borderlands by burning castles and farms, the other half would soon advance to Edinburgh itself to place Albany upon the Scottish throne.

Several leagues from Channelkirk, he heard the rattle of drums and the wailing of pipes long before he saw them and a smile split his tired face.

It was more than a mile later that he rounded a bend in the road to see a great many horsemen bearing down upon him from the north with the banners of the House of Stewart unfurling in the wind.

Cameron had moved the clans.

12

THE HANGING

As the last rays of the sun fell across the land, Julian leaned against an ancient spreading oak, his gray eyes sweeping over the vast numbers of horsemen and foot soldiers setting up camp between the parish kirk at Lauder and the old village bridge.

He was exhausted and beyond weary of the entire situation. Or mayhap it was more than just this particular situation. Could it be that he was weary of political intrigue altogether and simply retiring to Castle Huntly wouldn't be so dull a prospect after all.

Aye, if he had a lively lass there with him, one with stunning hazel eyes, it might be a delightful adventure!

A light touch on his arm caused him to jump and instinctively reach for the knife safely tucked in his belt.

"Stand down, lad!" Cameron's easy laugh filled the evening air. "And where was your mind? 'Tis quite unlike ye to allow me to startle ye so!" His brow was raised in mild curiosity as his keen eyes swept Julian from head to toe.

Julian grunted. He wasn't about to admit what he'd been thinking. Instead, he pointed to several Scottish nobles some distance away. The men were agitatedly waving their hands and exchanging heated words. "What has them so angered?" he asked.

Cameron followed his gaze and then expelled his breath in unmasked contempt. "'Tis James. The daft fool sought to make Thomas Cochrane the captain of the cannoneers. Aye, I told him 'twas best to remain in Edinburgh, but there are rumors both the king and Thomas are on their way."

"Ach!" Julian made a sound of disgust. "We've no time to let fools parade on the battlefield in fine velvets when we've the English to fight!"

"Aye, I fear the king willna listen," Cameron murmured grimly. "I cannot guarantee his safety should he come here with Thomas."

"Then I almost wish he would come," Julian admitted dryly.

"Nay, Julian," the Earl of Lennox disagreed with an elegant shake of his head. "Scotland cannot yet withstand a civil war. You know this."

"Aye, I know," Julian replied, somewhat chastened. And then he added truthfully enough, "I wish for peace. I'm weary of these turbulent times. Ach, I would this was already over."

At that, Cameron heaved a sigh. "Soon enough, lad."

And then one of the agitated nobles drew his sword and began shouting at the others.

"If ye'll excuse me, lad? It seems I've a matter to settle," Cameron said, nodding at the man with his chin. And then clapping Julian's shoulder in farewell, he set off in the man's direction.

Shaking his head, Julian heaved himself off of the tree and returned to where he'd staked Ewan's black charger out to graze. 'Twas time to return the beast and to use it as an excuse to ask Ewan if he'd heard word of Liselle.

Liselle. He'd been fretting far too much over the lass of late, and dreaming of her too.

Scowling a little at himself, he grabbed the horse's halter and headed back to camp in search of the MacLeans.

They weren't difficult to find.

He had only to listen for the loudest band of men singing raucous drinking songs around their evening campfire. And because of the sheer number of clans gathered upon the field, it was quite a feat that they still sang the loudest.

Chuckling, he stepped around a half-drawn tent to come upon Ewan standing apart from the others.

Julian paused and eyed his cousin.

The young man's feet were braced wide apart, and his arms were folded tightly across his broad chest as his unseeing gaze locked upon the horizon. Again, the sadness was etched upon his handsome face, plain for all to see.

Julian frowned, wondering what burden his young cousin carried, but it was fair impossible to escape the lad's eagle sense for long. Almost immediately, Ewan's fair head turned his way, and he raised an arm in silent greeting.

Stepping forward, Julian hailed him warmly and held out the reins. "I've come with your horse, cousin. 'Tis a fine animal, and I'm sore tempted to steal him from ye." As he said the jest, a brief vision of Liselle fled across his mind, but he quickly pushed it aside.

Ewan gave the horse a fond slap on the flanks and replied mildly, "I think ye still have need of him, aye? Your gray mare has yet to be found."

Julian clenched his jaw.

"I'm sure the lass is safe, cousin," Ewan reassured. "Ye should—"

"Ach, her safety is not my concern," Julian grated roughly.

It was a lie.

They both knew it.

And then the resounding cry of "A MacLeod! A MacLeod!" split the air.

Thrusting the reins back into Julian's hands, Ewan urged, "Take the lad, cousin, and return him only when ye've need of him no longer." Tilting his head in the direction of the commotion, he added, "I've words that must be said to Ruan, so I'll leave ye to your thoughts."

Julian grimly watched his young cousin thread his way through the crowd to where the dark-haired Ruan MacLeod, Laird of Dunvegan, waved a strong arm in greeting.

Turning away, Julian passed a hand over his face.

Liselle was clearly capable of handling herself. Aye, the lass leapt through windows. Most assuredly, she could ride across the heath upon the back of his sure-footed gray mare.

He had no cause to worry.

Shaking his head, he'd just made up his mind to greet Ruan MacLeod himself when he heard a familiar laugh.

Instantly alert, he scanned the sea of faces about him and spied a burly form and a glimpse of red hair flashing from under a black cloak.

Shoving the horse's reins into the hands of a nearby MacLean, Julian slipped through the crowd and fell into step behind the cloaked man. Aye, he'd recognize him anywhere. Stepping forward, he tore the man's hood from his head, and grabbing him about the throat to half-choke him, hissed into his ear, "Might I have a word with ye, traitor?"

Archibald Douglas, the Earl of Angus, looked back at him, gasping, as his eyes bulged in surprise.

"I'd wager your presence here is as rotten as it smells!" Julian growled, making little effort to disguise his disgust. "You're no better than Albany! Ye both should hang from yonder bridge along with any man who conspired with ye to burn the villages of good honest folk!"

He twisted his hand tighter around the man's thick neck.

"Hold!" The Red Douglas wheezed, clawing at Julian's hands. "I come at Cameron's bidding, by way of tidings that ye delivered with your own hand!"

Julian searched his eyes before shoving him back roughly. "Then I'll personally deliver ye to the man," he said, his voice sharp-edged and hard. "I'll not have your ilk wandering about here unescorted!"

Catching his balance, Douglas nodded and straightened his collar, feeling his neck as if to make certain it was still in one piece. "Aye, then, lead on," he replied with an uncustomary meekness.

With a curt nod, Julian motioned for the man to precede him, but they had scarcely taken two steps when the sound of a horn split the air.

At once, the voices in the camp fell into muted whispers as all eyes riveted upon a party of men approaching in great state.

Four trumpeters with golden horns bearing the royal crest marched before two elaborately dressed men on horses. And they were in turn followed by several hundred soldiers, all on foot, clad in white livery, and armed with gleaming battle axes.

The two horsemen were the king and his favorite, Thomas Cochrane.

Julian's lip curled in disgust.

King James rode a splendid roan with crimson ribbons plaited in its mane. Swathed in a fine ermine-trimmed mantle and wearing boots adorned with silver braid, the monarch looked frail and nervous as he surveyed the clans gathered before him.

But, at his side, the long-faced Thomas Cochrane sat proud, and with a smug smile, swept aside his black-velvet cloak bedecked with precious stones to reveal a silver hunting horn overlaid with gold.

"Aye, James and Thomas bring three hundred while Cameron can summon fifty thousand," Douglas growled at Julian's side.

"And just *whom* are we here to fight?" Julian spat in reply. "I think ye just might know the army, intimately!"

Douglas' jaw clamped. "You may not understand it, lad, but what I've done is for the good of Scotland herself!"

"Burning her villages is for the good of her, aye?" Julian rejoined sarcastically. Nodding toward Thomas Cochrane, he added, "There are other ways to fight the likes of him."

They watched Thomas dismount and smooth his trimmed, sleek beard. And then his nasal voice could be heard giving the soldiers orders to raise the king's tent alongside his own.

Still hushed, the Scottish army of clans watched as Thomas' silken tent was brought forth and raised with cords entwined with silk and gold. And as a matching tent for the king was raised—only slightly larger than Thomas' own—another small party of silk-clad men arrived.

Julian turned away in disgust as he recognized the king's other favorites. Among them were his rumored former lovers, the English musician, Roger, and Torfifan the fencing-master. Clearly, these men cared only for pomp and prestige and nothing for the suffering of the honest folk whom they'd plundered to dress themselves in such finery.

"Aye, let's speak with Cameron," Douglas muttered at his side.

But, as they made their way to Cameron, rumors began to circle amongst the gathered men, rumors that the king had placed Thomas Cochrane in charge of the cannons after all. And by the time they found Cameron standing before the Lauder Kirk, an old stone building covered in vines, he was surrounded by furious nobles.

"The king was to stay in Edinburgh!" one of them was shouting.

"Along with the treacherous vermin crawling around him!" cursed another.

Catching ahold of Cameron's arm, Douglas demanded, "Can this be true? Has the king truly placed a mere mason in command of the artillery?" He was so outraged that he'd apparently forgotten his own treachery.

Raising a cool brow, Cameron pointed toward the stone kirk. "Let us gather within to discuss these matters, for the defense of our country is at stake."

His calm order had the desired effect, and falling silent, the men obediently filed into the building.

Joining them, Julian cast a backward glance to where James and Thomas spoke with Roger and Torfifan. 'Twas hard to fathom. Even now, the king surrounded himself with lowborn favorites and focused more on matters of love than the protection of his own country.

Drawing his lips in a line of disgust, Julian ducked into the kirk and closed the wide wooden doors behind him.

As soon as the heavy doors shut, the nobles burst into heated conversation.

For the most part, Julian ignored them, he was fair exhausted.

Propping his booted feet upon a pew, he leaned back and closed his eyes for a time, but as the minutes passed, their repetitive bickering grated on his nerves.

At a sudden lull in the debate, he gave a dry laugh. "Ach, the lot of ye are like the mice in *The Tale of the Mice and Cat*!" he observed in a derisive tone. "Aye, and the king is nothing but a *royal* mouse manipulated by the cat, played, of course, by Thomas Cochrane!"

Several of the nobles drew back in insult, but Cameron asked calmly, "And what tale is this, Julian?"

Slowly, Julian sat up to dangle his arms over the back of the pew. "'Tis the one of the mice who met in secret to plan how they would defend themselves against their great enemy, the cat."

From the corner of his eye, he saw Cameron smile as the rest of the lords waited for him to continue.

"Aye, they could never win against the beastie," Julian continued, thinking the gathered lords before him did indeed have much in common with mice. "The cat prowled so quietly on its paws that once they knew 'twas there, they'd no time left to run away. Finally, they agreed a bell must be hung upon the cat's neck to warn them sooner of its approach."

"And?" Douglas pressed when Julian paused again.

"They failed, and all were eventually killed," Julian replied sarcastically. "But only because they couldna ever find a mouse courageous enough to fasten the bell."

There was a stilted silence.

And then Douglas leapt to his feet, and pulling his sword from its sheath, roared, "Aye, *I'll* bell the cat!"

Several nobles cheered enthusiastically. Julian rolled his eyes. How could the man forget his own treason so quickly?

But then the massive doors of the kirk creaked open.

"Who goes there?" Cameron called out as they all leaned back to look.

"'Tis I, the Earl of Mar," came Thomas Cochrane's nasal reply. Kicking one of the doors back in a gesture of great authority, he stepped inside the kirk.

He'd taken the time to change his clothing and now donned a blue-feathered hat and mantle of crimson satin embroidered with pearls enough for a king. And about his neck, he once again wore the broad gold chain that some claimed was a lover's gift from James himself.

In less than an instant, Douglas had seized the man, and reaching over, he ripped the gold chain off of Thomas' neck. "A rope will become yer neck better, ye fool!"

"What is this?!" Thomas' mouth, at first smiling, suddenly twisted, and his eyes blazed in anger.

"Ye've saved us the trouble of seeking ye!" Douglas cried, shoving him forward into the circle of nobles. And snatching the silver hunting horn hanging from the man's belt, he added, "Ye've been the hunter of mischief long enough!"

But Thomas was not easily intimidated. He brushed his sleeves and peered at the men in astonishment. "What cause have ye to subject me to such rough usage? Is this a jest?"

And then Cameron rose slowly to his feet, and the others fell silent.

"This is in good earnest," Cameron answered in a low voice, and his face was fierce and stern. "Your time is at an end. Now, ye shall receive the reward for your misdeeds. Aye, and ye'll pay for spilling the blood of Mar and for the pain ye've caused many, among them, my own wee Kate."

At the mention of her name, Thomas paled, and a flicker of genuine fear entered his eyes. Falling down on his knees before Cameron, he raised a pleading hand, and his voice took on a wheedling tone. "Save me! Ye are a kind, just lord! I see that now! Forgive—"

But Cameron cut him short in an even, deadly tone. "Ye are little but a thief, murderer, and traitor. And I'll see your name erased from history!" Raising an elegant hand, he ordered, "Bind the man! He'll be taken to Edinburgh to stand trial for his crimes against the people. They have suffered enough in order to fit him into robes made for kings."

"Aye," the nobles muttered in agreement.

"Nay! Let us finish this now!" Douglas disagreed with a shout.

The bitterly angry tone in his voice made Julian suddenly wary.

"'Tis time for justice!" Douglas insisted. Grabbing Thomas by the throat, he bodily lifted the man to his feet. "I'll wait no longer! I'll see ye hang this night! Ye and the king's other favorites! Ye've stolen from the people of this land for too long!"

As the other nobles took up the cry, Douglas seized Thomas and began to drag him out of the kirk.

"Hold!" Cameron cried. "We'll have our justice, Douglas. We'll take him to Edinburgh forthwith!"

But his words were lost as the other nobles took up Douglas' words to chant, "Hang him! Hang him on the bridge!"

And then, as Thomas was dragged screaming through the camp towards Lauder Bridge, madness ensued.

Cameron and Julian fought to calm the nobles, but it was too late. They could do little but follow the men as anger raged through the gathered clans and into the nearby village like a wildfire.

They had nearly reached the bridge when a few of the villagers gathered to pelt Thomas with spoiled vegetables and small stones.

"No more Cochrane Plack!" they cried.

"Then, if I must be hanged, hang me with a silken cord from off my tent, as a man of my station deserves!" Thomas Cochrane screamed in a thin, wavering voice that betrayed his fear. "I canna perish like a common thief!"

"Ye deserve no better than a rope of the roughest kind!" Douglas roared in response, the vein on his temple pulsing.

"Aye!" another man cried. "I've a rope of horse hair for the likes of ye!"

"Ye canna hang me as a thief!" Thomas wailed. "I'm untouchable! Ye canna do this!"

"There's not a man who is untouchable!" Douglas cried, and the men about him roared in agreement.

"Save me!" Thomas screamed a high-pitched sound. And then his thin pale eyebrows arched in disbelief as a man stepped forward to place a rough noose about his neck.

Julian watched grimly. It was hard to watch, but it was justice. The man had murdered more than one innocent man and had ravaged the land for his own gain. Aye, it was fair payment for Mar's death alone. Finally, the king's youngest brother would see his murder avenged.

It was then that Julian heard Cameron's quiet words for Thomas.

"For the pain ye caused mine, and the harm ye've done to my country, I'll not be saving your worthless head, Thomas Cochrane. I warned ye. Aye, 'tis justice for Mar and for the people of Scotland."

He didn't mention Kate's suffering, but Julian knew it was ever-present in his mind.

And then the rope drew tight, and Thomas Cochrane's scream ended abruptly as he was thrown over the bridge.

There was a moment of silence

"May God have mercy on your soul," Cameron murmured. "For I cannot."

And then a mighty roar rippled through the gathered clans. But as the sounds grew louder, an even deeper madness seized them as they began to chant, "Hang them all! All of the king's favorites! Hang them all!"

At that, Cameron and Julian exchanged looks of alarm.

There was no controlling the men surging to where the king's tent had been newly erected.

Julian and Cameron shoved their way forward but could only see glimpses of the king as he stood behind a fine wooden table laden with silver platters of delicacies. Beside him hovered Roger, the English musician, and Torfifan, the fencing-master, clutching bottles of wine and half-eaten tarts.

"What is the meaning … of this…" The king's voice started strong but ended in a nervous sputter. Even he could not fail to read the vengeance in the eyes of the men confronting him.

"Why do the royal Stewarts believe so fully that they are immune to danger?" Douglas asked incredulously, pushing his way to the forefront.

The crowd burst into laughter, drowning any words that might have been said in response.

The vein on Douglas' temple throbbed yet again as he shouted,

"Have ye not seen who is even now swinging from Lauder Bridge?"

The king went deadly white.

And then the men surged forward, grabbing Roger and Torfifan and pulling them from the tent, all the while ignoring Cameron's direct orders to stand down. As the crowd swept back towards Lauder Bridge, the king found Cameron and desperately clawed his sleeve.

"Stop them, Cameron! We command ye to stop them!" the king begged.

But there was no one who could stop the madness that had seized them.

"I command ye!" the king was shouting, and then he abruptly fell silent as his gaze riveted upon Thomas Cochrane's body still twitching in its death throes on the rope suspended from the bridge.

It was a gruesome sight. And in minutes, Roger and Torfifan had joined the mason.

But as several more of the king's favorites were bound and gagged, and ropes were being fitted over their necks, Cameron once again raised his voice, commanding the men to stop.

But still, his call went unheeded.

"Douglas is caught in a bloodlust," Cameron said through thinned lips as he desperately pushed through the crowd in an attempt to reach the red-headed earl. "'Tis not the way it should be done! This madness must stop!"

Shoving the man in front of him aside, Julian unsheathed his dirk, and taking careful aim, launched it towards the red-headed earl.

As it grazed the man's cheek, he whirled angrily in their direction.

"There will be no more killing this day!" Cameron's strong voice thundered.

And then Ewan appeared with Ruan MacLeod at his side, and giving a great cry, they raised their swords to beat them against their shields. And as every highlander followed suit, the rhythmic sound of metal clashing upon metal caught the attention of all, until finally it was the only sound that could be heard.

Then Ewan raised his arm, and the beating stopped.

Thanking him with a gracious nod, Cameron's powerful voice rang out in the ensuing silence. "What great folly is this? Are we no better than the English? The time for killing cowards is done! Now is the time to defend our country. Make ready! We ride to Edinburgh at once!"

By his side, the king gasped and repeated, "Ride to Edinburgh? We've given no such orders!"

But Cameron's face was impassive. Turning to his cousin, he replied, "Ye no longer have the right to give orders, James."

The king blanched and then clutched his heart. "It was prophesied that the Lion of Scotland would be devoured by its own whelps!" he whispered through white lips. "Ye haven't the right to subvert the divine right of kingship given by God himself! Ye didn't make us King!"

There was a pregnant pause. One in which every eye turned to Cameron as a slow, scathing smile formed on his lips.

"Aye, I didn't make ye king, James!" he agreed in a lethal tone. "But I've kept ye king. Never forget that! For now, ye'll be my prisoner, and we ride for Edinburgh afore ye and Albany drown our fair land in rivers of blood!"

Julian glanced up in surprise and voiced the question in everyone's mind. "But the English?"

"Aye, I dinna fear the English. Gloucester dinna bring the resources to besiege the castle," Cameron stated calmly. "And after hearing the doings of this night, even Gloucester himself will believe that we want Albany as king. They'll come running to Edinburgh with haste to put him on the throne. 'Tis a far better trap then the one that I'd planned."

"But we outnumber them now, aye?" Douglas pointed out. "Let's take the fight to them and kill them all!"

Both Julian and Cameron looked upon him with raised brows.

It took the earl a moment to recall the reason for their response. "Ach, what I've done, I've only done for Scotland!" he swore, pounding his fist in his hand. "And now that Cochrane and his kind are dead and the king in our hand, I belong here, lad, ye know it!"

Cameron eyed him with disdain. "Then bring Albany to Edinburgh and bring him right quickly!" And then raising his hand, he issued a crisp order, "Bind the king. He'll walk to the village as penance for the neglect of his own country."

The king balked.

But the gathered clans appeared pleased by this, and as Douglas grabbed a length of rope to tie the king's hands, they roared in approval.

With the look of a hunted animal, the king fell into step behind them as they lead him into the darkness, through the dale and into the village of Channelkirk.

And as the villagers carrying torches lined the road to watch the bound king stumble past, a mule with a worn leather saddle was brought to carry him back to Edinburgh.

No one spoke as the king slowly mounted.

13

LADY GRAY

Julian yawned and stretched, glad to be back in his chamber in Edinburgh Castle once again. With the king now a prisoner, the nobles were in an uproar. Not because they wished to free James. Nay, quite the opposite. Most were seeking his head on a pike.

Aye, Cameron had his hands full. 'Twould be a miracle if he avoided a war between the angered clans calling for blood.

Yawning again, he wandered to the window.

'Twas time to hunt down the MacLeans for any tidings of Liselle's whereabouts. He'd spent far too much time worrying about the wee devil. And even though his mind calmly informed him that she was a highly skilled and trained assassin, his heart refused to listen.

A clatter of hooves sounded outside, breaking into his thoughts. Cocking a brow, he leaned out the window to see a messenger clad in the livery of the House of York, surrounded by Scottish royal guards.

Watching as the man was led away towards the royal apartments, Julian threw on his plaid and left his chamber.

Unable to find Ewan or his men for news of Liselle, he headed across the inner cobblestoned courtyard towards Cameron's section of the royal apartments to sate his curiosity over the content of the Yorkist message.

The afternoon sun was overly warm, and the shutters of the windows along the passageway were thrown open wide to catch any hint of a cool breeze. Undoing a button of his collar, he ran up the steps two at a time and knocked with a quick rap on Cameron's door.

It opened almost immediately.

A bright-eyed lassie with amber ringlets and apple cheeks peered up at him. "Come in, my lord!" the child invited with a curtsey.

Julian hesitated as the squealing sound of more children met his ears. He winced and moved back. Opening his mouth, he prepared to excuse himself, but alas, he was too late.

"Julian!" Kate's cheerful voice ensnared him.

Coercing his grimace into a smile, Julian took a deep breath and stepped inside.

The chamber was filled with females, big and small. Most of them sat on cushioned chairs with sharp embroidery needles in one hand and fine bits of silk in the other.

It was most certainly not a place he desired to be.

But Kate gave him no opportunity to escape. She descended upon him at once, grabbing his hand and pulling him even deeper into the depths of the femininity surrounding him.

"Cameron will be here any moment," she assured, wrinkling her nose into a smile. "Have a wee oatcake or a nip of wine to refresh yourself whilst ye wait, Julian!"

With that, she pushed him towards a long table holding an array of large silver bowls filled with pears, almonds, and oat cakes, alongside several bottles of fine Rhennish wine.

Absently selecting a pear, he took a large bite and turned to lean against the table, his mind set to identify the fastest route of escape. But the women were watching him. There was much fluttering of the lashes, many doe-eyed smiles, and plenty tilting of the heads as they strove to catch his attention. But he wasn't interested.

Taking another bite from his pear, he'd just made up his mind to leave hastily by the side door when a familiar alto voice spoke by his elbow.

"How delightful to see you again, my lord!" Liselle's husky voice said.

Julian choked.

Gasping for air, he gaped at Liselle in surprise, even as relief overwhelmed him to find her standing safely by his side.

Standing on her tiptoes, she pounded him helpfully upon the back.

And though he struggled to breathe, he couldn't stop his gaze from roving over her. Never was there a more bonny lass! Clad in a silver gown embroidered with stars that shimmered like opals, her hair was braided and caught to the nape of her neck by a bejeweled net, dotted with silver beads.

She stood there, watching him. And as he finally caught a long, dragging breath, the corner of her lip lifted in a secretive smile.

"Ach, ye wee devil!" he half-choked, clearing his throat even as his cheeks creased into a wide grin.

Her presence at the Scottish court was not a good thing, so why couldn't he stop smiling? Mayhap it was her sultry looks, or her low, seductive voice. Or her lips.

Thinking of her kiss, he gave a low chuckle. "Aye, but ye are a wickedly sinful lass. But clearly, joining forces with wickedness has its place now and then."

Her lashes dipped in amusement, and then she lifted her hand and in it was a goblet of wine. With a challenging gleam in her eye, she said, "Pray take some refreshment, my lord."

He snorted.

But then she licked her bottom lip, and he was undone as a hot wave of desire washed over him. Had she just suggested another type of refreshment, or had he shaped her words to fit his own longing?

Aye, he was tempted to taste the wee imp's lips then and there, even though he knew he should focus on such matters as discovering just how many weapons she had upon her and for whom they were destined. But, 'twas fair impossible to think of anything more than the soft, seductive pull of her lips!

Plucking the wine glass from her hand, he set it down upon the table and raked her with a deliberate, smoldering gaze. And then unable to resist, he rumbled suggestively, "Ere the next time I leave ye, mayhap I should strip ye first, Lady Gray, to see what ye might be hiding, aye?"

Shocked gasps greeted his scandalous words. He wasn't all that surprised. After all, he'd just spoken of stripping the lass naked, but then it was his turn to be shocked as the most unexpected and dreadful response circled through the chamber.

"*Lady* Gray?"

"Lord Julian has *wed!*"

Julian's eyes widened in alarm as every head turned upon him.

And then he glanced down at Liselle. She was staring at him with an expression in her eyes that strangely demotivated him to correct the misunderstanding.

And then her low, throaty voice broke the silence.

"You have been sorely missed, my lord," she said, selecting an almond cake and daintily nibbling at the edge. "The pain of parting your company was sharper than the edge of a finely honed blade."

Julian's eyes lit with humor at the reference to her escape. Aye, she was a sharp-witted minx. "'Twas your choice to leave that night, Lady Gray," he replied with a half growl. "But 'twas not the choice of my own gray mare!"

"She is safe in the stables, Lord Gray," she answered. And then picking up the goblet of wine, she offered it to him once again, lowering her lashes in private amusement. "Please, drink, my lord."

Deliberately sweeping her curves in a lazy manner, Julian couldn't resist a provocative response. "But 'twill it cause me to wake up unclothed once again?"

Conversation exploded in the chamber.

She sent him a slight scowl, but he responded with a wink.

And then her pouting lips parted slowly, and it was suddenly fair difficult to focus on anything else as she touched the goblet to her lips and took a sip.

A drop of wine beaded at the corner of her mouth, and he fought the temptation to lick it off. Catching his breath, he closed his eyes and forced his thoughts to clear. The wee devil was playing him again.

But he was a master at the art of seduction himself. And had he not played with the heart of many a lass, enemy or no?

Something cool touched his mouth and his lashes flew open. She was standing on her tiptoes, holding the cup to his lips.

"How can I refuse ye, Lady Gray?" he asked, taking the cup. He drained it in a single draught and slammed it down onto the table.

And then with a charming smile and a roguish lift of his brow, he trailed his finger over her collarbone and ran the back of his hand down her arm. Weaving his fingers through hers, he brought them to his lips and planted a soft kiss on a single fingertip.

"I thank ye for the wine, lass," he rumbled softly.

She was staring at him. Her eyes wide. "Would you care for more, my lord?" she asked.

And then she swallowed with apparent apprehension.

He suppressed a grin.

So the wee minx *was* affected!

"I can never have enough of ye, Lady Gray," he whispered as he lifted his free hand and brushed his thumb lightly along her jawline.

Her breasts heaved, and the delicate fingers he held trembled a little.

And then, he no longer heard the tittering of the women surrounding him. And he was no longer playing a game.

He saw nothing but a complicated, mysterious woman before him.

As if in a dream, he pulled a lock of hair through her jeweled net and entwined it around his fingers. But then the net slipped and he found the resulting spill of her golden locks oddly intoxicating.

Freeing her hand, she reached up and softly cupped her palm against his cheek. The vulnerability in her eyes was laced with desire, and he knew then that she was no longer acting.

But neither was he.

He'd kissed many a lass, but never had he experienced anything as seductive as the simplicity of her touch. Growling low in his throat, he slipped his hands around her waist and pulled her close.

And then, Cameron's amused voice broke the spell. "Please introduce your wee wife to me, Julian!"

Julian froze.

And then Liselle was pushing away.

Quickly gathering his scattered thoughts, he turned to face Cameron's dark eyes which were rife with amusement.

But Liselle was already stepping forward, and with a deep curtsey, she said, "Allow me to introduce myself, my lord. I am Lady Liselle di Franco." She paused a moment before adding, "Wife to Lord Gray."

Cameron's brows arched in surprise. His dark gaze swept over Liselle in open curiosity before moving in astonishment to Julian.

Ach, the jest had gone too far. It was one thing to allow the gossiping ladies to believe he'd wed Liselle, but it was quite another to deceive Cameron. But even as he opened his mouth to contradict, his throat inexplicably constricted.

"'Tis such a delightful surprise!" Kate laughed, appearing at

Cameron's side to slip her arm through his. "And 'tis right glad I am to see ye, Lady Liselle! I'd almost given up hope for our Julian!" Her brown eyes sparkled in excitement.

Closing his eyes, Julian ordered his senses to return.

Dimly, he heard Kate's warm tones insist, "Tell us every detail, Lady Liselle! Every one! First, where did ye first meet?"

"It was at my brother's home," Liselle answered sweetly while Julian replied at the same time, "In bed!"

There was a moment of stunned silence and he smiled. He liked his version better. Besides being the truth, it was considerably more provocative. Opening his eyes, he felt the strange haze in his mind dissipate. Aye, 'twas only a game of wits. He'd explain everything to Cameron later.

Treating him to a slight frown of displeasure, Liselle skillfully corrected, "Yes, I met Lord Gray whilst he lay ill in bed at my brother's house."

The dismay in the chamber quickly shifted to simpering sighs, and Julian rolled his eyes. The lass was a quick thinker. He had to grant her that.

"'Tis like a poem!" someone cooed.

"Ach, ye nursed him back to health then?" another one sighed.

"It was a trying time," Liselle said, punctuating each word with a delicate shudder. "We did not think he would live."

A chuckle escaped his throat as he remarked, "Mayhap my life was most in danger when ye stuck a blade betwixt my ribs?"

Liselle didn't hesitate. "It took more than one blood-letting before his fever would lift," she explained, pounding her hand dramatically on her chest and lifting her eyes heavenward. "*Santo Ciélo*, but it was a trying time!" Glancing at him sideways, she pursed her lips into a sly smile.

Julian sucked in a quick breath. He'd not let the wee trickster win. "Your brother was fair anxious to be rid of ye, no?" he asked, flashing a quick grin. "Mayhap 'twas your habit of stealing horses or jumping from roofs?"

A fan flew into her fingers from some hidden place in her sleeve, and she opened it to hide her face in shy embarrassment even as she graced him with a warning glance. "'Twas only to see you, my lord!" she chided softly. "And were you not there to catch me in your arms?"

A chorus of wistful sighs circled about the room.

She was proving adept at spinning tales. He opened his mouth to challenge her once again, but she was ready. Popping an oatcake betwixt his teeth, she rapped her fan on his nose in a threatening manner even as she fluttered her lashes.

"Take more refreshment, my lord!" It was clearly an order.

"Tell us more!" the women around them insisted.

Liselle smiled demurely, but when her lips parted he blocked her reply by slipping an almond cake into her mouth. "I canna eat whilst ye have no sustenance of your own, my sweeting," he muttered around his mouthful of dry crumbs.

Chewing their cakes, they exchanged competitive smiles as a multitude of questions burst forth around them.

Julian was the first to swallow. Leaning down to rest his cheek against hers, he whispered, "Use your mouth for eating, lass, not spewing wild tales!"

He felt her smile, but he was quite unprepared for what came next.

Suddenly turning her head, she caught his lower lip lightly between her teeth. And though the kiss was quick, heat flooded through his veins like liquid fire, whetting his earthly appetites for more.

He stared into her eyes as inexplicably, once again, his razor-sharp wit vanished. He could do nothing but watch as she drew back and curtsied deeply to all in the chamber.

"Pray forgive my youthful indiscretion," Liselle requested shyly. "I fear that we've caused more than enough tongues to wag this day. Please do not allow my foolishness to cause further interruption."

Julian watched, as with visible reluctance the women broke into smaller groups, and then he glanced over to see Cameron observing him in rank amusement.

"Allow me to pour ye a drink, lad," the Earl of Lennox suggested in a cordial tone. "To congratulate ye on wedded bliss."

But before Julian could reply, Kate swept forward to claim his arm.

"Afore ye leave, shall I read your future?" the wee countess teased as she plucked a nut from a silver bowl. "The future of your love shall be revealed in this nut, Julian!"

"Yes! Show us!" the ladies in the chamber exclaimed as they gathered close to the fire.

Julian eyed the nut suspiciously as Liselle raised a perplexed brow, but they obligingly followed Kate as she led Julian to stand before the hearth.

Placing the nut in her palm, Kate waited as everyone drew near. And then in a theatrical voice, she explained, "If the nut burns quietly, their love will be soft and gentle and grow stronger with each passing year. But if it cracks, they will face hardships aplenty!"

The women held their breath as Kate held the nut up for all to see.

And then she tossed it into the fire.

For several long moments, nothing happened.

Julian had just opened his mouth to make a sarcastic comment when the nut suddenly exploded and burst into flames.

Everyone stared in surprise.

Tossing his head back, Julian laughed. "And what does it mean if the nut bursts into flames?" he asked Kate dryly. "'Tis bound to be worse than hardships aplenty, aye?"

The women sent him sour looks and even Liselle seemed strangely disappointed. Only Cameron shared his humor. He could read it in his eyes, but the man was far too much of a diplomat to allow his lips to lift into a smile.

Clearly disappointed, Kate looped her arm through Liselle's. "I've never seen a nut burst afore in that manner!" she admitted ruefully. "'Tis clear your love is of the most extraordinary kind!"

"Aye, I'll agree to that," Julian granted in a playful manner.

Liselle dipped in another polite curtsey.

"Princess Anabella will meet me in Inchmurrin soon. Ye should come with me, Lady Liselle," Kate offered with a bright smile. "Cameron insists I leave Edinburgh straightway and return home to rest afore the bairn arrives." She patted her belly as a glowing smile crossed her lips.

At Liselle's alarmed expression, Julian chuckled. "Yes, do go, Lady Gray!" he insisted out of perverse amusement.

"I couldn't leave you, my lord," she replied with feigned meekness. "My heart would miss you so."

But then Cameron stepped forward, and with an elegant wave of his hand, suggested, "Shall we leave these ladies to their needlework, Julian?"

Without waiting for a reply, he threw an arm around Julian's shoulders and guided him out of the chamber and into the next.

As the door clicked shut behind them, Cameron raised a conspiratorial brow. "I'd wager there is more to this tale," he said, his lips crooking into a rare broad smile.

Julian hesitated. Now was his chance to explain, but crossing the chamber, he settled into a Spanish leather chair placed before the window and chose to remain silent instead.

Pouring two goblets of spiced wine, Cameron approached to hand him one and took the empty chair opposite his.

"When ye love a woman, she becomes your world," he mused, taking a sip of wine.

Strangely reluctant to offer any explanation, Julian shrugged instead. "A more saucy, brazen lass I've never met," he said and then added, "Aye, lovely, lively, and … evil."

Cameron raised a brow and tilted his head to the side. "And such are the strange ways of love."

Clenching his jaw, Julian circled the lip of his goblet with a finger. "I'm not in love," he said, more to himself than to Cameron.

The earl said nothing. He merely watched him with a twinkle in his dark eyes.

Julian grimaced and deliberately switched subjects to ask, "And what of the king? What have I missed whilst napping? I saw the Yorkist messenger."

Cameron drained his wine and gave a humph. "Aye, I'll pretend I dinna know ye wish to evade the matter of Liselle for now, lad. But that in itself speaks volumes," he said in amusement, but then his face grew serious all at once. "The king lives still, safely imprisoned in his chambers, and Albany will likely arrive on the morrow. Gloucester still suspects a trap and has tried to stop him, but it seems Douglas has been useful after all and is bringing him against the duke's wishes."

Relieved to discuss simpler matters, Julian drained his wine. "Aye, the fool willna listen, even though he should, aye? And what will happen on the morrow when he arrives?"

"'Twould be best that the brothers reunite as neither carries the full support of the country," Cameron answered, drumming his fingers lightly on the arm of his chair. "I'll not allow Scotland to be devoured by internal strife."

"'Twill be gall in Douglas' mouth if James still sits on the throne," Julian observed. "He won't stop plotting."

"Aye, but already the Scottish lords know of the Red Douglas' treachery. He'll have no choice. And now that Cochrane is gone, the man's ire has eased somewhat," Cameron said, dismissing Julian's concern with a wave of his long-fingered hand. "'Twill be accept James or die a traitor's death."

"Ach, to him a traitor's death just might be better," Julian answered with a dry chuckle.

Cameron smiled.

And then the sound of a horn from far away filtered through the open window.

Julian and Cameron exchanged a look of surprise.

Albany had arrived early.

* * *

And so it was that Albany rode under the great gates of Edinburgh Castle with Douglas, the Earl of Angus, at his side. But he had no sooner passed through the gates then they closed behind him with a resounding boom, and the Scottish prince knew in that moment that he had been betrayed.

"Traitors!" he roared, drawing his dark brows into an angry line.

Cameron stepped forward and eyed the man with marked disfavor. "Why should ye—of all men to walk this fair earth—find treachery astonishing?" His deep voice rang through the air.

"I've brought him as ye asked," Douglas inserted, dismounting from his horse to greet Cameron with a brotherly embrace.

"Ach, ye betrayed me as well, Douglas?" A murderous expression flickered over Albany's face. "God's Wounds!" he thundered. "But ye'll pay, both of ye!"

But Douglas only responded with a bark of laughter. "Ye have no power to make even a bairn pay, ye daft fool!"

Albany faltered, and then his face turned bleak all at once. "Then 'twas all a ploy to ensnare me? Do ye seek to try me for treason?" Still sitting on his horse, he began to nervously twirl his ring.

"While ye deserve no less, 'tis not a matter we need to discuss here. Come," Cameron ordered, and waving his hand towards the royal apartments, he waited for Albany to dismount before whisking him away.

Julian turned away in disgust.

He much preferred Albany to be accused, tried, and sentenced for betraying the crown. Never was a man more worthy of a hangman's rope. But he knew well that such an action would plunge Scotland into a civil war. But mayhap there was no avoiding it.

Though in any case, he'd had more than he could stomach of the affair for now.

Thinking of his favored gray mare, he made his way to the stables and found her—as Liselle had promised—contentedly chewing hay.

"Aye, ye wee lassie," he crooned, tossing her a handful of grain. "There's not a beast more surefooted than ye! Not one!" He shook his head, slightly amused. Why had he fretted so? He should have known Liselle was safe in her care.

After dispatching a message to Cambuskenneth Abbey for news of Dolfin, Julian spoke with the MacLeans for a time until the wailing of the pipes announced the midday feast, but by the time he finally made his way to the Great Hall, the feast was almost done.

There was no sign of Albany or Cameron, or many other nobles for that matter. He supposed that was a good thing. It meant that Cameron was negotiating, and that usually meant well for Scotland.

The tables were littered with dishes of mostly-eaten fruit and platters of fowl with their bones picked clean. A young minstrel sang to the accompaniment of a flute, as a line of servants, bearing large trays of savory roasted boar and venison, brought in the last course.

It took him a moment to find Liselle near the king's empty dais. And as he threaded his way towards her through the servants, he couldn't prevent his gaze from raking over her boldly.

Aye, she was a bonny lass. And a dangerous one. And he knew right well that it was the combination that caused a thrill to run down the back of his neck.

Sliding into the empty chair at her side, he wasn't even certain himself on what he'd planned to do until he'd unsheathed a small dagger from his boot and lightly pressed the tip of the blade betwixt her ribs.

For the briefest moment, her long lashes fanned her cheeks in surprise and then she merely reached for a plum as if she'd been eating in his company the entire feast.

Leaning close, he deeply inhaled the intoxicating scent of her hair and warned in a low rumble, "I'll not let ye or Pascal harm Dolfin, lass. 'Tis time for Orazio to acknowledge his defeat."

He felt her spine stiffen even as she looked up at him, and a soft smile spread over her lips.

Aye, but her mastery of emotion and deceit was just as impressive as her other skills! A searing jolt of desire—stronger than he'd known could exist—rocked through him.

Reaching for a goblet of wine, she laughed. It was a sinfully rich sound, and more than one curious eye turned their way.

She waited until the onlookers glanced away before saying in a low musical voice, "You should not seek my company, Lord Gray. I am caught in a web of conspiracies, betrayals, and masquerades. I am a creature of treachery. I know nothing else."

Her voice was strong and filled with humor, but underlying it all, he couldn't fail to hear a desperation in her tone that wrenched his heart even as his eyes lingered a moment upon her delicious curves.

Forcing himself to focus once again, he whispered a warning, "Ye should tell Orazio that I'll not allow the Vindictam to practice their craft here, lass. Aye, and as much as I despise the man, I'd not even allow harm to befall the king."

And then she was looking into his eyes again, eyes he could drown in.

He shuddered.

The lass held an unnatural sway over him.

"What ails me?" he murmured into her hair. "I should send ye away on the first ship that sets sail!"

Her laugh was low and bitter. "For the first time, Lord Gray, those words do not fill me with dread."

And then reaching down, she grasped the handle of the dagger he still pressed against her. He didn't resist as she plucked it free from his hand and used it to spear a haunch of venison.

"I'll not idly stand by and watch my country serve as a playground for the Vindictam, lass," he said, breathing upon her neck.

And then her lashes fluttered, and her eyes darkened seductively. "And are you asking me to defy him, my lord," she asked low in her throat.

Ach, but he was losing the battle of concentration. Her expression was whetting his appetite for more than food. "Aye, but ye have beguiling and deceitful ways, ye wee minx!" he accused hoarsely, letting his hand slide up her back and tangle itself in her hair. "Are ye trying to bewitch me?"

"Can you be bewitched, my lord?" she asked, curving closer.

Sweet Mary, but she clearly sought to distract him with her feminine wiles. And it was working right well! It was fair impossible to think of anything other than her bewitching eyes, alluring curves, and soft skin.

"I should send ye straight back to Venice this very night," he said, breathing hard. He knew he should leave. The lass was dangerous and untrustworthy, he supposed, but why did his heart not care? Clenching his jaw, he hissed, "Sweet Mary, what ails me? I'm a mead-drunk fool to look for food that I canna eat!"

Dipping his eyes over the curve of her neck, he wanted nothing more than to claim those lips, to make her his own with a tantalizing slowness until he had caressed every inch of her skin.

Their gazes locked and held as in a voice scarcely above a whisper, she asked, "And why can you not eat, my lord?"

It was too much. With a low moan, his hand dropped slowly around her waist and over her hips. And pulling her half out of her chair, he lightly traced her lips with his tongue a moment before breathing heavily into her hair to moan, "I need to know how I feel about ye, lass."

And then with a lazy, sensuous mastery, his tongue swept past her lips to ravish her mouth in a searing kiss.

She responded at once, permitting her tongue to tangle with his for a deliciously wicked moment even as her hand caressed his cheek. For a timeless moment, there was nothing but the warmth of his mouth melting into hers and the touch of his hands softly skimming her curves.

And then, he shivered and pulled away with a groan. "Aye, but I dinna know what I should think of ye, ye wee beastie! What power do ye hold? I've no doubt ye could bewitch me with a kiss even whilst slitting my throat!"

Liselle recoiled in a reaction so violent, that he drew back in surprise.

And then to his outright astonishment, she pushed back from the table, and fled the hall without a backward glance in his direction.

Julian blinked.

Rising to his feet with thoughts of pursuit, he'd taken only one step when a shout sounded outside the hall and a group of royal guards entered, escorting a man dressed in fine clothing.

It was the English duke, Gloucester.

The hall fell silent. All eyes watched the man approach, his twisted spine causing his shoulders to dip dramatically with each step.

And then Cameron and several other nobles appeared to greet him, and Julian turned away in disgust. He didn't have the temperament to deal with such matters. They were better left to Cameron's skills.

Choosing to clear his thoughts and escape the political intrigue for a time, he headed out of the castle and into the cobblestoned streets of Edinburgh in search of a distraction.

14

RETRIBUTION

Liselle stood in the center of her assigned chamber in Edinburgh Castle and bitterly turned in a slow circle. She was no true lady-in-waiting. The canopied bed, writing desk, and a carved wooden chest belonged to an assassin.

Again, she heard Julian's words play through her mind, words that had whispered in her thoughts often of late. It was becoming painful to even think of him. Every time she did so, she could only hear: *What cause could ye possibly have to harm an old man? Have ye no heart?*

She had a heart. An aching heart. If only he knew how heavy her heart *was*.

And how much it hurt to hear him even jest about slitting his throat.

Moving to the window, she peered out. Her chamber was on the second floor, facing the chapel not far from the gates. In the distance she could see the rooftops of Edinburgh spreading out below her.

And then shaking the pall that had settled over her, she donned her finest green satin gown with a bodice gleaming with pearls, and taking up a small woven basket, left her chamber to run the Countess of Lennox's errands.

The afternoon was quite warm, and she fanned her cheeks as she made her way to the market square. The countess had wished for several skeins of silken yarns along with several new quills and a pot of ink.

Liselle had just purchased them all and had stopped to tuck the packages safely in her basket when she heard several women's voices coming from around the corner of a nearby shop.

"Aye, 'tis a sad day when ye cannae buy tallow candles nor salt for the table!" one said.

"Ach, and the goats have gone dry," another one grumbled.

"Those goats of yers are ancient crones, Maggie!" The first one snorted. "Ye'd have more luck getting milk from a buck! Just butcher the auld things and have done!"

Shaking her head, Liselle moved forward when the second woman's response made her pause.

"Did ye hear of the Venetian prince at the butcher's near the city gates? 'Tis a secret, 'tis!"

"Ach, Maggie!" the first woman chortled. "If 'twas a secret, then why would ye know of it? Yer as gullible as a wee lassie!"

"I heard him myself!" Maggie's voice took on a wounded tone. "I've a wee bit of skill with the herbs, I do. And the butcher fetched me to care for the man. Even his purse is made of velvet. And he spoke of the prince—"

"Aye, *spoke* of a prince," the other woman interrupted with a scoff. "Yer such a dreamer, and those goats of yers are proof of it! They'll never give ye milk, ye daft woman! They're too auld!"

As they began to quibble about the goats, Liselle hesitated.

What Venetian was this?

Glancing at the sky, she knew she could spare time to investigate, and patting the stiletto in her sleeve, she hurried down the Cannongate towards the city gates.

The butcher's place was easy to find; she could smell it from some distance away. The faded sign hung by a single nail, and a pig wallowed in the mud at the entrance. The water in the wooden trough was green and murky.

Pursing her lips in disgust, she craned her head around the side of the building to see the butcher himself passed out in a drunken stupor near a pig's carcass. Several heaps of animal entrails and decomposing heads were tossed about the yard, giving off an overwhelming stench that made Liselle gag. Flies buzzed and crawled everywhere.

Covering her nose with one hand, she pushed the door open enough to peek through the crack.

The walls of the small room were blackened with smoke and grime. A hutch holding a collection of earthenware bowls along with several knives stood behind a trestle table, which was piled high with various animal parts. They were crawling with even more insects than could be found in the cloud of flies outside the door.

Sliding her bone-handled stiletto from its hidden pocket, she stepped inside.

The place was empty.

Frowning, she spied a curtain in the corner, and with a cautious step, pushed it aside to reveal a narrow flight of stairs. She eyed them suspiciously and almost turned away, when she heard the sound of singing coming from above.

She would have left, had she not recognized the gondolier tune, a Venetian *barcarola*.

Overcome with curiosity, she tiptoed up the creaking steps to hesitate at the top where three doors stood before her.

With a pounding heart, she opened the first one.

The room proved empty.

She had just moved towards the second door when the sound of a man's hacking cough came from behind the third.

Gripping her stiletto tightly in her hand, she squinted through the cracks to see a man lying forlornly on a straw pallet.

Santo Ciélo! It was Dolfin. And he was clearly ill.

Masking her surprise, she slipped into the room, and kneeling by the old man's side, placed a light hand upon his fevered forehead. Her brows knit with concern; his flesh was burning.

Dolfin's eyes opened then, and his dry lips twitched into a smile. "Am I at death's door?" he asked in a weakened voice. "I see an *àngiolìna* at my side."

"An angel?" Liselle laughed a little taken aback. An angel of death, mayhap. Wrinkling her nose, she eyed the squalid room and shuddered before turning back to him. "Why do you stay in such a place?"

"Then have you been sent by *Le Marin*?" A look of confusion crossed his face.

Liselle drew back sharply. "You know … *Le Marin*?" she asked even as it suddenly fell into place. Of course! Julian had been aiding the old man all along!

"You must tell him of the prince, *àngiolìna*!" Dolfin whispered. Gripping her arm with a shaking hand, he repeated in a stronger voice, "The prince!"

Arrested by the earnestness in his face, Liselle gave his hand a comforting pat and leaned closer. "The *Doge*?" she asked curiously.

"The prince!" he said again, and then caught in some strange delirium, he began to sing again until a series of wracking coughs seized him. But when he was finally done and had caught his breath, he pointed a feeble finger to a leather pouch at the foot of his pallet. "I would never betray them. *Inposìbile*!"

Liselle turned her head speculatively to the side. "And whom might *they* be, *bón pare*?" she asked softly.

His eyes lost focus as his voice trembled in reply, "The Vindictam!"

She drew back in surprise.

"I would never betray *La Serenìsima* to Ferrara," the old man continued. "I must send the word to the Vindictam. They should know the

Saluzzi have betrayed them. The prince, the Electus, is in danger. Find him by his mark. I have drawn his mark, there—" He waved trembling fingers to the leather pouch at his feet.

Liselle's brows rose even higher as comprehension dawned. He was speaking of the ruling elite of the Vindictam, matters so secret that not even Orazio would know of them!

Another bout of coughing seized his frail frame, and she could do nothing more to ease him other than to pat his back and murmur more comforting words. "Rest, *bón pare*. Take rest. Do not speak." Indeed. For her to hear such things would only be a danger!

"Rest, *sì*, I can rest, *àngiolìna*," Dolfin murmured. And then closing his eyes, he dropped into a feverish sleep.

Liselle stared down at the old man's pale face in shock.

No wonder Orazio had been seeking him! With such knowledge the old salt spy would certainly be an enemy to the Vindictam. But did he truly know the identity of the Electus, the man who had been chosen to replace the Grand Master, the *Dominus Granditer—the* iron fist to rule over them all?

She shivered and eyed the leather pouch with trepidation. Whatever it held, she was safer not seeing it. Such knowledge was death.

The identity of the Dominus Granditer was a closely guarded secret, a necessity for his own survival.

Yes, she should destroy the pouch with its contents unseen. Dolfin would be killed on sight if he were found with such a thing.

But she picked up the pouch anyway and her fingers untied the loop and slipped inside. At first, she found nothing unusual. A comb, prayer beads, and an iron ring of lock picks.

There was nothing with a mark upon it.

She pursed her lips and lightly tossed the pouch away.

The man was most likely delirious.

But after a moment, she picked up the pouch again and ran her fingers along its velvet interior.

It was then that she felt the hidden seam, and in the next moment, she was looking at a strip of parchment with the single word Electus written above a symbol of a 'V'.

She frowned, never having seen such a thing before.

And then Dolfin woke again, his shaking hand clawing her arm. "Water, *àngiolìna?* Do you have water?"

Liselle glanced about the room, but it was bare. Rising swiftly to her feet, she promised, "I will fetch some for you right quickly, *bón pare.* Hold tight."

Hurrying down the steps, she twisted her lips, perplexed. She could only pity such a helpless old man. How could Orazio expect her to slay him?

* * *

Approaching the Mercat Cross, Julian squinted at the postings, reading the latest one declaring the reconciliation of James and his brother. He rolled his eyes in disgust. And as a clap of thunder echoed in the sky above his head, he squared his shoulders, thinking it was time to head back up the Royal Mile to the castle high on the hill above him.

But he'd only taken a step when the flash of Liselle's green dress caught the corner of his eye. Stepping into an archway, he allowed his gaze to travel over her slender figure.

Even though he'd seen her jump out of a window, the wee vixen looked like a fragile doll, a creature of the court with her pouting, kissable lips. But she possessed a strength that he'd seen in few.

He was fair tempted to step forward and claim her lips once again, but then she set off at a brisk pace.

Intrigued, he followed her along a narrow twisted route through Edinburgh's wynds, keeping to the shadows as she hurried down the Cannongate to finally pause in front of a decrepit butcher's house. On the step, she glanced over her shoulder several times before cautiously stepping through the door and disappearing inside.

Peeking through a dirty window, he watched her slip behind a bedraggled curtain hanging in the back.

He glanced about and lifted his lip in disgust.

The air reeked of urine and filth. There was no sign of the butcher. Stepping inside, he took one look at the rickety staircase and knew he'd never be able to reach the top without announcing his presence to all.

But it was a simple enough matter to solve.

Returning outside, he quickly scaled the back wall and approached the windows from the roof. But it was only a slightly better solution. The ancient tiles cracked and shattered beneath his feet.

And then he heard Liselle's distinct voice followed by a man's hacking cough. And leaning over the edge of the roof, he peered through the top of the window to see her kneeling before a pitiable figure of a man lying on a straw pallet.

"And take another, *bón pare*," Liselle was saying as she dipped a silver spoon into a wooden bowl of what appeared to be gruel.

The clatter of hooves sounded on the street below, and Julian drew back a little as a company of royal guards galloped by, escorting several men dressed in the livery of the House of York. They were clearly headed towards the castle.

By the time he peered through the window once again, Liselle had moved, blocking his view of the man as she leaned forward to lift his head and press a cup to his lips.

"'Tis barley water sweetened with honey," she murmured

encouragingly. "It will give you strength."

Julian lifted a curious brow even as his eyes dipped over her seductive curves. His gaze strayed to the curve of her neck as she once more began to spoon gruel into the sick man's mouth.

Aye, her neck called for a man's kiss.

And then the man on the pallet lifted a feeble hand and said in a weak voice, "You have returned, *àngiolìna!*"

Julian's eyes widened in alarm as he instantly recognized Dolfin's voice. The man was supposed to have travelled to the Cambuskenneth Abbey! How was it that he'd ended up here?

"You must leave this place at once. You cannot stay, *bón pare*," Liselle was saying. "It is too dangerous. You will be found."

"My weary old bones cannot travel, *cara*," Dolfin answered with a shaky laugh.

"Would you rather die a traitor's death?" she asked with a firm shake of her head. "I will arrange for someone to take you from here. You must go with him, and you must leave this night!"

And then rising gracefully to her feet, she dipped a respectful curtsey and sailed through the doorway, heading back down the creaking steps.

Julian didn't hesitate.

Dropping through the window, he landed lightly on his feet, and in a moment was kneeling at Dolfin's side.

"How do you feel, *Istruttore?*" he asked without preamble, laying an uneasy hand upon the old man's sweating brow. Had she poisoned him?

Dolfin was clearly surprised to see him, but he managed a weak, welcoming smile. On his thin, unshaven face, it looked almost ghoulish.

"You are well, *caro!*" he croaked.

"Aye! And why would I not be?" Julian asked grimly, frowning in concern. "How long have ye been ill? And why are ye here? Did I not tell ye to travel to Cambuskenneth? Why did ye come here?"

"So many questions," Dolfin's voice trembled as he struggled to prop himself up on an unsteady elbow. And then he knit his brows. "What did you ask?"

Julian eyed him in concern. The man was confused and frail, but he didn't appear to be poisoned. "Dinna fash yourself over it," Julian muttered under his breath. "I'll see ye safe myself and right quickly."

Dolfin reached out and patted his hand. "My strength is returning, thanks to yon *àngiolìna*. You just missed her, *caro*."

Julian grunted. He could hardly tell the man that the lass was a Vindictam assassin.

"I must leave this place—" Dolfin began, before a fierce bout of coughing consumed him.

"Aye, of that there is no doubt," Julian murmured with a stern brow. "Tarry a moment more, *Istruttore*. I will find help right quickly."

It didn't take him long, and soon enough, Julian found himself standing in the center of the road, waving a relieved farewell to Dolfin, who was safely tucked beneath a plaid in the back of a friar's cart. The friar was a trusted friend and had vowed to see Dolfin safely to the monks of Cambuskenneth Abbey. Aye, the good brothers would see the old man properly tended to.

And only when Dolfin and the friar had rolled out of sight, did Julian turn back towards the castle, pondering the strange turn of events along the way.

Liselle's deed was an odd one. She had no cause to aid a man her brother sought to kill. Unless it was part of some devious scheme he had yet to uncover.

* * *

Liselle hurried back to the castle, planning to find Julian at once to warn him of Dolfin's dire circumstances and perhaps gain a measure of his trust along the way. The feeble old man filled her heart with pity. How could Orazio even think to kill him?

Frowning, she had just stepped out of a narrow close when a red roan reared before her, and she immediately fell back, her instinct unsheathing her stiletto in an instant.

"Do you recognize me?" a man's voice asked harshly.

Startled, she glanced up into the face of the thick-browed Saluzzo from Fotheringhay, the man she had injured. *Santo Ciélo!* Why had the man accosted her? Was it vengeance?

"Should I know your face?" Liselle asked haughtily, holding her head high even as she gripped her stiletto tighter.

The man threw back his head with a short bark of laughter. "You know well who I am, you foolish woman! You may think you've outwitted me and prevented this war, but you are sorely mistaken! I and my brother will see this truce broken and the Saluzzi honor restored! We shall free the Saluzzi from the spell you've cast over them!"

"War?" Liselle repeated, feigning ignorance as she stalled for time. *Santo Ciélo!* How had the man found her out?

The man rolled his eyes and glanced away in disgust before turning back to laugh, a hard, cruel laugh. "I'll not let Antonio uphold this truce! I and my brother will prevail. We shall open Antonio's eyes and make him see the treachery of the Vindictam at last!"

Liselle fell back a step. The name of Antonio Saluzzo was a fearsome one. Unlike the Vindictam who kept their ruling elite shrouded in secrecy, the Saluzzi made their leader known to all.

"You make little sense!" she whispered, feeling suddenly ill. She *had* rekindled a war! "I have done nothing—"

"My brother saw you in Fotheringhay," the man replied, his squinty eyes narrowing into slits. "Antonio demands retribution for your attack, but my blade cries for your blood! Even now he wastes his time discussing with the Vindictam a fitting punishment for you. But there will be no justice for me until I see a river of your blood flowing down the street!"

"You are *un demònio*!" Liselle said through white lips. The man was clearly consumed by hatred, almost to the verge of madness.

"Mayhap I am!" The thick-browed man's eyes glittered with contempt. "Know you that I'll be watching your every move, and I only hope that you will fail, because then I will see what I truly want. Your blood upon my blade!"

Liselle's head snapped back.

With that, the rogue Saluzzo wheeled his horse around and galloped away, but at the last moment suddenly leaned back to hurl a slim blade directly at her.

Arms of steel banded about Liselle's waist, pulling her back to safety, but not entirely quick enough. The blade grazed the side of her neck, leaving a wide scratch, but she scarcely felt the pain.

She sheathed her stiletto. The man was already out of range, and within seconds, out of sight.

"Diàmbarne!" Liselle cursed under her breath, shaken.

And then, she turned upon her rescuer, and her lips parted in surprise. It was Julian.

He was looking at the scratch upon her neck, and his brows furrowed as he wiped the blood away with his thumb.

"I dinna care for the sight of your blood, lass," he murmured.

But she scarcely heard his words. Her mind raced over what the Saluzzo had said. Antonio Saluzzo was even now discussing retribution? Was the man here in Edinburgh?

"What cause did he have to attack ye?" Julian asked, his brows knitting with worry. "Is this about Dolfin?"

Pain lanced through her heart upon hearing Dolfin's name on his lips yet again. She could hear the disapproval in his voice. Would he even believe her that she had planned to seek him out in order to aid the old man?

"Dolfin—" she began, but then a party of Yorkist horsemen clattered through the streets towards them, led by the Earl of Angus, the Red Douglas.

And as the man hailed Julian, Liselle slipped from his grasp.

She did not have the time to listen to the red-haired blustering earl, nor could she afford to be overheard by anyone discussing Dolfin. Such things had a way of finding the ears of the Vindictam.

The old man was safely hidden at the butcher's house for the moment. And with the Vindictam and the Saluzzi discussing retribution, the old salt spy was most likely far from their minds. She had to find Pascal, and she had to find him quickly. Mayhap he would know the truth of the matter.

Hurrying back to the castle, she looked everywhere for her cousin, but he was nowhere to be found.

Finally, she left a message upon his desk, and wiping the sweat from her brow, exited his chamber and tiptoed through the passageways of Edinburgh Castle as silent as a wraith. *Òsti*, but she found the situation almost unbearable, nothing like she had imagined it would be when she'd dreamt of receiving the tongue on her viper tattoo. Becoming an assassin had all seemed so dazzling then. She sorely needed to calm herself. Mayhap she would ask the maids to draw a lavender bath.

But first, she must leave word for Julian, for *Le Marin,* concerning Dolfin's location.

It didn't take long to find Julian's chamber, but the door was locked. Slipping a long hairpin from her netted hair, she used it to pick the lock of his door and quickly slipped inside.

The room was empty.

A ripple of disappointment coursed through her, a ripple that was met by a chagrined twist of her lip. What had she secretly expected? That the man would be waiting to sweep her into his arms and claim her lips with a passionate and unending kiss?

Putting her hand to her chest, she rolled her eyes at her thoughts.

How could she think of such things with such weighty matters to deal with? Blowing a strand of hair away from her cheek, she eyed his desk.

She'd leave him a message and then she'd have her lavender bath. Moving to his desk, she rifled through a stack of books, searching for parchment and a quill, but her search proved fruitless.

With a sigh, she prepared to quit the place when her gaze fell upon the canopied bed, a massive creation with crimson-velvet curtains and a matching counterpane that all at once summoned her memories of Sarlat and their first meeting.

He was a handsome man. The way his cheek creased when he grinned, and the fiercely honed muscles of his chest made her pulse quicken. *Santo Ciélo*, the man was seduction itself!

As if in a dream, she moved to his bed and absently traced a finger down the length of his bedcover. Mayhap she should return later, when he would be lying in it. She shivered at the thought.

It was then that she felt a blade against her throat.

She froze, startled that she hadn't heard a thing.

And then Julian's silken burr whispered into her ear, "And have ye come to slit my throat whilst I sleep? Ye should have waited until dark, ye wee devil."

As the heat of his breath traveled down her neck, Liselle jerked uncontrollably.

The movement caused the tip of his blade to almost prick her flesh.

"Sweet Mary!" he swore, withdrawing the weapon at once.

But she scarcely heard him as his words finally registered. *Have ye come to slit my throat?* A pang of despair stabbed her heart, and for the first time, she saw her family as a curse. Julian would *never* trust her.

She moved as if to step away, but he caught her about the waist and pulled her close against his chest.

Disheartened, she said, "I merely came to give you tidings!"

"Aye?" his voice sounded coarse.

"Dolfin is ill and in danger," she replied, heartsick. "If you truly care for the man, move him to safety—"

And then, his scorching lips grazed the back of her neck, gently kissing her neck wound, and she fell abruptly silent, stunned.

He stood closely behind her. She could feel every inch of him.

"Lady Gray," he groaned, softly nuzzling the back of her ear.

A thread of fire raced down Liselle's spine.

And then he moved back, drawing her with him. "Yon bed is too tempting a thing in your presence, ye wee minx," he said as he twirled her in his arms. Leaning close, his cheek creased in a smile as he added, "Though we *are* wed, aye?"

Liselle swallowed, speechless. His lips were close, too close. And his lashes were exceptionally long and dark. Her finger twitched with the temptation of touching them.

They stood there, breathing hard.

And then he crushed her to his chest and buried his face in her hair. Inhaling deeply, he tilted her head back and proceeded to kiss his way down the side of her neck and along her collarbone, leaving a trail of burning skin.

A soft moan escaped her lips.

His chest rumbled, and catching her earlobe in his teeth, he sucked the tip. And as he licked the sensitive skin of her neck, the fires of passion burst between them.

Desperately, her lips sought his, and he obliged her at once. And as his tongue plundered her mouth, she was held captive in breathless wonder in a kiss as raw and powerful as the man himself.

With her shaking knees threatening to give way, she dug her fingers into his arms to steady herself. Locking an arm about her waist, his other hand dropped to caress the swell of her hips.

She had no idea how long she stood there, lost in the torment of his kiss, before he abruptly tore away, breathing fast and ragged.

Entwining her hair around his finger, the corner of his mouth lifted in a sensual smile. "I dinna know where 'tis we're headed with this, lass," he murmured, trailing his thumb down her jawline and slowly over her bottom lip.

She looked up at him, a little dazed.

He seemed quite dazed himself, and he swallowed several times before he stepped back and said gruffly, "Ach, ye'd best leave afore I'm tempted to claim more than those sweet lips."

Liselle's breath caught in her throat as an expression crossed his face, an expression of unbridled lust that she knew matched her own.

But then he spoke again. "Ye've no cause to concern yourself over Dolfin. I've already seen him safe."

Dolfin.

The man's name shattered the mood as the weight of her situation came crashing down upon her all at once. Suddenly, she wanted to be gone, and gathering her skirts, she pushed past him, and without a backward glance ran out of the chamber.

15

THE TATOO

Seeking to cool his heated blood, Julian stepped out into the frigid evening air. Storm clouds continued to gather overhead, threatening rain. Taking to the castle walls, he let his thoughts wander over Liselle, over her puzzling actions and what role she might be playing in the Vindictam's plots. But most of all, he thought about her sensuous kisses.

Time passed.

It began to drizzle, but the rain would not last long. Already, he could see the break in the clouds illuminated by the light of the moon.

After a time, he found himself staring up at the window of Liselle's chamber. Her shutters were open, and she was pacing back and forth, clearly upset.

He frowned, wondering at the cause of her agitation, and then knowing it really wasn't a good excuse—but seizing it anyway—he entered the stone building. And taking the steps two at a time, he arrived at her door.

It was locked.

He'd just decided to turn away when he heard the approach of a grumbling woman.

"Find peace, aye?" the woman was muttering under her breath. "What daft fool could find peace from sitting in a tub of water, aye? Foreigners! I swear, these foreigners and their foreign ways will make my bones auld afore their time!"

Slopping two buckets of hot water down before Liselle's door, the woman gave it a vicious knock. But as the door opened, her cantankerous scowl switched at once into a meek smile.

"Yer water, my lady," she said, bobbing a cheerful curtsey. "And if it please ye, the laddies are bringing ye more as we speak."

Raising his brow, Julian peered from the shadows as the woman pushed her way into the chamber, swinging the door wide open.

Liselle stood nearby, a frown creasing her brow and with her hands tightly clenched. Suddenly, he wanted nothing more than to reach out and to fold her into a comforting embrace–to whisper into her hair that *he'd* handle whatever it was that caused her to fret.

And then several lads appeared, lugging more buckets, and after quite a few mumblings and more than one complaint, they filled the tub before the maid shepherded the lot out of the chamber and back down the stairs.

The door clicked shut, and silence reigned once more.

Hesitantly, Julian laid his hand on the latch again.

This time, it was unlocked.

He hesitated. As *Le Marin*, he would scarcely barge into a lady's chamber under such circumstances. But with Liselle, much had passed between them. Mayhap it was time she knew that she could trust him to aid her.

With a strong desire to protect her washing over him, he silently lifted the latch and peered inside.

The chamber was dark, illuminated only by the dull orange glow of the fire. The fragrant scent of lavender filled the air.

Liselle stood before the wooden tub, and for a brief moment, he caught the sensuous curve of her hip in the dim light as she sank into the steam rising invitingly from the water.

Grimly, he took a deep breath and prepared to shut the door. Aye, he'd wait until she was done. Her honey-colored tresses gleaming in the firelight made his pulse leap a bit too wildly.

And then there was a splash, and she lifted her leg out of the water, and rubbing a dark spot upon her ankle, she gasped in a strangled whisper, "Forever branded! Forever marked! *Eternità!*"

It was the desperation in her tone that propelled him forward. It was enough to make a man's heart break. And enough to dispel any lustful thought he might have had. Concerned only with her welfare, he entered the chamber, and shutting the door behind him, crossed the room in three long strides.

He heard Liselle's horrified gasp, and from the corner of his eye, he saw her jerk her foot back into the water and sink down into the tub so only her eyes peered over the edge.

But he strode first to the fire and only when he'd kicked it back into life with his booted foot did he turn to catch Liselle's eye. Never breaking her gaze, he advanced to kneel on one knee beside the tub.

Ignoring the sounds of her protests bubbling from under the water, he plunged his hand into the tub, and firmly grasping her submerged foot, pulled it out.

In the bright firelight, he could see a black tattoo of a viper gracing her slender ankle.

She twisted her foot but to no avail. His grip was strong.

The mark was a finely wrought one. He could see the fine scales of the snake and its venomous tongue curving around her flesh.

And then Liselle rose up enough out of the water to say, "Leave! At once! Pascal would strike you dead without question if he saw you now!"

But he paid little heed to her warning.

Curious, he rose to sit on the edge of the tub, and gripping her ankle even tighter, he drew it across his knee and rubbed his thumb along her skin.

"This mark. What is it?" he asked in a soft rumble.

For a moment, he didn't think she would answer, but then her alto voice replied, "Something that is death for you to see."

His quizzical gray eyes met hers.

Jerking her foot free, she immersed it quickly. "I am not free, as you are," she said bitterly. I am forever cursed, marked as an assassin."

Sorrow washed over him. Then it was true. The lass truly was an assassin.

And then she turned her head away to plead again, "Please, leave."

"Nay, I'll not go," Julian swore with deep intent. Nay, he'd not let this lass be used in games of power. She was more than a tool for the Vindictam. "Tell me how ye might be freed from this curse, lass. 'Tis clear that it is your wish, aye?"

Her hazel eyes dilated, and for a moment, he thought he saw the glitter of tears in them, but when she spoke, her voice was strong and harsh. "I cannot leave, Lord Gray."

"And why canna ye leave, lass?" he asked tenderly, his voice sounding thick to his own ears.

She drew her brows into a line and remained silent.

He couldn't fault the lass for her loyalty. Aye, he respected it. But, mayhap if she understood that he already knew some of her secrets, she might reveal more. "Tell me more of the Vindictam and the Electus, lass," he said.

"Those are words that you may not know!" she gasped, horrified.

"Yet, I know them," he said gently.

Her face was suffused with fear and dismay. "These are unspeakable secrets, secrets that I cannot betray! Already, I have revealed far too much," she whispered, closing her eyes. "Already, you know too much. They will not allow you to live."

Sliding his hand along the rim of the tub, he chuckled and replied lightly, "Then what's the harm of knowing more if I'm a dead man even now?"

"I do not jest, Lord Gray," she replied with a firm scowl. "And if you are gentleman, you would leave me to my privacy at once!"

Her eyes were large in the dim light, and then with a bitter twist of her lip, she said, "I would that I had never left *La Serenìsima*. Life was simple then, living for the promise of the future. Had I known then …" Her voice trailed away. And then she turned on him suddenly and said, "Leave. You shouldn't be here."

"I'll not be leaving, lass," he said, rising to his feet and walking to the window. He opened the shutters a crack. The clouds had fled to reveal the face of the moon, lighting up the castle grounds. "I'll fix my eyes upon the moon long enough for ye to make yourself decent, Lady Gray."

She didn't hesitate.

He could hear the soft lap of water as she exited the tub, and then the rustle of clothing. 'Twas strange. He would have thought such a circumstance would have filled him with lusty thoughts, but instead, he was only consumed with worry over Liselle's safety. He didn't stop to think exactly what that might mean.

"You should fear Pascal," her voice filtered through the darkened chamber.

Turning, he spied her standing in the shaft of moonlight falling from the window. She looked magnificent in a simple blue gown with sleeves that swept almost to her knees, her long hair twisting down her back in shimmering waves of silk.

"I've never once run from the face of fear, lass," he assured, his cheek creasing into a wry grin. "Come with me." He held out his hand.

"It is not so simple, Lord Gray." Her laugh was bitter. "For the women of the Vindictam, there is no way out. One of us tried to leave once. Pippa."

"Pippa?" he repeated the name curiously.

Her eyes took on a distant look. Floating to his side, her voice dropped into a low storyteller's whisper. "Pippa was an assassin of the Vindictam, Lord Gray. Her knowledge of herbs was exceeded by no one. She was unmatched in both beauty and the art of poison. And she was greatly revered and respected by all, but even *she* had to pay the ultimate price when she fell in love with the man she had sworn to slay." Her eyes took on a distant look.

"And?" Julian prompted when she did not continue.

She shook her head a little, as if shaking herself awake, and then she turned her face up towards the moon and closed her long lashes. "A nobleman. A Scottish nobleman was to die by her hand, but she refused. A trap was laid for her. Her lover was betrayed and imprisoned. She rescued him and lost her life for it, but not before she'd enacted vengeance. Painting poison upon her lips, she kissed each corrupt lord and won her lover's freedom, leaving a legendary trail of bodies along the way."

"If her lips were as beckoning as ye claim, then 'twas not a bad way to die," Julian inserted lightly as she lapsed into silence once again.

Liselle frowned. "In the Vindictam, the women are the assassins, Lord Gray. We are raised from birth to kill, and once we have the tongue ..." She paused a moment, and then lifting the hem of her skirt, pointed to her ankle. "Once we have the tongue upon our mark, there is no room for failure, my lord. If we fail, we become the hunted. Hunted by our very own brothers, if need be."

A cold chill washed over Julian. Could it be true? The women of the Vindictam? At once, an image of Nicoletta fled across his mind. The Scottish Court had harbored an assassin for many years.

"An unusually cruel fate, Lady Gray," was all he could think to say.

She turned to him then and grasped his shoulder earnestly. "Should they discover you know this, they will hunt you down. You must leave. Leave at once! Go very far away from here!"

Her eyes held an unmistakable plea, stunning eyes that seemed to devour him. He saw many things there. Fear. Desire. Despair.

Gently, he closed his hand over hers. "Then come with me, lass," he said, surprising himself with the genuineness of his request. Aye, he could think of nothing he wanted more than to have her at his side throughout the years.

"I ... may not," she said with a hiss of indrawn breath.

"May not, or will not?" Julian questioned, searching her face. "What aren't ye telling me, lass?"

"I may not choose ..." she began, but then grimaced and said instead, "What does it matter? You are now a dead man. You know too much, Lord Gray."

"So ye insist upon telling me, lass," he replied with a shrug. Catching her by the wrist, he pulled her close and tucked a wayward strand of hair behind her ear. "Come with me. I'll see that ye willna be harmed."

With a snort, she placed her hands upon his chest and pushed him away. "Even *Le Marin* is no match for the Vindictam. Go before you are found here."

"And your tongue?" he asked, indicating her ankle. "If ye fail in assassinating Dolfin, what then?"

She glanced at him sharply, and her eyes widened in surprise for a moment, but then she replied, "I have not been chartered to kill him, my lord—"

There was a knock on the door.

Jerking back in alarm, Liselle gasped. "You must go! It must be Pascal!"

He was loath to leave her presence, there was still so much to say.

"Liselle?" Pascal's distinctive tone filtered through the wooden door.

Planting a soft kiss on the back of her hand, Julian briefly folded Liselle in his arms, and then throwing the shutters open wide, he promised, "I will return. This isna' over, lass. Not at all."

And then without waiting for a reply, he swung his booted feet over the window ledge, and finding a purchase for his toes, climbed down far enough to drop safely onto the ground below.

Over his head, he could hear her speaking with Pascal for only a moment before the door slammed shut.

With a muffled oath, he sprinted for cover, heading for the chapel. Aye, he'd follow the lad. As Electus, Pascal was a key to be used.

And as he waited, bits and pieces of Liselle's conversation played through his mind.

The lass was trapped. Nay, she was enslaved. A victim. A victim who could be forced to kill his mentor, Dolfin. And if she failed to escape her charter … he refused to finish the thought. He had to find a way to save them both.

He waited for a time, but Pascal did not appear.

And when he finally went in search of him, he found no sign of the lad. It was as if he'd never been there at all.

Disconcerted, Julian returned to the chapel and positioned himself near the window with a good view of Liselle's chamber. Propping his booted feet on the back of a chair, he settled in for a long night.

Dawn arrived, and with it came the English army.

As Gloucester's men covered the heath outside of Edinburgh, any support that Albany had gained evaporated in an instant. He was left with no choice but to reconcile and concede the throne to James with a public declaration of brotherly love and kindness.

But Julian wasn't interested in royal politics.

He sought Liselle. He had to find a way to aid the lass.

He found her in the company of Kate and her ladies as they sat in the morning sun, taking up their needles to embroider upon bits of silk. And for a time, he watched her from under his brows.

How could he truly set her free? And if he were to set her free, what then?

Different possibilities whirled through his mind, most of them centered upon whisking her away to Castle Huntly, to be held safely in his arms. But then Cameron's deep voice shattered his concentration.

"Albany's not entirely daft," the earl observed as his lips crooked into a smile. "Now he sees that his plans for the throne have unraveled."

"Then he's switched sides?" Julian asked, clearing his mind of Liselle—at least for the moment. "And Gloucester?"

"We'll surrender Castle Berwick to the English," Cameron replied, the slight twist of his lip revealing his annoyance. "And forfeit Princess Cecily's betrothal. We'll repay what coin we've received for her dowry to Edward, and then 'twill be the end of this mad affair."

"Albany won't stop." Julian arched a brow riddled with disdain. "He'll only have enough when his mouth is filled with earth from his own grave. The man doesna know the meaning of loyalty. I'm sure this is no more than a mere pause between acts in a play, a play that will soon see him trying to seize the throne again."

"Mayhap," Cameron agreed readily enough, but then his voice adopted a humorous tone. "But at the moment, lad, I'm far more curious over another matter."

"Aye?" Julian grunted.

Cameron's dark eyes sparkled with amusement. "Why do I find ye spying on your wee wife?"

Julian drew back sharply.

And then Cameron reached over to clap him on the shoulder and laugh. "Aye then, I've a truce to finish, lad. But we'll speak soon. There's a tale here that I must know." And then with a cordial nod, he excused himself.

Drawing his brows into a line, Julian turned back to Liselle.

But she was gone.

* * *

Begging a headache as an excuse, Liselle left the company of the countess and returned to her chamber. She was scarce in the frame of mind to push a needle through cloth.

The evening before, she had told Pascal of the Saluzzo's venomous words.

Her cousin had responded with a blasé shrug and the comment that if the man started a war, then he would rejoice. Frankly, he had seemed disappointed that only a few of the Saluzzi were obsessed with breaking the truce.

But then, what had she expected from Pascal?

And after making her swear, once again, not to mention the matter to Orazio, he had slipped away into the darkness.

Liselle scowled.

If only Orazio were here, he would know what needed to be done.

Frustrated, she struck her palm against the stones. And then falling back upon years of habit, she channeled her frustration into action. Slipping her bone-handled stiletto from her sleeve, she took aim. The stiletto flew through the air, hitting the chamber door, dead center.

Marching across the room, she yanked the slim weapon free and targeted the beam above the window.

Again, her aim was true. And again. And again. But each time she heard the thud of the blade striking home, her frustration only grew.

Lord Gray was dangerous to her peace of mind! *Come with me!* How dare he say that to her. She could never do so. The Vindictam would never allow it. She had behaved so foolishly of late, spending far too much time dreaming of his kisses and the touch of his skin on hers.

And Orazio! How could he expect her to kill an old man? The thought was abhorrent. She had to find some way of keeping Dolfin out of harm's reach for good, before Orazio appeared again to give her the final order.

Santo Ciélo! Why couldn't her brother simply let the old man be? He would die a natural death soon enough.

She could only hope that her next target would be someone clearly evil, a far more palatable proposition.

And then a sudden knock on the heavy wooden door shattered her thoughts. Sliding her stiletto into its hidden sheath, she opened the door and gasped.

It was Orazio.

Flinging her arms around her laughing brother's neck, Liselle cried out in a mixture of relief and delight.

"Let me see you, *cara mia!*" Orazio finally ordered, stepping back to hold her at arm's length as his noble face took on a stern look. Peering down at her along his angular nose, he asked, "Are you well? Where is your color? Have you been ill?"

His lip twisted, and she could tell he wasn't pleased with her appearance, but she was so thrilled to see him that she brushed his concern aside and instead asked for news of Nicoletta and the rest of the family.

For a time, Orazio humored her requests as he folded his ebony-hooded cloak and brushed the lint off of his black-velvet doublet. And then seating himself in a chair, he stretched out his fine leather boots and let out a whistle.

Liselle blinked in surprise as the door opened once again to reveal Pascal upon the threshold.

Clad in a white, long-sleeved muslin shirt with black hose and a wide leather belt, her angelic cousin stared down at her through half-closed lids. "Good day, *bábia*."

"*Bábio*." Liselle frowned in response.

Gracefully propping the door open with his foot, he leaned back into the hall and reappeared with a covered cage.

Liselle's heart stood still.

Pigeons.

"Your time has come, *bábia*," Pascal muttered in overt disapproval as he pushed past her to set the cage upon the writing desk.

Liselle held her breath. Her time to kill had come at last. But strangely, she felt only apprehension and despair. There was none of the eager enthusiasm that she had long dreamt would accompany the moment.

Woodenly, she turned to face Orazio.

Her brother watched her closely as he drummed his fingers on the arm of his chair. His eyes, always so warm and welcoming, were now cold and hard as he said, "You know that you cannot fail."

Liselle's mouth went dry, but she managed to nod all the same.

Could she kill an old man? She *had* spent her whole life preparing for it. She stared into her brother's eyes. She had always wanted his approval and acknowledgment of her skills.

There was truly no choice for her in this. She would *have* to kill Dolfin.

Orazio straightened his black doublet with calm authority and began, "A di Franco does not shy away from duty. You will not fail. I have faith in you."

"Pah!" Pascal inserted darkly. "She is not a killer. How many times must I tell you not to do this? She does not have the heart to truly be one of us."

Orazio's eyes merely flicked at him before falling back expectantly upon Liselle. "Then are you ready to receive your orders, *sorèlina*?" he asked.

What could she do? Numbly, she unsheathed her stiletto and nicked the tip of her finger. And as a single drop fell from it, she whispered the expected vow: "My life is yours to command. I am *Vindictam*. I am revenge."

Suddenly, Orazio caught her chin and held it still to search her face. "I fear for you, but I have no choice, *cara sorèlina*," he said in an almost desperate tone. "I have been told that you spilled Saluzzi blood on behalf of Lord Julian Gray."

Liselle grimaced.

So the Saluzzo had been speaking the truth.

"The Saluzzi yet again," Pascal interrupted with a dangerous smile. "Are we their puppets?"

Orazio raised a mild brow his direction. "This matter is none of your concern, Pascal."

Thankful for the distraction, Liselle reminded herself that she was well-practiced in the art of deception. *Òsti*! This was a most trying test! Taking a deep breath, she was ready when Orazio turned upon her once again.

"I do not know what you speak of—" she began.

But Orazio cut her off brusquely. "Antonio Saluzzo himself informed me that Lord Gray carries the stiletto that saved him close to his heart."

Liselle's lips parted, strangely thrilled at the thought of her stiletto in Julian's keeping.

"And Antonio demands retribution, a heavy price that you alone will pay," her brother continued harshly. "To keep our fragile peace, I have agreed to his demands, even to that of hosting the Saluzzi at my lodgings until the matter's been settled. They will ensure that the retribution has been paid by no one other than you, *cara sorèlina.*"

"Are we to answer to the *Saluzzi?*" Pascal asked in a deadly tone.

Orazio turned upon his cousin. "*Basta!* If this is all an error then let me see the proof." And turning to Liselle, he commanded in a voice that brooked no argument, "Show me *both* of your stilettos, Liselle. At once."

But Pascal stepped forward before she could respond. "This is a Saluzzi trap, Orazio, can't you see that? They merely found out that I took one of her stilettos to be repaired. The pommel had cracked," the youth lied boldly. And with a contemptuous tilt of his chin, he added, "But I find it strange that you trust the words of a Saluzzo so readily! Has the Vindictam become their plaything to toss about at will?"

Orazio sent him a sharp glance. "For the last time, Pascal, this is not your concern. Be quiet, and if you do not heed my words, I will order you to leave this chamber."

Pascal's eyes narrowed. For a moment, it appeared that he would object, but then he moved to gracefully slouch against the wall and idly inspect his fingers. But there was anger in his dark eyes.

"I will do anything to see the Vindictam uphold the peace with the Saluzzi, as Antonio will do for his part," Orazio said, adopting a somber tone. "He could renew the war over this, but he has refrained."

Pascal snorted.

Ignoring him, Orazio moved to lay a heavy hand upon Liselle's shoulder and demanded, "You must not become enamored with Lord Julian Gray*, cara sorèlina.*"

"I will not, I swear it!" Liselle replied, desperately summoning her training once again. *Gexondìo*! But he was now going to give her the order to kill Dolfin. Could she truly do it?

"Do you not remember the tale of Pippa?" Orazio asked softly.

Ignoring her rioting emotions, Liselle forced her voice to remain strong and calm. "I am not Pippa, Orazio!" How many times had she said those words?

But Orazio continued, as if he hadn't heard her. "Pippa fell in love with the man she was to slay and lost her life for it!"

"I am not in love!" Liselle protested, but the words sounded weak even to her own ears.

"*Diàmbarne*! What secret do these Scottish men hold that breaks the bonds of blood?" Orazio asked almost to himself. His face was pale.

Liselle pressed her lips firmly together. Orazio clearly feared that she would fail, but she could not let his apprehension consume her. Forcing her lips into a smile, she insisted once again, "But I am not Pippa, Orazio!"

The nostrils of his angular nose flared, and his fingers gripped her shoulders even harder. "You cannot fail me, Liselle! You must accomplish this mission!"

"I will, Orazio," she vowed, still smiling even as her soul cried out in anguish for the old salt spy.

"Then hear your orders," Orazio intoned.

Nothing could have prepared Liselle for her brother's next words.

"You must kill Lord Julian Gray."

16

THE CAGE OF PIGEONS

Masking her turbulent emotions behind cool eyes, Liselle faced her brother, but before she could speak a word, Pascal interrupted.

"Why Lord Gray? The man is just a drunkard. Why do we care of the fate of such men?" His voice was calm and courteous. Strangely so. "This is not the way of the Vindictam."

"Though I owe you no explanation, I shall answer," Orazio replied, sending Pascal a curious yet annoyed look. "Antonio desires to test Liselle's loyalty to us all."

"Then Antonio is our puppet master," Pascal observed, his lips curling into a slight sneer.

Liselle swallowed. The words of the thick-browed Saluzzo made sense now. She bowed her head. He had wanted her blood, but had settled for her heart.

Orazio's voice took on an aristocratic tone. "I see no fault in his demand. Liselle has spilled Saluzzi blood and thus must prove her loyalty to the truce by taking Lord Gray's life."

At that, Pascal's tranquility fled. His dark eyes flared with passion as he practically spat, "Why do we care a fig for what the falling house of the Saluzzi desires? Even a suckling babe can see the Saluzzi for the treacherous fools that they are! This truce was an error that will soon be remedied!"

"Do you *hope* for war, Pascal?" Orazio asked harshly as his face hardened. "Know that I will not allow it! And neither will Antonio! If either of us sees treachery even amongst our own brothers, we will root it out for the greater good of all!"

"It does not matter how you sweeten things. The Saluzzi are nothing more than vultures feeding from rotten carcasses!" Pascal's tone was cold and deadly. "They are undeserving of peace. Their hearts are black and their deeds foul, and not one is worthy of walking the face of this earth."

At that, Orazio made a chopping motion with his hand and ordered, "*Cestìl*! Enough of your hatred. Do not force me to cause you harm, but such words are traitorous now!"

Their gazes locked.

And then Orazio sighed, and glancing away, said in a softer voice, "When I was younger, I would have said such words myself, but now I see that it's time to end such wanton bloodshed. And if the blood of a drunken fool such as Lord Gray can preserve this peace, then it will be done!"

"*Òstrega!*" Pascal swore, and then lifting his lip in dark amusement, he continued, "The latest tidings from Venice have all but proven the Saluzzi have broken this farce of a truce already. Liselle should be applauded, nay, greatly rewarded for drawing the blood of traitors!"

Liselle stared at her cousin in astonishment. Never had she seen Pascal speak with such vehemence.

Even Orazio was surprised, but for quite a different reason. "And what tidings from Venice are these?" he asked stiffly. "I have received none. If there was such proof, indeed, I would know of it before you."

Pascal didn't even blink. With a haughty tilt of his chin, he brushed Orazio's question aside as if it were of little consequence.

But their gazes locked again, and for an even longer time they glared at one another in awkward silence.

And then Orazio's shrewd eyes fell upon Liselle once more, and he ordered brutally, "Lord Gray dies before the sun sets, Liselle. This very evening."

It was all Liselle could do not to shrink back from his penetrating stare. Gripping the edge of the desk to steady herself, she forced her voice to reply evenly, "As you wish, Orazio."

Pointing to the pigeons, he said, "I will be staying with the Venetian salt merchants in town, and the Saluzzo will be my … *guest*. The bird that you send when the deed is done will find us there."

Liselle swallowed.

She knew very well there was only one reason the Saluzzi would insist upon having one of their own stay with her brother until her message had been received. If she failed to send the pigeon by sunset, the Saluzzi would force her family to slay her. And if they refused, the truce would be broken, and the war would begin again. Orazio would be the first to die.

Orazio read the fear in her eyes, and a sympathetic expression crossed his face. Giving her shoulder an encouraging clasp, he urged, "I have faith in you. Stay strong and wary, *cara*. You can do this and do it well in the manner befitting a di Franco."

Liselle bowed her head. And even as a despair stronger than she'd ever known to be possible washed over her, she whispered, "May I prove worthy of the honor."

"You have not disappointed me, *sorèlina cara*," Orazio said, more to himself than to anyone else. "You will honor our family."

A month ago those words would have made her heart soar. Now they felt like leaden weights. Never before had she lied to her brother. Every word she had spoken had been false. Blood and loyalty? *Òsti!* There was no solution to this! How could she spill Julian's blood? But if she did not, could she see her own brother and cousin die?

"Then send us word when the deed is done," Orazio repeated crisply, indicating the caged pigeons again with a curt nod.

"Yes, Orazio," she murmured woodenly.

"Then I must be gone," her brother said with one last encouraging smile.

Discipline allowed her to compose her features and escort him to the door. But upon the threshold, Orazio paused, sending Pascal a questioning brow.

"Allow me to tarry a moment," Pascal answered the unspoken question.

Orazio hesitated, but then with a nod, spun on his heel and quitted the chamber.

As his footsteps faded away, Liselle's veins turned into rivers of ice. But she could not panic yet. She still had Pascal in the room, watching her every minute expression.

"*Diàmbarne!*" he swore, striking the wall with his fist. "Why does Orazio insist on dancing to whatever music the Saluzzi play?"

Liselle bit her lip, unable to trust her voice to form a reply.

And then Pascal's voice cut through the chamber. "You find this order ... distasteful?"

Composing her face, Liselle turned to meet his sharp gaze. In a firm tone, she replied as he would have expected. "I belong to the Vindictam first."

He didn't believe her. That much was clear. "Then I will observe with interest what harm you can do," he drawled with a mocking smile. "Particularly to the one you love."

Love.

The word was a powerful one, and suddenly she couldn't trust herself to speak. Ducking her head, she smoothed her skirts and fought to control her emotions.

But if Pascal noticed her discomposure, he didn't show it.

Moving to the window, he peered out of the shutters and shook his head in disgust. "And I thought England to be a land forlorn of refinement,

Scotland is even more barbaric. I fail to see how Nicoletta survived here for so long. 'Tis no small wonder she took ill rather than return to this purgatory!'"

As his litany of complaints continued, Liselle closed her eyes, grateful for a moment to regain even a shred of control.

"I grow exceedingly weary of this place. The sun never tarries for long, but at least they do not even attempt to make wine here," Pascal commented as he abandoned the window to lounge against the door once again. And then peering down at her through half-shuttered eyes, he warned suddenly, "Have a care with Lord Gray. I'd wager the man is not what he seems, *bábia*. I would fain prefer to keep my blade clean of your blood this night."

Liselle swallowed. Lord Gray certainly *was* much more. And not because he was *Le Marin*, but because she loved him. She closed her eyes as the magnitude of her situation truly began to take hold of her.

And then Pascal's hand snaked out to grab her forearm tightly, his fingers digging into her flesh. "Can you do this?"

Liselle gave a bitter laugh that rang hollow. "I was born for this. How can I not?" It was a lie, but how could she say anything else?

"Walk away," he ordered with a dark look.

Startled, her eyes went wide. "What are you saying? I cannot run. I am being watched, and I have received the tongue! Orazio *himself* would hunt me!" *O ciélo*, but was there a way out of this?

"I would see that you were not hunted," Pascal vowed, his dark eyes blazing passionately.

Liselle wrenched her arm free. "And who are *you*?" Her voice was unsteady. "Why speak such drivel? You cannot change the laws of the Vindictam!"

He gave a rich laugh before whispering under his breath, "No. Not yet."

"Yet?" She laughed herself, but there was no mirth in it. "Even with your strange connections, Pascal, you have no real power here. No one can stop this save the Dominus Granditer." She swallowed, catching her shaking breath.

Pascal drew his lips into a thin line as he clamped both hands upon her shoulders. "Then outwit them all, *bábia*. Do not disappoint me! Ever have you excelled in games of treachery! Your presence of mind and skills are unparalleled. Outwit them all!"

Again, Liselle glanced up at her cousin, surprised at his genuine tone of concern. Pascal was only growing more complicated and mysterious each day. And he hadn't betrayed her to Orazio. But did that mean he was an ally, or was it merely that his hatred of the Saluzzi was so strong that he cared for nothing else?

"Or," Pascal continued, his voice dropping into a familiar belittling pattern. "Or you can do what you are most likely to do, *bábia*. You can pretend you cannot find the man and pray that he stays away."

And with that parting barb, he opened the door and was gone.

Liselle wasn't certain how long she stared at the empty passageway before the cooing of the pigeons gradually broke through her thoughts. Closing the chamber door, she returned to stand in the center of her room.

She would not kill Lord Gray. Her heart would not allow that. Nor would it allow her to betray Orazio.

"Why does heaven hate me so?" Liselle heard her own voice gasp. It sounded thin and far away, as if it belonged to someone else.

She stood there a moment as a wave of panic threatened to consume her, but she closed her eyes and steeled her resolve. She could not waver now. To waver now would be to lose.

But what could she do?

No matter which path she took, it could only end in death.

She left her chamber in a daze. Somehow, she had stumbled her way down from the castle and onto Edinburgh's streets, and was only dimly aware of the afternoon sun beating down upon her face.

Numbly, she wove through the crowds.

A fanfare of trumpets sounded from the castle above, and as the last notes died away, she was dimly aware of the mighty gates creaking open and a company of horsemen riding forth led by Albany and King James himself.

And as the Royal Stewarts approached, the crowd of shopkeepers and bystanders thronged around her, craning their necks as they jostled and bumped elbows, striving for a better view.

As if in a dream, she watched the parade of royals.

Albany rode at James' side, his head held high and his lips curved upwards in a smile, but his green eyes glittered in anger. And then the Royal Stewarts had passed, proceeding down the Royal Mile to enter Holyroodhouse as the bronze bell sounded from the church tower.

17

THE BONE-HANDLED STILETTO

There was no denying it. She had failed. The words rang in her head, over and over. She could think of nothing else.

And then Liselle found herself standing in her chamber once more, having no recollection of how she had gotten there. The window was open, and the rays of the afternoon sun made sharp shadows on the wall. Behind her, she could hear the cooing of the pigeons.

Woodenly, she smoothed her skirt and tucked her stray curls beneath her bejeweled hairnet. There was no hope. She felt it like a fist in her belly. She would truly die this night.

With her hands involuntarily clenching, she moved to stare down at the gray birds in the cage.

Mayhap it was not too late to give the Saluzzo his chance at revenge.

The sun had not yet set.

Yes, she would die, but not at the hand of her brother. She would spare him that pain, at least. And she would do her best to protect his life should he refuse to slay her.

With a numb sense of resignation, she took a sheet of parchment from her writing desk, and tearing off a narrow strip, dipped her quill in the ink and wrote the words of defeat:

Saluzzo, I give you my blood for his. I await my fate at the feast.

Sprinkling sand over the wet ink, she read the message several times, feeling nothing. And then reaching into the cage, selected one of the birds and carefully tied the message to its leg.

Orazio had said the Saluzzi would be waiting with him for her pigeon at the salt merchants. It would not be the message they expected, but she knew it was her only choice.

Cradling the pigeon's softness against her cheek, she moved to the window and opened her hands.

The bird bounded away, ascending to fly in lazy circles in the sky before suddenly turning east to swoop over the city and disappear amongst the rooftops.

She didn't know how long she had stood there until she was shaken from her reverie by the church bells tolling in the distance. And then there were shouts at the castle gates, and Albany and James reappeared with great fanfare, apparently finished with their parade of unity.

The feast would start soon.

She did not know how quickly the Saluzzo would arrive, but the salt merchants were not far away.

With a heavy sigh, Liselle closed her eyes.

Her fate was sealed. By now, her message had been read.

It was done.

A ripple of anger washed over her. The Saluzzi were despicable. She could understand Pascal's hatred of them now.

And Nicoletta. Tears threatened when she thought of her sister. She squeezed her eyes shut and forced the tears away. Nicoletta had been so worried for her. And as usual, Nicoletta had been right.

Returning to her desk, she dipped her quill in the inkpot once more to write her sister a letter of farewell, but she had only succeeded in writing Nicoletta's name upon a fresh sheet of parchment before tears blinded her eyes, and she could not write more.

Instead, she unsheathed her bone-handled stiletto and placed it on top of the page.

Her sister would understand.

Gathering her courage, she stood, preparing to leave for the feast when a hand caught her elbow and spun her around.

"'Twas ye in Fotheringhay, lass," Julian's soft burr whispered, but his gray eyes were riveted upon the stiletto on the desk.

Strangely, she felt nothing upon seeing him. Not even surprise as she observed the irony. Yes, she had saved his life in Fotheringhay, but it had only brought about the current events which demanded that she take his life now.

"*Santo Ciélo!* What curse *is* this?" she whispered.

Julian's fingers gripped her shoulders hard to give her a little shake. "Tell me what this is about, lass! Sweet Mary! Dinna hide this from me! Let me help ye!"

But Liselle cold only stare at him, feeling nothing more than a cold detachment.

Through the window, she could hear the wailing of the pipes announcing the feast. She could not risk being late. This was her last chance to save Julian.

Slowly, she lifted her hand to cup his cheek and whispered, "Dream of me." Yes, she could die this night if she knew she would live forever in his heart.

And then twisting free from his grasp, she picked up her skirts and ran, ignoring his calls for her to stay. She was no coward. She would face her fate with her chin held high.

Quickly, she made her way to the castle hall.

Pausing on the threshold, she searched for any sign of the Saluzzi, but the great hall was crowded, and the light was dim. The place was bedecked for a sumptuous feast, a feast to celebrate the renewed peace between James and his brother, Albany. Fine linen graced the tables, and the enticing fragrance of fresh bread mingled with the scent of cloves and oranges. Musicians played their lutes.

But still, she saw no sign of the Saluzzi or the Vindictam.

And then trumpets sounded, announcing the arrival of the king and his royal brother, and Liselle quickly found a seat.

As if in a dream, she watched the Royal Stewarts parade in their regal trappings through the hall.

This was her last feast.

With a removed interest, she noted the king's satin doublet was trimmed with a lace collar in the fashion of the French, and that the man appeared pale and sad.

From the corner of her eye, she thought she spied a black-cloaked figure, but when she whirled there was no one there.

Frowning, she turned back as the king passed by her less than an arm's length away. She could smell the distinct odor of whiskey.

Spirits.

Her eyes strayed over the table and lit upon a bottle of wine.

She didn't hesitate.

Grabbing the bottle, she filled her goblet and drained the contents in a single draught as Cameron and a number of Scottish lords arrived to take their places at the king's high table.

Pouring more wine, Liselle sipped slowly as she scanned the faces in the hall.

And then King James rose from his canopied chair and called for Albany.

The announcement was almost too garbled to understand. Apparently, Albany had received the titles of both Mar and Garioch. But the king had scarcely said the words before he succumbed to a bout of hysterical weeping, clutching his chest and calling out the name of

Thomas.

And then as Cameron drew the king away to escort him back to his apartments, Albany gladly stepped up to command that the feast should begin.

She had swallowed the last of her second goblet of wine when a man clothed in a black cloak appeared by one of the arched windows. Liselle's stomach lurched, but he only proved to be some Scottish lord with bright red hair and his arm in a sling.

Taking a deep breath, she poured another goblet of wine.

Òsti! Why did they make her wait? Was it for the enjoyment of the Saluzzo who sought her blood?

She closed her eyes and for a moment, let her heart ache for the simplicity of her life before, of gliding in gondolas through the narrow canals of Venice and drowsing in the sun to the lull of the gentle waters. She had watched the latest plays, dined on fresh figs, and perched on the clay-tiled rooftops at night with her feet bare, dreaming of the day she would venture forth as an assassin.

Her future had seemed so romantic then. Before she understood what it really meant to *be* an assassin.

But it was too late now.

Reaching for wine, she had half swallowed it when Julian's light-hearted laugh rang a short distance away.

The sound was like a knife through her heart.

She couldn't bear to look at him, yet she could not stop from glancing over her shoulder to watch him approach, impeccably clad in the white shirt and plaid that he seemed to favor.

She loved him.

She had for quite some time. There was no point in denying it now.

Seizing her goblet, she drained the rest of the sweet, heady wine only to desperately refill it yet again. Wine would numb the pain. Already, she felt its warmth coursing through her veins. She had just touched the goblet to her lips when Julian slid into the seat by her side.

"Mayhap ye should eat a little with all that wine, aye?" he asked with a playful grin as he tossed her an orange.

She watched it bounce and roll off the table.

Julian's brows knit in concern as his gaze grew hard. "Is your honor in need of avenging, lass?" His voice was soft and gentle but held a dangerous undertone.

The thought was preposterous. She was hardly helpless. She opened her mouth to retort, but hiccupped instead.

"*Santo Ciélo!*" she finally managed to say. "I would gut the man that tried! Yes! I would welcome it!" Especially this night. She slammed her fist on the table in emphasis even as she frowned a little at herself for her unusual response.

Mayhap it was the effects of the wine.

At her side, Julian chuckled and his cheek creased into a grin.

But then, a group of musicians arrived, followed by jugglers and jesters, and it was simply too much effort to shout over the noise.

And then more pipes began to play, and she winced at the sudden pain ringing in her head.

What was taking Orazio and the Saluzzo so long? Surely, they had gotten the message? Had the Saluzzo refused her bargain?

The wine bottle was empty, she reached for another, but Julian caught her wrist.

"Ho, lass!" He looked outright worried. "Ye've had a wee bit too much, aye?"

"No," she snapped with a glare, and slapping his hand aside, reached for the bottle anyway. At the moment, becoming drunken out of her wits was far more preferable to anything else she could think to do. It would make the entire thing easier for everyone involved.

It was difficult to refill her goblet, most of the wine splashed out, but she swallowed what remained in one huge gulp.

Julian waited until she had finished and then offered her a bit of roasted fowl on the tip of his dagger.

She scowled at him and turned her head away, feeling dizzy.

After some time, the performers went away, and the servants arrived with another course.

"Are ye feeling better now?" Julian's soft burr rumbled in her ear.

Liselle winced. His voice seemed unnaturally loud. Reaching for her goblet, she stretched her hand for the bottle of wine, but it danced away from her grasp.

"Hold still!" she snapped at it peevishly.

"Ach, 'tis enough wine, ye wee minx," Julian announced, reaching for the bottle himself.

"Leave me be!" Liselle bellowed.

He chuckled a little, but in a worried way. "If ye insist then!" he muttered under his breath.

Ignoring the weight of his steady gaze, Liselle tipped the bottle, mesmerized by the light of the candles playing in the stream of red wine pouring into her cup. It was a thing of beauty. She watched with numb appreciation as the deep red wine spilled over the edge and onto the white tablecloth to form a crimson pool.

"Ach, lass. 'Tis clear that ye are done." Julian's hand closed over hers.

"No!" she disagreed, shoving him back but knocking her goblet over in the process.

Stupefied, she watched as the goblet rolled off the table, and then she reached for the bottle to drink from it instead.

"No more. I insist," Julian said, firmly plucking the bottle from her fingers.

Liselle heaved a sigh, suddenly too tired to even be annoyed. "It will be over shoon," she said. Her tongue was heavy in her mouth, and it took some effort to enunciate the word again. "Soon."

"And what will be over, Lady Gray?" came his soft query.

Liselle closed her eyes. Already, she was weary. How had Nicoletta lived with the weight of her viper's tongue for so long?

"What are ye saying, Liselle?" Julian's deep voice asked.

Liselle. She smiled sadly. "I would that ... I had heard my name more upon your lipsh." She frowned and then corrected with a hiccup, "Lips."

"*Had?*" Seizing the word, he gripped her by the shoulders and twisted her around, forcing her to face him as he rested his arm protectively on the back of the chair.

"So bold and dangerous," she said wistfully, trailing a finger along his bottom lip. "I couldn't kill you. Pascal knew it. He knew I would fail."

And then realizing what she had said, she quickly covered her mouth with her hands to stem the tide of words. She was still a di Franco. She had failed as an assassin, but she could not betray the Vindictam.

Julian went still. "Pascal?"

Her hand dropped and she answered anyway. She couldn't stop. "He told me to run," she said, slurring the words, but she kept speaking. For some reason, it was simply a relief. "But the Salus ... the Saluss ..." She paused, frowning. When had her tongue become so difficult to control?

"The Saluzzi?" Julian supplied softly.

"Ah, yes. They forced Orazzzio ..." She almost giggled. Why hadn't she noticed before that her brother's name was so amusing to say?

"Forced your brother to …?" Julian probed gently.

"Make me kill you. As retri … retribu …" She frowned and then chose easier words. "Because I saved you in Fothin … Fothinhay. I spilled Slaushee blood, so I have to spill yours to stop the war." She blew her hair out of her face, relieved the difficult words were over. But then feeling nauseated, she leaned her head upon the table, closed her eyes, and added, "They said before the sun sets. Run! You should run. Be shafe and run."

But he didn't run.

Instead, Julian dropped his cheek next to hers. "Bonds between men and women dinna end that easily!" He growled in her ear. "Your kiss tells me that I've naught to fear from ye."

"*Bábio!*" she replied in a tormented whisper. She didn't want to think of his kiss. It just might wake her from her stupor, and she didn't want to wake up. The end would be easier to face if she were asleep. Desperately, she reached for another bottle of wine.

"There's no need to make yourself ill, Lady Gray." Julian chuckled as he slipped his arm around her waist and pulled her into a close, protective embrace.

Wearily, she laid her head upon his shoulder.

"Aye, 'tis been a strange road with ye, lass," he said, his voice rumbling deep in his chest. "How can I love ye?"

Love?

A shiver rippled down her spine, followed quickly by nausea and a pain ringing through her head. *Santo Ciélo!* Why had she drunk so much wine? And then clamping her palm on her forehead, she answered in a wounded tone, "Love? It is too late for love."

"I think not," he said, chuckling again.

She found his humor irritating. "I failed."

And then Julian swept her onto his lap with an easy arm and

murmured into her ear, "I'll settle the matter with Orazio, lass. And I'll be speaking with Pascal on the matter of your freedom."

She could only stare into his eyes. "Orazio will sh… shl…slay you on sight," she finally managed to say, wincing all the while. Each word felt like a dagger in her skull.

"Have faith in me, aye?" His tone was light and encouraging.

"I'll speak with Orrraazzzio," she insisted, and sliding from his lap, rose to her feet. But the world began to spin, and she desperately clawed at the table to regain her balance.

"Aye, and if ye canna even walk?" He was laughing outright.

Santo Ciélo! But how could he find so dire a matter humorous?

Sending him a dark scowl, she took a step forward. She didn't get far. The stones beneath her feet seemed to be moving.

"Aye, I'll just carry ye, lass," Julian's amused voice reverberated in her head as she was suddenly swept off her feet and tossed over his shoulder.

"But Orazzzzio will slay you on sight!" she protested and pounded his back with her hand. The movements made her stomach roil.

"Aye," Julian agreed easily enough and then added, "'Tis why we will speak with Pascal."

Why did he care to speak to her arrogant cousin? Pascal would do nothing to stave off this disaster, even if he could!

And then the world around her began to spin even more, and a wave of blackness rose to carry her away.

* * *

Liselle opened her eyes to the sound of Pascal's voice.

"Lord Gray," came her cousin's cool tones. "Your presence is … unexpected."

"Aye, 'tis not often ye speak with a dead man, aye?" Julian asked dryly. "Come in, come in. Allow me the pleasure of your company."

Pascal made a disagreeable sound, and there was a creaking of a door. "You are most considerate to invite me into my own chamber, Lord Gray."

Liselle opened her eyes.

She was lying on the bed in a chamber lit only by a few tapers. Julian lounged against the bedpost with his arms folded across his broad chest, and she could see Pascal's face as only a pale blur in the darkness near the door.

"I've waited for ye quite some time, lad," Julian informed him calmly. "Ye should know that neither Liselle nor I will be dying over this Saluzzi matter, and I'll be freeing your wee cousin from the web of the Vindictam this very night."

Pascal approached slowly and paused in the circle of light before replying, "Just hours ago, Albany was forgiven and his lands restored to him. Is that not so?"

"Aye, 'tis true enough," Julian admitted.

"Then you should know, Lord Gray, that we are neither as trusting nor forgiving as the Scottish," Pascal said, gracing him with a distinctly haughty gaze. "When we are betrayed, we seek vengeance. There are no exceptions."

"And what of loyalty, lad?" Julian raised a brow. "Do not the Vindictam care for such things?"

"Vengeance comes before loyalty, *bábio*," Pascal replied as a cool mask descended over his face.

Julian shrugged and adjusted his plaid. "Then ye'll never understand true power, lad. A man's fear is no match for a man's loyalty. Men who fight from loyalty canna be stopped."

Pascal hesitated.

Julian's cheek creased with a grin as he continued, "Blood loyalty is what ye've witnessed concerning Albany, not forgiveness. Ye've witnessed clan loyalty in uniting against the English, men setting aside their feuds to prevent a greater enemy from rising to destroy them all. Aye, there will be vengeance aplenty when the threat has gone."

There was a short silence, one in which Liselle struggled to a sitting position. Her effort was reward by an acute wave of nausea.

Pascal glanced at her, and waving a hand in her direction, said, "This is not something I can stop. I told her to run. She did not. Already, they are searching for her." His tone foretold only of doom.

"Then your rule will be a short one," Julian replied with a glint of ill humor in his gray eyes.

Pascal's head snapped back. "Rule? You clearly suffer from some delusion, Lord Gray."

"Do I?" Julian asked. Boldly meeting Pascal's gaze, he rose to stoop and adopt the gruff voice of the priest he'd pretended to be in Fotheringhay. "'Tis right glad I am, to see ye escaped the swine unscathed. *Forgive me, my child.*"

Pascal's dark eyes widened at the implication

"I'm done with this nonsense," Julian said, tossing his head. "Keep her safe, for I will return, and should one hair upon her head be harmed, 'twill not end well for ye, lad. Be ye Electus of the Vindictam or not."

"Do you think to threaten or to order me?" Pascal asked in soft outrage.

"Aye, I dinna fear ye." Julian's tone was self-assured and confident. "I know ye strive to speak in words harsh to the ear, and ye may not know it yet, lad, but ye've a bit of Scottish loyalty running through your heart. 'Tis the only reason ye would have told your wee cousin to run. Running stands against your precious rules of vengeance, does it not?"

Pascal remained still.

And then Julian leaned over Liselle and twisted a stray lock of her hair around his finger before bending down to kiss her lightly upon the forehead.

"Dinna worry, lass," he said as deep dimples accented his grin. "I'll see this undone this very night." He caught her fingers and pressed them to his lips.

"But, it is not that simple!" Liselle protested in alarm. "Orazio will slay you on sight! And the Saluzzi as well!"

"They are no match for me," he said, flashing a wicked grin.

"This is madness!" Liselle insisted, rising from the bed to grasp his arm.

But Julian adamantly removed her hand. Leaning forward, he whispered softly for her ears alone, "Nay, far from it, Lady Gray. I've a wee bit of proof that I gathered after ye saved me from the Saluzzo in Fotheringhay. 'Tis evidence of his treachery that'll stop this madness and set ye free. But stay here with Pascal. 'Tis the safest place for ye to be for now. Ye must trust me, lass. I swear I will not fail ye."

She wanted to trust him, but how could she? She knew the Vindictam better than he. But then with a bow, he strode through the chamber, out the door, and was gone.

There was no way she could have stopped him.

Desperately, she turned upon Pascal. "We must go after him! At once!"

"Why?" Pascal asked, looking down at her from dark, hooded eyes.

She turned away. There was no reason Pascal would help. Why should he? And then her eyes caught on the sky framed by the open window. The sky was still dark, but dawn was clearly peeking.

"What time is it?" she asked in alarm.

Pascal followed her gaze and shook his head. "A new morning arrives soon enough, *bábia*."

"Morning!" she echoed in a horrified whisper. "Then I have become the hunted already. It is too late!"

Her cousin snorted. "I expected so much more from you! I had really thought you would outwit them all." He shook his head in disappointment before explaining with a scowl, "We searched for you the entire night, Orazio and I."

She shuddered and closed her eyes, not wanting to think. They had been searching for her. "Then ... will you slay me now?" she whispered hoarsely. "Let Julian go, please. He has done nothing—"

"It was fair difficult for Orazio to escape his Saluzzi escort upon receiving your message. That man from Fotheringhay is mad!" Pascal interrupted her with a dark laugh. And then unsheathing a stiletto, he viciously drove it deep into the wooden surface of a nearby table.

Liselle jerked back in surprise.

"*Diàmbarne!*" Pascal swore. "Orazio destroyed that foolish message and searched for you in order to save you, *bábia*, not slay you! But by the time Orazio had evaded the Saluzzi and made it to the castle, you had left the feast and were nowhere to found. Orazio and I broke every law of the Vindictam this night. Every law that will see even me—*me*—become the hunted, should my betrayal be discovered!"

Liselle's mouth dropped open in surprise.

"I take offense at your astonishment," Pascal muttered under his breath.

Suddenly, there was a pounding at the door.

Pascal's dark head whipped around, and he warned her to be silent with a finger to his lips.

"I know you are there, Pascal!" a man's gruff voice replied. "Open the door at once! *Ale!* Orazio has been taken hostage by the Saluzzi! We must end this!"

Liselle gasped in alarm and would have cried out had not Pascal clamped his hand down hard over her mouth, the gold ring about his finger almost bruising her lip.

"Silence!" he hissed into her ear. "That man would see you dead. You must hide. He cannot see you."

She drew in a shuddering sob. *Santo Ciélo*, but this night was accursed!

"Hide!" Pascal whispered, shoving her towards the bed.

As his hand fell away, her eye caught on the ring glittering about his finger. It was an unusual ring with a bold symbol of a "V".

She recognized it immediately.

It was the same symbol she had seen upon the parchment from Dolfin's pouch, and it was suddenly difficult to breathe as the pieces fell into place. Her cousin's strange meetings with dark-cloaked men. His half-finished sentences. Julian's words just moments before.

Pascal was the Electus!

Her arrogant cousin was soon to be the Dominus Granditer over them all!

She stood there in shock.

"What are you doing?" Pascal's dark eyes widened in alarm. "Hide! For my sake, if not yours! I would not see you dead before I can stop this madness!"

But it was too late. The man had picked the lock.

The door banged back with a crash to reveal a man she recognized from the churchyard in Fotheringhay, a man she knew could only be one of the Quattuor Gladiis. And as his hand fell to his waist, she suddenly knew what to do.

Trusting her instincts, she darted behind Pascal, and placing the tip of her blade to his neck, applied enough pressure to draw blood.

"Halt!" she warned in her deadliest voice. "You must do as I say, or the Electus shall die!"

18

THE SALUZZI

"Bravo, *bábia!*" A dark smile crossed Pascal's lips. "Now, *this* is treachery! Though I fail to see your plan—"

"Hold still!" Liselle hissed in his ear. "Or else I'll not be able to save your worthless life for failing to slay me, *bábio.*"

"My lord?" The member of the Quattuor Gladiis gasped in alarm.

"Do as she commands, Venerio!" Pascal ordered curtly.

Liselle didn't allow herself to think, lest she lose her resolve. Summoning her haughtiest tone, she boldly met Venerio's gaze and lied, "I have poisoned my blade, and I alone know the antidote. So, heed my words well if you wish to cure the Electus of the poison that even now works its way towards his heart."

Venerio ran his hand through his graying hair, and his lined face was clearly shocked, but he managed to nod quickly enough. "As you wish."

"Then escort us to Antonio Saluzzo and his men with haste," Liselle continued imperiously.

"*Antonio?*" Pascal asked in astonishment.

Liselle didn't hesitate to press her blade deeper into his neck. "You are in no position to question me!" she replied in an imperious tone.

He scowled.

Turning back to Venerio, Liselle commanded, "Inform the Saluzzi we are coming and that we bear a great gift for them! But if they harm one hair upon Orazio's head, their chance for true retribution will have been lost forever! And you must find Lord Julian Gray. He has proof of a Saluzzi deception which might aid us."

The man hesitated.

Liselle raised a cool brow. "If you hesitate, then know that the blood of the Electus is upon your head."

"As you command! As you command!" Venerio waved his hands in a chopping motion. "I will saddle the horses and escort you myself, but it will take time. Our sources say Antonio has taken to the Carmelite catacombs near Linlithgow Palace which is some hours ride away!"

Liselle hid her surprise, but hardened her voice. "Then let us ride while the world still sleeps. We leave at once."

As she prodded Pascal forward, he waved her hand aside impatiently.

"Put your blade away, Liselle," he said with a sneer. "The poison already courses through my veins. You have my word that neither I nor my men will disobey your command, lest you withhold the *antidote*."

At first, Liselle hesitated, but then at Pascal's nod, she reluctantly complied. They would move quicker that way.

As they exited the chamber, Pascal sent her a dark scowl, mouthing the single question, *Antonio*? But she could not explain herself to him. Not yet. Not when she was relying on instinct alone.

Praying that she had not just made the biggest blunder of her life, she donned a black cloak and filed silently behind them as they slipped through the passageways and out into the cold darkness. The castle gates were closed, but Venerio bribed the guards with a few coins, and they were swiftly allowed to pass.

Hurrying through the deserted streets, Liselle glanced up at the remaining stars twinkling as the dawn approached. Closing her eyes briefly, she implored the heavens to aid her as Venerio guided them to the city walls. And after announcing he would fetch horses and see her orders delivered, he left them there to wait.

"Antonio?" Pascal asked again the moment Venerio was out of sight.

Liselle took a deep breath. Her cousin's hatred of the Saluzzi had blinded him to the implication of their request for only Julian's death as retribution for her deed. Antonio had clearly wished to avoid breaking the truce, else new war between them would have already begun.

Or so she hoped to believe.

If she were proved wrong, then she would offer her life to the Saluzzi again. She would give it up in exchange for her brother, as she could not see him die any more than she could Julian.

But she could scarcely share these thoughts with Pascal. Taking a deep breath, she faced him and said, "We must give Julian the chance to reveal the treachery of the Saluzzo who tried to attack him. Then all will be made right."

Pascal's dark eyes narrowed. "Lord *Gray?* You trust that scandalous drunkard?"

"Yes," Liselle whispered, clenching her fists tightly.

He snorted, tossing his head a little, and his dark eyes glittered. "I'm not a fool, Liselle. 'Tis clear the man is more than he seems, but what if some mischief were to befall him this night? Even *Le Marin* can fall victim to misfortune in a town overrun with Vindictam and Saluzzi."

Liselle took an involuntary step back. Pascal *knew! Santo Ciélo!* But her cousin was proving uncommonly keen of late. "Since when?" she asked in a strangled whisper.

He knew what she meant and smiled. "Before you, I am certain," came his reply.

"Then you must know that he will not fail," was all she said. What else was there to say?

They were silent for a time, but as the first rays of sun spilled over the horizon, Pascal began to pace.

In the dim light, she could just see his face. His expression was strangely withdrawn.

"The blade isn't poisoned," Liselle assured him softly, wondering at his odd mood. "It was the only—"

"Pah!" Pascal interrupted, becoming animated all at once. "I know that well enough, *bábia!* You do not have the heart to harm anything, even your most loathsome cousin."

For a moment, they stared at one another without words.

He had changed. Or perhaps they both had. For all of his obnoxious barbs, he had never truly betrayed her and somehow, along the way, Liselle was surprised to discover that she had grown fond of him.

She smiled then and gave a little laugh. "Most loathsome cousin? Insufferably arrogant and troublesome, to be sure, but … hardly loathed."

Pascal's lip lifted in a warped smile, one that she matched, and then his face grew serious all at once. "How did *you* find out?" He held out his hand and glanced down at his ring.

Liselle looked at him and lifted her chin. "You, above all, should know that a member of the Vindictam never betrays the source of their information."

He raised an amused brow and then replied softly, "There is something you should know, *bábia.*"

Liselle tensed at the gravity in his tone.

He folded his arms and focused on the ever-brightening sky above them. "The end of Pippa's tale," he whispered.

"I know it well," Liselle retorted in aggravation. "She died for the love of her Scottish lord. Are you likening—"

"But she did not," he interrupted softly.

Liselle's lips parted in surprise.

"Pippa is a da Vilardino, and though the Vindictam ordered her family to kill her for her treason, the da Vilardino do not *ever* kill their own," Pascal informed her coolly.

Liselle could only stare at him in shock.

Pascal met her gaze with rank amusement. "To all but a handful, she truly is dead. But she changed her name, wed her Scottish lord, and has been known here for many years as the gracious Lady Sutherland—a skilled healer with herbs."

Still stunned, Liselle could only look upon him. Pippa's mastery had been in the art of poison. What irony that she'd turned her wisdom to healing!

Pascal shaded his eyes with a graceful hand and nodded at the rising sun. "I cannot fathom how this day will end; only that I hope it will end badly for the Saluzzi. But should something happen to … should you need help, you would do well to go to her."

Feeling strangely numb, she merely nodded.

"She will be pleased to see you, because there is one other thing that you should know," he said softly, searching her face. "Pippa is sister to my mother and to yours."

Finding her voice at last, Liselle gasped. "My … *aunt?*" Pippa the legendary assassin was her *aunt?*

"Yes, I have visited Pippa often at my mother's behest over the years," Pascal was saying as he glanced around him and shuddered in mock horror. "If you only knew how many times I've been forced to suffer this godforsaken country that they even bothered naming 'Scotland', then you would truly pity me."

And then a clatter of hooves announced the arrival of the Vindictam at last, and Liselle whirled as a party of riders on horses approached. She searched the faces of the men, recognizing Venerio and two others from Fotheringhay and the Abbey, and a fourth whom she did not know. They could only be the Quattuor Gladiis, the Four Swords. Julian and Orazio were not amongst them.

Liselle took a deep breath and willed herself to remain calm.

"Nicolo will bring Lord Gray," Venerio informed her as he handed her the reins of a black horse. "And I have spoken with the Saluzzi. They swear Orazio will be there. Shall we ride to meet Antonio?"

Liselle hesitated, eyeing the members of the Vindictam who watched her intently from under their stern, expressive brows, but she knew that she had no choice.

"Yes, let us ride with haste," she said, thankful that her voice sounded strong and sure.

As she mounted her horse, a crow flapped overhead to land on the city wall nearby, and as its harsh caw scolded them, a shiver ran down her spine.

"*Santo Ciélo!* It is an omen of death," she said.

"Yes, *cara*," Pascal agreed from her side. "But not ours."

* * *

He truly loved her. He knew that now. The ache in his heart at the mere *thought* of losing her was already too much to bear.

Clearly, there was little good in being that undone over a lass, but just as clearly, there was no way to prevent it now. 'Twas too late.

He loved her.

Aye, she was complicated, mysterious, and unpredictable—a highly trained mistress of deceit. And he wanted her to be nothing else.

"I love ye, lass," the whisper escaped him.

There was a time that he'd believed those words would never pass his lips. Now he wanted to hold her close and to tell her such for the rest of his life.

But first he had to secure her safety and freedom.

Julian slipped through Edinburgh's narrow wynds in the chill night air. Already, the sky was graying in the east. Dawn would arrive soon.

He knew he would pick up Orazio's trail at the shop of the Venetian salt merchants.

Keeping to the shadows, he made his way past the Mercat Cross to a tall, elegant house; unique, in that it was roofed with imported clay tiles. A wrought iron sign depicting a Venetian gondola beneath a spoon of salt proclaimed the place to be the domain of the salt merchants. He eyed the building with wry amusement. Aye, most likely, the entire house was crawling with the Vindictam, ruthless assassins masquerading as simple salt-traders amongst the unwary masses of Edinburgh.

Low voices sounded from the close behind him, and darting under a shadowed archway, Julian watched as a man in a black cloak rushed past him to pound on the door of the house.

It was opened almost immediately.

Voices rose. Emotions were high.

Clearly, something was afoot.

Moving under the cover of darkness, Julian slipped closer, just in time to hear the man inform the occupants of the house that Orazio was now in the *safekeeping* of the Saluzzi.

Julian arched a brow.

As the door was slammed in the Saluzzo's face, the man laughed and hurried away, with Julian close upon his heel. Fishing a length of gray cording from his sporran, he began to weave a Turk's head knot as he followed the man through the winding streets of Edinburgh to the other side of the city.

As dawn arrived, the Saluzzo paused before a narrow house near the city gates, and casting a quick glance over his shoulder, knocked on the door and slipped inside.

Julian paused to study the house, seeking entry.

He could see shadows moving before the windows. Clearly, men were on guard.

Cocking a brow at the roof, he grinned and several minutes later, he stood upon the lead tiles to pry the shutters of an attic window open, and vaulted inside.

Julian squinted as his eyes adjusted to the darkness surrounding him.

He stood in a storeroom filled with bags and wooden crates resting on boards spanning the rafters. Voices came from the floor near the far wall.

Moving carefully across the beams, he silently crouched to peer down through the cracks in the wattle and daub ceiling that afforded him a view into the room below.

There were three men in the chamber.

The thick-browed Saluzzo from Fotheringhay sat at a table cluttered with candles while a man who could almost be his twin stood by his side. A third man paced by the window, but as he moved to the table the candlelight reflected upon his face.

It was Orazio.

And as he began to speak, Julian strained forward to hear their conversation.

"Antonio will discover your treachery," Orazio was saying. "He will demand your heads for such a betrayal to your own kind!"

"Then so be it!" the thick-browed Saluzzo growled. "If it comes to that, then Antonio has outlived his usefulness. Mayhap it is time for a new leader of the Saluzzi to rise! A new leader like myself, who is not afraid to spill the blood of the Vindictam!"

"Shall we begin with yours, Orazio?" the other Saluzzo asked with a hissing laugh.

There was a rasp of a blade.

Julian acted at once.

Shoving his booted foot through the wattle and daub, he dropped between the rafters.

His first action was to kick the table over, pinning the seated Saluzzo against the wall and knocking the man's head sharply back, rendered him unconscious. He then disabled the second man by kicking him hard behind the knee and striking his head in quick succession. With a gasp, his victim sank to the floor, joining his companion in oblivion.

And then Julian heard the rasp of a blade leaving its sheath, and spinning, he artfully dodged Orazio's stiletto as it flew past his head in a surprisingly close miss.

Leaping onto the side of the table, Julian vaulted over Orazio, and a moment later, had the man's head securely locked in his forearm.

"Do not think to harm me," Julian said, tightening his grip. "I am not your enemy!"

"Lord Gray!" Orazio wheezed.

"Aye, 'tis time ye knew me by my other name," Julian interrupted grimly. Releasing his chokehold, he shoved Orazio forward. And pulling the Saluzzi belt from his sporran, he slapped it onto the table before dropping the Turk's head knot upon it.

Orazio stared at the Turk's head and then turned white.

A series of expressions crossed his face. Astonishment. Horror. Disbelief. And after what seemed like ages, his lips formed the words: *"Le Marin!"*

"Aye, I am *Le Marin*," Julian acknowledged sharply and pointed to the belt. "But we've little time to discuss it. Liselle is in danger, and I'll see her safe this very day. This belt provides proof that the Saluzzi have betrayed ye. These men seek to kill the Electus. Ye've no cause to take your sister's life for the honor of a traitor!"

Orazio's eyes widened in shock, and then grabbing the belt, he quickly wrapped it around a candlestick and scanned the incriminating words.

"*Diàmbarne!*" he cursed, slapping the flats of his hands upon the table. "It is as I feared! These men are mad!"

"The identity of the Electus is safe for now," Julian inserted quietly. "And I'll see that it remains so ... *if* ye set Liselle free."

Orazio's jaw dropped open. "Dare you to extort the Vindictam?" he asked, astonished.

"Aye, I dare!" Julian responded passionately. And boldly meeting Orazio's penetrating gaze, he added, "I love the lass and I've every intention of wedding her forthwith—"

It was too much for the man. In a flash, Orazio had drawn another stiletto from his belt and lunged forward with a roar.

Sidestepping him, Julian twisted his arm back and wrenched the blade free of his grasp. "Liselle loves ye," he said between clenched teeth. "And I place what she loves above my own desires."

"And your own desires would be to slay me?" Orazio grated as he broke free of Julian's grip.

"I wouldna slay a man for personal cause nor for coin," Julian hissed. "I seek only to protect my country!"

"As do I," Orazio growled in reply. "And I have the courage to do what is necessary!"

Their gazes locked and their chests heaved, but then suddenly, one of the men on the floor groaned and sat up.

Orazio laughed. It was a cold, chilling laugh.

Moving to crouch next to the man nursing his sore jaw, Orazio clamped a hard hand down upon his shoulder.

"Can you tell me what attracts a swarm of flies, Lord Gray?" he asked in a deadly voice as he glanced at Julian from over his shoulder.

Julian arched a curious brow.

Turning back to the man, Orazio's lip lifted in a sneer. "Is it not something that gives off a rotten stench?"

The man had only a moment to frown in confusion before Orazio's fist connected with the Saluzzo's jaw. Dropping back onto the floor, the man went unconscious once more.

"I must be gone from here," Orazio said, grabbing the belt. "I have words that must be said to Antonio!"

"Then I'll be coming with ye," Julian inserted in a voice threaded with steel. Stripping the belt from Orazio's grasp and stuffed it back into his sporran. "I'll be keeping this until I have what *I* want."

They glared at one another yet again, but this time it did not last long. With a curt nod, Julian sprinted down the stairs and out into the streets. Orazio fell into step beside him, matching him stride for stride.

They had scarcely arrived at the Salt Merchants' shop when they were met by several men on horseback gathered before the door.

"Magno Duce!" one of them gasped. "Liselle has taken the Electus as hostage to the Saluzzi in Linlithgow!"

With a curse upon his lips, Julian grabbed the nearest man by the belt and pulled him down from his horse. Ignoring the man's protests, he vaulted into the saddle.

"The Electus?" Orazio replied in astonishment. "The Electus is here? In Scotland?"

"Aye, ye know the Electus intimately," Julian informed him. "And if ye wish him to survive, follow me now with haste!"

Orazio did not have to be told twice, and moments later, he was galloping at Julian's side, headed for the city gates.

At full speed, Julian left the city of Edinburgh behind him, riding low over the neck of the horse as he streaked towards the royal burgh of

Linlithgow with Orazio and his men close behind him.

Dark clouds rushed across the morning sky as they rode through the soft rolling hills of the lowlands, across rivers and burns, and around hamlets and kirks.

He knew right well where they were headed. The secretive brotherhood of the Carmelites farmed the land near Linlithgow Palace. And Julian was quite familiar with the secret passageways running beneath the fields near the friary. He'd hidden there on more than one occasion himself.

A few miles shy of Linlithgow, the clouds above their heads unleashed a torrent of rain that slowed their progress. Thunder raged across the sky, frightening the horses as they slipped in the mud.

Cursing under his breath, Julian urged his horse on.

It was almost noon when they finally galloped down the grassy hillside, past the formidable towers of Linlithgow Palace and across the empty fields to the Carmelite friary nearby.

Maintaining a breakneck pace until he had reached the line of trees on the far end of the field near the friary, Julian pulled his mount up short, its sides heaving and its muzzle lathered with foam.

"There!" Julian said, pointing to a small mark of a "V" carved in the trunk of a tree. "The mark of the Electus! Pascal was safe then, at least until this point."

Shock registered upon Orazio's face.

"Aye," Julian said, "Your young cousin has been harboring a secret, Orazio."

But the man could say nothing in response, so great was his surprise.

And then dismounting, Julian led them through the trees to a small hillock where a granite ledge thick with moss and lichen covered a gaping maw leading into darkness.

It was the entrance to the catacombs of the Carmelite monks.

Julian frowned.

The monks were not ones to leave the place unguarded. Peering into the dark hole, he listened for any sound, but only heard the light patter of the rain striking the leaves above their heads. Making up his mind, he unsheathed his dirk, and motioning the others to follow, led them into the gloomy network of hiding places and escape tunnels.

The passageway was arched, made of hand-hewn stone, and ran straight ahead for quite some time before veering sharply to the left to branch in several directions. Pausing to allow his eyes to adjust to the darkness, Julian was about to step forward when a torch moved in the blackness ahead.

Silently, he altered course and they crept forward, following the torch until the distinct buzz of voices could be heard, and rounding a corner, he could see the torchlight reflecting off of a barrel-vaulted ceiling.

They had arrived at the secret meeting chamber, the largest room in the catacombs. Torches burned in iron sconces embedded upon the wall, and at the far side stood a large doorway with stairs winding upwards into the darkness.

Moving closer, Julian peered from the shadows to see the place filled with monks and men in dark cloaks sitting at a long wooden table. Around the neck of each, monk and man alike, hung a length of wooden beads.

"The monks are Saluzzi!" Orazio whispered in shock from his side.

Julian arched a surprised brow. Was Scotland crawling with foreign assassins? Ach, he'd have to tell Cameron. Something must be done!

It was then that he spied Pascal a short distance away, leaning against the wall and observing the men in the center of the room intently.

And at his side stood Liselle.

Even in the dim light of the chamber, he could see that she was worried.

Aye, the lass walked a path fraught with danger, but he'd see that she was never placed in such a position again.

"I will wait for Orazio," a man's voice rose above the others in the room. "This matter is a puzzling affair, and I would not make so hasty a judgment. I will hear the truth from a man I trust."

There were protests, among them demands for blood justice.

Julian drew himself up and turned to Orazio. "Let's get this done, aye?"

Setting his lips into an uncompromising line, Orazio nodded.

Silence blanketed the chamber the moment they entered, and all eyes focused on Julian as he boldly strode to Liselle's side.

She looked exhausted. Long, sweeping strands of her hair spilled from under her hood, hair so dark with rain that it almost looked black. A streak of grime trailed down her cheek and the dark circles under her eyes announced the decided lack of sleep, but the expression of relief and joy upon her face made his heart sing.

"This will be over soon, lass," he promised, lowering his head to place a kiss on the delicate slope of her nose.

"True enough!" a harsh voice sounded from beside him.

Julian turned as a fist connected with his jaw, and he reeled back a step from the unexpected impact. Wiping the salty taste of blood from his lips, he peered down at the thick-browed Saluzzo from Fotheringhay in surprise.

The man was covered in mud, apparently he had just arrived.

Several men leapt forward to pull the man back as voices erupted in outrage and accusation, with Orazio's among the loudest.

And then a tall man stepped forward. Julian could see the outline of his aquiline nose, but the rest of his face remained shrouded in the shadows of his hood.

"Let Orazio speak," the man ordered in a voice of authority.

As Julian extended the Saluzzi belt, Orazio snatched it from his hand and held it up for all to see.

"This belt reveals treachery!" he announced without preamble. "Treachery of some of your brethren, treachery in the hope of breaking the truce between our families!"

The tall man drew back sharply. "Such accusations are dangerous, Orazio di Franco! But if they are true, I will shed the blood of these traitors myself!"

"Then let us read aloud the words upon this belt!" Pascal demanded, pushing himself away from the wall. "The Vindictam have danced for the Saluzzi like puppets on a string long enough!"

A chorus of Vindictam voices agreed with him even as the Saluzzi objected.

"You do not dance for us!" The tall man's voice was riddled with disdain. Holding up his hand for silence, he drew back his hood and revealed a distinguished face framed with gray hair. "I am Antonio Saluzzo. Who are *you* to speak for the Vindictam?"

The hatred in Pascal's eyes burned hot, but Orazio stepped in front of him before he could reply.

"Pray do not let my young cousin distract us from the matter at hand," Orazio said, skillfully taking control in the obvious attempt to protect the identity of the Electus and Quattuor Gladiis. "I am the Magno Duce here. And I will speak for the Vindictam."

The look Antonio sent Pascal was a chilling one. "Be wary, arrogant youth," he warned harshly. And then snatching the belt from Orazio's grasp, he began to loop it around the sheath of his sword.

As the others crowded close to read the words, Julian saw the thick-browed Saluzzo from Fotheringhay inch towards the stairs leading into the darkness. And as the message on the belt became clear, the outrage of both the Vindictam and the Saluzzi ignited, and the man bolted.

Leaping over the table, Julian was after him in a moment. Aye, he'd not let the man escape justice!

The stairs wound in a tight circle, spiraling to the ground above. Taking the steps two at a time, Julian dashed upwards, but as he neared the top, the stones grew slick, causing him to slip.

Stumbling out of the catacombs, he saw the Saluzzo sprinting for the Carmelite friary a short distance away and quickly set off after him.

The man was short and no match for Julian's stride, thus by the time he'd neared the chapel, Julian had almost closed the distance between them.

Glancing over his shoulder, the man's face registered desperation. Abruptly changing course, the Saluzzo ran down the cloister walk, dashed inside a small tower at the corner of the friary, and barred the door shut just as Julian arrived.

Pausing to catch his breath, Julian eyed the tower.

There was no place the man could go. He was trapped. And the tower was a small one that could be easily scaled.

Standing back to eye the jagged stones, Julian glanced up to see the Saluzzo glaring down at him from atop the tower, wiping the sweat off his brow with his forearm.

"Be gone!" the man shouted from above. "Do not even step upon my shadow if you wish to live!"

Julian snorted at the empty threat, but at the sound of approaching feet from behind, he cocked a brow and turned to see Pascal, Orazio, and the gray-haired Antonio arriving at a run.

Exchanging silent looks, Orazio and Antonio skirted the tower as

Pascal joined Julian to address the treacherous Saluzzo above them.

"Prepare to die!" Pascal thundered.

Lifting an amused brow at the youth, Julian then looked up at the man and warned sharply, "Tread carefully lest ye find yourself beyond prayer! Come down at once. There is no place for ye to hide, ye daft fool!"

But the man's attention had focused on Pascal, and the anger in his voice was unmistakable as he shouted in reply, "Have a care, Pascal da Vilardino! I will see your blood stain the ground, and I will extinguish the cousins of your cousins—"

Pascal's chilling laugh cut him short. "Whoever dies this day, Saluzzo, you will certainly be amongst them," retorted the youth.

The Saluzzo roared, "*Ah sì?*! You are naught but the walking dead!"

And then shouts were heard, and Orazio appeared at the top of the tower next to the man, and a struggle ensued.

"Ah, they must have gained entry from the other side! I must join them!" exclaimed Pascal, and he set off at a run

And then without warning, a knee slammed into Julian's spine, and as he pitched forward, a blade whizzed past his ear.

Rolling to the ground, he drew his dirk in a fluid motion and twisted around to face his attacker.

It was the *other* Saluzzo he'd fought in Edinburgh.

Angling his dirk, Julian blocked the vicious blows of his attacker and sparks flew from the force of the clashing blades. They struggled for a time, neither able to gain the advantage.

And then, seeing his opportunity, Julian lunged, and it was over.

The man let out a cry like a wounded animal as Julian's dirk struck home, and with a gasping gurgle, his assailant sank into the grass, dead.

Scanning the grounds for any more attackers, Julian held his dirk at the ready, but when no more appeared, he turned his attention to voices now shouting from the chapel.

The thick-browed Saluzzo had managed to escape the tower. Having eluded Orazio and Pascal, he'd taken up a stance near a section of wall surrounding the chapel. Armed now with a crossbow and a quiver of bolts, he'd taken Antonio as hostage.

"His blood will be upon your hands!" the Saluzzo threatened, aiming the crossbow mere inches from the man's head.

Pascal laughed. "And why would I care if the Saluzzo should kill one of their own? It simply means one less problem for us is walking the earth!"

Even Orazio seemed nonchalant to the threat.

Suddenly, the Saluzzo hitched his shoulder and grinned. Shoving his hostage aside, he dove over the wall even as the stilettos of both Orazio and Pascal bounced harmlessly off the stones, missing him by a mere hair's breadth.

And then with a maniacal laugh, the Saluzzo reappeared on the wall, standing with his feet braced wide apart, and a bolt notched on his crossbow.

But he was aiming over the heads of Orazio and Pascal.

In confusion, they turned to follow his aim, and as horror spread across their faces, Julian slowed his approach and turned himself to look.

And then his heart stopped.

It was Liselle.

The shaft was pointed straight at her.

Pascal roared and dove for the Saluzzo, but with a sickening realization, Julian knew the youth would be too late to stop the bolt on its flight.

There was only one way to ensure Liselle's safety.

And the decision was a simple one.

In three large strides, Julian threw himself into the bolt's path, spreading his arms wide. He heard it whistle, and he closed his eyes, praying that it would meet him.

A breath of wind kissed his cheek.

And then his prayers were answered.

The bolt struck him in the chest with such force that he was knocked backwards into the wet grass.

But he felt nothing. He only heard Liselle's screams.

For a brief moment, he was horrified that the bolt had found her after all, but then his chest exploded with such burning agony that he could only smile, knowing that he had succeeded.

Liselle was safe.

For a brief moment, he opened his eyes to see Pascal running towards him, horror etched upon his face as he shouted, "Have you lost your power of reason, Julian?"

Behind him, Julian was dimly aware of Antonio with a drawn sword, towering over the body of the thick-browed Saluzzo, now lying still on the ground.

And then Liselle's warm arms were about him, and her face filled his failing vision.

"I love you," she cried, her hazel eyes bright with tears.

Julian drew his breath sharply as agonizing pain surged through his body. With every ounce of his strength, he managed to wheeze, "Aye, and I love ye, lass."

And then consciousness slipped from his grasp, and darkness swallowed him.

19

WE ARE REVENGE

Consciousness came to Julian in momentary flashes.

His chest throbbed in pain. It was difficult to breathe.

There was the soft intonation of a man's voice giving him the last rites, and then blissful nothingness swept him into its embrace once again.

He woke once more to voices shouting around him. Someone pressed hard upon his chest. The resulting wave of pain caused him to faint.

The moments of lucidity were rare after that. He was distantly aware of someone forcing a bitter liquid between his lips. Repeatedly.

He only knew that it was too hard to breathe. Each breath taxed his strength to the point that he only wished for his agony to end, but it did not. His lungs felt as if they were made of lead.

Time passed.

A woman's voice that he did not know whispered through his mind, a low voice, speaking as if from a great distance. She spoke words of comfort, words that brought peace.

During the worst of it, he distinctly heard Pascal's arrogant tones ordering, "You belong to the Vindictam. You cannot die. I will not allow it."

And then everything became dreamlike and peaceful, seeming to stretch into eternity, until gradually, he became aware of the warmth of the sun upon his face.

Too tired to lift his lashes, Julian lay as he was, enjoying the heat on his skin as he listened to the song of the birds before drifting off to sleep.

When he woke next, he finally succeeded in opening his eyes. He saw first the blue sky framed by a narrow arched window. In the distance he could see Linlithgow Palace, so he realized he must be in the Carmelite friary. Puzzled, he turned his tired gaze upon his bed. He lay under a fox-fur coverlet with his head resting upon the soft luster of a satin pillow.

Moving as if to rise, he gasped at the sudden pain ripping through his chest and collapsed back, overwhelmed by a bout of dizziness.

A soft rustle of skirts hurried to his side, and he opened his eyes long enough to see an ageless woman with raven hair threaded with silver. Her bright blue eyes were kind and intelligent as she placed a cool hand over his forehead.

"Rest, *caro*." She sent him a comforting smile. "You will grow strong now. Love has brought you back from death's door. I knew love would not fail!"

He was too weak to ask who she was or what she meant. His eyes were already closing, and then the peace of sleep carried him away again.

After that, there were several brief flashes of a cowled monk clad in coarse woolen robes, but the thought of love gave him comfort, and he slept for a very long time.

* * *

Julian woke to the soft light of morning.

The heavy weight in his chest was gone, and for several long minutes, he savored the simple joy of breathing.

The ageless raven-haired woman stood at a small table a short distance away. For a time, he watched her select flowers from a basket to grind the petals and stems before she sensed his eyes upon her.

"Good morning, Lord Gray," she greeted him warmly as she wiped her hands upon an apron covering her skirts. Tucking a silver-threaded lock of hair behind her ear, she picked up an earthenware cup from the table and approached his bedside.

"Drink this, *caro*," she ordered briskly, supporting his head with her

292

hand, she pressed the cup to his lips.

Recognizing the bitter taste, he grimaced, but drank half the cup in one gulp.

"Much stronger! Yes, you are much stronger," she announced, quite pleased. And then with a slight frown, she clucked and shook her head. "You stayed at death's door far too long, *caro*."

Julian frowned, attempting to recall the circumstances of his injury.

And then the events of the Saluzzi and Liselle returned with a rush.

Choking on the remainder of the liquid, he half sat up and gasped, "Liselle! Where is she? Is she harmed—"

"Hush, *caro*!" The woman laughed. Pushing him back gently, she placed a finger upon his lips and nodded to the other side of the bed. "Liselle is safe. You saved her life. And she has never left your side for many, many days. Not once."

The effort of turning was a draining one, but worth it upon seeing Liselle's honey-colored locks fanned out about her delicate face. Though still sitting half in her chair by the bed, she lay sound asleep, her head cradled upon one arm on the pillow next to him.

"She is exhausted," the raven-haired woman said. Her skirts rustled as she moved to stand behind Liselle's chair, and a soft expression crossed her face. And then bending down, she lightly kissed the top of her head. "*Mia bèla.* I had never thought to see her."

Julian raised a quizzical brow.

Straightening, the woman noticed his curiosity and smiled, a soft dimple graced her cheek. "I am Lady Sutherland," she said, answering the unspoken question.

Julian's eyes lit in recognition. While he had only seen Lord Sutherland's lady once before, he knew her husband quite well. The distinguished noble was one of the most honorable, upright men in

Scotland. But Julian's curiosity only deepened. Why would Lady Sutherland hope to see Liselle?

"My husband has always spoken highly of you," Lady Sutherland said, moving away and patting his blanket as she headed towards the door. "We can speak more later, *caro*."

Julian opened his mouth to call her back, but then a familiar alto voice whispered his name.

"Julian."

With a one-sided smile creasing his cheek, he turned to see Liselle staring at him in surprise.

Reverently, he lifted his thumb to trace the tears falling down her cheek.

She held still, too overcome to speak for a time. But finally, she reached for a cup and asked, "You have been so feverish! How is your thirst?"

His eyes glinted at that. "Unquenchable," he said, unable to resist a suggestive reply, but he was taken aback by the weakness in his own voice.

Liselle blinked but did not smile. Instead, she moved to lay her cheek lightly on his shoulder. "We thought you would die," she said, her voice quivering.

With great effort, Julian lifted his hand and stroked her cheek. "The softness of your skin is powerful medicine, lass. I'll mend quickly now," he promised.

And then exhausted, he closed his eyes to let sleep carry him away.

After that, his strength returned rapidly, and on a damp gray afternoon several days later, a familiar voice sounded from the door of his chamber.

Glancing up, Julian grinned as Cameron stepped through the

doorway. Folding his blue-velvet mantle over his arm, the Earl of Lennox drew his dark brows into a stern line.

"Ach, Julian," his deep voice disapproved. "But ye fair scared us all, lad! There are less painful ways to lie in bed all day with your lady by your side." His words were polite, but Julian caught the teasing twinkle in his expressive eyes.

Laughing, Julian cast a quick sidelong glance at Liselle, but she had merely risen to curtsey.

However, Lady Sutherland, sitting in the corner, rolled her eyes, but her words were warm as she said, "My dear earl, it is a pleasure to see you yet again and so soon."

As Cameron bowed graciously to them both, Julian queried, "So soon?"

Cameron moved to tower over him. "I dinna care to witness a priest reading ye the last rites, lad." His eyes were serious and filled with deep concern.

"Aye, well, clearly, 'twas a misjudgment and a bit premature," Julian replied lightly. Glancing at Liselle, he sent her a reassuring smile.

Following his gaze, Cameron's carved lips crooked into a smile. "Aye, 'tis time ye took up other important matters, lad. And I'll have the king issue ye a decree if that is what it takes."

Julian raised a questioning brow.

"I do believe Castle Huntly is in need of an heir," the Earl of Lennox replied with a sly smile.

Julian chuckled, noting a slight shade of pink stealing over Liselle's face as Lady Sutherland rolled her eyes once more.

"Shall we leave these boys to their discussion, *cara*?" she asked, looping her arm through Liselle's to sweep her away.

As they left, Julian watched Liselle with a smile upon his lips. Aye, he could think of nothing more pleasant than to lock himself away with her in a castle. But she had scarcely gone before Cameron turned to tidings of the court.

"Albany has betrayed Scotland yet again," the earl informed him with a shake of his chin. "And we've had reports from England that Edward's health is failing."

Julian sat up in bed. Aye, 'twas invigorating to be enmeshed in the web of intrigue once more. Surprisingly, he had missed it. "Then Gloucester will become King of England," he observed thoughtfully, and then smiled. "And after these recent matters, he'll not support Albany nor muster an army to bother Scotland any time soon."

"Aye," Cameron agreed, permitting his eyes to smile in return.

Julian eyed his friend in admiration. Cameron was ever the wily statesman. "Well played," he said. "We've staved off another English threat then, aye?"

Cameron nodded, but then grew serious. "But dinna forget, now we have Albany loose again. He has withdrawn to Dunbar and has just this day been named a traitor to the Scottish crown."

"He'll never stop until he's dead," Julian said grimly. "Ach, but ye need me, Cameron! I should be riding, not lying abed!"

Julian slapped the bed with the flat of his palm, but the gesture made him wince in pain.

"Ye'll ride soon enough, lad," Cameron assured him and then settled back in his chair.

They spoke of other things then, and when Liselle returned after a time, the afternoon passed pleasantly with Cameron regaling her with tales of Julian's follies throughout the years.

Julian didn't mind. Hearing Liselle laugh warmed his soul. And though he desperately fought to stay awake, it was too difficult in such a peaceful atmosphere.

He was not even aware he had fallen asleep until he woke to find himself staring into the dark eyes of Pascal standing at the foot of his bed.

"I trust you are feeling better, Lord Gray?" the graceful youth queried in a guarded tone.

Easing himself onto an elbow, Julian gave a dry laugh. "The fact that I yet live tells me the Vindictam has rescinded my death sentence." With a gracious nod, he added, "And for that I thank ye, lad."

Pascal's lips curved into a smile. "You are protected … for now. But it is an easy enough matter to make someone disappear," he said, caressing the hilt of the sword belted about his slim waist.

Recognizing the glint of humor in the lad's eyes, Julian merely arched a brow.

Pascal remained silent for a time, and then began to pace thoughtfully before the window. "You were delirious for quite some time, Lord Gray," he said at last. "And in the heat of your fever, you spoke of what I had long suspected in France—and knew for sure in Fotheringhay."

"Aye?" Julian prodded curiously.

Pascal's dark eyes riveted upon him. "You are *Le Marin.*"

A smile creased Julian's cheek as a memory flashed across his mind, and he said, "Aye, and in that fever, I distinctly recall hearing the voice of the *Electus* ordering me not to die."

Their gazes locked, and then Pascal dipped his chin in graceful acknowledgment. "An order that you dutifully obeyed," he pointed out. And then his intense eyes grew serious. "Join us, Julian. Your fingers will flow with gold. Work with us in the fair city of *Le Serenissima.*"

Julian chuckled. "Nay, lad, I serve Scotland alone," was all he said.

"Dare you stir my anger?" Pascal's grim tone was at odds with the smile on his lips. "Mayhap I should tell you that the Quattuor Gladiis has not yet decided upon the fate of *Le Marin*—whoever *he* may be.*"*

"And mayhap I have faith that the Electus—whoever *he* may be— will introduce a wee bit of Scottish common sense into his men. Loyalty before vengeance, aye?" Julian replied easily.

Pascal's dark eyes lit with a smile, but it took some time for his reluctant reply. "Then we have an understanding."

"Do we?" Julian asked, easing back onto the pillow. "Orazio and ye should know that I'll be wedding Liselle."

"Do you have a death wish, Lord Gray?" Orazio's distinctive voice sounded from the doorway.

Glancing up, Julian watched the man enter the chamber and approach the bed, his hands folded behind his back.

"Tread softly, Orazio," Julian warned, boldly meeting the man's piercing gaze. "I've already proven that I'll protect her with my life. I'll not live without the lass. I love her."

Orazio exhaled strongly through his nose. "Loyalty is the pillar of our family, Lord Gray," he began.

"Aye, as with any clan," Julian agreed.

"And blood ties can never be severed," Orazio continued grimly, joining Pascal at the foot of the bed.

"The tie of a brother, aye," Julian granted, but then his voice hardened. "But the ties of the Vindictam have been severed already."

Orazio's head snapped back. "Never has the Vindictam released one of its own!"

"Truly, Orazio?" A woman's soft voice filtered through the chamber.

As one, they turned to see Lady Sutherland hovering in the doorway.

"Do not uncover the past, my lady," Pascal warned quietly.

Her blue eyes impaled him. Stepping into the chamber, she shut the door firmly behind her and then crisply addressed Orazio and Pascal,

"Liselle was never made to shed blood, you two young fools!"

Orazio's mouth gaped open as Pascal expelled a breath of annoyance and moved to slouch against the wall, clearly preparing for what he knew would come next.

Wagging her finger, Lady Sutherland took them to task. "Orazio, you must open your eyes. And Pascal, if you truly wish to restore the Vindictam to its former glory, you must be strong, *caro!* A strong leader assigns tasks to only those who can succeed at them. As Electus, the responsibility lies with you!"

Pascal's lip curved into a smile. "I see why they let you go free," he said softly.

A look of outright alarm and astonishment crossed Orazio's face. "Who is this woman? These matters are of the highest secrecy! We must—"

"Mayhap you would know her better by another name," Pascal interrupted calmly. "Orazio, allow me to introduce you to your *Sia* Pippa. Pippa da Vilardino."

Julian's lips parted in surprise as Orazio choked.

But Lady Sutherland graciously inclined her head. "Pippa," she repeated softly. "It is a name I'd nearly forgotten, *caro.*"

Julian raised a brow at her perfect English accent. This woman was the famed Venetian assassin in Liselle's tale?

Orazio was the first to recover. Motioning towards Julian first and then to himself, he said, "These matters should not be discussed here. Nor even—"

"Nonsense!" Lady Sutherland retorted, waving her hand. "We are bound by blood and Lord Gray through love. If Pascal cannot speak to us of such matters, then he can trust no one. And he will not remain the Dominus Granditer for longer than a fortnight!"

"Should I even ask how she knows of this?" Orazio turned upon Pascal, clearly taken aback.

Pascal merely gave a humorous sigh. "There is little that Pippa does not know, Orazio. And I wasn't jesting when I said the Vindictam was relieved to be rid of her."

"Then set Liselle free, Pascal," Lady Sutherland insisted, tucking a silver-threaded lock behind her ear.

Emphasizing his displeasure with a deep frown, Orazio stepped forward. "May I remind you, *cara sia*, that Pascal is not someone you can simply demand—"

"Nonsense!" Lady Sutherland cut in with a smile, though her voice was powerful. "Pascal is my nephew. As are you, Orazio. And did your mother not teach you to respect your elders, and above all, the women elders of your family?"

As her sharp eyes turned upon Orazio, Julian was amused to watch the formidable man take an involuntary step back.

"Respect, certainly, *mia sia* ..." he faltered, searching for words.

Perversely entertained by Orazio's discomfiture, Pascal held out a hand. "Please take Orazio to task elsewhere, *sia cara*. I shall join you shortly."

As Lady Sutherland obligingly guided Orazio from the chamber, Pascal turned to Julian once again.

"Then I want something in return, Lord Gray," he said, his dark eyes turning hard. "Dolfin."

Julian lifted a wary brow. "Ye needn't fear he'll betray ye, lad."

"And what assurance do I have of that?" Pascal's eyes narrowed.

"I should think the word of *Le Marin* should be enough," Julian replied, locking gazes with the youth. "Dolfin is dead to ye. Let him go. Ye owe the man a debt, lad. Without him, ye never would have exposed

300

the Saluzzi corruption."

Pascal's lips drew into a hard line, but his voice was calm as he asked, "Is it true that his mind has grown weak?"

Julian heaved a sigh. He hadn't wanted to admit it, but there was no denying it. "Aye, the man is old and frail."

Pascal moved to stare out of the window for a time. "Liselle is willful, Lord Gray," he finally said before turning to face Julian. A smile graced his lips. "It is not too late for you to run to the highlands. Allow me to be of assistance. I owe you that much, at least."

Julian's mouth shifted into an answering smile. "I'll not be running from her, lad. Besides, I have no doubt she would find me."

At that, Pascal gave a cutting laugh. "True enough," he said. "She followed only you from the beginning it seems. It is unfortunate that Dolfin died before the hand of justice could find him."

Julian's smile broadened as he dipped his chin in thanks.

"But know you this, Lord Gray," the dark-haired youth continued with an arrogant lift of his brow. "It is you who weds into the Vindictam. I will not slay Liselle, even in name. And even though she will not be called upon to practice her craft, she remains one of us. Protected. Loved. Cherished. Never forget the meaning of the Vindictam." He paused a moment before adding, "We are revenge."

The threat was clear. But Julian could do naught but smile. "Aye, I knew ye had a Scottish heart, lad," was all he said. And then suddenly weary, he waved a tired hand. "Now, if ye'll excuse me, I'm in sore need of rest. Ye've quite taxed my strength."

And then ignoring the assassin threatening him from his bedside, Julian yawned and fell asleep.

* * *

White clouds scurried across the blue sky as Lord Julian Gray stood on his ancestral lands and surveyed the gray-stoned castle rising before him. Dew glistened on the tender leaves of the trees and shrubbery. Nearby, he could hear the bleating of goats and the lowing of cows.

He took a deep breath of the crisp spring air.

His family had lived on this land for generations. And for the first time in his life, he felt he belonged there as well.

Adjusting his plaid, he smiled.

Castle Huntly was filled with his closest friends and kinfolk, all of them waiting for the arrival of the bride before proceeding to the kirk a short distance away.

Aye, this very day he would wed Liselle.

Today, she would truly become Lady Gray.

He'd spent a peaceful winter—nay, a wondrous winter—courting the lass in Edinburgh. She had wanted to be wed immediately, but he had insisted upon a proper courtship. Never had he cherished a woman so. And he knew in his heart that he would love her until his dying breath.

"I'm certain they will be here soon, my son," his mother's voice sounded from his side.

Julian turned to see his mother and Lady Sutherland standing behind him.

His mother was a lovely woman in her own right, and her calm green eyes and lined face were alight with excitement. Wearing a blue satin gown and her flaxen hair bound by a jeweled net, she was ready for the wedding she had spent months preparing for with Lady Sutherland. A wedding she had dreamed of for years—a wedding that Julian knew his mother hoped would turn her scandalous son into a respectable man once and for all.

And then Lady Sutherland's blue eyes widened. "They are here, Lord Gray."

Spinning on his heel, Julian saw a party of horses approaching at a mad pace. He scanned the riders quickly, but the moment he caught sight of the familiar honey-colored tresses flying loose in the wind, he saw nothing else.

It seemed but a moment later that he was swinging Liselle down from her horse. Sweeping her close in a warm embrace, he buried his face in her hair.

"I've missed ye sorely, lass," he whispered.

"It has only been a week, Lord Gray," she replied with a husky laugh.

"A week is long enough to make a man mad," he teased lightly. "I have to see ye to return to my senses, lass. I can't stand to be apart from ye."

Capturing a handful of her hair, he rubbed it against his cheek and then stood back to eye her in open, frank admiration. Her green-velvet gown hugged her figure in the most seductive of ways. And her lips were as full and kissable as they always had been.

With his mouth curving into a wicked grin, he began in a low suggestive rumble, "Aye, 'tis time I kissed ye rough and slow—"

"It is good to see you hale and hearty at last, Lord Gray," Pascal's amused voice cut in.

Startled, Julian whirled on his heel.

Ach, how had he forgotten the dozen or so horsemen who had accompanied Liselle? And judging by their wary demeanor, rich black attire, and piercing eyes, every one of them belonged to the Vindictam.

"I shall leave you now," Liselle whispered in his ear.

With a capricious smile, she attempted to dash away, but he snagged her by the wrist and pulled her close once again.

"Are ye leaving me to face a dozen assassins on my own, ye wee devil?" he asked lightly.

"You are *Le Marin*, are you not?" Her hazel eyes sparkled. "Surely, the ruling elite of the Vindictam will be no match for you."

Slipping from his grasp, she darted away to join his mother and Lady Sutherland. He watched them disappear into the castle before turning to face the Vindictam once again.

Pascal and Orazio had dismounted and were moving his way.

It had been nigh on six months since he'd last seen them.

Pascal had grown broader of shoulder, and he moved with an air of authority that most likely meant he was now the Dominus Granditer, but Julian knew it was not something he could ask.

With an obvious reluctance, Orazio clasped arms with Julian in greeting. But then leaning close, he warned in a voice heavy with emotion, "If you even make her weep, Lord Gray, you will shed tears of blood."

Had any other man said those words, Julian would have been insulted. But from Orazio, he knew it meant the man had accepted the marriage at last.

Pascal confirmed it with a dark smile, but he couldn't resist adding, "And should you try to run and hide, we will find you, Lord Gray."

"Aye, fair enough." Julian chuckled, recognizing his twisted humor. "I've no need to hide from ye, lad." And then turning to Orazio, he nodded once. "Your wee sister will never weep because of me."

For several long moments, Orazio locked gazes with him. But then his expression softened, and his chin dipped in the minutest amount in acknowledgement.

Behind them, the dark-clothed horsemen had dismounted to scan the area critically. Their tense movements spoke of a barely contained ferocity.

Julian suppressed a sigh.

Life with Liselle was not likely to get easier. Not with her vigilant brother and her cousin the Dominus Granditer of a powerful family of assassins.

But the lass was well worth the trouble.

"Welcome to Castle Huntly," Julian said, bowing to them all. "My home is yours."

They had almost reached the entrance when Pascal's sharp eyes spied an old man sitting in the sunlit garden a few steps away.

It was Dolfino Dolfin.

The old man glanced up and tottered to his feet.

Pascal froze.

"And who be our guests, *caro?*" Dolfin called to Julian, waving a trembling hand at the Vindictam.

But before Julian could reply, the old salt spy laughed.

"Ah, I know right well. I may be old, but I am not blind." With a wide smile, he shuffled towards them to stop in front of Pascal. "Guests! We have guests, Julian. Guests for the wedding. It is the season for love!" With a laugh, he kissed the air. "*Amór!*"

"*Amór!*" Julian repeated with a fond smile.

Dolfin's mind had grown weaker with each passing month, and the moments of clarity were few now. It was surprising that he had even remembered the wedding.

"*Amór, bón pare,*" Pascal said softly.

A brief expression of compassion crossed his face, but it was so fleeting that Julian wasn't entirely certain he had seen it.

And then Pascal turned his sharp eyes upon Orazio and exchanged a meaningful look with him.

"The man reminds me of someone I knew once, long ago." Pascal's tone was cool. "But that man is dead now." And then holding out his hand, he said, "Do we not have a wedding to attend? Let us not tarry here. I would leave this barbarous land as soon as I may."

As Pascal turned on his heel and walked away, Julian led Dolfin back to his chair in the sunlight, and after seeing the man settled, straightened his plaid and made his way to his castle to wed his bride.

The events passed in a whirlwind.

More guests arrived and among them were Ewan and the highlanders from Mull, Cameron, his wee wife Kate and their newest bairn.

The wedding and the feast was everything his mother had hoped it would be. She spent the entire day and evening, weeping tears of joy.

As for Julian, he spent more time keeping a watchful eye on the members of Vindictam at the feast than not, but for the most part, Liselle's kin mingled easily enough amongst the highlanders. And after observing them for the entire day, Julian supposed the two groups had much in common. Fierce loyalty, protection, and honor ran as thick through the Scots' blood as with the Vindictam.

Soon enough, the bride was carried to the bedchamber, and Julian was laughingly escorted by a group of men so drunk they couldn't successfully navigate the stairs.

"I relieve ye of your duty, lads." Julian laughed, shooing them back down the steps. "I know the way well enough."

Amidst their cheers, he dashed up the remaining flights and slipped inside his tower bedchamber.

The room was dim, lit only by the dull glow of the dying fire and the light of a single taper, but it was enough to illuminate Liselle standing by the window.

He paused a moment, watching the candlelight flicker, casting shadows over the rich tapestries and brocade, curtained bed, but most captivatingly, playing on the soft satin folds of the gown gracing Liselle's slender hips in a way that made his blood boil.

Aye, the lass was bonny, and the long creamy expanse of her throat called for his lips. Coming up behind her, he wrapped his arms about her waist and pulled her close against his chest, and with a soft growl, he kissed the back of her neck.

He felt her shiver and then she laughed. "Lord Gray, you are quite bold!"

His hands stayed upon her hips as she twisted in his arms.

He could drown in those hazel eyes.

"Ye are bonny beyond measure, lass." He groaned softly, and then catching her chin in his hand, he lazily investigated her mouth in a long slow kiss.

Her lips were soft and pliant under his, eagerly opening to allow her tongue to dance with his.

After a moment, he pulled back to breathe lightly against her cheek. "Aye, but your lips are a sinful pleasure, lass."

"You speak too much, Lord Gray," she whispered with a sultry smile.

"And what would ye have me do instead, Lady Gray?" he asked with a playful wink.

Wild desire burned in her eyes as she pulled his head down and caught his lips lightly between her teeth.

Crushing her even closer, he reclaimed her mouth in an instant as he allowed his hands to explore her soft curves. And then placing feather-light kisses along the curve of her neck, he traced a long slow line down the side of her neck and over her collarbone with his tongue.

Liselle shivered uncontrollably, and a soft sigh escaped her throat.

Julian chuckled.

Sweeping her up into his arms, he carried her to the bed. And removing her slippers with a low growl in his throat, he bent down and kissed the viper mark upon her ankle.

She gasped in pleasure.

Slowly, his kisses moved upwards, but when she slid her hands beneath his shirt to run her fingernails over his skin, it was his turn to shiver with desire.

"It is too bright," she whispered, nodding at the candle.

Pulling himself away, it took him a moment to focus his eyes on the flickering flame, and when he moved to oblige her, he heard her soft laugh.

"Please, Lord Gray!" she murmured in amusement. "Allow me."

He heard the soft rasp of metal as a bone-handled stiletto appeared between her delicate fingers. And then she took aim.

Unerringly, the blade flew through the air to slice the wick from the wax.

And as darkness fell, he heard the laughter in her voice. "Pray continue, Lord Gray."

With a grin creasing his cheek, he pulled her closer and whispered his reply, "As you wish, Lady Gray."

EPILOGUE

Julian stood on top of the wall of the castle, commanding a fine view of Lochmaben.

Below him stretched the dark waters of the loch mirroring the summer trees as ducks arrowed through its surface in the afternoon light.

It was St. Magdalene's Day, and the villagers had chosen to celebrate with a fair. From his position on the wall, Julian could hear the laughter and calls of the hawkers selling meat pies and other treats. The place was a hive of activity. Gypsies wearing red and green attire awed the crowds with feats of skill on horseback whilst clansmen tossed cabers and played the pipes.

Idly, Julian watched as a man wearing a russet cloak guided his shaggy garron towards the castle entrance. He gave the man little thought, instead choosing to think of his wee wife. He missed her sorely. He prayed this business would soon be over, so once again, he could ride north and spend his time in her company. He shook his head, amused. Lord Julian Gray was in danger of becoming a homebody.

And then the shaggy garron turned to trot along the castle wall and pause directly beneath him. Curiously, he watched from above as the man dismounted, but then he heard a familiar husky laugh.

It wasn't a man at all.

It was Liselle.

Shaking out her mass of honeyed tresses, she squinted up at him and waved.

"Ach, lass! Ye shouldna be here!" he rumbled in disapproval, and swinging his legs over the edge, promptly climbed down the wall to kiss her warmly in welcome. "I left ye safe in Huntly, ye wee minx!"

Locking her arms around his neck, Liselle murmured between kisses, "Buy me some ribbons and sweet cakes from the fair, Lord Gray."

The soft shimmering waves of her hair and her pouting lips made his blood run hot and it was with some difficulty that he set her firmly aside.

"Ye have no cause to be here, lass!" he chided softly. "'Tis business—"

"*Santo Ciélo,* Julian! Can you not admit that you were wrong?" she teased as she began plaiting her hair to one side. "There is no sign of Albany or the Black Douglas. King Edward of England is dead and his brother Richard now sits on the throne. He is busy with internal strife, Lord Gray, and has no time to pester your Scotland!"

"Albany rides to unleash a rebellion, lass," Julian corrected with some difficulty. Aye, but her soft curves were distracting. Shaking his head a little, he added, "Albany's hoping there are yet those who might feel loyalty to the Black Douglas in spite of his many years of lurking in England."

Liselle smiled, and walked her fingers up his arm. "But I do not see them now. Mayhap we can find better ways to spend your time, Lord Gray?" She lowered her lashes provocatively.

Aye, 'twas fair tempting.

"And even if they should arrive, Ewan MacLean is ready for them, is he not?" She suggested and gestured towards the men standing on alert about the castle and beyond.

Even from this distance, Julian could spot the flaxen hair of his cousin, Ewan. Aye, the lad was a natural-born leader and unholy swordsman. Albany didn't stand a chance against such a fearsome highlander.

But then his wee wife's words played back in his mind.

"Should?" he repeated, turning back to her in wry amusement. "Dare ye doubt the word of *Le Marin* that Albany will arrive soon with five hundred men?"

"It is the number five hundred that has me wagering *Le Marin* is mistaken this time, Lord Gray." Liselle laughed outright. "Five hundred is such a paltry sum, he would not dare!"

"But I told ye his stratagem is different this time, lass. He hopes to start a civil war," Julian rumbled as he moved to join her. And then wrapping his arms about her slim waist, he rested his chin upon the top of her head and asked in a suggestive tone, "But tell me, just what are ye willing to wager?"

But she didn't answer. Instead, she grew serious all at once.

Following her gaze, he saw horses, helmets, and spears on the horizon.

"Sweet Mary," Julian cursed beneath his breath. "I had hoped to be wrong."

And then ordering her to take safety in the castle behind them, he appropriated her garron and urged the animal down the gentle slope towards the fair.

He had covered only half the distance before he spied Ewan vaulting onto his horse, and as he watched, the young man pulled back the string of his bow and let loose an arrow.

As the shaft whistled over the heads of the crowd in a clear signal of warning, the battle cries came, starting first with "A MacLean!" but soon resounding with the names of other clans.

Men shouted and horses reared. The air crackled with danger. As the women and children fled to the surrounding hills, the village men took up their axes to gather behind Ewan and his men.

"Aye, Albany doesna stand a chance." Julian nodded grimly. "Not when even the townspeople rise to take up arms against him."

And as he joined the fray, Albany and the Black Earl bore down upon them.

The battle was a short one.

Ewan led the men forth, engaging Albany head on. And before the clouds of night had even gathered, the rebels were routed and Albany was captured, bound, placed upon a horse, and taken as prisoner to the castle.

"Well done, lad," Julian greeted Ewan with a fond clasp on the shoulder.

"Julian," Ewan acknowledged him with a crisp nod. "Your tidings bore true. 'Tis fortunate that Cameron called us here in time."

For the most part, Julian was satisfied to find that the young man was unharmed—suffering only a scratch upon his cheek—but there was a coldness in his eyes that was worrisome.

"Your skills played no small part in this swift victory, lad," Julian inserted, tilting his head speculatively to the side. "Walk with me a moment, Ewan, will ye?"

Ewan said nothing, but joined him to move a short distance away.

"Are ye well, lad?" Julian asked abruptly.

The young man merely lifted a cool brow before glancing briefly over his limbs. "As you can see, I am unharmed, cousin."

Julian snorted softly. "I meant your heart."

At that, Ewan's head snapped back, and an expression that Julian had never seen before crossed his face—an expression of anger and pain. But it was gone before he was even certain that he had seen it.

"Heart?" Ewan repeated icily. "Have ye not heard, Julian? I have no heart."

Astonished, Julian merely stared at him.

And then Ewan smiled, but there was little warmth in it. Gesturing to the battlefield, he added coldly, "How can a man who wields a sword that has killed so many even have a heart?"

And then without a further word, he pivoted on his heel and was gone, leaving Julian to stare at his departing figure in consternation.

The next few days were eventful ones.

Albany and the Black Douglas were escorted to Edinburgh, and upon entering the city gates, the town folk pelted them both with vegetables and small stones. Soon, Albany was imprisoned in the David's Tower to await justice, and jubilation abounded in the city below; the common folk, weary of his treachery, called for his head.

But Albany wasn't through yet. It was only a matter of days before he'd escaped by getting his guards drunk. He had then lowered himself from a tower window with a rope made of sheets and had fled once again to France.

The entire affair provided the Scottish court with plenty of gossip, but there was no longer any real danger. The French were as angry with him as the English now. The man had succeeded only in making enemies of those who would help him.

The summer waned, and the hint of fall was in the air.

With Albany's latest doings safely behind him, Julian found himself growing restless in Edinburgh. In the past, he would have set himself off to a foreign land to let adventure take him where it willed, but now he longed instead for his ancestral lands.

Slipping into bed next to Liselle, he drew her close and chuckled. "I no longer recognize myself. Ye've made me far too respectable this past year, ye wee vixen. I fear *Le Marin* will fade into the realm of stories."

"Never!" Liselle protested, flipping onto her stomach to nuzzle his ear. "But I see no harm in him staying by my side until next spring before venturing forth again."

Julian frowned. "And why only till next spring? Will ye weary of me for good so soon?"

A softness crept over her face, and then pulling his head down, she whispered into his ear.

His gray eyes widened in shock.

A bairn.

Aye, but it seemed adventure had found *him* this time. And finding himself grinning like a daft fool, he caught Liselle up into his arms and kissed her passionately.

* * *

At any other time, Liselle would have enjoyed the sweet autumn and the crispy crackle of the fallen leaves as she stepped upon them, but she found little joy as the days marched on.

She was worried.

Nicoletta was more than a month overdue and winter would arrive soon. Only the most persistent yellow leaves clung desperately to the naked branches surrounding the castle.

"Ach, lass, fretting 'tis harmful to the bairn," Julian murmured against her neck early one morning as he lovingly caressed the small curve of her belly. "And if I know Nicoletta, she's most likely harping on Pascal or Orazio this very moment. Ye've no cause to fret over her. Stay here and rest a while."

She knew he meant to comfort her, but she was too restless to listen to reason. "Nicoletta has only just regained her health," she said, frowning a little.

Rising from the bed, she pulled on her gray-leather boots and a cloak trimmed with fur, and leaving the castle, trudged across the frost-tipped field to stand near the road.

But Nicoletta did not come that day.

Nor the next.

Time passed. Winter arrived.

And each day, Liselle wandered restlessly. And each day, Julian faithfully rode his horse behind her, waiting until she grew tired to lift her with a strong arm into the saddle and carry her safely back to the castle.

"Ach now, ye wee devil, ye'll catch ill!" he chided gently each afternoon.

Yet, she could not bear to sit still.

And then one particularly cold afternoon, Julian swung her lightly down from his horse when a willowy beauty wearing an embroidered lavender silk with a jet and silver brooch clasped about the graceful curve of her throat swept from the castle doors to greet them.

It was Nicoletta.

Wordlessly, Liselle ran into her arms and the two of them set about wailing and weeping tears of joy until Julian stepped between them.

"Mayhap ye'd care to continue this in the warmth of the hall, ladies?" he suggested with an uneasy eye cast in Nicoletta's direction.

Her head swiveled his way. Placing a finger upon her lips, she responded coolly, "Silence will be your friend, Lord Gray."

His brows arched in surprise. "Are ye ordering me to be silent in my own house?" he asked in astonishment.

"*O cièl!*" Nicoletta rolled her eyes. "Is the man deaf?"

Bursting into laughter, Liselle pulled her sister into the hall, and then tossing her cloak aside, grabbed both of Nicoletta's hands in hers. "Tell me the news! All of it, Nicoletta!"

But Nicoletta's face registered shock. "Are you with *child*, Liselle?" Her lips broke into a smile that quickly withered as her gaze fell upon Julian.

He grinned.

"Osti!" Nicoletta wailed before turning back to Liselle and hissing with a gleam of hope, "Please tell me that *macaròn* is not the father!"

"Nicoletta!" Liselle gasped, but more in amusement than anything else.

Pipes keened, announcing it was time for the midday feast, and as Liselle drew her sister towards the high table, Nicoletta sighed heavily.

"I worry for you!" she said, her voice taking on a dire tone. "You are cast alone in a savage land!"

"Alone?" Julian repeated in a tone of derision.

Politely holding out Nicoletta's chair, he waited until she had taken it before playfully shoving it forward a bit with his booted foot.

Nicoletta sent him a dark look, and glancing up at Liselle, she repeated, "And you are cast *alone* in a *savage* land, *sorèlina cara!*"

"My lady, please sit." Julian smiled warmly at his wife, assisting her with exaggerated care and kissing the top of her head before taking his place by her side.

Liselle watched the two of them, amused.

The meal passed pleasantly enough, and when Julian finally rose to excuse himself on estate matters, Nicoletta turned excitedly to Liselle.

"Have you heard the news of Albany?" she whispered.

"Albany?" Liselle blinked in surprise. "Is he not in France?"

Nicoletta tossed her head back and laughed. "He *was, cara.*" The smile on her lips was a smug one.

The way she said the word *was* spoke volumes. "He is dead then," Liselle said.

It was the hand of the Vindictam. She could tell by the expression in Nicoletta's eyes.

"Soon, you will hear the tidings," Nicoletta said a bit proudly. "They will say that he was killed in a tournament in Paris—from a splinter entering his eye. They will never discover how he truly died. And Orazio! His hands flow with gold. England, France, *and* Scotland, they each secretly paid him to see the deed done!"

Orazio had ever been the wily one in such matters, but Liselle could only stare at her sister in slight horror. "You?" She swallowed.

"Not I!" Nicoletta shook her head, but her denial rang false.

Liselle glanced away. "Albany caused many to die," she said finally. "I suppose it is only fitting."

At that, Nicoletta reached over to cup Liselle's face between her hands. "Forgive me, but I forget, *cara!* You do not have the assassin's heart. Let us speak of other things."

Liselle took a deep breath. She had changed. Far more than she had realized.

Across the hall, she saw the tall form of her husband clad in his white shirt and favorite plaid. Sensing her eyes upon him, he turned and grinned. *Santo Ciélo*, but his smile alone weakened her knees.

And then glancing down at the small curve of her belly, she closed her eyes, and for the first time in her life, she felt complete and at peace.

She was where she belonged.

Reaching over, she hugged her sister tightly.

"You and Orazio were right from the start, Nicoletta. I should have listened," she said softly. "I was meant for other things."

The End

The next book in
"The Highland Heather and Hearts
Scottish Romance Series":

The Bold Heart

"Moridac is beyond skilled as an archer, I'll grant him that," Ewan agreed, eyeing the slim, dark-haired youth playing a rowdy game of dice in the corner with several of Ewan's men. "And his heart is as brave and valiant as any. But we are at war. There's no place for a lad to ride amongst us."

"Ach, Ewan!" Alec MacGreggor protested mildly around a mouthful of oatcake. "I'd wager my finest dirk that he's older than I am!" Tipping his chair back on two legs, he raised his voice, "Moridac, lad, how many summers do ye have under your belt?"

Across the room, Moridac craned his neck in their direction. "And why do ye care?" he challenged, his lively dark eyes brightening with interest.

"Why canna ye answer a simple question?" Alec snorted, slamming his chair down. "'Tis always a challenge with ye!"

"Ye've the patience of a nit, MacGreggor!" Moridac retorted in reply.

As their banter continued, Ewan crossed his arms and observed the raven-haired Moridac from beneath furrowed brows.

There were times of late that he had thought the lad would make a better lass. He was far too slender, too graceful, and his skin too soft. But Sweet Mary! This evening in the dim light of the burning embers, he didn't look like a lad at all. The curve of his throat was downright womanly!

And then Moridac's dark eyes met his, gleaming with amusement, and Ewan glanced away.

There it was again. The odd effect the lad had on him.

Abruptly, the lad threw in his hand at the dice and left to care for the horses, and it was with some measure of relief that Ewan watched him go.

"He's old enough—" Alec began.

But Ewan cut him short. "The lad leaves on the morrow."

Several of the men gasped.

"Ach, but ye've grown downright disagreeable of late, Ewan!" Alec's tawny brows knit into a line. "If 'tweren't for Moridac, we'd be feeding the crows now, and well ye know it!"

"I'll brook no argument. Give the lad coin and send him on his way!" Ewan ordered, a little surprised himself at the harshness in his tone.

At that, Alec rose abruptly to his feet, knocking his chair to the floor. "Nay! Not after what he's done for us," he said hotly. "Tell him yourself!"

All eyes followed him as he stalked out of the room, slamming the door behind him.

There was a stilted silence, one in which Ewan moved to prop his booted foot on the table. And keenly aware of the disapproving glares of his men, he turned to his own thoughts and settled in for another long, sleepless night.

There was no doubt he owed his life to the young Moridac.

They all did.

But 'twas precisely for that reason that he'd see the lad go. The battlefield was too grim a place for such a gentle soul.

A mirthless smile played on Ewan's lips.

Over the years, his reputation as a renowned warrior and a

swordsman unmatched had only grown with each battle he fought. But few saw the scars upon his heart and fewer still knew that his sleep was haunted with the screams of dying men.

He would spare the tender Moridac that pain at least.

After a time, both Moridac and Alec returned, and as the men rolled into their cloaks upon the floor, snores gradually replaced all other sounds.

The night passed with interminable slowness. For Ewan, sleep came only in fits and starts. And it was with his customary relief that he saw the dawn break.

And when Moridac rose to tiptoe over the sleeping men to slip outside, Ewan made up his mind.

He'd tell the lad now.

Fastening his woolen cloak over his leather hauberk with a large round brooch, he stepped out into the cold morning air.

Frozen peat crackled beneath his feet as he shaded his eyes and scanned the dun-colored hills spread out before him.

There was no sign of the lad.

A bitter gust of wind lifted the hem of his cloak. The thin sunshine would do little to warm the day. In the distance, clouds gathered on the horizon, heralding more snow. It would be a cold ride.

It was then that a movement near the trees in the distance caught his attention.

Ewan hesitated, suddenly recalling the awkward encounter the last time he had spied upon the lad's peculiar habits. His own reactions had been disconcerting to say the least.

But he had little time for such concerns, not with a storm approaching.

Steeling his resolve, he swiftly set off down the narrow path towards the forest.

He didn't go far. By the time he heard the sound of the murmuring brook tumbling over the rocks, he spied Moridac through a gap in the ancient, gnarled trees.

The lad was kneeling by the water, his cloak and his tunic had fallen off his shoulders, and he appeared to be concentrating upon unwinding a bandage wrapped around his chest.

Ewan's mouth tightened in concern.

The lad was injured!

Alarmed, he stepped through the underbrush just as the bandage fell away.

It took Ewan a moment to recognize what he was seeing.

The soft swell of a breast. The gentle curve of a hip.

And then his jaw dropped open.

This was no lad!

Moridac was a *woman!*

Relief coursed through him, a relief so profound that he chuckled outright.

At the sound, Moridac whirled, tripping back over the exposed roots of an ancient oak to sprawl headlong into the damp earth.

"Aye, now, lass!" Ewan laughed, stepping forward with an outstretched hand. "'Tis no cause for alarm!"

Rolling over, she sprang to her feet and gathered her cloak close about her. "Stand back, Ewan!" She glared.

The cloak slipped a little, exposing her bare shoulder, and all at once his blood ran hot. Aye, it had been too long since he'd allowed himself lusty thoughts over a lass. He could only grin. How had he not seen from the start?

She was downright bonny! From her willowy height, short-cropped curls, to the perpetual mischievous gleam in her brown eyes.

And then she scowled.

And that simple knotting of the brows effectively doused any impulse he might have had. For in that instant, he knew *exactly* who she was.

Sweet Mary, but she had changed since he'd helped to rescue her as a lassie from her aged and cruel husband!

His heart sank.

How could he even dare to think one lusty thought over Ruan MacLeod's wee sister? Aye, he'd almost preferred that Moridac was a lad!

Half-choking, the name was torn from his lips:

"Merry MacLeod!"

The Introduction of a New Romance Series
"The Vindictam":
Revenge

Venice 1491

Pascal drummed his fingers on the side of the gondola as it traversed the maze of canals.

He hadn't been back to Venice since the Black Death arrived six years ago.

Many had died during that scourge, even the Doge himself. The Vindictam—arguably the most powerful family of assassins in Europe—had fled at once, knowing even they were no match for the plague.

He leaned back in the cushions for a time and simply enjoyed the soft splash of the oars dipping into the water. The smoothness of a gondola on the quiet canals of Venice was a far superior way to travel than the perpetual jolting rattle of a carriage on London's bustling streets.

It was good to be home, and he had always meant to come back, but upon receiving his mother's summons, his vague intentions had turned into speedy actions.

Pascal's lip curled in dark amusement.

As the Grand Master, the Dominus Granditer of the Vindictam, men followed his orders without question. He answered to no one.

Save his mother.

His smile widened.

He was nothing more than a slave to her happiness. She was prickly, overbearing, and demanding. And she ruled her children with an iron fist. But she truly loved them, and they knew it well.

So when his mother demanded his appearance no later than noon of St. John's Day, he had dropped matters of the gravest importance to go home at once.

But the journey had been a rough one, and judging by the sun's arc in the sky, noon had passed some time ago.

He tapped the side of the gondola a little impatiently. "A silver coin for you should you get me there sooner!" he said, tossing the coin at the man's feet.

The gondolier grinned and put more muscle into the oar, and as the magnificent buildings on the Grand Canal flew past him, his thoughts wandered once again.

His mother hadn't stated the reason for his summons, but he could guess well enough.

Several months ago, he had succumbed to her pressure and to that of the Quattuor Gladiis, his four right-hand men.

They had demanded that he marry.

He had signed his name to the parchment as a show of good faith, knowing full well that with his mother involved, he had no say in the matter. They would choose the appropriate bride, one with the needed political ties.

No doubt, they had made their choice, or several, and had called him to meet his prospective brides. And most likely, the woman would be dull and tedious to deal with, but if it kept his mother appeased and the Quattuor satisfied, then what did he care if he had a wife?

It was just a marriage. How could that affect him?

He would be traveling again soon enough. There were matters in France that required his attention.

And then the gondolier called out, shaking him from his thoughts.

Leaving the Grand Canal, they glided into a new waterway, and as they passed under the arched stairs spanning the canal, Pascal beheld his ancestral home.

He eyed the place in dry amusement.

Returning home never failed to fill him with a wondrous yet disquieting sense of barbaric gloom.

The familial home of the da Vilardino was a striking marble creation perched on the water's edge. In his mind's eye, he could already see the rich paintings adorning the walls, the heavy velvet curtains hanging above the Moorish windows and the ornate frescos gracing the ceilings.

Yet there was another side to this luxurious domain.

The place was a virtual stew of plotting, scheming men engaged in the never-ending quest to gain more power and gold.

And then the gondolier maneuvered the boat to the landing, and Pascal stepped out onto the marble stairs leading from the water to the door.

He had arrived.

Dusting the slashed sleeves of his white travel-stained shirt and his close-fitting leather-studded breeches, he eyed his clothing with a wry twist of his lip. He far more resembled a highwayman than a Venetian noble, but he was already late.

He'd pay homage to his mother first before changing into proper attire.

But he had taken only a step toward the door before it was yanked open to reveal his elder sister, Anna.

A lithe dark-haired woman of proud bearing, she viewed him with her customary frown and a chilling gaze rife with disapproval. "You are late."

"And how have you fared these years, Anna?" Pascal asked in a dry undertone.

Anna's dark brows knitted into a frown. "This is a matter of the utmost importance, Pascal," she warned.

Pascal lifted a single brow in query. "Cristofo? Rigi?" he asked in a soft, dangerous voice.

Angry that he, the youngest of the sons, had been chosen as the Grand Master of the Vindictam, his elder brothers had never ceased plotting against him. They were sly and wily, and though it had never been proven, all knew it was they who were behind the attempts to unseat him in the past few years.

Anna's harsh tone cut into his thoughts. "You have been wed, Pascal. Rigi stood in as proxy for you."

Pascal nearly missed a step.

But then reaching the door, he slouched gracefully against the frame, folded his arms, and peered down at his sister from under hooded eyes. "And who did I wed?" he asked in an even tone.

At that, her lips thinned. "Mama's choice! The Quattuor Gladiis brought her this very day." Her critical gaze took in the state of his clothing and she added, "Come as you are, you are too late already."

"And why such haste?" he began.

But she had already turned away in a rustle of silks.

With a growing sense of apprehension, Pascal followed his sister through the hall and down a narrow twisting passage that led to the garden.

But as he approached the walled enclosure, he heard the sound of his mother's angry voice engaged in a heated argument.

"I am truly home," he murmured under his breath with a snort of private laughter.

Stepping through the door, a sea of faces turned to greet him. The voices around him were hushed, and a cloud of anxiety hung in the air.

With a heightened sense of vigilance, he scanned the gathering, recognizing only a few of the guests.

And then his mother's displeased tones sounded again, and he saw her standing near the statues clustered around the massive bronze cistern on the far side of the garden.

She was a sharp, shrewish, bony woman with a steady hand and dark hair despite her advancing age. The expression on her face was a fierce one, and her brown eyes flashed as she wagged a finger at a tall gray-haired man standing before her.

"And by what authority do you even dare *imply* that my son is disobedient?" Her voice rang throughout the garden as loud as a church bell.

Pascal's lip lifted in amusement.

And then spidery, wizened fingers clutched his sleeve, and he glanced down into the wrinkled face of his aged grandmother.

"Be brave, my sweet boy," the old woman encouraged in her weak, gravelly voice. "Be brave! I do not know why she has done this to you!"

Pascal patted her hand in warm affection. "Do not fret, *nòna*. I will not suffer!"

"Pascal! Attend!" his mother's voice ordered sharply.

Leaving his grandmother to the care of one of the guests, Pascal approached his mother and bowed. She had aged since he'd seen her last. Frowning with concern, he gently took her hands between his.

"Are you well—" he began.

"You are late," she observed with a crusty smile. Squeezing his fingers in a brief gesture of affection, she snapped her fan open, and waving it near her face, she turned to the tall gray-haired man still standing before her. "He is here, so I'll hear no more libelous words from you!"

Curious, Pascal glanced over his shoulder.

And then froze.

He recognized the man at once.

It was Antonio Saluzzo, the leader of the Saluzzi.

For years, the Vindictam and the Saluzzi—the rival assassins of Ferrara—had been the bitterest of enemies. That is, until Pascal's father had forged a treaty, an exceedingly fragile and uneasy one.

Clasping his hands calmly behind his back, Pascal smiled, but it was a dangerous smile and one that few would fail to recognize as a threat.

"Antonio Saluzzo," he said the name slowly. "And why, pray tell, is a Saluzzo present during the marriage festivities of a da Vilardino?"

Antonio did not answer him. Instead, he folded his arms and peered down at him silently from the lengths of his large aquiline nose.

And then a soft musical voice spoke from behind him. "How much longer will you insult me, husband?"

Startled, Pascal turned to behold a young woman clad from head-to-toe in black. She was standing beneath a gnarled olive tree in the center of the garden.

"Your bride," his mother murmured from his side. "Gemma."

But Pascal scarcely heard her.

His attention was captivated by the stunning creature dressed in black.

Moving forward slowly, his eyes raked her in ironic amusement. The fact that she was dressed in funeral attire was not lost upon him. Clearly, she was less eager to wed than even he had been.

But she was certainly not what he had expected.

She was a woman of breathtaking beauty. Her hair fell in soft golden waves and her eyes reminded him of the sea. And the black lace of her attire only accentuated her ivory slenderness, giving her the appearance of an exquisite carving.

She stood there, haughty and aloof, meeting his bold appraisal with one of her own.

"Black suits you," he said softly, intrigued in spite of himself.

Her eyes flickered with a deep emotion that he could not name as she informed him with the utmost scorn, "I care little for your compliments."

Pascal's lip curved upwards in response, and his dark eyes lit with challenge.

And then she extended her hand in a royal gesture as if she expected him to kiss it. "My name is Gemma," she said, lifting her chin defiantly. There was a distinct pause before she added, "Gemma Maria Elizabeta Saluzzo."

Pascal recoiled, and his mouth went dry at once.

And then staring down at his bride, he suddenly recognized the expression in her stormy eyes.

He knew it was mirrored in his own.

Pure hatred.

Venetian/Latin Glossary

ah sì?! – oh really?!

ale! – go!

aimèi! – oh, woe is me!

al diavolo! – to the devil!

àngiolìna – Little Angel

bàbio/a – male/female fool

basta! – enough!

bón pare – good father

bravàso – brave

cà de dìa! – good heavens!

caro fradèl – dear brother

cestìl! – be quiet!

che scalògna! – what bad luck!

ciò – hey / huh!

dedìa! – my goodness!

diàmbarne! – devil's house!

Dominus Granditer – Grand Master

Electus – Elected One

eternità – eternity

esumìmi! – Jesus help me!

gexondìo! – hexes!

gòfi – clumsy

gramersè! – many thanks!

indilaménte – immediately

Inghilterra – England

macarón – blockhead, literally macaroni

Magno Duce - Great Captain

marcìa via! – go away!

mercànte – merchant

mi digo! – I believe it! For sure!

nòna – grandmother

O ciél! – oh heavens!

orponón! – damn!

òsti – good lord!

Quattuor Gladiis – The Four Swords.

ridicolóxo - ridiculous

Santo ciélo – heaven help me!

Sia – Aunt

Santa pazienza! - God give me patience!

smoroxéto – lady's man

sorèla cara\sorèlina cara– dear sister\dear little sister

Sò falimènta – I'm a failure

un demònio – a devil, demon

un farabùto – a scoundrel

Vindictam – Revenge.

ABOUT THE AUTHOR

Like many of us on this planet, Carmen Caine/Madison Adler is from another world. She spends every moment she can scribbling stories on sticky notes that her kids find posted all over the car, house, and barn.

When she is not working as a software engineer, she is busy ferrying her kids to various appointments, writing lyrics for her husband's songs, raising her new puppy Ajax, attempting to tame her three insane cats, scratching her three Nigerian Dwarf Goats behind the horns or coddling her flock of thirty bizarre chickens from around the world.

And although I am terrible at tweeting and posting on Facebook (though I do strive to improve), please follow me on Twitter - twitter.com/CarmenRomances or visit my Facebook page: facebook.com/Carmen.Caine or CarmenCaine.com

The "Glass Wall" is the first book of her new quirky paranormal series about ancient beings, Tulpas and different dimensions:

"The Glass Wall" (Now Available)

"The Brotherhood of the Snake" (Now Available)

"The Inner Circle" (2013)

"The Egg" (2014)

Her Scottish Medieval series, "The Highland Heather and Hearts Scottish Romance Series" covers the span of years ranging from 1478-1488:

"The Kindling Heart"(Now Available)

"The Bedeviled Heart" (Now Available)

"The Daring Heart" (Now Available)

"The Bold Heart" (2014)

And her new series about the Vindictam, beginning with the book:

“Revenge” (after the above ...)

www.ingramcontent.com/pod-product-compliance
Lightning Source LLC
Chambersburg PA
CBHW070735180626
46818CB00007B/2857